PENGUIN BOOKS

LEADING MEN

Christopher Castellani is the author of three previous novels. He is a Guggenheim fellow, on the faculty of the MFA Program at Warren Wilson, and the artistic director of GrubStreet. He lives in Boston.

* * *

Praise for *Leading Men*

"Vividly reimagines the relationship between Williams and Frank Merlo, and offers intricate thoughts about the nature of fidelity, the artistic impulse, and estrangement . . . Its author knows a great deal about life; better, he knows how to express what he knows. . . . This book is a kind of poem in praise of pleasure . . . To hold it in your hands is like holding . . . a front-row opera ticket."
—Dwight Garner, *The New York Times*

"Real and imagined lives collide as Tennessee Williams and his longtime lover Frank Merlo befriend a young Swedish woman named Anja on the glittering Italian Riviera in July 1953. Though entirely fictional, the enigmatic Anja, who goes on to reluctant fame and fortune as an actress, propels this story of desire, ambition, and heartbreak."
—*People*

"Spectacular . . . Castellani's novel hits the trifecta of being moving, beautifully written, and a bona fide page-turner. This is a wonderful examination of artists and the people who love them and change their work in large and imperceptible ways."
—*Publishers Weekly* (starred review)

"A seductive, steamy novel of Tennessee Williams and his lover . . . Castellani's quiet portrayal of Merlo has a deep, aching appeal. . . . [His] prose has a beguiling lilt and color, whether he's evoking his characters' evasive or erratic emotions, or conjuring the far-flung locales where these globe-hoppers touch down."
—Michael Upchurch, *The Boston Globe*

"With extraordinary artistry and grace, Christopher Castellani interweaves history and invention to show us both the depths great artists are driven to and the love that draws them back. I know of few books that give such a moving account of the indispensable value of genius and its intolerable human cost. This is a novel of rare insight and beauty, and Castellani is a writer of brilliant gifts."
—Garth Greenwell

"A daredevil of a novel, like the prettiest boy in the gay bar doing a backflip off a stool and not spilling his drink."
—Alexander Chee

"Gorgeous and sweeping . . . [A] sumptuous work of historical fiction. . . . [*Leading Men*] manages to capture the lightning of these massive artistic figures on the page with such force, it does feel as if you have tiptoed around Williams's desk in Rome while he was busy writing a masterpiece."   —Christopher Bollen, *Interview*

"Audacious . . . [Castellani's] novel not only exults in the historical synchronicities and proximities he has discovered but catches the reader up in its rapture."
—David Leavitt, *The New York Times Book Review*

"*Leading Men* is a finely rendered narrative . . . broad in scope and lush in detail, without every tipping into sentimentality."   —*Lambda Literary*

"*Leading Men* is glorious, a meditation on the ravages of fame, an investigation into the private lives of public artists, and one of the most moving love stories I've read in ages. By bringing to life these literary visionaries, Christopher Castellani proves himself their eminently worthy heir."   —Anthony Marra

"Castellani . . . [injects] the book with a gravitas and a precariousness that recalls the authorial finesse of his own character, Tennessee Williams, harnessing a talent not only for forming tragic heroes, but allowing them to exhibit the kind of complexity that remains utterly real to readers."   —Chris Campanioni, *Brooklyn Rail*

"Castellani elegantly weaves together Merlo's final days with memories of a dramatic (and delicious) Italian summer in 1953 that changes his world forever."
—Hannah Tinti

"This is a tender, psychologically devastating, and gorgeously precise novel. Extraordinary."   —Lauren Groff

"*Leading Men* is a novel as moving as it is entertaining, a book that restored my faith in the old cliché that only through fiction can we reach the truth. Christopher Castellani has written an astounding novel of great imaginative empathy that, by the end, had this cynic weeping."   —Peter Orner

"*Leading Men* is a clever, allusive, multilayered novel filled with wit, insight, and heart. I loved it."   —Justin Torres

"This is a tale of love and loneliness, the personal costs of genius and its attendant fame, and of the ultimate, inconsolable pain of loss. In its depiction of Americans in Europe, its closest literary cousin might be F. Scott Fitzgerald's *Tender Is the Night*."   —*Library Journal*

"Lyrical, restrained, and affecting. This is a book to savor."   —Taylor Jenkins Reid

---

Look for the Penguin Readers Guide in the back of this book.
To access Penguin Readers Guides online, visit penguinrandomhouse.com.

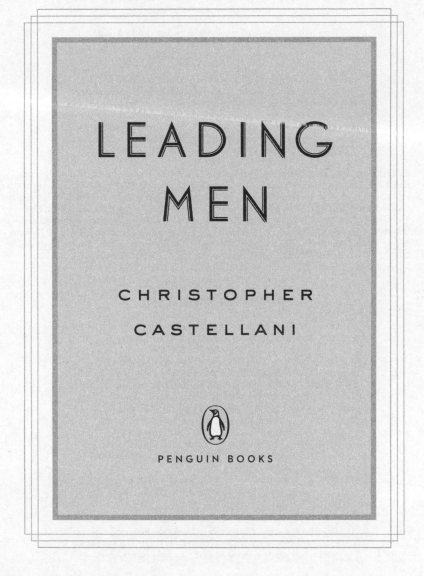

LEADING MEN

CHRISTOPHER CASTELLANI

PENGUIN BOOKS

PENGUIN BOOKS
An imprint of Penguin Random House LLC
penguinrandomhouse.com

First published in the United States of America by Viking,
an imprint of Penguin Random House LLC, 2019
Published in Penguin Books 2020

Excerpt from letter from Tennessee Williams to Elia Kazan, c. June–July 1953. Excerpt from
"Little Horse" by Tennessee Williams, copyright © 1964, renewed 1993 by The University of the
South. Excerpts from *Memoirs* by Tennessee Williams, copyright © 1972, 1975 by The University
of the South. Excerpts from *Notebooks* by Tennessee Williams, copyright © 2006 by The
University of the South. Excerpts from *The Selected Letters of Tennessee Williams, Volume One,
1920–1945*, copyright © 2000 by The University of the South and *The Selected Letters of Tennessee
Williams, Volume Two, 1945–1957*, copyright © 2004 by The University of the South. Reprinted by
permission of The University of the South. Excerpt from letter
from Truman Capote to David O. Selznick, June 23, 1953. Reprinted with
permission of The Truman Capote Literary Trust.

ISBN 9780525559078 (paperback)

THE LIBRARY OF CONGRESS HAS CATALOGED THE HARDCOVER EDITION AS FOLLOWS:
Names: Castellani, Christopher, 1972– author.
Title: Leading men / Christopher Castellani.
Description: New York, New York : Viking, 2019. |
Identifiers: LCCN 2018029036 (print) | LCCN 2018031769 (ebook) |
ISBN 9780525559061 (ebook) | ISBN 9780525559054 (hardcover) |
ISBN 9781984877642 (international edition)
Subjects: | BISAC: Fiction / Literary. | Fiction /
Biographical. | Fiction / Gay.
Classification: LCC PS3603.A875 (ebook) |
LCC PS3603.A875 L43 2019 (print) | DDC 813/.6—dc23
LC record available at https://lccn.loc.gov/2018029036

Printed in the United States of America
1   3   5   7   9   10   8   6   4   2

DESIGNED BY MEIGHAN CAVANAUGH

to Michael in return for Italy

There are some simply extraordinary people in Portofino—the place is rampant with the kind of Goings-on Jennifer never really believes Go-on. There is an Australian girl who ran away with her stepfather—and a Swedish mother and daughter who share a fisherman between them, etc. But these are very ordinary instances. Altogether, the place is fraught with peril.

—TRUMAN CAPOTE, IN A LETTER TO DAVID O. SELZNICK, 23 JUNE 1953

My name for him is Little Horse.
I wish he had a name for me.

—TENNESSEE WILLIAMS, *Collected Poems*

1.

THE LITTLE HORSE

Truman was throwing a party in Portofino, and Frank wanted to go. The invitation came in mid-July, slipped between parentheses in the long, gossipy paragraphs of his letter to Tenn, as if daring him to acknowledge it. Frank read the letter in Tenn's absence. He'd been stuck for weeks in their stuffy fourth-floor apartment on Via Firenze, waiting for him to get back from Spain, while, on the loud streets below, the real Romans escaped for the mountains. He replied to Truman with a brief telegram, and then he called the finest hotel in town, the Splendido, to book a room. He auditioned various linen jackets and swim trunks and hats in the mirror above the dresser, mended two pairs of Tenn's socks, and walked their silks down to the cleaners. When Tenn returned home to find their bags lined up in the hall, packed for another trip, he didn't protest. He was sweet on Frank again after three weeks apart. A drive in the Jag up the coast of Liguria, far from the melting heart of the *centro*, could only make things sweeter.

They took one last walk through the Villa Borghese. They followed two boys, the dark one Tenn's, the blond for Frank, down the Spanish steps and out the eastern side to the Corso, pulled along by the smoothness of their elbows. Not a hint of saggy skin on Tenn's boy, his long arms tanned by lazy days on the beach at Ostia, or on Frank's, a Swiss. Who could say where the Swiss got that scar, new and pink across the knob of the elbow, or where he spent his own empty afternoons? Who could say he was a Swiss at all and not from some disappointing place, like Minnesota? Who could say the scar didn't come from an iron fence he'd tumbled over, running from a cuckold in Lugano, his wife in the doorway clutching her robe and pleading for mercy? *They* could say, Frank and Tenn, walking at a safe distance behind the boys, as they liked so very much to do evenings after dinner those summers they lived in Rome, inventing lives for the Italians, inventing lives for themselves. It's what Tenn was famous for. It was one of the many happy ways they passed their time together.

They brought back the dark one, Mario, to Via Firenze. A Sicilian, like Frank, it turned out, but at least he wasn't American. As he hastily slipped on his espadrilles, color rising in his cheeks, Frank said to him, *You've just slept with one of the world's greatest writers*, and because Mario had heard of Tennessee Williams, he stayed for the coffee and pastries Frank brought onto the terrace. Soon Mario grew tiresome, as they all did, talking of his mother, who expected him home, who worried—there was always a mother—and they watched with relief as he and his tight elbows descended the stairs.

He wasn't the first Mario, of course. Over the years, they forgot their names, but not their scars or their attitudes or the stories they told as they lay between them late into the night. Sometimes, on their evening walks, the streets sultry and flickering with shadows, they'd spot one of the Marios in a piazza with his pack of friends, laughing, his arm slung over a girl's shoulder. If the Mario noticed them, he'd turn his face away or shoot back a look of defiance and shame and fear, which enlarged them.

They left Rome like this, big as elephants, the heat and storms behind them, the top down on the Jag, for Portofino. Frank slept most of the way, his head on Tenn's lap, and then again on the skiff from Rapallo, though Tenn kept nudging him awake to point out the houses on the cliffs. You like the orange? he asked. The yellow? No, that blue, up top! I'm shopping, Frankie. Any of these can be ours.

Truman had rented an apartment a few steps from the harbor, above the Delfino Restaurant, which Frank and Tenn passed on their way up the hill to the Splendido. Tenn paid the boat guy to carry their luggage, and, when the hill got too steep, Frank grabbed the heavy case with the typewriter. He didn't like it when another guy did work for him that he could do himself, a guy who would have been him if he'd never left Jersey. The Splendido was first a *monastero*, the boat guy told them, and now look at it, *che spettacolo*, the place Clark Gable drinks his brandy to a view. Tenn went straight to the desk as usual and Frank arranged their dress shirts on hangers and brought their shoes down for shining and stole another hour for a nap. He'd never felt so tired in the middle of the afternoon, and he chalked it up to being thirty, but it's possible—no doctor was ever able to tell him for sure one way or the other—that the trouble had already started in his lungs. When he woke, Tenn offered him a pill. Tenn had as many pills as Italy had houses on the water. But Frank wasn't taking pills, not then. Instead he smoked another cigarette and paid the boat guy to drive him over the mountain to Paraggi Beach, where he swam to find his strength and clear his head.

They didn't like Truman much, but Frank didn't hate him the way Tenn did. Or maybe Tenn didn't hate Truman. It was hard to know for sure with Tenn. It was a job in itself keeping track of who he was angry with, and who was jealous of him, whose parties he was looking forward to and whose they'd have to make up some excuse to get out of. Frank's official job was as Tenn's secretary, but even his secretary didn't have a reason for being in Portofino other than to stop by Truman's party, and he didn't know when they'd be leaving. There wasn't much Frank knew in the summer of 1953, least of all how long he and Tenn might last.

In those years, there was no such thing as early, late, or on time. They went from place to place on a magic carpet. Dropped here, dropped there. Women in electric dresses, men in monkey suits and bow ties made of white silk. Cognac, cigars, wine. The sky turquoise even when it was gray. Because Tenn had no mind—and little use— for schedules and logistics and coordinates, he needed Frank to organize the day they woke to, and the coming days, and even the days before. The dinner they'd had in London, Tenn swore on Mother Edwina's grave they'd had in Chicago. The party for the *Sweet Bird of Youth* tryout in Philadelphia he remembered as the one in New Haven for *Camino Real*. The life of Tennessee Williams was a memory play in which memory was a jumble. It was bodies he remembered, bodies they remembered together. His body and Frank's, the Southern Gentleman and the Little Horse. The bodies of all the Marios, from Key West to Marrakech. When it came to matters of the body, Frank and Tenn trusted each other like soldiers.

At the Delfino, Frank lost track of him the first minute. Tenn couldn't walk into a room without someone sweeping him up and into a crowd. How many times had Frank stood at the edge of the crowd as if on a shore, watching him drift farther and farther out, his head bobbing on the waves, glancing back just once to meet his eyes. How many times had Frank found himself in an overflowing room like this one, greeting guests as they arrived, recognizing their faces from movies and the backstages of theaters. How many times had these people walked in, looked around, saw Frank, saw nobody, spotted a somebody over his shoulder, and then headed upstairs.

A brass band started up. Frank danced with a French girl whose uncle watched from the bar. Girls liked to dance with Frank, and he with them; he had a way with a spin and a twirl and a catch and a bow, and this French girl, she could follow. That wasn't always the case with girls, even the fancy brought-up girls, but dancing with the clomping ones—the Clydesdales, he called them—even *that* was better than dancing with a guy, which he and Tenn never did anyway, not with each other at least, not even in Provincetown. He saw the world like that a lot then: what he did with Tenn, what he'd done with girls.

He had his hands all over the Frenchy—Martine—until he noticed the uncle giving him the stink-eye. He let her spin into some other man's arms. He brought a whiskey over to the uncle, not bad looking himself once he relaxed and the stink left his eye, and they got to talking. They'd both been at Guadalcanal. They traded stories loud over the music. When it became clear to the uncle that there was no money in Frank for his precious Martine, he took off in a cloud of leathery cologne. It was then and there that Frank first saw Jack Burns.

Frank knew a drunk when he saw one. In a few years, he'd have good reasons to become one himself, to crave that slow blurry kill. That night, he craved only a cigarette and the sea air, but for the air he had to get past the drunk slouched against the doorway of the Delfino. From across the room, in the low smoky light, with the band playing "Lazzarella," he might have mistaken the man for handsome, but as he walked toward him from the bar, into clearer focus came his pink, bloated face, his world-hating mouth, his body heavy and lifeless as a sandbag. Frank stopped, looked him in the eyes, and asked if maybe he'd come to the wrong place.

"This isn't Portofino?"

A man appeared behind him and put his hand on his shoulder, to steady him or claim him or both. "We are here for the party upstairs," the man said to Frank in Italian. "It is *privato*."

"This is the party, downstairs and upstairs," Frank said in English, using his hands for emphasis. He spoke enough of his parents' native language to converse with the man, but there was no reason to make the effort. "Not as *privato* as you might expect."

Whatever the Italian then whispered into the drunk's ear had no effect on his scowl. "We drove from Firenze," he said to Frank. He put out his hand. "I am called Sandro. This is John Horne Burns. The novelist."

In just a single night in Portofino, Frank had met Rex Harrison the actor, kissed the cheek of Daisy Fellowes the heiress, eyed the not-so-secret boyfriend of Arturo Lopez-Willshaw the Chilean magnate, and posed for Cecil Beaton the photographer. He had never heard of John Horne Burns the novelist. From the looks of him, Frank doubted anyone else had, either. Truman's parties drew all sorts of hangers-on, parasites, and wannabes, even in this remote little cove at the tip of the peninsula.

"Nice to meet you, John Horne Burns the Novelist," Frank said, more out of politeness to Sandro than affection for the surly fellow.

"Jack," he said.

Frank looked around for Tenn. If he was already upstairs, he wouldn't be down for hours. Upstairs was where the glitter was. The most glitter was hidden behind the closed doors of bedrooms. He and Tenn had once spent an entire party on Maureen Stapleton's king-size bed, the three of them sprawled on the coverlet with their shoes still on passing around a liter of vodka, while her party clinked and boomed on the other side of the door and the glitter-hungry mob banged and shouted to be let in.

"*The Gallery*," Sandro said. "The great war novel. A great work of American fiction. And two just-as-great novels since."

"Quit it," said Jack.

"Great," said Frank.

"He is *modesto*," Sandro said. "He is working now on his great fourth novel. I force him this weekend to take a break. I say, go to the party of Truman Capote. We meet him in Firenze in June and last week receive the telegram with this address. Everyone in Italy knows his book, so I say, we take the car and drive to see the little man with the funny voice. Our first time in *questo bel posto*."

"This place is lousy with writers," Frank said to Jack. "You'll be in good company. Clare Luce is over there. Jack Dunphy." He paused. "Tennessee Williams."

At those glittering names Jack merely rolled his eyes and swayed. "We going in or not?" he said, and headed for the bar.

Sandro turned to Frank. "Please forgive," he said. "He has trouble with his book. He is a great man." Then he rushed to the great man's side.

To get an uncluttered view of the water, Frank followed the stone sidewalk around the bend of the harbor. White yachts crammed the shallow cove, their lights blazing, tinny music pouring from their radios onto their crowded decks. In Portofino in midsummer, Truman's was not the only invitation to be had. It was even possible that these people standing along the railings talking and dancing in pairs had never heard of Truman Capote or Tennessee Williams, not to mention John Horne Burns; that they'd never gone to the theater or finished a book or attended the symphony; that they were rich without culture. Frank would rather be poor. He might rather be dead.

A dark-haired woman waved to him from one of the swankier yachts farther out, and for the delicious moment he mistook her for Anna Magnani, he brightened; he lifted his arm to wave back; but she wasn't Anna at all, of course, just another overflowing *signora* in an evening dress and a smile too big for her face. They'd just left Anna in

Rome, and even she in her fierceness didn't pick up and leave without a plan unless she had a new lover, and if she had a new lover she'd have made sure Frank knew. Frank missed Anna. He could talk to her and she would at least make a show of listening before she brought the subject back to herself. In Rome, she called their apartment every morning first thing. "*Ciao ciao*," she'd say, already in a hurry. "What's the program, *ragazzi*?" Frank often forgot she was an actress in the big time and not one of his sisters in Peterstown, busting out of her brassiere and squeezing his face with her hands when she needed to get a point through his thick skull.

The buildings in the harbor glowed like giant jewel boxes, pink and yellow and orange. The archways along the curve shone down their own lights, making little stages where people stood on their tip-toes staring back at the boats for a glimpse of the rich and famous. Frank could have rooms in one of the jewel boxes if he wanted. Did he want jewel box rooms? Did he want to stay here, stay anywhere? What was the program?

No matter how most of Tenn's friends treated him, Frank was anything but a hanger-on. Did a hanger-on earn his keep as a personal secretary, managing the ledger and booking passages and choosing jackets and ties? Did he hold Tenn's shaking body against his long into the nights he lay sleepless and terrified, pressing tight against him to keep the demons out? Would the great Tennessee Williams dedicate *The Rose Tattoo*, his most beautiful play, his opera of a play, his love play, to a parasite? "To Frank in return for Sicily," Tenn wrote for the dedication, which would stay printed forever in bookstores and libraries all over the world.

Frank was too young to be almost thirty-one. His body was still tight, but from what he saw of men in their bathing trunks or less, in every country Tenn took him to, all those beaches and saunas and walks in the park, it wouldn't be long before his skin came loose from his legs and upper arms and his face dried to a prune. Who'll want him then? He had no money in the bank. Tenn signed his meager paychecks, which barely lasted him until the end of each month. Though he'd gifted Frank a fat percentage of the profits from *The Rose Tattoo* in perpetuity, if Frank had learned anything in their six years together, it was that plays had shaky legs and that perpetuity wasn't so long in the end.

If he stayed in New York for more than a few weeks at a time, he could start going to auditions again. He'd had ten walk-ons in movies in the forties, but nothing since he'd met Tenn. If he worked up the nerve, he could use Tenn or Audrey Wood or Kazan to get him through the door on Broadway or in LA. He'd set his sights on a leading man role, but he'd settle for a speaking part, or even a spot in a dance company, something—anything—to build on. He wasn't a bad dancer. He was just getting started in ballet back in '49. He missed how dancing made his body electric and numb at the same time, how he used to swim through the air, and how the swimming turned his head calm and clean as a fishbowl.

He looked around. Tossed his cigarette into the water. Alone in the darkness of the pier, facing the twinkling harbor, he stood on the tips of his white loafers and stretched out his arms. Held the pose. His middle wasn't as strong as it once was, but his legs had the same power. The muscles in his chest strained his shirt buttons. He lifted his head to the sky, drank in the stars. He wished he could see himself.

When I'm gone, Frank thought, Tenn will have his pick. There was never not some starry-eyed wannabe trying to elbow him out of Tenn's light. If he could see from here on his tiptoes into Truman's apartment, surely he'd find one of the wannabes with his head thrown back in laughter at one of Tenn's wicked remarks. "Oh Mr. Williams!" the boy was saying now, his thin wrists going limp. "Oh Mr. Williams, you are *too much*!" Half the men they met at those parties wanted to be Tenn; the other half wanted to be Frank; the difference was that none of them remembered Frank's name the moment after hearing it. Why bother, they figured, a new one will be along soon.

"What do *you* do?" Jack Warner had asked him, four summers ago now, almost to the day. Tenn had brought him on the *Menagerie* trip to LA. They'd been lovers for close to a year.

"I sleep with Mr. Williams," Frank had said, straight into the producer's shocked eyes. He'd rehearsed the line, if not for Jack Warner then for the next person who asked. He'd intended to get a rise. To make an impression. He meant: I do that, yes, and I do it well, but I do much more. He meant business. When he'd rehearsed the line, the meaning seemed obvious, but it came off wrong. Nobody, Warner especially, took it for anything but a punch line. Tenn told that story a thousand times. It was one of his favorites. Just last week, in Anna's kitchen, it came up again. Tenn leaned over and whispered something in her ear, and they both laughed and laughed. Then he slapped Frank on the back. "Isn't that right, baby?" he said. The slap shrank him to the size of the dog. But Tenn and Anna were right to laugh. Other than sleep with Mr. Williams, what had Frank Merlo done with his life?

Tomorrow he'd come up with a plan. Tonight, maybe he'd have a drink after all. See how Tenn was making out upstairs. Take Martine for another spin, squeeze her ass when he dipped her, put a real scare in the uncle. Frank liked to play games. To perform. To be watched. He'd do more of all that, starting tomorrow. He figured he had one good decade of youth left in him. On the walk down the hill to the party that evening, Tenn had mentioned visiting the set of Visconti's *Senso* back in Rome sometime in the next couple months, before they sailed to Barcelona, before they sailed to Tangier. Visconti was making two versions of the film, one in Italian and one in English, with Tenn and Paul Bowles contracted to write the American script. If they needed a speaking part from an equine Italian-American man at the last minute, then square in their sights the Horse would be, found money, a revelation.

Back inside the Delfino, the crowd had thickened. You could tell the crashing tourists from their day clothes and stiff guilty postures and darting eyes. They took up precious space in the corner and giggled at their luck. Why wasn't there someone to give them the boot? It was past eleven; by midnight it would be anyone's party, with the uninvited pouring in from the square, smelling the rich blood. If Frank had Truman's fame and fortune, he'd run a tighter show. A quality show. He'd invite Maria Callas to sing for them, if only so he could finally see her in person. He'd clear a space for the dancers he'd studied with in Manhattan. The best parties didn't skimp on the entertainment.

He took the stairs to the apartment, which should have been kept more *privato*, but the door was wide open and the room just as packed. The only faces he recognized belonged to Jack, passed out in a rocking chair, and Sandro, the Sentinel, standing beside him with his hands in his pockets. When he finally found Tenn, he was in the doorway of Truman's bedroom, talking to the two palest, blondest women Frank had ever seen, one of whom was holding a white Maltese the size of a football.

"*There's* the Horse!" Tenn said, and grabbed Frank by the elbow. "And just in time! These gorgeous ladies have me spellbound with the most delicious tale. A scandal if I ever heard one, and I've heard them all." He pulled them into a tight circle. To Frankie he said, "One of these women is the mother and one is the daughter. I dare you to tell me which is which."

It was obvious, but Frank politely shook his head all the same. "Impossible," he said, and introduced himself with his broadest, toothiest smile and a wink for the daughter. Already, these fierce and delicate greyhounds, with their taut slender necks and their blue-gray marbled eyes set wide apart, had him spellbound, too. They wore identical white iridescent shift dresses and pearl chokers, the shorter one (the mother) in silver high heels that brought her up to her daughter's exact height. They'd pulled their hair back in the same au courant style, which had the effect of tightening the mother's skin almost enough to hide the telltale signs of age. A ringlet of the daughter's hair had come loose and stuck out from the side of her head like an antenna.

"Bitte Blomgren," said the mother.

"Anja Blomgren," said the daughter.

"And this is Maja," Bitte said, lifting the Maltese up to Frank's lips as if he'd asked to kiss her. He scratched the back of her neck.

The presence of Maja irritated Frank. Truman had not extended his party invitation to Mr. Moon, Frank and Tenn's black bulldog; he had his own bulldog, Bunky, currently waddling through the crowd, shining shoes with his mess of slobbers. Bunky didn't much like the company of other canines, Truman had explained to Frank on the phone, least of all those of the same breed, and so Frank had been forced to abandon Mr. Moon to Anna's divided attentions and the company of her vicious German shepherd. What made these ice queens so special that they were allowed to smuggle her in?

Weeks ago, Bitte was saying, the three of them had come to Portofino from their aunt's cramped Vienna apartment, by way of a sightseeing trip in Paris and the Loire, by way of their home in Malmö, to stay with a widower of obscene and obscure wealth who'd set his sights on making Bitte his third wife. He'd set up mother and daughter in separate rooms above the kitchen on the eastern side of his villa. The widower slept until noon, due either to his advanced age or to late-night carousing or a combination of the two, but the girls were early risers. Each morning, a local fisherman, a brute with a smashed nose and hook-shaped scars on his bulging forearms, dropped off the day's prime catch in the widower's kitchen. From their shared terrace, Anja, sipping coffee and reading a novel while her mother wrote postcards inside, gave the *beau laid* fellow a little wave as he came up the walk; then, another day, Bitte, leaning over the railing to admire the view while Anja bathed, wished him a *buon giorno*. His subsequent visits to their respective rooms were quick and rough and wordless. They had yet to determine which of them had him first. In fact, they were still unsure whether he was aware they were not the same woman.

She would leave her door slightly ajar so that he'd find her sitting up in bed, pretending to be caught by surprise (that was Anja); or she'd stand in the doorway in her white silk robe, pull him in from the hallway and rarely make it as far as the bed (that was Bitte). Bitte recounted the details with matter-of-fact directness: the briny smell that lingered on her skin, his oily sunburnt chest covered in black hair coarse as wires, the filthy boots he never removed. His callused hands that sometimes bled. His animal grunts. She was bragging. Trying to impress them. This happened all the time around Tenn. Auditioning. Frank believed little of it, least of all that this insatiable sea-wolf couldn't tell the two apart. We men are connoisseurs of bodies, he wanted to inform these Blomgren girls. No matter how many we've tasted, they are as distinct to us as species of flowers.

"Our new friends have gone native," Tenn said to Frank.

Anja remained quiet and perfectly still during the story, embarrassed, maybe, by her mother's gaucherie. Yet she kept her head up, regarding Frank and Tenn with a neutral radiance, and with a tranquility rare among the women in Tenn's set. Starlets, agents, hangers-on, socialites, Mother Edwina, and even poor Rose Williams; Frank always sensed in them, as he did in Tenn, anxiety churning like a motor in their throats. The motor was at a constant whir, warping their voices into a tremulousness everyone but them could hear. It kept Frank on alert. Next to them, he was as steady and plush as a child's toy. He was the man they turned to for comfort, or to confess, or simply to rest. Was this because he had no motor, or because he had no significance? Or did the absence of the motor confirm his insignificance? Whichever it was, Frank was the reliable kind, and he sensed that Anja was, too.

The widower was no longer in the picture, according to Bitte. He'd turned out his guests upon hearing of the sea-wolf's visits. (But did he keep bringing the fish? Frank wondered.) It was the cook, the loyal cook, who'd betrayed them. The Blomgrens then befriended Truman, who found them an apartment in town until they could determine their next move. Money was a concern, but not an immediate one. For Bitte, the most pressing question was, *Who will we be?* The longer they stayed away from Sweden, the louder this question echoed in her dreams, and the more possibilities opened up before them. No one waited for them in Malmö, and she had no desire to see it again, especially during the dark months. Anja was a model who aspired to act; Bitte an artist who aspired to marry. For herself, Bitte wanted love and money in equal measure, by which she meant she wanted to swim in them, to drip with them. For her daughter, she wanted fame in proportion to her astonishing talent. But how? Where? Much of what they wanted they might find in Italy and certainly in the States, and possibly Spain or the south of France, but never in Sweden, not at the intensity they craved.

"Our country is dull, dull, *dull*," said Bitte. "To live we require brightness. We are mad for it."

Bitte spoke for Anja the way Tenn spoke for his lobotomized sister, Rose, as if Anja were too precious or too limited to choose her own words. Frank wondered if brightness was indeed what Anja required, and if anyone had asked her, and what exactly it meant. In the hour or so that Frank stood in the corner listening to her mother, fending off the parasites trying to break into their tight circle, the only words Anja had spoken had been her name.

That is, until Bunky, Truman's prince of a bulldog, toddled into their field of vision, her head bowed to lick up crumbs, and Maja leapt suddenly from Bitte's arms to greet her. The white puffball falling like a bomb startled Bunky, and his first instinct was to bite. Maja, fierce Blomgren girl that she was, bit back, but she was no match. In the span of a moment, Bunky went stiff, bared his teeth, lunged, and took another chunk out of Maja's side. In a single motion, Bitte scooped her into her arms, turned her back to Bunky, and rushed across the room and down the stairs, her little dog whimpering and yelping and smearing her dress with blood.

Sandro rushed over and dropped to his knees. *"Sono un veterinario!"* he said, and "I will help!" as he cradled the still-raging Bunky at his side. He turned his head away from the direction in which Bitte and Maja had escaped.

"Why help this dog when our Maja is the one who is hurt?" Anja said to Sandro, which is when Truman appeared, hysterical, pushed Sandro out of the way, and sank to the floor. He lifted Bunky above him to inspect him, twisting him this way and that. Truman was so slight, so much a tiny creature himself in his round glasses and floppy hair and flailing skinny wings. Not yet thirty, he seemed far younger than Frank, a gawky child with practiced refinement and an alien brain. "Where'd she get you?" he cooed to Bunky in that impossible voice. His eyes and ears were all for him, as Frank's and Tenn's would have been had Mr. Moon initiated such a brawl, which of course he never would.

"She should be fine, Signor Capote," said Sandro, standing over him. "There is no break of the skin. Thank you for this nice party."

"Who the fuck are you?" said Truman.

Sandro opened his mouth to answer, but, before he could, Anja grabbed him by the arm and pulled him across the room.

Through all this, Jack remained out cold in the armchair.

An assortment of twittering parasites crouched down beside Truman and Bunky, rubbing Truman's back, scratching Bunky behind the ears. "We saw it all," they said. "We got here as soon as we could. Poor little Bunky! Poor Truman!"

Frank and Tenn rolled their eyes at each other, smiling. This was how it always was: after a night apart, lost in a parade of strangers and giddy acquaintances, they reunited in the final hours, faded into a corner, the faces and lights and music and clinking glasses becoming a silent blur around them. A brief intermezzo, scripted for them alone. Soon someone would interrupt, lure Tenn away, ask Frank to dance; or they'd stumble home together too drunk and tired to do much but collapse on the bed still in their clothes; or they'd argue over some perceived slight, and one of them, more often Tenn these days, would storm off; but until then, for the brief time after they found each other at the ends of these parties, they held one another's attention entirely, hungry for stories and kisses and gossip, as enraptured as they'd been on the porch of the Atlantic House in Provincetown the night they met, their mutual rediscovery a reminder of who really belonged to whom, and of the falsity of both the gods of glitter and the demons of anxiety fighting that very moment to come between them. Two lovers locking eyes across a room: this was theater, yes, but it was something else, too. Brightness, maybe.

On that particular night, it was Jack Burns who came between them. "You see that guy I came with? Sandro?" he asked Frank. Sleep had sobered him up some, but he still wobbled. He had a bright pink crease across the side of his face from the piping in the armchair.

"There was some excitement," Tenn said to Jack. "Of which the party was in sore need."

"He's helping out a lady's dog," said Frank.

"That sounds like him," he said bitterly.

They led Jack through the crowd and down the narrow stairs, eager to rid themselves of him but also wanting to make sure he didn't cause trouble, and that he found his . . . lover? Patron? They owed Truman that much. But Sandro and the Blomgrens were nowhere to be found. The bartender hadn't seen them. Martine and her "uncle," his hand on the small of her back, her neck arched as he touched his lips to it, stood dreamily at the edge of the dance floor. The trombonist, on a smoke break, shook his head. The kitchen was dark. Only the crashers, on the lookout always, had answers: first the old blonde lady came down crying with the little dog and then the younger one that looked like her in the same dress and the man in the blue suit with the curly hair met her and calmed her down, and then the three of them ran out in the piazza and see, there they are, on the beach.

They looked up, and out of the windows of the Delfino they saw Sandro holding Maja above the water. Anja and Bitte stood watching on the sand, two shadows, one with arms outstretched, one with arms folded, as Sandro dunked Maja in the salty water and held her in it up to her neck. He then wrapped her in a large white towel—a tablecloth from the restaurant, Frank guessed—and handed her to Bitte. Maja continued to wail, a carnival baby in a Baptism gown, as Sandro dried her and applied pressure to her wounds in the floodlight of a moored yacht. He'd rolled up his pants to his ankles, but his shirt was soaked to the skin. He looked like a fisherman himself, trudging out of the sea with a curious catch.

You couldn't call what Maja was doing barking or even crying; what came from the creature's mouth was more like the mournful

and knowing fade of a siren. Only when Bitte handed her back to
Sandro did she go calm again. He cradled the dog to his chest, gently cupped her left cheek with his right hand, and rested his chin on
the top of her head. It's possible she fell instantly asleep to the beat-
ing of his heart. When Sandro saw Jack approach with Frank and
Tenn, he said, "Are you OK?" to which Jack shrugged and looked
away.

"The little monster will live," Sandro whispered, with a smile for
the Swedes. "But bring her to me in the morning. I have things in my
bag to help her. Things not for dogs, but won't hurt dogs. Will stop
the infection."

"Sandro and his potions," said Jack. "Just your luck you meet a
warlock."

The women ignored him. Sandro said that when they came to visit
in the morning, he could introduce Maja—gently—to Jack's dog,
Lucky, who was currently under the care of their cook in their small
hotel up the hill, on the Via del Fondaco. They were staying tonight
only. By noon tomorrow, they planned to be on the road to Marina di
Cecina, where they'd rented a bungalow for a much-needed holiday.
They came to Portofino on a whim, not deciding for sure on the de-
tour until minutes before they turned north at Livorno.

When Sandro handed Maja back to Bitte, she clawed for him and
wailed again until he took her back in his arms. Her little chest heaved
under the white tablecloth, her eyes wild and afraid. Bitte cocked her
head at the dog and sneered.

"We give her a few minutes more," he said to Bitte. "She is still
very scared."

Bitte walked off, producing a cigarette from some mysterious
pocket inside her dress. Jack provided the lighter. It was a dry windless
night, the waves not so much crashing as crinkling at their feet, then
shyly retreating, as if embarrassed to have appeared at all.

"Smart girl, that dog," Anja said to Frank. "She sees an escape and she makes it."

"Who can resist a strong set of arms?" said Tenn. He came up behind Frank and squeezed his biceps. "She's not the only smart beast in this menagerie."

"She's afraid of your mother," Frank said.

"I was hoping to leave them both here with old Signor Ricciardi," said Anja, watching Bitte remove her shoes with one hand and maintain her cigarette in the other. "The fisherman she told you about? Vittorio? He was not the disease, he was the symptom, if you understand me. And he was mine first."

She had begged Vittorio not to make so much noise, Anja told them, her mother now far out of earshot. She had been fully aware what could happen if they were discovered. If the fisherman couldn't be silent and quick, he shouldn't come to her at all. He liked to say Anja's name, over and over, but she forbade it. The first few mornings, he followed her instructions, but they went out of their heads a few times, and they were lucky nobody heard. For her he removed his boots, though it was unwise and took up precious minutes. They had the timing down to the second Bitte stepped into her long bath. But then one morning Bitte woke early, which was unlike her, and threw off their timing. She saw him from her terrace and waved. He understood her wave, and that she was like Anja but not Anja. Vittorio was not picky. The idea appealed to him. He must have had a good laugh about it with his friends. But not with Anja, not in her presence. She never let Vittorio in her room again. Her mother misled them on that score. It was not a share, but a theft. The disease, not the symptom. Anja had learned a long time ago how Bitte fashioned her life stories to make herself bigger than she was, and that it was not only pointless to contradict or even clarify them, it was a betrayal.

"And you loved this man, Vittorio?" Frank asked.

Anja laughed at the question. "How old are you, Signor?"

"Our Frankie is a romantic thirty and a half," Tenn said, now squeezing his shoulders. "A young man with the heart of a schoolboy."

It was how most people, not just Tenn, knew Frank then: dreamy, fun-loving, the cutup easily seduced by the promise of a good party— all of which he was—and carefree, which he was not. Sincere and instinctively honest, he expected the same of others. He rarely questioned their intentions. As a result, Frank had been taken advantage of; he'd had his schoolboy heart broken again and again by girls who sniffed out the weakness in him. He'd always gone for the hard, inscrutable ones like Anja. He'd ask one on a date and then, when she didn't show up, he'd spend countless hours waiting around for her, his resentment quickly turning to worry she'd come to some harm, then to the certainty he'd gotten the time or place wrong, and then ulti- mately to disappointment. If Frank had the talent to paint a self- portrait, he'd paint his face looking out a window at that moment hopefulness gave way to concern.

Though he hated when people failed him, he forgave easily, except when he had to forgive himself for failing someone else. So he made it a point not to fail anyone. To always agree. To say yes to every adven- ture, especially of the romantic sort. Of all the people in Frank's life, Tenn was the only one who knew how tightly he clenched his fists over his hours in the window, through his adventures of love. Only Tenn knew how Frank braced himself at all times for disaster, and to fight off whoever stood in his way. Tenn once said that, yes, Frank was a little horse, the name fit the shape of his body, but that he wondered sometimes if the horse was made of porcelain. Frank preferred to think of himself not as a horse at all, but as a fine but common instrument, a mandola or a *chittara battente*, carved from dense solid wood, banged up from night after night of being lugged around to parties. No one expected much from this dented common thing. When played, though, how sweet it sounded. What pleasure it gave. What comfort.

Love and affection is what I got to offer on hot or cold days in this lonely old world, says Alvaro Mangiacavallo, the hero of *The Rose Tattoo*, the leading man Tenn based on him. Had Frank once said as much about himself, about their affiliation, or did Tenn simply understand Frank's purpose on earth better than he did?

Tenn's hands on Frank's shoulders, there on the sand in Portofino, soothed him. The muscles in his neck and upper back were like rubber bands stretched at all times to the point of snapping. Sometimes— at parties, on a stroll, even at the breakfast table across from Tenn or Anna—Frank caught himself with his shoulders tensely hunched and realized, again, that he'd been going through the world like that for hours, for days, for years. Relaxing the muscles was like telling himself very good news; his lungs filled with nourishing air; his eyes closed in sweet relief; but then moments later the bands pulled tight again. He did not consider himself an anxious person; he was simply *on alert*. Something terrible could happen at any moment, and for that inevitability he needed to be ready.

"You see, Frank," said Tenn, "the Scandinavians age at a faster rate than the men and women of the sunburnt countries. The difference is in dog years. When were you last a romantic, Miss Blomgren? Age . . . ten?"

"Fourteen," she said quickly.

"What happened at fourteen?" Frank asked.

She blinked. "Here she is," she said, as Bitte rejoined them.

It was long past midnight, and crowds were still pouring steadily down into the square from the hilly streets. In this way, Portofino was like the dozens of other port towns Tenn had taken Frank to on their summerlong stays in Italy. People stood around with their ice cream cones telling jokes and flirting and swaying to the music. Every once in a while, a startling burst of fireworks filled the sky over the fleet of boats. A car appeared out of nowhere and honked its way through the square, the driver shouting and pumping his arm angrily out the window. Then, slowly, as the ashes fluttered away and the eggy firework smell wore off and the yachts cut their radios, couple by couple staggered back up the steep narrow inclines, men in each other's arms, men with women, packs of friends, their songs and shouts and laughter bouncing off the stone in hollow echoes. The colored lights strung from the lampposts blurred in the mist. The lights stayed on until dawn, when the guys setting up the fruit stands and fish stalls and flower markets unplugged them, and the mist burned off, and the boats whirred to life. That's how it was the night the six of them and the patched-up dog crossed the square to a nameless bar for a nightcap that none of them needed, and stayed so long talking, dreaming, planning—one nightcap turning into three, to four—that the owner, whom Tenn paid a handful of lire not to kick them out, fell asleep slumped in a chair waiting for them to release each other. They emerged, squinting, into the second day of August, 1953.

Ten years ago.

Jack was gone now, of course, and Sandro lived blameless and cozy and unreachable in some Tuscan hill town. Anja's most recent letter came posted from Madrid, where she'd been filming. She couldn't get to New York until the fall, she wrote, but surely Frank would be out of the hospital long before then; the cobalt treatments would do the trick this time. She'd enclosed a Polaroid from a recent shoot in Marrakech, her head wrapped in one of those Moslem scarves, looking bored and triumphant astride a camel. She insisted on seeing him—"and Tenn?"—in Spain for the holidays. She loved Madrid so much that she'd purchased a floor-through apartment in a ramshackle building in La Latina, though she rarely spent more than a few nights in a row there. Sometimes Frank imagined this apartment, which he'd seen only in Anja's exuberant descriptions, as his next home: the sloping stucco butter-yellow walls, the tall windows dripping with flowers, the wrought-iron balcony that overlooked the tight oppressed streets of the Plaza de San Andrés. He'd roam these streets in the evenings on his way to late-night resistance meetings. He'd provide aid to the artists. He'd run money, arms, whatever the Movement found necessary. In this next life, he is put to good use.

He set the photo on the little table next to the vases of flowers. With the last of the day's strength, he turned a page of the letter over and scribbled *Come now please I need you*, one word per line, like a madman's ransom note. He tucked the page back in the envelope, sealed it with a little spit and what was left of the glue, wrote RETURN TO SENDER on the front, and handed it to the nurse. For the rest of the day, a thousand hollow hours, he slept. He had no trouble nodding off, though he woke often and couldn't dream. The men in his ward, their sudden shouts and strangled gurgles, kept him in that shallow pool of sleep. He didn't mind the men. Their bodies and voices and breath kept him company, as they had in his Navy days. You couldn't convince him he wasn't back with his squadron, that they weren't sailing out first thing. *Quit clowning, Merlo*, one of them said. Nicky? Sea Hawk? *Get some shut-eye. We need your legs.*

When the night nurse woke him, she told him that he'd had a few visitors: Al and Dan, his sister Connie, the priest. There was always a priest. To the priest Frank was carrion. He'd be back. The others, too. Vivien Leigh, who'd thrown a party in his honor weeks before. Irene Selznick had dropped off an expensive tin of sweets. Someone else had called on the phone, the nurse said, but didn't leave a name or a message.

"Man or woman?" Frank asked her.

"Woman."

"Woman," Frank repeated. What was it this time, he wondered. A crisis of staging? Some diva actress pitching a fit? Was his precious Angel reading from a book of poems? No, Tenn had sent Angel back to Key West. This time it was the premiere of *Milk Train*, down in Virginia. Frank pulled the sheets up to his chin and turned on his side, wincing at the pressure of his ribs on the mattress. The nurse's shadow disappeared from the wall. He pushed the button to get her back. He needed a blanket. He needed two blankets, and the oxygen. Every shiver turned the vise tighter on his chest's tender bones. He could feel the necrosis in his lips, blue as ice, his skin cracking. He pushed the button again. This place couldn't hold him. He would get to Spain. Anja would come and smuggle him out.

Tenn used to tease Frank about his daydreams, his giddy contemplations, how he always jumped ahead to the happy ending, a different way of ending happy each time. Even that night in Portofino, in the nameless bar, drunk to high heaven, Tenn had proclaimed to their new friends, with pride, *There are roses tattooed in my Frankie's eyes.* And he was right. Never, not for one moment, did Frank fear what Tenn feared—what most men feared—which was that he'd die alone. It was funny how it had all turned out, wasn't it, Tenn? Wasn't it almost funny?

2.

THE MUSE IN WINTER

For thirty years, Anja has lived in his city. Now that he is gone, it turns to her an unfamiliar face. From the safety of the train, behind the thick-paned window, she recoils from its lopsided mouth, its filthy eyes. When she steps off the platform, it looks away in recrimination. Hatching a plan. Lying in wait. She would apologize or confess if she had cause, but she has no cause. What is the old saying? The heart takes no commands. She loved him, but she has never loved where he brought her.

She climbs the hill toward the house they shared. She is coming from a meeting at the university, which has taken the last of his papers. In her bag is a letter on heavy paper signed by the chairman of the board of trustees, explaining the terms of the transaction. It has taken three weeks to pack up his effects, and now his books are all that remain of him in their house. To Goodwill went his clothes, to his daughter in Leiden the few letters and photographs he'd saved at Anja's insistence. Pieter Meisner was a man entirely devoid of sentiment, and she was, if not his wife, the partner of his mind. Vacated by his body, she and their rooms have suffered little substantive change. The house had no claim on his body, and so it does not register the absence of his breath or his excretions or the touch of his tremulous fingers. They miss his ferocious brain, that generator humming all the days and nights, emitting its invisible vibrating vectors. She would vibrate, too, and return her own waves, the two of them hurling energy back and forth at each other even as they slept. Mornings they woke already buzzing.

How still she feels now.

But the city. The city grieves all of him, and has shifted from its halfhearted attempt to woo her to its campaign for revenge. The brick buildings narrow wrathfully as she walks between them on her way up the hill. If she does not quicken her pace, reach the square at the end of the block, the walls will squeeze her last breath out of her. Already she has slipped once and fallen on the cobblestones, spilling her bag of oranges, where they sizzled and foamed in the burning snow until, stumbling to her feet, she stuffed them back in the bag. She hurries on, her gaze fixed on the broad square, asking humbly, silently, for the protection of the dogs and the Jamaican nannies and their shrieking charges, but they cannot register her plea. She is just another rich old white lady carrying her groceries in a neighborhood of rich old white ladies busy with their projects.

The little peace in her life Anja has found in only two places: a crowd, or with him. Everything else—all that in-between—has bedeviled her since Italy brought her into being. Now she dreads the party of two, being seated across from any person who is not him, a woman especially, her hand clasped clammily in hers, her face beseeching, besieging, digging her hollow. There is equal terror in the party of three, in negotiating the conversation, steering it one way or the other, trying to ensure that no one stays too long in the cold. If she must choose, give her a movie set or a stage. Give her an audience of eager nameless strangers drinking her in. Or, best of all, these days, give her her empty rooms—two blocks past the square, one block north, almost there almost there—where she will be, if not admired, then, at the very least, safe.

She sees the young man on her front steps the moment she turns the corner, before he sees her. He rises at her approach. "You are Anja Bloom?" he asks.

Without meeting his eyes, she sets down the grocery bag and reaches into her purse for a pen. "You have something for me to sign?"

For this reason alone, she should have kept her name out of the newspapers after Pieter's death. Apparently, it has not been enough to answer by hand the letters her manager forwards her each quarter, to autograph head shots and film stills, to, once, in a rare flare-up of sentimentality, walk to the hospital on the other side of the hill to grant the dying wish of a man in his fifties wasting away in his bed. Now, because she was too weak to believe Pieter would ever die, and prepared not at all for the aftermath of his going, she will be compelled to entertain in her front yard actors and film students and all other manner of the curious and needy, until she decides on her next and final city.

But this young man produces no yellowing playbill, no decades-old glossy photo bought from one of those vintage shops at the bottom of the hill. "I am not a regular celebrity fan," he says, with an attitude and affect she recognizes but cannot quite place. The most she can identify is that unmistakable mark of the Italian man: bold imperiousness shot through with shame. *"Le mie condoglianze per la perdita di suo marito,"* he says, with careful formality. Not a Sicilian, for sure. A Florentine, maybe. Educated. Or a skilled impostor.

"Common-law," she says, studying his face.

"My father was Sandro Nencini," he says in English. "That is my name also."

The lone tree in her yard shakes its fists at her. She picks up her bag and shoves it into the arms of the young man. "We can talk upstairs," she says, and, as soon as they are inside, she slams the front door and turns the lock. Breathes deeply. Here, finally, in the stairwell, her back against the solid wall, she can gulp the sweet life-giving air.

His boots drip brown salt on the living room rug. "Please," she says, motioning to remove them. The west-facing windows drown him in light. His large and ungainly feet, sheathed in multiple pairs of multicolored woolen socks, are incongruous with his slender body. He unwraps his scarf to reveal a pleasing mutation of his father's face, one made kinder by a softened Roman nose and blunted cheekbones. His mother must have been a girl from the country, plump and sweet and adoring. Likely against her wishes, he has decorated himself with a beard and mustache and the feminizing long hair favored by the youth of film departments since her day.

He is very sorry to bother her, he says, helping himself to Pieter's leather chair. The last thing he wants to do is to trouble her in her grief, especially given its recent onset, but he has come because he hopes he might be of some comfort, or at least an agreeable distraction, or maybe even a happy walk down what he calls—with no apparent discomfort with the cliché—"Memory Lane." He couldn't resist the chance to see her in person, he says, once he read the name Anja Bloom in Professor Meisner's obituary in his university's newspaper. Who would expect to find such a name in such a place, dropped into the history of the great astronomer's life as casually and matter-of-factly as one of his distant stars? But of course, he says, in a phrase he must have scripted, *she* was one of Meisner's stars, too. Did people tell her that all the time?

Once, yes.

"No," she says.

"Do you mind talking about him? About your life before him?"

"What I mind are your television questions," she says, coldly, though she likes him, and liked him immediately, even after he spoke his name. Italians have always won her over without effort. (If this were an Italian city, she would have been in its throes from the first.) It is obvious that he is using his father's connection to her to seek wisdom and instruction, so she might as well get on with the lesson. "On television they say 'Memory Lane,'" she explains. "Or in *People* magazine. The serious film-maker does not let such a sentimental concept enter his head. He despises sentimentality. Nostalgia is his mortal enemy. What he seeks is disharmony, friction, the conflict of heart and mind. Not connection. The viewers make the connections if they wish."

In other words: Square One. And yet the boy seems to pay no attention to her lesson. His films will be schlock.

"I am in graduate school for neuroscience, Signora," he says, interrupting her, as if in apology. "On the medical side. I have seen many of your movies—most of them, I think, the ones that came to the theater. The library has a large collection, too, some even on the reel-to-reel—but I am not in the business of movies. I have much respect for them, of course, for work like yours. Artistic work. *Film.* And your husband's contributions to his field."

"Your father was a doctor," she says, not because it will be news to him but because she has just remembered.

"Yes, he was. A veterinarian. But he helped people, too, with ailments not as serious. Fevers, asthma. He wrote prescriptions and set bones. He could even fix teeth. The last few years of his life, he also sold antiques out of a little shop. My mother used to joke, 'I don't worry when the fresh young girls come in. Your father likes only what is old and broken.'"

She looks at the boy more closely: the smooth skin in the corners of his eyes, the faint rouge of acne on his cheeks. "He must have had you when he was very old."

"Is sixty-two very old?" he asks, and there is Sandro's smile coming for her all the way from Portofino in 1953, the smile of the doctor, the weak-willed lover, the murderer. Sixty years, and still she recognizes it. How much of his father's history does he know? "When he died I was seventeen," the boy says. "He went to sleep after lunch and never woke up. The phone rang, an emergency at the clinic, and my sister tried to wake him. My mother and I were on the terrace smoking when we heard her scream. He didn't like us to smoke. Every day we waited for him to sleep, and then we'd sit outside with a pack of Embassies and gossip about the neighborhood and the girls in my school and what my life was going to be."

Though she knows from his breath, she asks anyway, "Do you still smoke?" When he nods, she produces a pack of Camels from her purse. "I will join you."

"Inside?"

"Why not?"

She flicks the lighter and draws in the first earthy breath, more delicious than the purity of the stairway air, craving the poison of it. She has given up on her body. She wants to punish it for keeping on so stubbornly, as if out of spite.

"I'd like to stop," Sandro says, not stopping.

Until his father died, he tells her, he had no interest in medicine. He was a young man already drifting. His job after school was to make deliveries for a family friend who owned a flower shop. When school ended, he planned to work full time making deliveries. If he had any ambition at all, it was to open a second flower shop in the next town, or to wait until the death of the family friend, who was childless, and take over his shop under his own name. But the day his father died, he said, it was like a switch turned on. As for the antiques, they'd never appealed to him; it was the potential for life, what you could *do* with it, the *more*-ness of it, that suddenly became the puzzle he must solve. The shell of life, what had been done and could not be undone—he was talking about history, about chipped figurines and grandfather clocks and handmade lace—held significance, but, for him, no romance.

"Let me guess, then," says Anja. She does not have to hear any more. "You discovered your calling was to save people. To help them. To give them that potential for life you speak of. So that they would not die before their time, like your father." She has heard this story, or versions of it, a hundred times, an individual history presented to her as if it were singular, an original invention. She longs for a new story, for someone to convince her that his life has not already been led by a thousand men just like him in the years that have just passed. She longs for someone to surprise her. It is one of the many reasons she stopped making films; not only does she know the ending from the first page of the script, she knows the middle and the music and the minor characters as well. There is always a mother, and always a bed on which a loved one has died. There is always a decision resisted and then embraced. There is always a striking out on one's own.

"That would be the television reason, no?" he says, and there again is Sandro's smile, except this time accompanied by the pulling back of his hair over his ears. A kind face, framed by soft waves, will get you only so far, she could tell him. As will charm. As will youth, and the privileges of your sex. And those eyes. If she were cruel, she would say: you will not be as lucky as he was, to die in peace in your bed after decades of sins, your country wife and dutiful children tiptoeing around the house in deference to your sleep. The Fates are less forgiving now. The century has beaten them down.

"To help people wasn't my reason," he continues. "I don't know if I had a reason. I know only that the switch turned on and filled me with light. But my education is taking a long time. Just after I started, a year into the university program in Perugia, my mother became sick. Lung cancer. Another reason to quit these. She went fast, but not so fast to save her the terrible suffering. It is her money that brought me to America. Here I have a better chance. The Italian university system—" He waves his hand as if swatting a fly. "It is full of superstition still. Hard science comes second to them. I want to be at the edge of the research—the cutting edge, as the expression goes. If you can't be at the cutting edge, why bother to be anything at all? Open a flower shop. Make movies for Hollywood, and not the black-and-white kind they study in film school." He sits tall against the back of the chair. "Can I ask you to guess what I have made my specialization?"

"Why? Will it surprise me?"

He shrugs. "I am interested, what you think I would choose to study. I feel that you know me, and that I know you. Is that strange? All I have are some pictures of you, and a few letters of my father's that mention you by name, and this hour, so far, of conversation." He picks up his knapsack, as if he is about to pull the memorabilia from it. Instead, he rests it on his lap. "And your movies, of course. *Films*, I apologize. I have seen more of your films than I pretended to see. My favorite is *Echo*."

"Your feelings of connection to me—if we can agree on that word—do follow," Anja says. "You have watched me on screen. You have seen my body without clothes, a version of my body at least, with the light in all the right places. You have watched me live many lives and die each time. Did you notice I died in every film I made with Martin Hovland? It was a joke, almost, between us. To Hovland, there was no peaceful death. Your grandmother who passed with grace into the next life holding your hand, inside she was screaming. To make it otherwise on film was to perpetuate a dishonest myth. And so I screamed and clawed and won awards for the effort. I can show you stacks of letters

from men and women who have written to me claiming to know me
better than I know myself, just from how I have screamed and clawed.
My Greek chorus with their unsolicited misinformed advice, trying to
convince me that they alone saw what Hovland's camera did not capture. That is your connection to me, Sandro; it is logical, but it is still
an illusion. My connection to you, though—you say, 'I feel that you
know me'—has no logic. It is just your fancy."

"I don't know that word," he says.

"It means your whim."

He considers this. "Maybe," he says. "But I felt it the moment you
recognized my father in me. I was nervous to come here, and to show
you the things I have to show you." He turns the bag over in his lap.
"But as soon as you saw Papa's face in mine, my nerves dried up."

"Because you are a homosexual, too?"

Without hesitation, he says, "That's a word I know." He smiles,
holding her gaze. "But it's not the one I use."

"Which one do you use?"

"We say queer now, Signora."

"We said queer then."

He gives her an uncomprehending look, which may or may not be
for show. Anja has always had trouble distinguishing genuine naïveté
from the kind put forth as a bluff to buy time or to force the other
person to show his hand. It was a strategy best suited to the young,
though most people take too long to perfect it, and by then it is no
longer as effective. He says, "It was under my impression that there
were no words at all for us in those years."

It is possible that young Sandro is right, Anja thinks, that her time
in Italy passed before language. The years certainly make no sound
now. She does not envy his twenty-first-century generation, the
weight of the voices and images they carry with them at the tap of a
finger. Still, how it would please her to hear them, the voices of Frank

and Tennessee, even Jack, even Sandro, any one of them. She can find videos of Tenn's interviews, of course, in the library or from the internet, but in none of these videos can he call out again to her, or to Frank, by name from across the terrace above the Roman Opera. In none of them can he place his hand on the small of her back and lead her to the bar, saying, ladies and gentlemen, I give you Anja Bloom. Tenn was the last of these men she touched, in 1982 in New York, fat and doped-up and wearing an absurd beret. Of the four of them, Sandro was the one to whom she had paid the least attention, certainly the last she had ever expected to see again. But now here he was.

"I would like to know this," she says to him. "Did you come here to ask me something, or to tell me something? Or are you not sure yet? What are you so excited to show me that you think I am not already aware of?"

"To show you something was my plan," he says. "But maybe I am also looking to get something. And to learn something."

"That is many somethings," she says.

"You don't want the company, then?"

"This is more of an intrusion than company," she says, but—and this surprises her—she does it in a way that signals, if only to herself, that she welcomes both.

In *Echo*, her most recent film, her final film, she played a disgraced wife exiled to a seaside town in the Curonian Spit. For sixty-five minutes, she wandered the beach in an evening gown, encountering other abandoned women in various forms of dress, until she came upon her older sister, missing since their childhood. Wordlessly, her sister took her by the hand and led her through a marsh to an empty farmhouse, where they slept side by side, as they had done as children, and fused their dreams into the action-adventure plot that constitutes the third act of the film. In this plot, a deliberately jarring shift in tone and genre, the two sisters roamed Eastern Europe hunting war criminals and, in between kills, sang torch songs in roadside bars. *Echo* was not only Anja Bloom's farewell to the screen twenty-four years ago, but the last film written and directed by Hovland, the man who had made her his muse, whose brain exploded in his sleep the month of its release. Fourteen films they made together, starting with *Mercy* in 1954. They had disagreed on some of the particulars of *Echo*, but in the end Anja admired it enormously, as she had all of Hovland's work, and she even admired herself in it, which was less often the case, and to this day no one questions the influence on world cinema of both the film and her portrayal of the nameless exile.

Anja's mother brought her to Italy—there is always a mother—and Italy brought her to Frank, and Frank and Tenn brought her to Hovland, and Hovland brought her to Pieter, and then Pieter went screaming into oblivion and left her alone in this hateful city, and now Italy sits across from her again crossing and uncrossing his legs.

3.

WHITE

Before the six new friends parted, at long last, outside the nameless Portofino bar in the purple dawn, they made a plan: sleep all morning, pack sandwiches and wine, and meet in the early afternoon on the beach at Paraggi. There was no time for one of those elaborate Italian lunches that dragged into midday, not with rain expected in the early evening. Jack grumbled about delaying their road trip to Marina di Cecina—they'd already paid for the bungalow, it was unfair to Lucky the dog and Marika the cook to keep them cooped up in the dreary *albergo*, he liked the rain, he didn't want to come here to begin with—but, in this matter, as in life, he was weak-willed and darkly indifferent, and Sandro was a man of persuasive passions, and so they stayed on in Portofino one more day.

Tenn had managed to sleep a couple hours, and by nine he was at the desk in their room at the Splendido. A telegram from Visconti had arrived, demanding an update on the *Senso* script, but it was *Battle of Angels* he was smashing up again that morning, inspecting each of the broken pieces for how it might be repainted, reassembled into a new shape, or tossed permanently on the trash heap. In four years, that play, retitled *Orpheus Descending*, would hit the Broadway stage, starring Maureen Stapleton, and flop. In between would come *Cat on a Hot Tin Roof*, the last knockout Frank had seen, and probably ever would see. Strange to think that *Cat* was just a few months away then, forming itself in the back of Tenn's brain as, hungover from Truman's party, he picked through the wreckage that became *Orpheus*. Tenn never missed a day of work, no matter what debauchery had transpired the night before. If a new play wouldn't come, he'd take up one from the trash heap, or he'd scratch out a poem or a story or ideas or a few sketches in his journal. He showed up to his job in the early mornings like a stonemason to a cathedral. When Frank woke each day—in Key West, in New York, here at the Splendido in the bed under the soft covers—it was always to the music of the man at his labor: the clatter of the keys, the slam and ding of the carriage return after return, the shuffling of papers, the sighing and stomping and creaking of the chair.

Frank seldom got the chance to watch Tenn work, as he was doing now. Back home, Tenn had a separate office with a door he kept closed even when he was alone. He'd come out for another cup of black coffee, nod dazedly in Frank's direction, then retreat back into his world of silent voices and invisible companions.

He watched Tenn stick a pencil in his mouth, tip his chair back, prop his bare foot on the desk, and close his eyes. His pants were rolled up below his knees, his hair a mess of matted curls. He sat that way a long while, his hands folded at his waist, unmoving, deep in thought, the clock on the mantle ticking loud. In profile like this, without both of his baby-boyish cheeks visible, he looked older and more distinguished, the man of letters he was born, if not bred, to become. An artist should paint him from this angle, in this soft morning light. They should put him on a postage stamp. Tenn shook his head vigorously, as if eavesdropping on Frank's thoughts. Then his lips softened into a faint smile over the pencil. They remained there in a long moment of self-satisfaction. Of peace. Confidence. To witness such a moment was like catching a wild animal taking a sunbath.

Frank should have told him then and there that he loved him and would never leave him. Not how *much* he loved him, which was very much, but that he loved him at all, a fact Frank took for granted but Tenn claimed not to know. He should have told Tenn that he admired his stonemason life, that he was in awe of the churches he'd built and was building, their beauty and permanence, the sacred hearts that blazed within them. He should have said, I'm grateful for all you've brought to me, and for all you've brought me to, for all that you bring out of me. But Frank had never said anything of this sort to Tenn. He had never spoken the word "love." The time was never right. He didn't want to disturb him. His bad poetry embarrassed him. Frank was a tough guy from Jersey who worked construction, fought for his country, and imagined he might still have a kid or two someday, not to mention a woman to go along with those kids. He was afraid that once you gave something a name, it would turn on you. And maybe he knew, even then, that love was a currency he hadn't spent all of yet, while Tenn had gone broke on Frank the first moment he saw him.

The clock ticked louder. The sun forced itself on the windows. Up from the town came the clang of the church bells. It was Sunday, after all.

In the clamor of the bells, Tenn lunged for his desk. His chair dropped behind him with a thud. He stood and riffled through the stack of pages next to the typewriter and scribbled something, and he didn't seem to notice when Frank, now keenly aware of the late hour, climbed out of bed and walked naked in front of him on his way to the toilet.

Was this lunging the lightning strike of the new title, *Orpheus*

Descending? The first lines of *Cat*? Or just a scrap of dialogue he threw on the heap a minute later? Frank knew only as much of Tenn's draft pages as he'd tell him, which some days was a lot—a character's buried shame, a third-act revelation—and other days was nothing. Frank learned fast that to ask was to be denied, that the less interested he acted, the more likely Tenn was to pull a page from his typewriter, walk it out to the porch, and read it aloud to him. Mostly what he told Frank was that his writing was shit, that he was washed up, that he didn't have another *Streetcar* in him and even *Streetcar* wasn't the masterwork everyone thought it was, that no one worth a fig would finance another one of his plays, that he'd die poor and forgotten and not even Frank would come to his funeral, glad—giddy, in fact, relieved, *ecstatic!*—to be free of him. He'd fly into a rage at Frank for betraying him so heartlessly, for his secret wish to abandon him, and then, minutes later, he'd beg Frank's forgiveness, remind him through tears of their many good years together—of Mr. Moon, of Duncan Street, of stepping off the boat in Genoa—and how many more of the good years awaited them if only he'd grant him one last reprieve. Please, Frank, please, he'd plead. Find it in your heart . . .

Frank was the palm tree in the hurricane, slashed and bent by the wind, pushed to the point of splitting, as he waited for the calm of the inevitable eye. This life with Tenn, though far from tranquil, taught him patience. Like Tenn, he fixed his hopes on the greatness of whatever tomorrow might bring—the next knockout, the next trip abroad, the next party, the next boy—and dismissed or distrusted what came before simply for belonging to the black-and-white past. Their future together promised color in bright bursts: an orange house in Liguria to return to next summer, the costumes on the set of *Senso* in the fall, one day the green rooftops of Marrakech, the turquoise water off the coast of Key West when they finally made it home.

"Let's not make them wait," Frank called from the bathroom, though it was he who'd slept too long, as usual.

"You go on ahead," Tenn called back. "I'll meet you on the beach."

"I don't want to go alone."

"Hitch a ride with the lovebirds. They need a referee."

"They're awful to each other, aren't they? What do you make of them?"

Tenn gave no answer. When Frank got back to the room, he was hunched over his desk again, biting his lip as he crossed out lines and wrote between them in his mad scrawl. Another lightning bolt. Frank gave him a quick kiss on the top of his head and stood another moment at his side, the only sound now their breathing and the shushing of pencil on paper. How lucky Tenn was, Frank thought, to have another world to tunnel into. No matter that it couldn't hold him or love him back. It was far more real to him, more urgent, more alive, than the world in which Frank buttoned his shirt, took one last look in the mirror, opened the door to the hallway, and shouted back, "Don't be long."

"WHAT DO *YOU* THINK OF them?" Frank asked Anja and Bitte as they waited on the beach for their new friends.

"I think they won't show," said Bitte. "The mean one got his way."

"Which is the mean one?"

They laughed.

"Maybe his books are very good?" said Anja. "You hadn't heard of them, either?"

But then there they were, in the distance, walking toward them in sunglasses, loud-patterned boxer swimsuits, Sandro with a short-sleeved shirt unbuttoned at the navel, Jack with a long-sleeved shirt covering him to the throat. Sandro waved wildly at them with both hands, like an immigrant from the deck of a steamer. Jack carried a canvas bag over his shoulder, his head bowed in defeat.

They found the private section reserved for guests of the Splendido and angled their chairs toward the sun. The Splendido section was so close to the water that the sand was cool. Frank saved the chair to his left for Tenn. Anja was on his right, then Bitte, then Sandro, then Jack and his translucent skin at the far end under a striped blue umbrella. They lay side by side in a perfect row, surrounded on all sides by perfect rows, a grid of bodies presenting themselves for the delectation of the gods.

The first time Frank encountered an Italian beach, its military precision shocked him: the sections organized by color and pattern, the cabanas numbered to correspond with the umbrellas, the young men who came through twice a day to rake the sand. In Jersey, you brought an old bed sheet and a cooler and six cousins and set up shop on the first free spot you found. Your knees rubbed up against the hairy back of the guy next to you, and nobody squawked about it. He couldn't decide which he liked better. There was pleasure in the Italian order—you knew your place and your color and pattern; nobody stole your watch or kicked sand at your scrawny nephew—but he missed the messy collage of Monmouth and Asbury Park, where you tripped over radios and inflatable balls and the pots and pans people brought from their kitchens to make sandcastles.

Frank wasn't the type to lie around. He'd had plenty of sleep, not too bad a hangover, and an espresso that got his legs buzzing. Yesterday's weariness had burnt off with the morning mist. "Anyone for a swim?" he shouted down the silent row, loud enough for Jack to hear, though he ignored him. The Swedes shook their heads and smiled. Sandro was dozing. If Tenn were here, he'd at least be telling a story.

Anja said, languidly, "I'll go in with you, but not for a little while. I'm still cooking."

Today she and her mother wore tight-fitting one-piece swimsuits that barely covered their thighs and which tied behind their necks in little bows; in their hair, matching white bands framed their faces and exposed their foreheads to the rays. Did they own any clothes that weren't the brightest white, and did they only buy them in pairs? In their identical uniforms, they were a blank canvas inviting you to paint them, and yet they were also forbiddingly pristine. You wanted to drown them in colored ink and you wanted to protect them from the slightest smudge. Their skin was smooth and unbroken by moles or blemishes or hair, their legs and arms shellacked with oil that smelled of rosemary. They wore no makeup or nail polish. No adornments or jewels of any kind. Bitte's skin was tanning at a faster rate, a shade darker than her daughter's, which accentuated the streaks of age barely visible at her throat and the corners of her mouth.

Until then, Frank hadn't fully appreciated the beauty of the women. What had looked last night like flecks of gray in Anja's eyes were now, in the bright sun and at the edge of the brilliant sea, a chalky white, like little chips in a blue plate. He wanted to tell her that the white was like the crashing surf and her eyes like the water, but that was more bad poetry, and besides, the surf was dull in comparison and God had mixed the water with too much green, and, on top of that, he didn't want to give her the wrong impression. He flirted too much with women, Tenn said, but he did it more out of habit and manners and genuine appreciation than desire. When he flirted with men, it was usually toward some end—professional or otherwise, sometimes both—but, even then, the flirting was often unintentional, maybe even unconscious; only midway through a conversation would it occur to Frank that the man was in a position to help him in some way, or that what he'd taken as interest in his acting and dancing were naked attempts at seduction. In general, Frank wanted people to feel good about themselves; when they did, they made better company, and he had more fun.

And wasn't having fun the point of everything?

It was no fun to sit around on a beach chair. It was a waste of time, no conversation, Sandro now snoring, Jack in hiding under the umbrella with his arms folded staring grudgingly at the waves. The dog would have made better company, but they'd left her in the apartment to lick her wounds. Frank stood and looked around for someone else to talk to, someone he'd met at Truman's or spied on the yachts, but the only person he recognized was Luca, the boat guy turned luggage guy turned driver guy, who'd been taking him everywhere.

Luca stood with his fellow *ragazzi* over by his truck. Frank gave him a little wave. Should he approach him, introduce himself to his friends, propose a game of soccer? Luca lifted his chin at him as if to say, *What do you need now?* By which he surely meant, *What do you need now, pervert?* It was always a walk across fire with these men, for even the most innocent of purposes—a drink, a few rounds of *briscola*—and it was even riskier without Tenn. A pack of younger boys, too young by far, children really, were gathered behind Luca and his friends; they offered scooter rides to the tourists and rented them bikes by the hour. In a few years, they'd graduate to driving the tourists around in little vans. Frank wondered what, if anything, Luca would graduate into, or whether he'd just stay here driving starlets and rich queens around for the rest of his life.

To Anja he said, "I'm here to tell you you're burning already." He put his finger on her shoulder. "Ouch!" he said. "Come cool off with me."

"The skin burns faster in the water, no?"

"That's a myth," Frank said. "True for regular water maybe, like in a pool, but salt water protects skin. It coats it in a kind of film. Look at me." He took a step back into the aisle of sand so she could see his entire body, bronzed from head to toe. "I spend hours a day in the ocean, and I never get sunburned."

She eyed him skeptically.

"Trust me," he said. "I lie only to men."

"Go now," Bitte ordered. "You've rested enough."

In the blue-green bay, Frank and Anja floated beside each other for a long time. She was a good swimmer who, like him, favored the breaststroke. You could still look around and talk as you did it, and it moved you more quietly and elegantly among the others. Mostly they sculled back and forth from the deeper end to where they could stand and rest a bit. Every so often, Anja cupped handfuls of the salty water, splashed it onto her face, and then rubbed it in like cold cream. "Next you will tell me the Paraggi is the fountain of youth," she said.

"It's beautiful enough to be, isn't it?"

She adjusted her white bathing cap and looked back at the rows of chairs. "When I am her age, I will return here."

"You might never leave."

She considered this. "Depends."

First, she said, she had to find Bitte a husband. Only after she was settled could Anja breathe and choose her city and make her own way in the world. It was something, she said, bringing up a mother. It took patience and a hard heart. You had to give her the illusion of control and maintain a clinical distance from the decisions you made for her, decisions she believed to be her own but for which she took no responsibility. Only then would she release you. She had every intention of outliving you, of living forever, in fact, which gave you plenty of time—years upon years—to muck around in New York or Paris or wherever your dreams took you, as long as your dreams were big and had no chance of coming true. One day far into the future, broken but not destroyed, you could return to her, and she could mother you again, except that it would be the first time.

Anja hated modeling, she told Frank. If she did aspire to act, as Bitte claimed, it was only to give her brain and her limbs something to do while the cameras were on her. Becoming an actress was more Bitte's dream for Anja than her own dream for herself, and as such it would propel her out of her mother's orbit. In whatever city Bitte eventually landed, cuffed to a rich man, drowning in bejeweled dresses and suffocating through garden parties, Anja would stay for a brief time to ensure it would last, but soon it would become clear to Bitte that her daughter's future as an actress lay elsewhere. "Preferably on the other side of the farthest ocean," Anja said, with a laugh. Then, once her mother insisted that Anja go build her life and career in some distant city, she'd say her goodbyes, buy a small apartment with the money she'd surely be given, learn a trade or take up secretarial work, or do whatever she had to do so that, at night, she could gorge herself on art and ideas. History, science, music, poetry, dance, painting, theater, sculpture, she hungered for it all. She was twenty-two. By her own admission, she knew everything and nothing. She would never marry, she said, not unless the man allowed her to be a glutton in this way, not just on art and ideas but on other men, too. He would have to be very strong, and, from what Anja had already seen, strong men with an appreciation for art and ideas seemed to prefer the company of other men and not of women, especially women who required that particular form of strength.

It was not the conversation Frank hoped for or expected from his new friend. He tried to interrupt with stories of his own mother and sisters—their small, aproned lives he'd looked upon with pity and a kind of envy, so sure they were of their place in their house, their square block of Jersey, the world. At Anja's age, he'd fled from their sights each morning in his uncle's truck to make his deliveries; in the afternoons, he'd pick up his buddies and park at the beach for hours, smoking and whistling with them from the front seat of the truck at the girls stepping down from the boardwalk. Then he'd fled from them, too, those flightless boys, first for the war and then, when the war spit him back onto shore, for the city. It was the city, he told Anja, where his eyes finally adjusted, where he could see men as if for the first time, leading him into unmarked doorways and the bright life behind them.

"I am trying to imagine you behind the wheel of a milk truck," said Anja.

Frank hunched his shoulders. "You think I'm too short, don't you?" he joked. "Admit it! All you see is the top of my head."

"No!" Anja said, embarrassed. "It is just—"

"I'm teasing you," he said.

They were far out in the bay at this point, and his arms were growing tired. He guided Anja back to where they could stand. The sun beamed down on the backs of their necks and bounced back in their faces off the mirror of water, but she barely seemed to notice. Was now the right time to confess that the salt would not protect her? She stood neck-deep beside him, squinting, facing the beach. As she talked, she tapped little circles on the surface with her fingers like it was a piano.

She had no one to confide in, she said. No one to wrestle with, to discover, to tease back. For all her ambitions, Bitte kept them at a remove from the friends they made on their travels, inexplicably declining their invitations and distrusting their gestures of friendship. If Anja talked too much at parties, her mother would pinch her arm to warn her. Once, at a formal dinner, she'd pressed a fork into Anja's thigh under the table until she went quiet. Bitte believed young women should remain mysterious, an unwritten story; whereas older women needed to perfect the art of storytelling in order to remain visible, to survive.

Anja was an only child. She evaded all of Frank's questions about her father except to say that he was dead, a fact that seemed to give her comfort, or at least definition. Some of the other specifics of her situation—the blind aunt in Vienna, the family's ample savings, the quiet childhood of ice-skating and Christmas markets and ponies and months of rainy days she spent indoors without friends—Frank knew already from their all-night conversation at the piazza bar; what surprised him was not the bitterness with which Anja referred to her life, and to her mother's influences, but how desperately she wanted Frank to believe her. Until he sensed this undercurrent of desperation, Frank had had no reason to doubt that she was telling him anything but the truth.

"We should go in," he said.

"I am boring you," said Anja. She lay back and floated again.

He flicked a little water, gently, at her toes. "Secrets never bore me," he said. "For some reason, people are always telling me theirs. Gossip's more fun, though. And gossip about other people's secrets? There's nothing better than that."

He didn't know if it was just how the light was hitting her, but, from this angle, he could see through the fabric of her swimsuit. To spare them both this embarrassment, he got on his back, too.

She stretched her arms out and took his hand. "What I find from men of your type is that you always want women to perform for you," she said matter-of-factly. "We did this for Truman and his Jack in the weeks after Signor Ricciardi turned us out. We did this all over France. Vienna, too. What we wondered out loud to each other, though, my dear mother and me, walking all the way to this beach up the hill and then down from Portofino because no one offered to drive us, is what happens at the end of the performance."

"You walked here?" Frank asked. "To Paraggi? Why didn't you tell me? I'm sure Luca could have picked you up along the way. I'm sorry, I should have checked. There are other drivers if you need one . . ."

"Will we have a place to go after the curtain? Will we be safe there? Will we have enough to eat? Will we still interest you?"

"I consider myself a gentleman," Frank said.

On the other side of the beach, Luca and his friends had taken off their shirts to play soccer with the younger boys. At this hour, all of Italy was at rest: asleep, frolicking, digesting, making love. Frank craved not rest but adventure. Joy, at least. Thrills. He liked Anja, he wished her well, he felt bad about her long walk and her inevitable sunburn, but, for someone so young, she was short on joy and long on complaints. He wondered what, if anything, might give her joy, and if they'd been brought together so that he could introduce her to it.

"Is there a place to dance in Portofino?" he asked her, hopefully.

She said there was a small club, but that it was too loud to hear yourself think.

"Why do you need to think if you're dancing?"

When they saw Tenn step from the truck—it must have been four o'clock by then—they waved to him and pointed to the Splendido section.

"I have to go in now," Frank said. "Did you want to stay?"

"No," she said. "It's time." But she made no move toward the shore. Frank offered to race her, intending to lose by a length. She shook her head.

"Are you really leaving us this week?" she asked.

He reminded her of the trip to Verona for the *Senso* script, which Tenn had described in detail the night before. Visconti, the director, was insisting on the poetry of the dialogue, and Tenn needed to hole himself up in a hotel to write it. They were meeting Paul Bowles and his new lover, Ahmed, who were on their way to Verona from Rome. "Tenn's one of the busiest writers in the world," he told Anja. "Busier than Truman, that's for sure, no matter what Truman says. Every day he gets an invitation to write something for someone, to appear here or speak there. Half the time when he wakes up he doesn't remember what city he's in."

"That's him," she said. "What about you? Do you go everywhere together?"

"Not always."

"Do you have a lover waiting for you in Verona?"

"No."

"Then there's a chance our show will go on here in Portofino," she said.

"I suppose there is," he said.

Finally, they swam toward the beach. When their feet could touch bottom, they walked and, to his surprise, she took his hand again, which was when he remembered, the level of the water now at their waists, the transparency of her swimsuit. He looked down and saw how little to the imagination it left, and then, in a horrible flash, how the people in the front rows, their chairs turned to the west, gawked at her. Awkwardly he moved in front of her to shield her as best he could without blocking their forward progress. He shot a look at an old man uncouth enough to point. Luca and the boys stood shoulder to shoulder in a line, the shorter ones on their tiptoes, as if at a parade. None of this Anja appeared to notice, not his efforts to conceal her and not the old man and not the eyes roving from her breasts to the dark patch between her legs to Frank and then back again. To the people on the beach, Frank must have seemed to be presenting her, putting on a show, while all the while she babbled girlishly in his ear of cities she longed to see—Rome, Athens, Tangiers—and had Frank and Tenn traveled there? And which of these cities did they love best? And how soon could she join them? And did the beggars really come right up to you with their open mouths?

He led her over the sand to their row, pulling her close behind him. His snarling eyes dared the crowd to utter a word. She continued her incessant chatter into his left ear. She was glad Tenn was finally here, she was saying. She found Tenn dashing, not only because he was the most famous artist she'd ever met but because it was the first time she'd heard that cowboy accent in real life. She almost didn't believe Americans really talked like that. Her father had liked westerns. She'd never had the honor of attending one of Tenn's plays in the theater, but she'd seen the film of *Streetcar* twice and fallen in love, like every girl, with Marlon Brando. Really, though, she said, she was in love with Stanley Kowalski, because Stanley was the brute she and every other woman longed for in spite of themselves, in spite of what was good for them. . . .

It was at that moment, at her mention of the brute, that it occurred to Frank that Anja was ashamed, and that, rather than being oblivious to what was happening to her on the beach, she was all too aware of it, of the effect of the water on the bathing suit her mother had bought for her. She had repeated Bitte's exact words about Stanley from the night before as if they were her own. It was possible she only half knew what she was saying since she emerged from the water, that she'd been talking so much in order to distract herself, maybe even to distract Frank. When she had taken his hand, it had been for protection. "*Go now,*" Bitte had ordered. "*You've rested enough.*"

"You two look refreshed," Tenn said now, as Anja quickly wrapped a towel around herself. She settled back into her chair and tilted the umbrella for shade.

"What do you say we get the hell out of here?" said Frank.

"Typical Frankie," Tenn said to the group. "Just as I arrive, he's ready to move on."

From the corners of his eyes, Frank could still see the pointed fingers, all the drooling men and outraged old ladies and giggling children. He heard their giddy whispers. But it was also possible those people had gone back to their naps and their magazines, Anja's display already forgotten. Had Frank imagined the entire scene? Was he so modest and prissy? Was the heat getting to him? Luca's soccer game had resumed on the grass beside the parking lot. Sandro and Jack argued over a piece of paper, which Jack had torn from a book and held up to Sandro's face.

"Where do you propose we go?" Bitte asked. "Everything is closed at this hour."

"Can't we rest a bit?" said Anja. The towel covered her from her chin to her knees.

"Frankie doesn't know the meaning of the word," said Tenn.

"There has to be something to do here," said Frank. "Something to get our legs moving."

Sandro grabbed the piece of paper from Jack's hand, crumpled it, and turned his back to him. "Our *padrona di casa* told us of a walk along the sea," he said to the rest of them. "She says it is the best view of Portofino from up high, very beautiful. There is a wild garden of statues."

"Testa del Lupo," said Anja. "On the other side of the mountain. Toward Santa Margarita. We have seen it." She added, "We have had to do a lot of walking."

"The head of the wolf," said Tenn.

"Bravo!" said Sandro.

"The walk there and back is very long," said Bitte. "But the view is worth it enough for a second trip. At sunset the colors must be even more spectacular, don't you think, Anja? If we're going to go together, and eat a little something first, which we should do so I don't faint, and stop by the apartment to change clothes, we don't have all the time in the world. Just to get to the walk takes a little drive."

"Luca will take us," Frank said.

4.

FALLING

He comes for her on Monday evenings, between six and seven. His habitual tardiness annoys her, but only enough for teasing, not enough to make it a point of contention. Possibly if he spent less time grooming and choosing his clothes—he is always impeccable, as if he has a date afterward, which maybe he does, Anja has never asked, it is not her concern, and besides, she does not want him to interpret any interest in that regard as grandmotherly, because she is not his grandmother, she is his friend.

He wears a tailored coat and a long fur scarf he wraps multiple times around his neck. The fur of the scarf matches the fur on the sleeves of his leather gloves. His jeans are complicated by zippers in odd places. The level of his dress prompts her to walk for the first time in years to the flat street at the bottom of the hill, the site of if not the more fashionable shops of the day then the ones appropriate for a woman her age, shops that sell dresses and suits in classic cuts, smart cardigans in slate and beige and silver, nothing too flashy, nothing that draws attention.

She lets the salesgirl talk her into a thin wool-blend coat in a gray-and-black crosshatch design she calls "London Plaid." The coat will not be nearly warm enough, but its high asymmetrical collar gives it a certain daring, one that almost overcomes its frumpy below-the-knee length. At the register, Anja reaches over and grabs a red cable turtleneck from the holiday discount table and then a hat, scarf and gloves from the same line.

"Those are an incredible bargain," says the salesgirl. "And because you're buying the set you get an extra ten percent off!"

The last occasion Anja had to examine her accounts, at the settlement of Pieter's estate, she had more than ten million dollars at her fingertips.

She keeps the new items in their sturdy boxes, where they were lovingly wrapped in lavender tissue paper and sealed with a sticker that bore the name and insignia of the shop. It seems such a shame to break the seal and to tear the fine paper that she puts it off for three months, and of course by then it is officially spring and the clothes are too warm after all, even the coat, and she wonders if her association with Sandrino will last into the next winter. Little Sandro, she calls him, though he is taller than his father by at least a head, and she barely reaches his shoulders.

On the Mondays he comes for her, always Mondays, because these are the nights a professor she greatly respects at the other university curates a film series, she cleans the front rooms of her apartment, not because he requires her to do so or has once remarked on her untidiness, but because she takes pleasure in the acts of straightening up and disinfecting and polishing, and because she learned late in life the illogical fact that pleasure tastes better hoarded and swallowed in one sitting than divvied up like sensible slices of cake. The hunger in between is not only bearable, it makes for perfectly agreeable company, just as rage would if she were rageful.

Her legs give her some trouble from time to time, so she walks slowly in fear of falling. Once an old childless widow falls, she is done for. Anja will not submit to a bright-faced nurse with a rubber hand-bag of sponges and plastic pans. Sandrino tells her it is not the fall that breaks the bone; the bone breaks on its own and sends you down, there is no way to prevent it, you might as well dance. Still, she takes his arm and lets him walk her through the square and up the cement steps to his preferred coffee shop. She is sad to see how the snowdrifts in the park have shrunk since the week before. She can hear the in-sidious little rivers beneath them splashing into the drains.

The snow is the only thing she loves about this city. It reminds her of home. She has been thinking more about home since Pieter died, and this, too, is a fall she would rather avoid, because once an old childless widow starts reminiscing about the snow on the roof of her childhood home, the blinding quiet of the woods beyond the yard where the white wolves ran free, the bright eyes of her father behind the costume mask, his silly laugh, she is done for. In all of her world travels, Anja Bloom has not once returned to her native Sweden, not even for the grand opening of the theater in Malmö that bears her father's name.

When Sandrino comes for her, he smells of tobacco, cloves, mari-juana. His great love, more than food and beauty and sex, is the vari-ous gentle highs that come with the burning in his throat. She does not mind that he is often "elevated," as he calls it. At the café, they sit side by side on the cushioned bench, squeezed into each other by col-lege students pretending to study, so close that the scent of his Euro-pean cigarettes and bitter coffee lingers faintly in her hair and clothes for the rest of the week. The one night she shows her annoyance with him for arriving so late at her apartment that they miss the opening scenes of *The Blue Angel*, he responds by buying her a rose from one of those bins at a drugstore they pass on the way to the café. How silly she feels walking into the café carrying the rose in its clear cellophane tube in the company of this young elevated man, not that she pays any mind to what people might be thinking, not that anyone would think she was anyone but his grandmother.

It surprises her that they no longer talk much of his father and Jack Burns, and the events of Portofino and Livorno. After the initial run-through, the past has ceased to be a subject of their conversation. That first night, months ago in her apartment, he pulled from his bag with much ceremony a deck of Italian playing cards and a salt-stained copy of *Poems and Lyrics* by Percy Bysshe Shelley and a letter Jack had written to his mother in Andover but never sent. Sandro had kept the letter and the poems and the cards for himself, and after he died his wife passed them on to their son without explanation. The nature of the relationship between Jack and his father, if not the connection among the cards and the book and the letter, was clear enough, and not a shock to Sandrino or even, as best he could infer, to his mother. He only needed Anja to confirm it, which she did, and to tell him, if she knew, what became of the mysterious Jack. What was his last name? Perhaps he was still alive? Did this particular letter hold any special significance?

August 10, 1953

Darling mother,

I think the Eye-talians have finally turned me superstitious. I've convinced myself this bout of sunsickness I'm still fighting off came to me in direct retaliation for my last letter to you. Never should I have bragged so brazenly of my perfect health through that miserable Tuscan winter. Did you know gli Italiani *believe you can catch your death of cold if you sleep without a shirt on?*

And if the breeze blows in through your open window while you're lying in bed shirtless, you're a goner. Don't worry, I'm on the mend now and I'm still sporting the blue shirt you sent me. It has proven a good luck charm. Sandro's not much of a sailor or a swimmer, and he can't drive a car under a hundred kilometers an hour, but he makes a halfway-decent nurse when he puts his mind to it.

I've promised myself to write you more often after all those months of silence while I was finishing the book and the damp was seeping through the stones of La Bicocca. In the meantime, I'm waiting none too patiently for Warburg to come to his senses on Stranger, *and then it's just a matter of time before he sends the contract so I can set my sights on something new. I don't promise I'll make it back over when it comes out, not unless the Eye-talians make me a believer in miracles, too, while they're at it.*

I once worried that someday I'd have my fill of sensations, but now I've come to think such a satisfaction is an impossibility. I've become a warmer person in every way, and that's not just the fever talking. You can't live among a people for this long a time and not absorb them. They seep into you like the damp.

We have a buddy staying the week and he's standing over me as I write this. He wants my company on the beach now that I've recovered enough to venture back in the sun. Can you imagine a fellow wanting my company? I tell you, I'm going soft. Don't tell Dumps.

Will send a proper letter when there's something improper to tell.

All My Love,
Jack

From her bookshelf, Anja pulled out Jack's three novels—*The Gallery, Lucifer with a Book*, and *A Cry of Children*—and handed them to Sandro. She told him she had read every word of the first of these, and half of the second; she could get through only the first few pages of the third. John Horne Burns, this man his father loved, had won much acclaim in the late forties, she told Sandrino. He had a refined intellect and his books a wicked, satirical style. He was troubled and angry, arrogant and afraid, a genius and a washed-up drunk. The two men were not as kind to each other as he made it sound in the letter, not from what Anja had witnessed or what she had learned later directly from Frank Merlo. Anja had spent only three days with his father and Jack in Italy, though Frank had spent more.

Anja was not in the habit of withholding information, let alone holding her tongue, but that was what she did that first night Sandrino came for her with his bag of artifacts. She was moved by the tenderness with which he paged through the books written by his father's lover, by the pride in his eyes when they rose to meet hers. The next time he visited, he said, "I Googled Frank Merlo. I saw he was the boyfriend of Tennessee Williams and that he died young. You don't know how strange it is for me, my Papà hobnobbing with writers of plays and starlets. Reading poems in English. When I picture Papà, I see him down on one knee in the dirt, a cigarette hanging from one side of his mouth. I see him pulling a nail out of the hoof of a goat."

When she told him how and when the six of them had met, a matter-of-fact account of the fighting dogs and the all-night revelry in the bar, he exclaimed, "Truman Capote! *Breakfast at Tiffany's*? Impossible!" She held back what came in the days after their meeting, the trip to Testa del Lupo, the days Frank spent with them in Livorno, although—she reminds herself now—she never lied when Sandrino asked her a direct question. When she did not have a fact at the ready, she gave her opinion, and she made sure to distinguish one from the other. He wanted to know how his father and Jack Burns got along, whether anyone knew Sandro already had a wife. He wanted her to speculate what his father might have done if Jack had lived.

Eventually, Sandrino ran out of questions about those three days Anja spent with his father in Portofino in 1953, and he started asking what might be next for the two of them.

When he comes for her, the city sits back on its heels. For the evening hours she spends in his company—the walk from her house down the hill to the train, across the university quad, through the square and the park and up the stairs to the café, and then from there to the other train that takes her home—the city presents its upturned hands to her in supplication. But its forgiveness never lasts. Its mercy is temporary and conditional. The next morning, when she steps outside to sweep the trash from the sidewalk, it smells blood, and she hurries back in. Within the forty-four separate walls of her apartment, her hunger for his next visit, and for the city's concomitant offer of mercy, is an agreeable companion. And yet, she sometimes thinks, she would give anything for rage.

She tries to summon rage with memories of her mother, with a stark appraisal of her age-ravaged body in the full-length mirror, with the image of Pieter's blue gaping mouth, with the thought of Frank left to rot in Memorial Hospital, but the rage will not come. She has been too lucky; she is now too grateful. Her grief is no match for her hunger. Anja Bloom is beloved and proud and right of mind, a millionaire brimming with wanderlust, flush with the freedom and time to choose the next great place to spend her life. She will decide on that place soon—this summer, at the latest. The film series will end, and Sandrino will need nothing more from her, and she will release him.

Lima. Dakar. Melbourne. She will never run out of cities. If she continues in this manner of good health, there is a very good chance she will live long enough to punch one of those one-way tickets to

Mars. At the prospect of this, she smiles to herself. Pieter would be unbearably jealous. The man who studied dwarf stars. For him, she still follows the progress of Gliese 581g. He had hoped to prove it habitable in his lifetime. He had hoped for more answers in his lifetime. What is his lifetime? His colleagues who outlasted him on earth are poring over his discoveries this very minute. In six months, *The Astrophysical Journal* will publish his article on hypervelocity stars. Anja's films will still be playing in a hundred years. More. Both of their names appear in textbooks; they have been featured in documentaries that will be shown to generations of filmmakers and scientists. All this luck and gratitude, it does not cannot will not fill her. By the end, his skin went dry as paper. His gnarled knuckles were like mountains on a globe. She would give anything for rage. Her hunger is no match for her grief.

What Sandrino most wants to know is does she miss working. Twenty-four years is a long time, he informs her, which of course it is not, but to make that case to a young man is pointless. He says he can't tell how she really feels about her "life in show business" from the way she talks about it. In one breath, he says, she's relieved and emancipated; in the next, the longing weighs on her like regret. Which is it? They are in the café. They are in their seats waiting for *The Cabinet of Dr. Caligari*. They are standing outside her front door at the end of another Monday night. It does not matter where they are, his questions are the same, asked in different words but always with that disarming mix of exuberance and disbelief and privilege and concern.

"Don't you miss working?"

"How do you just let it all go?"

"You must be happier now than you were then?"

"Tell me *something* about it you miss."

But even at the height of her association with Hovland, she considered acting an indulgence—an arduous one, but an indulgence all the same. She has never believed the arts are a higher power than, say, science, or religion, or even athletics; and within the ranks of the arts, she does not put acting anywhere close to the top. She supposes that is because acting came so easily to her. If you cannot see the struggle in a thing, its intricate craftsmanship, the precious irretrievable hours it stole from a person's life, how can you determine its value? The complex machinery of an excellent film, written and directed with a clear and uncompromising vision, yes, she admires that; the novels of Henry James and Virginia Woolf fill her with awe; she marvels at the Imagist poets; certain classical and contemporary music; and of course, painting and sculpture, though not so much the modern fare, with its high concepts and low execution. She always resented being called a prodigy. She does not see the honor in doing expertly the thing you were born to do.

Even so, she reminds Sandrino, she has not been idle over these decades since *Echo*. She directed the stage version of *Angle* in London and in Amsterdam. She still sometimes tinkers with a collection of poems, though she fears they are derivative of the Imagists. She accompanied Pieter to various conferences and on extended research trips, including one to the South Pole. For two semesters in the late nineties, she taught an undergraduate course at NYU. She traveled far and wide to accept awards, and for each of them she wrote a new speech. It is only the past few years—she has lost track of exactly how many—that the city has held her hostage. Do not believe the press, she tells him; they are lazy with narrative. She is not Greta Garbo. The press makes history repeat itself so they are not forced to work too hard.

Still, he keeps asking. There's no other director who excites you? None of those Hovland disciples? He does not believe her when she tells him acting was not her first or even her second love, that it was simply a means to an end. It does not make sense to him that you can be preternaturally good at something—among the best of the twentieth century, if her various trophies can be trusted—if you do not love it, if it does not consume your very soul. He is a product of Italy, after all, his romantic sensibilities as reliable as the cheese and the olive oil. She is grateful to him for bringing Italy back to her, not because her time there was beautiful—much of it was not—but because it was the last place she lived as a young woman. Being a young woman exhausted her, but it was far less work than being a grown woman. And now that she is an *old* woman, mercifully invisible, finally granted the solitude and freedom she once feared, she finds that laziness is not the ugly word she was taught to despise. In fact, she has begun to experiment with laziness, to embrace its time-bloating vastness, its endless permissions. Lately, her Mondays with Sandrino are the only nights she leaves her house.

The days he does not come are long. It seems equally impossible that Pieter is gone and Sandrino has appeared only recently. More than once she calls Sandrino by Pieter's name, unnoticed until he corrects her, a flash of apprehension on his face. No, she is not going senile, she reassures him; she knows all too well who they both are; it is just that this is what they once did so much of, she and Pieter: sit beside each other and "mind-wrestle," as he called it, for hours upon hours, disagreeing fiercely, concurring ecstatically, until hunger or exhaustion forced them to remember they also had bodies to contend with.

Sandrino cannot blame her for falling back into a thirty-year habit, especially since she has not quite given it up. Anja has continued to wrestle with Pieter's mind, imagining his reaction to the day's news and then voicing her opposition or her commiseration. Pieter's mind is as familiar and accessible as her own: his frames of reference, his maddening biases and blind spots, his predictable bugaboos and sacred cows. Debating him does not require his physical presence. So far, in the nine months since his death, he has been in the right roughly half the time. "You saw that coming," she said to him the other day, turning over a page of *The New York Times*.

After all these weeks screening ancient films and enduring solemn audience talk-backs with the curator, she should have expected that Sandrino would ask to change the subject. "I want to show you a little bit of my world," he says, implying that he has so far felt confined to hers. His world is the graduate neuroscience program at the university, where he is completing his first year of coursework. It is also sushi restaurants ("What they do to those little fish!" he exclaims, "they are sculptures you can eat!"), predawn rowing on the river with a club of enthusiasts, craft beers, and drag bars. She feels equal parts relief and disappointment when it is the academic hemisphere he invites her into, by way of an upcoming lecture entitled "Learning and Memory in Drosophila."

"Fruit flies?" she asks him, laughing. "I give you the world of Marlene Dietrich and Fritz Lang and in return you offer me fruit flies?"

He holds the flyer for the lecture in his hand the way he once held the rose. With mock incredulity, he says, "You're not curious what those little buggers learn and remember?"

"By now you are well aware how curious I am to learn everything," she says. She accepts the flyer and folds it in half. "Of all the desires, curiosity is the only one capable of keeping a person alive." Until she says this, she does not know if she believes it. She starts to catalogue for him all the forms of desire she can come up with—ambition, sex, love, the whole taxonomy—in order to argue on behalf of curiosity, but then she remembers Pieter, the most inquisitive man she has ever known, and she stops herself.

"Something is wrong?"

"No," she says.

No desire, no matter how strong, can save a person once the body betrays him.

She unfolds the flyer. "It looks very interesting," she says.

"It's the final lecture of the term," says Sandrino. "Others have been more sexy—'Epigenetics' and 'The Prefrontal Cortex' and 'Hierarchical Behavior,' I think you would have liked those—but I was too nervous to invite you." He explains that she is an Important Person and he is merely her fancy. On a movie set, he adds, the prop does not get the privilege of asking the star to join him in the warehouse with the rest of the equipment.

"Is that how you think I treat you?" she asks him. "Like a prop?"

This wounds him. "Of course not!" Their time together is the highlight of his week, he says, a happy break from his difficult studies. She reminds him of his teacher of English in Florence, and yet she is unlike anyone he has ever met.

"I was Hovland's collaborator," she says. "Not his diva. Not his slave. With Pieter, too: a collaborator. He shared all his research and ideas and theories with me, even though I could barely speak his language. I think all I have ever wanted from another person, man or woman, was to collaborate with them, to wrestle. I do not want to be your teacher, Sandrino, and besides, you are too intelligent to be my student."

He smiles. "Then together we will learn everything there is to know about the fruit flies."

"Yes," she says. "Why not."

"And other things, too, I can show you. If you truly are curious about everything."

Those mischievous eyes, that curl of the lip. It could be any year. They could be in any country. He could be any one of them.

"I will meet you in the Marcus W. Lannon Lecture Hall," she says, reading from the flyer. "Thursday, the twelfth of May, four p.m."

"Let me give you directions."

She shakes her head. Lannon Hall. Across from Calderwell, across the quad from Meacham. The names of the university lecture halls are like cities they once lived in and to which she never expected to return alone. Pieter is standing at the lectern at the front of the cavernous trapezoidal room, the giant white screen behind him. He is looking out at the audience, holding his silver laser pointer—his lipstick, she called it—over his right shoulder to show them the stars. He knows the placement of the stars with such precision that he need not turn around.

"Will I meet any of your friends?" she asks Sandrino.

"I don't have friends in the program," he says. "The social life, it is hard. We are so busy. And they have girlfriends and wives and some, they even have little children. They come in for class or their rotations and then they go. The friends I have told you about—Trevor, James and Roberto, Bryce who collects the old cars—they are guys I met in the clubs, or with the rowing. Or . . . online." He shrugs. "We are not very close to each other. This city! Everyone tells me you must live here five years before you know for certain your friend is real. Five years is too long to wait!"

"They are wrong," Anja says. She means that it will take longer, or it may never happen at all, and that escaping to a better city is the only solution, but he has brightened, having taken her comment the other way, and so she does not correct him. Let him have hope. It occurs to her for the first time that Sandrino is lonely, though it is possible he has been talking of nothing but his loneliness from their first night together. His world, when he describes it for her (she is curious, she is always asking now, in these two weeks before the lecture), sounds full to the point of bursting: the frigid mornings on the river, the hours in the library, the dates three or four nights per week, the part-time data-entry job at the hospital for extra spending money, the English lessons to keep up with his classmates, the late-night shows and dancing and drinking, the occasional refuge of church on Sunday mornings when he craves the choir music. Half the people who overstuff life this way do it out of joy, because they cannot get enough of life's bounty; they are gluttons, gourmands. Frank Merlo was one of these. The other half do it to distract themselves from loneliness, from the pit that will open up beneath them if they stop running. Anja has taken Sandrino for the former. But his youth and good looks, his ease with his body, may have deceived her. Why else, after the initial rush of her celebrity and her connection to his father, does he continue to spend his Monday nights in the mostly humorless and imperious company of an old woman—bereft as she is, haunted, overbearing, starving—if he is not desperate for distraction?

"I have a confession," he says.

"How thrilling," she says. It is the Monday before the lecture. The days have gotten long. It is light when they walk to the train.

"My friend Trevor, he has been spying on us," he says. "On *you*."

Trevor is the one he likes best, the boy of whom he speaks most often, the one with the shrine to Tennessee Williams in his apartment, the poster of Marlon Brando above his bed. Sandrino claims he is handsome, though he is never in the pictures he has shown to her from his phone. Trevor played Brick in his college's production of *Cat on a Hot Tin Roof* and treated himself to orchestra seats he could not afford at the recent Broadway revival of *Streetcar*, but his favorite plays are the more obscure, experimental ones, the ones Tenn wrote after Frank died, the ones nobody loved: *Small Craft Warnings*, *Out Cry*, *Clothes for a Summer Hotel*.

"I told him to meet us one night at the Archive and say hello, that you are not a person who is cold, that you would shake his hand warm, but like me Trevor is shy for certain things." Here Sandrino lowers his head. When he is nervous, he loses his English. "A few of the

Monday nights, he is at the same time to us at the coffee shop. He sits nearby where he can watch you and hear you. His headphones are empty. *Off*, I mean. He wants to hear the voice of someone who was a friend of his idol, Tennessee Williams. He read to me once out loud from the biography about your time in Italy with him and Frank." Then he adds, quickly, "Of you he is a fan, too. You and Hovland. Trevor is a schoolteacher and an actor on the side in the community theater. Remember when I told you I saw *Angle*? It was Trevor who rented it for me pay-per-view and together we watch it. At the end we clapped like you were with us in person."

"Does he know my address, Sandrino?"

"No!"

"The neighborhood where I live?"

Again he lowers his head. "The neighborhood I did let slip out of my tongue by mistake. But it is a big neighborhood, yes? He won't find which apartment is yours. I promise you. Café Viva is enough. And the lecture. He is coming to the lecture. 'To see her in the light'—this is how Trevor talks! Very dramatic!—and to meet you, finally to meet you face-to-face. That is a piece of my confession. I mentioned to him that you were coming with me to see the fruit flies. Another slip. I'm sorry. Trevor is someone, I don't know—" He waved his hand at the streetlamp. "I can't say no to Trevor."

She manages a smile and says, "It's fine, Sandrino," though his confession, and Trevor's insinuation into their Thursday plan, stirs up a familiar but unplaceable unease.

Later, after the screening of *The Student of Prague*, in the hard-won back booth of Café Viva!—she forgot the place even had a name, or that exclamation point at the end of it, that loud aggressive wish, *Long may you live! We dare you!*—she scans the crowded room for Trevor, though Sandrino claims he is not there, and she imagines that all the headphones are empty, that everyone is listening to her tell Sandrino the story she has chosen to tell him tonight, the story of the last time she saw Tennessee Williams. Maybe she is performing for him a little, setting the scene of the Waldorf Astoria in 1982, of the hustler on whose arm Tenn arrived and departed, of his mysterious gift that arrived at Anja's house a few months after his death.

Sandrino's eyes go wide. "You will tell Trevor this same story?" he asks, with more eagerness than she has ever seen him show about anything, and it is this moment when she places the source of the unease she felt at Sandrino's confession, which is that particular sadness of loving a man who loves other men. It is this moment when she knows for sure that she will lose him, that she was always going to lose him.

Lately, everyone is talking about Iceland. Reykjavik is both close enough and far enough. To what? From what?

When she does meet Trevor, three days later in the hallway outside Lannon Hall, she recognizes him immediately. He is in every way Sandrino's opposite: blond and muscular, the American you see in cartoon posters, his features angular and patrician, his hair cut military-style everywhere but the front, where it crests and curls in a stiff wave. He wears blue jeans and a tight-fitting T-shirt. His voice is high, feminine, though he makes an obvious and clearly laborious attempt to modulate it. What a Brick he must have made. Anja has already met him a thousand times.

"An honor," says Trevor, and kisses her hand.

The professor behind the podium tells the audience that the head of a fruit fly is less than one millimeter across. The professor is not Pieter. He has none of Pieter's flair. But he is solid, convincing, a wonk. Each fly head contains approximately 100,000 neurons, he says, a manageable number to study and manipulate but not without its challenges. The professor who is not Pieter trained the flies to form long-term memories by exposing them to the smell of mushrooms. His

discovery was unexpected: the genes that helped create memory were
the same genes that sensed light. The room buzzes. Sandrino makes
notes on a legal pad in his mellifluous cursive; bent over the armrest,
he keeps tucking his hair behind his ear. Trevor catches Anja looking
at him and rolls his eyes as if to say, *I don't know what that guy's talking
about, either.* But Anja does know, or at least she believes she does. It is
common sense, the link between light and memory. Hardly worth a
study at all.

Afterward, the cubed cheese and sliced melon and sparkling water
and Trevor sitting at her feet like a lustful dog. He is unworthy of
Sandrino, Anja thinks, but simpatico enough, so she answers his questions with politeness and patience. That she has brought Trevor one
of her presigned head shots seems to give Sandrino the greater pleasure, as if the act has signaled her approval of him. Trevor has nowhere to put the photo, so he sets it faceup on a radiator behind him.
Instantly she wants it back. She doubts the photo will make its way to
the wall beside Brando. It is not Anja Trevor is after.

His questions are all about Tenn and Frank and Truman, the lowest of the television questions Sandrino has never once tossed at her,
even when he asked about his father. Anja would prefer to talk about
light and memory, about Reykjavik, about Gliese 581g, about *The Student of Prague*, about anything other than the glitter of Italy in 1953.
But look at the pride on Sandrino's face. Look how it pleases him to
be the vehicle that can deliver what Trevor wants. Look how he taps
his feet in rhythm to music that is not playing. In her seat between
Sandrino and Trevor, turning her head from one to the other, Anja
considers the corollary that accompanies that particular sadness she
has newly remembered: the corollary of electricity, the kind that can
pass from one man to another through a woman. Despite her wariness
about Trevor, it thrills her—in this moment, at least—to conduct this
current, to allow it to animate her.

"He told me you're sitting on a gold mine," Trevor says.

"Is that what he called it?"

"No!" says Sandrino. "I never said gold mine. Trevor!"

"*I* call it a gold mine, then," Trevor says. "It's true that you're the only one in the entire world who's seen it?"

"I believe so," says Anja.

"And you haven't done anything with it?"

"It was a gift to me," Anja says. "I showed it to my husband once, many years ago. We read it out loud together. It is short, more personal than commercial. Naked. I have arranged to donate it to the University of the South, but until then it belongs to me and me alone."

Trevor raises his eyebrows at Sandrino. Sandrino shrugs. The current shoots through her.

"I will tell you about the last time I saw Tennessee Williams," Anja says. "I will tell you about the play he wrote for me, because I promised Sandro I would. But before you ask, let me answer: no, you cannot read it."

5.

THE HEAD OF THE WOLF

Frank sat in the front seat, Tenn beside him, Luca driving. Jack and Sandro were in the back, one at each window, a mile of thigh-burning leather between them. The women followed close behind in Luca's brother's truck. At the switchbacks they waved to each other like children on a carousel. Frank's sweat-soaked shirt clung to his back. Tenn fanned himself with a handful of pages he pulled from his satchel. Sandro stuck his head out of the window like Mr. Moon did when they drove him down Duncan Street. The open windows gave them no relief, not even as they climbed toward the supposedly drier mountain air. They were fools to have left the beach, Jack said, and what was the point of a view when the sun baked and blinded you and heights made you dizzy? What was all the fuss about a view anyway? What did a view give you but a false and dangerous illusion of command over the world, shrunk down small enough to be pinched and flicked away? If only!

He went on like this until Sandro offered to switch places with him. When Jack refused, he offered his lap for him to rest his head. He refused that, too.

What kept two people together? On those turns, when the truck seemed to hover for a moment on the edge of the road over the rocky ravine, what kept Sandro reaching over to put his arm across Jack, though Jack offered no acknowledgment or tenderness in return, no hint that he even wanted to be saved? What better version of himself did Jack show Sandro when they were alone, and what, if anything, did he do to compensate for these times when he behaved like a bratty child, holding everyone hostage with his constant displeasure? Frank wanted to find out. More than that, he wanted Tenn, unprompted, to compare how Jack treated Sandro to how Frank treated him, and to be grateful; and he wanted to welcome Tenn's gratitude rather than immediately resist or distrust it; but most of all he wanted all of that welcome and gratitude to harden around them like a shell.

They'd already stopped once at Bitte and Anja's apartment for a change of shoes, then at Sandro and Jack's for Sandro's binoculars, and now, at the ladies' request, they were stopping again at a touristy *terrazza panoramica* for pre-hike *aperitivi*. The picnic lunch at Paraggi had been their idea, but they hadn't packed any food for it, relying on the men to provide for them. Anja hadn't eaten a thing over the hours at the beach, while Bitte had devoured half of Frank's mortadella sandwich, a peach, a handful of hazelnuts, and most of Sandro's wine.

Bitte invited Luca and his brother to join them at their table on the terrace. "We will wait," they said, without hesitation, putting up both hands to signal that they were on one side of this trip and that Bitte and her puzzling assortment of friends were on the other. Frank wasn't surprised. Everywhere he traveled outside the States, hired men not only knew their place, but they took pride in it, and in the particular service they offered, whether that was driving a car or carrying a bag or delivering groceries to a rented flat. The brothers were getting paid for their time, after all. To ask them onto the terrace for a Campari and soda with their employers implied that the terrace was higher ground, a privilege they hadn't requested and didn't necessarily desire. Instead, they stood within shouting distance in the parking lot, which was just a patch of dead grass between the road and the cliff.

Though it was now close to five, the sun was still so high in the sky that it felt like midday. They sat on the terrace under an umbrella at a round table draped with bright red linens, and which had a postcard view of the beach they'd just abandoned. "What a relief," Jack said when the drinks arrived. He took an ice cube from his tumbler and rubbed it across his forehead.

"Sometimes I tell my sick people," said Sandro, "'To cure yourself, all you need is Campari and soda.'"

"I thought you only cured animals," Frank said.

"He has human patients more and more," Jack said. "They flock to him. Our Sandro is something of a witch doctor in his little hamlet."

Sandro looked around the table. "What does this mean, *witch doctor*?" he asked, with an eager smile.

"I want to ask you, Sandro," Frank said, quickly. "Something I noticed, back in the truck. When we went around the turns, you put your arm across Jack. To protect him."

"It is silly, I know," said Sandro, laughing. "Like a father to a child. But it is instinct."

"What I noticed, though," said Frank, "was that you put your arm low, across his waist and not his chest—" He demonstrated. "As if you were hiding it from Luca in the rearview mirror. Every time you did it, you looked up at Luca afterward. Nervous-like. Do you think Luca doesn't know what we are?"

Sandro narrowed his eyes. "Instinct again," he said. "And you say 'what we are' as if it is a uniform we wear."

"It's not?"

"Luca's job is not to notice," declared Tenn. "And if he did notice, not to let on. The last thing in the world he'd ever do is sneer. These laborers pride themselves on their poker faces, you know. How they talk behind our backs is a different story altogether."

"They hate us," said Frank.

"I think they're just afraid," said Jack.

"Of you maybe," said Bitte, and they all laughed. Even Jack managed an almost-smile, though that was likely meant for the waiter who'd arrived with his second drink.

Anja leaned over and kissed Frank on the cheek. "Who could be afraid of this face?"

"Hear, hear," Tenn said. "Who could be anything but in love with my Little Horse?" He reached his own arm across and ruffled Frank's hair. "You should see how he charms all of Key West just by strolling down the sidewalk. Not even the cops are immune. I've often said that if Frankie ran for mayor he'd win in a landslide."

"*Un angioletto*," said Sandro.

Everyone was looking at Frank. He was conscious of the sweat on his face that Anja had tasted with her cool lips. He shook his head, trying not to blush. "I'm no angel," he said. He stuck two fingers in the bowl of olives and dug out a couple green ones. They were the little kind, leather-smooth and mostly pit, the pits sharp at both ends. The restaurant gave you these olives and the wrinkly black oil-cured kind on the house, along with oily potato chips and mixed salty nuts and cubes of provolone impaled with toothpicks. Food that stimulated both thirst and hunger, food that got you through those empty late-afternoon hours when most men were at work but you were lucky enough to have nothing in the world to do but jabber with your new friends who praise your angelic nature. How did he get here? What had he done to deserve such richness?

"Pay no attention to him," said Tenn. "Frankie is like all the truly

great actresses; the louder the applause, the more convinced they become of their worthlessness."

"Except Anna," said Frank.

"Anna Magnani is the exception to every rule," said Tenn. Then,
to Anja, he said, offhand, as he batted away a fly, "When you come to
Rome, we'll introduce you." He smiled at her.

"You will do that?" asked Bitte.

"Yes, of course," said Tenn. "Anna will despise her on sight."

"Oh, she will," said Frank.

"And that will amuse you?" Bitte asked.

"Endlessly," Tenn said. "The sooner your daughter learns to manage the contempt and subterfuge and mendacity of her fellow actresses, the better off she'll be. It's a necessary phase of her education,
which, if you ask me, is already behind schedule. We don't know yet if
she has the constitution for it, but Signora Magnani will make the
diagnosis."

Bitte nodded conspiratorially. "I have been trying to toughen her
up," she said.

Anja had turned her face away, toward the road, as if she were indifferent to their intentions for her, but Frank knew from their earlier
conversation that she registered every word. Tenn went on to script
the next fifty years of Anja Blomgren's life, from the walk-ons in Eu-
ropean films to her enrollment at the Actors Studio in New York City.
Then: supporting roles on Broadway. Then: the next Geraldine Page.
He said he knew just the place in Gramercy for them to camp out for
a few months; a friend of Kazan's had a white Persian longhair and a
spare room with two single beds. A friend, a cat, a situation Frank had
never heard of before or since.

"She is much prettier than Geraldine," said Frank.

"We're talking talent," Tenn said. "Not window dressing."

The stage would be wasted on Anja, Bitte argued, as if Kazan had already put an offer on the table. The camera gave her dimension you could not appreciate from fifty rows back. She expressed hope that more films would be made from Tenn's plays so that Anja could star in them and Bitte could fly to the premiere in a private plane.

Throughout all this, Frank kept his eye on Anja. She'd been watching a pack of young boys who'd appeared from behind the rows of cars. When they approached Luca and his brother, they kicked dirt at them and shooed them away.

"I did not expect gypsies here," Anja said, and they all turned to see who she was referring to. "How very sad."

There were nine of them. Shirtless. So thin their ribs glowed. Their shorts and calves were stained with mud. Some carried their shoes in their hands. One of the boys Luca pushed off twirled a wooden yo-yo around his head. His friends scattered, and then, in fits of mad giggles, tackled him in the middle of the street as the cars swerved around them honking and shouting.

"I hope they don't bother us," Bitte said. She pushed her chair back from the railing that separated the terrace from the road. The terrace was low enough that the boys could come right up to it and stick their bony arms through the slats.

"This isn't Africa," said Tenn. "It's not even *Sicily*. They're harmless."

"Quite," said Jack.

"You can never be sure," said Bitte.

"They do not look desperate to me, *Mor*," said Anja. "They look happy. Like little birds."

"Quite," Jack said again.

"Well, forgive me, all of you, if it's not so easy for me to recognize happiness," Bitte said.

Anja rolled her eyes at Frank. But Bitte had a point about the boys. There was something wild about them. They might have been happy, but their hands were filthy, as if they'd just burrowed into the light from underground. They'd tied pieces of colored string around their wrists and necks, like some sort of tribe. They reminded Frank not of birds but of angry raccoons, their dark, tired eyes rimmed with dirt, their little hands frantic as claws. They called to each other in little yelps in what was either a low-class Italian dialect, their own language, or gibberish.

"They give me the shivers," Bitte said.

"If they're Italians, they should be ashamed," said Sandro.

"And if they're not Italians?" Jack asked.

"*Boh*," said Sandro, with a shrug.

"*Boh*," Jack mimicked, in a high girly voice.

"You don't see such things in Sweden," said Bitte.

"Certainly not in New England," said Jack. "Where boys are conscripted at birth into the Anglican choir."

"It is very refined there, is it not?" Anja asked Jack. "My cousin Brigit told me New England is the most civilized region of the United States. She wrote to us from Boston. She was on a world tour. I remember seeing the words *New England* and thinking how hopeful they looked."

Much to Frank's surprise—and Sandro's apparently—Jack not only agreed with Anja, but he went on to describe, with a wistfulness they'd seen no trace of until that moment, the hushed greens and stern churches of Andover, the snow that was no match for the town's municipal order, the concentration of boarding schools and universities from Maine to Connecticut. The childhood he spent on cold wood floors gazing at books of paintings, the phonograph beside him playing Donizetti's *Don Pasquale*. The smell of incense that clung to the nuns' habits at St. Augustine's. His mother's hand, which he'd been required to hold just to cross the street to their neighbor's.

The small New England town had its charms, Jack admitted, but there was no place on earth more dangerous. "What is provincialism but the willful collective agreement not to keep trying?" he said, returning to form. "I'd rather be stabbed in an alleyway in Naples than rot on the leafy lawns of Phillips Academy." His mother was the only thing Jack truly missed about New England, about his hometown, about *the whole goddamned country*. He hadn't written to her in many months, he said, but lately she'd been on his mind more than usual.

They'd heard some of this the night before, but Jack said so little, and his tenderness was so rare, that they let him go on. "When he drinks," Sandro whispered to Frank, "he remembers most his *Mamma*. Then he remembers nothing."

Mother Burns was not dead. She was not even terribly old. She'd visited Jack in Florence as recently as last summer. They'd taken a trip with Sandro to the thermal beaches in Ischia, which required a train, a ferry, bathing suits, and blind denial of the queerness of their threesome. Sandro was nothing more than Jack's good buddy. *A real stand-up guy to pick up the check, wasn't he, Mother? Turning in early are you, Mother? Good idea!*

"He says the best good things about me when Mamma Burns can hear," said Sandro, again in confidence to Frank. "The rest of the time, I am . . ." He turned his thumb down.

When he bid farewell to his mother in Genoa, Jack said, he expected it was forever. There was little chance she'd return, and he had no intention of going back to the States, not even for the green lawns of Andover, and not even if his next book, *A Cry of Children*, was a hit, which it had not been. "*I* was the one crying when those reviews came out," he said.

"Bad reviews sell papers," said Frank.

"Then they must have sold a million papers," said Jack.

He'd just finished a draft of a new novel, though, Jack said, right on the heels of the last one. He worked hardest and produced his best stuff when he was counted out, when he had wounds to stitch. "These are my best pages since *The Gallery*," he insisted, which meant nothing to Frank or to anyone at the table, none of whom—not even Sandro, Frank would later learn—had read it. "And it's got a great fucking title: *The Stranger's Guise*."

He looked around at the circle of blank faces.

"G-U-I-S-E?" asked Frank. "Or G-U-Y-S?"

"I'm quite sure I prefer the latter," Tenn said.

"Laugh if you want," said Jack, all traces of tenderness suddenly gone. "My editor's gaga over what I've got so far. One or two months of tinkering and I'll get it into its final form. I should be working on it this minute instead of faffing up and down the coast like a tourist with you people. If this book never sees the light of day, the one to blame will be *him*."

Sandro, the accused, took Jack's half-full glass of whiskey from out of his hands and downed it in one gulp.

"What's the book about?" asked Anja.

The street boys had quieted down, but now, in a flash, the yo-yo kid took off up the hill. They watched his friends chase him into the woods, shouting those strange syllables. Along the way, they picked up sticks and rocks and stuffed the rocks in their pockets.

"They're just playing war," Jack said. He called the waiter over for another, and he answered no more questions about his book or anything else.

WHEN THEY GOT to Testa del Lupo, the sun was dropping fast and they had to rush to catch the colors. They were somewhere between Portofino and Santa Margherita, on an unpaved branch of an unmapped road, on the abandoned property of what was once an important family long died out. The only access to the cliff was through the sculpture garden, high-walled and forbidding, littered with statues that had been overturned or defaced or strangled by weeds. Luca walked them to the garden, then directed them to the white stone path on the other side that led to the point. He'd watched the sunset from there enough times, he said. It was where all the men brought their *fidanzate* to propose marriage, where one day he would bring his Teresa, of whom he spoke frequently and with great solemnity. In the meantime, he'd smoke. No one else was in the garden, but they could hear voices in the distance and a percussion that sounded almost tribal. "Probably a serenade," Luca said. He sat on one of the crumbling stone benches and struck a match.

With its high wall and neglected monuments, the garden resembled a necropolis. In the center stood the fountain that gave the place its name: a pillar ten feet tall with identical wolf heads carved into each of its four sides. Under the heads, cracked half-moon basins into which the water once flowed from the wolves' lips. At the top of the pillar, a creature with a wolf's head and torso and a fish's long tail, its teeth bared in the direction of the setting sun as if in rage against it. This was the only statue in the entire garden that had remained intact, that didn't have cracks or lichen or missing eyes staring up at it from the ground through the vegetation. Someone cared for the odd creature. Someone wiped its grooves of grime, polished its jagged teeth, scrubbed its scales.

They stood for a moment to admire it. It cast an elongated shadow on the far wall, which made it less menacing in its thinness but more imposing in its size. The shadow took up the entire length of the wall. A couple holding hands—a white-haired man with an impossibly young woman in a large floppy hat that concealed her face—hurried past without a greeting. The heat had broken, but the humidity gave the air vibrations. Frank leaned over and kissed the salty dried sweat on Tenn's neck. He rested his head on his shoulder, gazing at the strange fountain. *How you stand here all your days and nights yelling pointlessly at the sun I don't know.*

"What do you say, Bitte?" Frank asked. "Is our she-wolf here happy or sad?"

"Do not bait her," Anja whispered.

The fountain and the view were the only reasons to journey here, according to Bitte; the rest of the sprawling garden was common ruins. They passed under a low archway onto the path, which was surrounded on all sides by sparse woods and bursts of pink and yellow wildflowers in the brush. Couples lay on their backs on large flat boulders, their legs entwined at the ankles; they stared at the sky, kissed, slept, passed bottles of wine back and forth, climbed on top of each other. What Frank had been told about the old country had turned out to be true: everywhere you looked, even in the middle of nowhere, you found people in love.

They walked in pairs though the path was wide enough for six across. Bitte and Jack led the way. Tenn and Anja in the middle. Sandro dragged his feet, his hands deep in his pockets, his head low. Frank slowed his pace to keep him company.

"May I speak a few words to you in private?" Sandro asked, when the others were out of earshot.

"Me? Sure."

"I have been trying to get you alone, but you have not noticed me."

"I—"

"The first thing: It is not my fault about Jack's book," he said. "What he told you about it, the *Stranger* book, is not the truth. The editor, he writes from New York last week to say they cannot publish it. They *will* not publish it. It is no good, the editor says, even if Jack spends six months more on it, two years more on it. He can't make what's not good into something good."

"Does Jack know this?"

"Of course he knows this! He reads the letter. I don't hide his letters from him; he hides his letters from *me*. All night he drinks in the
bar in Firenze and when he comes home on the last bus he is angry
and flies to me with angry fists. And so the next night when he is gone
at the bar I read the letters from his desk and that is how I know what
they say to him about his book. Still I pretend because if he learns
what I know, he will be humiliation."

Frank put his arm around Sandro's neck and pressed close to his side.
"The less you know what's in their letters, the better," he said. "Trust
me. I've learned a few things living with a writer these few years."

Sandro shook his head. "I want to know everything or nothing."

"We'd have had it easier with actresses," Frank said. The actress
can learn her lines, go back onstage the next night, fix her makeup,
rethink the character's psychology, and boom! The audience loves
her. The writer has to spend months, years, in the tunnel between one
book and the next, with only his lovers and friends to shout at him in
the dark, *Keep going! It's good*, you're *good! Remember what so-and-so said
about that last thing you wrote!* "Except they don't believe a word we
say," Frank said. "I don't think they even hear us. They need desperately to hear it from us, but we're never the ones they believe."

"Jack gets very angry when I do this, when I try to build him up."

"Tenn, too. Except when he doesn't. Except when he begs me to
remind him, over and over again, what he is, *who* he is. Then he makes
me stop. I have quotations memorized from newspapers all over the
world. 'Go have a drink, Frankie,' he'll say, when I get revved up with
my quotations, pushing me out the door. 'I'm entitled to my misery.'"
Frank threw up his hands in mock defeat, smiling, as if to say, what
can we do? Might as well drink, dance, throw a party, find the nearest
opera house and buy a front-row ticket.

That wasn't the whole truth, though. It had taken Frank years to
learn the steps in this song and dance of need and resistance with

Tenn, and to sing along to the lyrics of the chorus: "I need you, now go away; chain me up, now hand me the key." By now, he was used to it all. And to be *used to* someone, to settle into his moods and demands and affections, wasn't that something? Wasn't that the best you could hope for, even when sometimes what you wanted most of all was to make love on a boulder for an audience of strangers, and to come back to the boulder every night at sunset to find that same man waiting there? Wasn't that, possibly, everything?

"Some nights I feel like the loneliest man on earth," Frank admitted to Sandro. "Especially when Tenn's in the tunnel." He could set a clock by these episodes, but what he should have told him was that a life of brief bouts of loneliness was far better than what he'd had before, which was one of love in a hundred desperate directions. If he'd been guilty of any crime before Tenn, it was of giving pieces of his heart to too many men who didn't deserve it. Now Tenn had all of it. It was only the shell of his body, those restless limbs and lips, that they let other men borrow from time to time, and that was less of a crime than it was a dive into cool water.

"Lonely is not the problem," said Sandro. "I can't worry about who is lonely and who is not lonely. The problem is that Jack is killing himself. Worse and worse he becomes with the drinking. The *Stranger* book was like blood flowing to his heart to keep him alive. But now there is no blood flowing. Before, he drinks and writes together. Anymore it is the drinking by itself all day in the bar in Firenze. After I read the letter is when I decide we must go to Portofino so he can talk to Truman Capote. To save his career. To get help for his mind, maybe, I don't know, I am desperate. He calls the writings of Capote 'nonsense,' but I tell him what does it matter if you like the man's books if he can make the right introductions? Instead we have a happy accident with the dogs and he meets the great Tennessee Williams, which is even better, and I meet you, you who are a gift to me because we are in, what is it called, the same boat. All day I try to convince Jack to stay even more days here with you and Tennessee Williams, to become friends more close, but he insists we must go tomorrow." Sandro was near tears, his hands talking loud though his voice was soft and breaking. "He says he will go by himself if he must, take the car and the dog and Marika and leave me here *abbandonato*."

"I'm sorry," Frank said. In a few minutes, they'd reach the cliff, where their group stood with their hands on the wooden posts for balance, their lips silently parted, looking up and out at the sky streaked with bands of pink and purple. The clouds were burnt red. The percussion sound grew louder from the woods or one of the villages below, Frank couldn't tell.

"I love this man," said Sandro. "You can't understand how, I know. I see the way you and the others look at him, like he is distasteful. He shows no kindness to me anymore, it is true. There are days when I wish him to disappear. And my heart is too big to disappear myself, to stay all the time with—" He shook his head. They walked in silence a few more steps. "You've had women before, yes?"

"Until the war," said Frank.

"Jack is someone in pain," Sandro said. "You do not have such pain. Not you, so full of life. Not me. Not Signorina Anja. But Jack has it all over his body, pain like his skin on fire. And he is my obligation."

They closed in on the others. "I will help you," Frank assured him, quickly, under his breath, though he had no idea what form that help might take. From all he'd seen and heard, Sandro was better off without the brute. Let Jack drink himself to death if that's what he wanted. He was entitled to his misery. Tenn had a life force that kept the words coming and the blood flowing, that got him out of the tunnel and the actors onto the stage and the audience to their feet. If you didn't have your own life force, no one could lend you his. No one could save you. But he didn't say any of this to Sandro, not then, and not later. All he could do was offer his vague promise of help.

"You two sure took your time," Jack said.

Other than the old man and his girlfriend with the floppy hat, who nuzzled close a few feet away, they were alone on the edge of the cliff. As the sky blazed and darkened, shadows swept across the towns and lights came on one by one in the houses and restaurants below, quietly welcoming the night.

"*Bellissimo*, no?" said Sandro.

"That breeze," said Anja.

"*Che spettacolo!*" said Tenn.

"What is all that *drumming*?" Frank asked, which was when, from behind the hill of trees on the other side of the path, the pack of boys from the street outside the café reappeared. They'd multiplied into more than two dozen bodies, some who looked as old as eighteen, others as young as ten, banging sticks and rocks together and singing in their gibberish tongue. They organized themselves in blocks of three or four, arm in arm, singing different songs, lifting their knees above their waists like soldiers as they marched down the hill.

"It's some kind of dumb show," said Tenn.

"It's hideous," said Bitte.

In moments, the boys had gathered in front of them, facing them, at the cliff. They inched closer and closer, pushing them in toward the railing with their bony little bodies, making that racket with the sticks and the rocks and their trilling voices and their eyes wide and wildly blinking. The old man pulled his girlfriend away and ran up the path on the other side unnoticed. The boys pointed their sticks at Frank and Tenn and Sandro and Jack, but their eyes and their broad toothy smiles were fixed on Anja and Bitte, still in their sheer sundresses over their white swimsuits.

Bitte covered her breasts with her arms and stood behind Tenn. "Give them some money or something!" she shouted.

"Stay calm," Tenn said, clapping along nervously to the beat of their weird drumming. "They just want our attention. It'll be over soon." Still, Frank reached into his pocket to fold the few lire notes he had left.

"But what *are* they?"

"They're just gypsies," said Jack. He reached out to one of the younger ones and pressed a coin in his palm. When the boy's friends surrounded him, Jack turned his pockets inside out and said, "*Vuoto!* No more!"

Their teeth were chipped and sharp, with gaps between them as if they'd been knocked out or had never grown there at all. Their ghastly concert went on and on, unbearably, even as, one by one, they handed over their money, darkness falling fast around them. The couples up on the hill climbed down from their boulders, approached the group curiously, then stopped and retreated to the garden. The boys were chanting by then, the chants blending into each other, unceasing, a nightmarish cacophony of nonsense. The voice of the one who appeared to be the leader rose sharp and loud over the others. His eyes were the wildest of the bunch. He had fleshy, pointed ears that jutted from his head like an elf's. They might have been singing in some obscure Italian or Slavic dialect, but no one, not even Sandro, could place it. They sang and chanted louder and louder, interrupting each other, competing with each other, stretching their mouths wide, baring their broken teeth.

Bitte tried to make a run for it, but after just a few steps the leader stopped her and held her in place. One of the other tall ones, his skin the color of walnut, then grabbed her from behind, his arm across her chest, her back pulled against him, and sang a slow sweet serenade in her ear. In his other hand, he held a long stick sharpened into a spear.

She closed her eyes hard. Her face was terrified. When she stomped her foot on his, he didn't flinch. Tenn looked to Frank desperately— "Do something," he said between clenched teeth—but behind them was the cliff and in front of them was the army of boys, whose faces showed a possessed exuberance. Was this some kind of horrible joke, or were they really dangerous? Frank had stared down the Japs without fear, line after line, but he could not imagine how to combat an army of children.

It was Sandro's turn to try. *"Vai via!"* he shouted, stepping toward them and waving his arms like a blind man finding his way.

The boys jeered at him. The ones with spears pressed them against Sandro's chest. Ten of them, maybe, had spears. Their faces were streaked with mud.

Sandro raised his arms above his head. *"Andate all'inferno!"* he shouted, ticking his chin up.

"Andate all'inferno!" They shouted back. They chanted his words, girlishly, mincingly, over and over, a queer chorus, as they marched in place. *"Andate all'inferno! Andate all'inferno!"*

Frank put his arm around Tenn's waist. He stood tall and stiffened his chest, muttering under his breath so that Tenn could hear, and then Tenn did the same. "Now!" Frank shouted, and they charged forward together to break through the wall of bodies. The boys swarmed them and brought them to the rocky ground three steps from where they started. They held their legs and pulled at their trunks, slicing into their thighs and backs with their sharp raccoon nails, digging under the skin as if trying to scoop out chunks of flesh. Frank tried to fight them off, punching at their chests and faces, but they kept coming at him. Jack and Sandro landed beside him, tackled easily, their arms flailing. The boys pinned Frank flat on his stomach onto a rock that bruised his ribs, a bare and putrid foot on the back of his neck and another on his shoulder blades to keep him down. Tenn's body lay on top of his. "What in holy hell is this?" Jack was yelling between gasps, covering his face with his fists, like a boxer, so that the boy kneeling on his chest couldn't scrape out his eyes.

"Anja, are you OK?" Frank called out. She and Bitte had been dragged to the edge of the cliff. In flashes, he could see them through the swarm of boy bodies. "Tell me you're OK!"

"Frank!" she called back, kicking her legs. She screamed as they pulled at her dress, choking her. "Help!" she shouted.

"Help us!" Bitte shouted.

Frank heard the sound of fabric being torn, and there, when he looked up, were the scraps of their white sundresses, bright as flames, being tossed into the blurry darkness. Anja's arms—probably they were Anja's arms—reached out for one of the wooden posts and grabbed onto it. He fought his hardest to get out from under the boys, but they kept coming at him to keep him down. Another bare foot settled on his right cheek, smashing the side of his head into the dirt. They'd rolled Tenn off him and, though he couldn't see him, he knew it was his whiskey-sweet breath on the back of his neck. He knew the rhythm of his lungs in his moments of terror and excitement. He knew the exact thickness of the chest he'd feel if he could only reach back and hold him.

Bitte had managed to get her arms around Anja's waist, but Frank had no clear view of what the boys were doing to them. There were too many boys surrounding the women. They piled on top of them, jumped back up, hung back for a moment, and dove forward again. Then Frank saw something he would never, for the rest of his life, be able to shake: one of the boys, his face indistinguishable from the others, opened his mouth wide, his teeth bared like a dog, lunged at Anja's bare leg and bit into it. She screamed. The boys started chanting even louder, and laughed, and shrieked like falling birds, a horrible noise that drowned out the women's cries. They took out their little cocks and stretched them, squeezing and pulling them toward the ground, a herd of bony cows milking themselves. Frank imagined the women's bodies stripped and mud-streaked, the boys, violent with lust, pressing limply into them, suffocating them. Devouring them. He tried again to hoist himself up, but he was immobilized and he was crying, and the crying made him weak. Never before had he felt so powerless, so trapped by the limits of his body.

Then Luca and his brother appeared, flanked by an army of men, from the boulders, and the boys stopped their chants and dropped their spears and flew into the dark woods. Only the leader, the one with the elf ears, stayed on. He was holding Jack by the throat when he saw Luca. The way Jack told it, the boy looked him straight in the eyes in a way that was tender and searching, as if he might gently press his lips to his, but instead he bent down, his left hand still clutching Jack's throat, picked up a rock the size of a fist, and bashed the rock into Jack's right temple. It swelled almost immediately into a bump the size and shade of a ripe peach.

Luca and his brother pinned the boy. They stomped on his groin and, when he curled up in pain, like a sow bug, they kicked at his face until it bled. They dragged his unconscious body, his eyes already bruised, the back of his head a seeping mess of gashes, to the edge of the cliff. Luca rolled him over it onto a ridge ten feet down, where he landed with his neck twisted the wrong way. The men stood there watching him, breathing hard. The boy didn't move. Then Luca slid down to the ridge and turned his head toward the towns and the boats in full glitter below.

A TOURIST FOUND THE BODY the next afternoon. The story was gossiped over for a few days, and then the police hushed it up quickly to protect Luca and his brother, Roberto, who would never have been charged anyway for ridding the world of a barbaric gypsy with no name and no papers. Who could prove he existed at all? No family came forward to claim him, no group cried out for justice. His tribe of boys disappeared into the woods, and then, Frank imagined, they dispersed among the low streets of the resort towns up and down the peninsula, where they targeted old women susceptible to pity. For years afterward, Frank searched the faces of gypsies whenever he passed them in various cities up and down Italy and North Africa, but he would have recognized only the leader by his eyes and ears, and maybe the tall boy with the walnut skin, who Bitte said smelled of cloves.

No detective followed Jack and Sandro from Portofino to the bungalow in Marina di Cecina, where they'd planned to swim and sail until the end of August. By then, Frank and Tenn and Anja were hundreds of miles away, and Bitte's rich old man, Signor Ricciardi, had set his sights on her again, because—and hadn't Frank known this all along?—the appearance of youth was as seductive as the real thing, especially when time was short and you were desperate for someone to lavish love on.

Now, lying again on his side, again crippled, again beaten to a pulp, with his cheek not in the dirt but on the nubby hospital sheets burnt with bleach, Frank was angry, he was furious actually, and it's possible he'd been furious for many years and transmuted his fury into desire, furious that never again would he come to possess youth or love. And though he hadn't wasted either of them entirely, neither had he protected them as fiercely as he could, if protection was even possible; and if protection had not been possible, then his fury came from the fact that no one had told him how brief the window would be. Or maybe they *had* told him—maybe it was obvious to everybody but him, maybe it's the message Tenn was sending with his neglect, his abandonment—but he was too romantic to believe any of them or to pay attention or to swallow his pride, in which case he hated himself more than he already did, he was angrier than he'd ever thought it possible he, sweet Frankie Merlo, could be, this man who was once a boy so in love with life that he believed he'd dance his way through it up to the very last day.

He looked to that night in the hills above Portofino as the beginning of his punishment. Since then, it had been meted out in gradual doses, slowly, one poisonous drop at a time, over the years he continued to dare to live free, to love with abandon, to chase beauty whenever it crossed in front of him like a deer on a country road. Not once in those years with Tenn did he question his right to gorge himself on beauty until he burst, and then to drop everything to chase the deer into the woods for more. He should have known better. No one gets away with such a life.

The note to Anja he'd scrawled yesterday on the back of her letter was currently flying across the Atlantic, all the way to Madrid, on wings of hope and desperation. Frank pictured the note like that, like a determined bird on a lonely mission, flapping furiously, its neck outstretched. It would get to Anja as fast as it could, and when she received it, she'd pull down the trunk from her closet, fill it with her multicolored print dresses, and make her own frantic journey over the ocean to Frank's bed in Memorial Hospital. From here, much restitution could be made. He could devote himself to Anja and her career—the way he had with Tenn's—but on this go-round with a kind of purity. He could be monkish in his service to her, his body cleansing itself with each day that passed.

For a time, in the years after Portofino, he considered having a go with Anja, trading the title of Mrs. Williams for Mr. Bloom. They would have lived companionably together, splashing around in the waves, managing the sun. Would he have minded so much? Would Fate—or the Lord, if his mother was right about His existence and

His judgment—have shown him more respect, or an ounce of mercy, for that sort of sacrifice? Would there have been a reward instead of this reckoning? Penance, his mother would call it. The priest has encouraged Reconciliation, that mystical sacrament Frank last practiced in grammar school.

Where was the priest, anyway? The next time he showed up, Frank would ask him why it was never too late to Reconcile, to confess, why God gave you a pass as long as, in your final hours, you admitted He was right all along. Frank and Father Kelly had little else to talk about over these long days and nights in the ward, why not introduce the subject of the Holy Lord's pettiness? Their visits were strained rituals, and yet Frank came to tolerate, if not enjoy, the old man's company. His ministry was a distraction from the endless wait for a single word from Tenn.

Over his time at Memorial, plenty of their friends had come or called on Tenn's behalf, each delivering his excuses and promises and his secondhand wishes for good health. "We expect a full recovery and nothing less," Audrey Wood had told him this very morning, in her dictatorial way, patting his icy hands, emphasizing the "we," as if she were Tenn's wife and not his agent, as if Tenn had just stepped into the next room and would be back in a moment with the tea and cookies.

The day Truman visited, he was sitting on the edge of Frank's bed when they carried out the corpse of Mike Murphy, who'd died a few hours before. The body floated by them covered in a sheet. The only time the ward went quiet was for those ghostly processions. As soon as Mike was gone, the screams and shouts started up again. Somebody tossed his empty bedpan into the hole that the absence of Mike and his bed had left. Then all the guys started throwing their bedpans. In tribute. In defiance. It brought tears to Frank's eyes. The clatter was like fireworks. Frank was in too much pain to get to his bedpan, so he motioned to Truman to do it before the nurses rushed in and put a stop to them. That was something: Truman Capote holding up Frank's plastic piss tub and tossing it, ever so gingerly, across the room. Afterward, he wiped his hand on the sheet. "I'll be back when you're feeling stronger," he said, and kissed him on the lips without shame.

Truman was the only friend who made no excuses for Tenn, for the cancer, for anything. "I hear he thinks you're contagious," he said, in the doorway. "Irene called him up the other day and gave him hell for it. For *this*—" He extended his arm to indicate the ward. "Now he's going to hear from *me*!"

Frank nodded and closed his eyes. Truman stood there a few moments longer.

"Just hold tight, Frankie," he heard him say, before he drifted off.

Frank and Tenn had both messed things up in the years since Portofino, but their mess was not unfixable, not to Frank, no matter what they'd said in the heat of battle. The shattered glass could be vacuumed up from the rug, or the rug thrown out, what did it matter, it was just cheap glass, it was just an old rug not even in fashion anymore. Their past may not be rewritable, but it was bearable. Frank didn't want to go back to his old life with Tenn, or even start a fresh one with him. All the negotiation required for that was too far ahead, with too many steps in between, too many characters on the narrow stage. He no longer allowed himself the luxury of future plans. The only luxury he'd allow himself, for now, was the hope that, sometime in the next few hours or days, the hand that nudged him awake would be Tenn's, that when Frank opened his eyes it would be Tenn's face that greeted him, Tenn's voice telling him it's OK, baby, keep resting, there's no party to get to anyway, no place more important to be than here, now let me catch you up on all you've missed. . . .

6

THE SKELETON OF
A SPARROW

Anja Bloom at fifty," said Tenn. "Still immune from the ravages of time!"

They stood facing each other in the restaurant of the Waldorf, his hands in hers. It was the summer of 1982. His hands were dry and cold, though he had just shuffled in from the sweltering street. Anja had been waiting over thirty minutes for their one o'clock lunch date, sipping mineral water and reviewing Hovland's notes on *Sequence* and searching her heart for the forgiveness she had narrowly convinced herself to show. Already her limp, reticent hands gave her away. Forgiveness had never come easily to Anja. Nineteen years had passed since Tenn had abandoned Frank to the desolate wards of Memorial Hospital, seven since he had explained away his actions in his *Memoirs* by turning himself into the devoted, heartbroken, misunderstood lover. In that time, out of loyalty to Frank, in revenge for his desertion, she had erased Tenn from her life.

She had spotted him immediately from the window in his wide-rimmed glasses and Panama hat. Broken as he was in that final act, his air of gentility still surrounded him like an atmosphere, thick with gravity and vapor. It permeated the glass. He had grown stout and now sported a bushy gray beard and what could only be called whiskers. There was a young man on his arm helping him to maneuver through the sweaty rushing sidewalk crowd, though Tenn seemed capable enough, at seventy-one, of doing so on his own. At the hotel entrance, the young man had kissed him on the cheek and pushed him gently but firmly toward the door the way a father does for his child on the first day of school.

Up close, Tenn's complexion was rutted, pocked, pale, his eyes heavy-lidded and wet, as if he had been crying or suffering a bout of allergic fits. His clothes, at least, were presentable and familiar: a pressed button-down shirt open at the throat, a gray linen suit in keeping with the pretense of an upscale midtown lunch, dress shoes appropriately shined, and a small Chinese fan poking from his jacket pocket. Anja had heard the stories and expected far worse.

That he'd read in the *Times* that she was back in New York for a spell, and that she had recently celebrated a birthday at a glitzy party on the Upper West Side, were the excuses he had given for his most recent letter with an invitation to lunch. The letter had sat unopened on her desk for two days until curiosity got the better of her. Most of the letter was nothing new. He didn't expect her to believe him, Tenn wrote, but every word of his *Memoirs* was true to the best of his recollection. He'd loved Frankie. Frankie'd kept him tied down to earth. Since Frankie, he'd been floating, flying blind, wandering willy-nilly. Everything he'd touched had turned to dust. He'd been fighting some sort of curse since The Horse got sick, he wrote, a curse he was just now surrendering to. He was bone-tired. Finished. This lunch would be the last time he'd see her before he moved to the Far East, said the letter. Before he left, he wished to surround himself once more with a person who knew his goodness. It was unclear whether the goodness he referred to was Frank's or his own.

Over the years, Tenn had sent Anja multiple iterations of this same letter. They had started in the months after Frank died. The letters waited for her at the front desks of hotels. Her manager forwarded them to her at her various new addresses in Madrid, in Amsterdam, in Los Angeles. The letters begged her to see him and to hear his side of the story. They talked big of parts he could create for her onstage, of film productions of *Sweet Bird of Youth* and *Suddenly Last Summer* that he could adapt to suit her great talent and beauty and range. It was possible Tenn did not remember writing these letters, that even this most recent one with his request for a lunch had been sent in a fog; it was possible that, last week, when Anja sent word to meet her at the Waldorf, he believed it to be her invitation to him and not her RSVP. If she trusted the stories, the pills and alcohol had finally taken their toll on Tenn's memory and judgment and concept of reality. He had grown more paranoid and desperate and afraid. His only reliable and devoted company were those in his employ.

Why did Anja agree to meet him in this state at this time? Why now did she choose to believe his version of history, and, possibly, to forgive him? She supposed it was because she had fallen in love.

Tenn ordered a martini—a "see-through," he called it—drank it all at once, and flagged down the waiter for another. He asked how long Anja planned to stay in New York. She said she was not sure. She did not mention Pieter Meisner, the Columbia professor of physics from whose bed she had just come, in whose apartment she had begun to keep clothes and books. Then followed a discussion on safe terrain: the lure of certain cities, the disappointments of others. He had recently become enamored of Bangkok, he said, one of the few places older gentlemen could go where they were still respected, where they were not lied to. The States showed men of his age and stature and proclivities no deference or loyalty, he said; neither did England or Italy, not anymore. Lose your youth, and you lose everything. Morocco had some promise, he said. Even Mexico offered intriguing possibilities. Thailand, though: it was Thailand where he must make his final settlement. Had she ever been, in her many exotic travels? She had not.

"I hear there is a problem with street crime in Bangkok," she said.

He waved this away. "You befriend the locals, and they protect you. You grease their palms so they don't clean your clock. Not the most honest system, I'm afraid, but its terms are clear. You pay one way or another."

She said that sounded like a perfectly fine plan.

"And how do you find Svoboda?" he asked, the unprovoked pivot she expected, though not so early in the conversation. They still had empty plates between them. Neither had yet to utter Frank's name. He gave her a thin smile and looked straight into her eyes, which brought on a wave of guilt she instinctively submerged. Jan Svoboda was the Czech playwright-director also mentioned in the *Times* article about her birthday party, the young phenom rumored to have written a new play of "magic and magnificence" and "extraordinary significance" especially for Anja Bloom, his favorite actress in the world. Anja had not yet appeared on any stage, let alone Broadway, though Broadway was where Svoboda could put her—or where she could put Svoboda, Hovland insisted—if she found the play worthy of her time and dedication. Hovland urged her against it; Mitchell, her trusted manager, was thrilled by the idea and by the play itself; Anja, the only person whose opinion mattered, was conflicted. Doing the play would mean staying in New York, a city whose grittiness and danger exhilarated her like a dare; it would mean many *grasses matinées* with Pieter, who stayed up all night to look at his stars and never taught before mid-afternoon; it would also mean eight shows a week in Times Square, which meant a long delay for Hovland's *Sequence*, a script that showed magnificence and significance of its own.

"I think Jan is brilliant," Anja said. "He reminds me of Visconti, precise and intellectual without the sacrifice of passion. Though this new play is not about the heart."

"The heart is out of fashion," Tenn said, gloomily. "It has been for some time."

She wondered for a moment if that was true. It was not. "*Crimes of the Heart*," she said. "I seem to remember it won the Pulitzer Prize last year."

Tenn rolled his eyes. "Third-rate watered-down Mississippi Gothic melodrama!" he said, loud enough for the woman at the table beside them to turn around, recognize one or both of them, and stare. "'A gruelin' nightmare' indeed! I walked out in the middle of Act Two."

"*Dreamgirls*?" Anja offered.

"Will you do it?" Tenn asked. "This brilliant heartless play of Svoboda's? Or will you finally let me write you something? I can have it for you quickly. Before the fall of the first autumn leaf. Before the end of August, if you can't wait that long! Give me the opportunity."

"I don't know what I will do with Jan," Anja said. "I am at a fork in the road."

"I'll write you something with heart and poetry and *muscle*," Tenn insisted, his right fist striking the table. "I don't understand life anymore, but I understand death. Death is the only thing that's comprehensible to me now. I'll write you something more transcendent and daring than Hovland and Svoboda combined could make for you."

"You tried that once already," said Anja, bitterly.

When the stage version of *Suddenly Last Summer* premiered off-Broadway early in 1958, Anja was in Germany with Hovland finishing *Angle*. At the time, she vaguely recalled being aware that a new play of Tenn's had been paired with another of his one-acts, and that the

entire production, called *Garden District*, was receiving mostly positive reviews. She recalled that she'd sent Frank a letter from Freiburg
to say she was sorry to miss the goings-on in New York, but that she
was nearly done with a film she and Hovland had great hopes for, and
that she wished *Garden District* a long run. In the middle of that year
came the release of *Angle*, the film that made Anja Bloom a star. She
got so caught up in the buzz of Hovland's worldwide vindication and
the explosion of her own career that she stopped following Tenn's and
Frank's and Visconti's and everyone else's.

One night in 1959, she agreed to go on a date with a minor actor.
She did not recall the name of the actor or the film he took her to see,
only that they were in Los Angeles and that it had recently become
necessary for her to wear dark glasses to keep from being recognized.
There on the screen, in the assumed safety of the theater, as the arm
of the minor actor found its way presumptuously around her shoulders, came the trailer for *Suddenly, Last Summer.* The naked native
boys rushed up the mountain, banging their strange instruments.
Elizabeth Taylor talked with agitation of her white and transparent
swimsuit, then fell to her knees on a sandy beach. Anja gasped. There
she was, exposed, assaulted without warning, by a memory she had
mistakenly assumed belonged only to her. She understood immediately why Tenn and Frank had never once mentioned this rape of a
play—now a major motion picture, now a vehicle for Elizabeth Taylor
and Katharine Hepburn—in their conversations and letters in the
years after Portofino. While Anja was finding her way as an actress,
Tennessee Williams was twisting her and her mother and Paraggi and
Testa del Lupo into a shameful nightmare to shock the world, purely
for his own gain.

Anja interpreted *Suddenly Last Summer* as Tenn's revenge on her
for going beyond him in fame, as her punishment for not following
behind him begging for scraps like an American actress. Hovland

helped her to see the wrongheadedness of this interpretation. Like every great artist, said Hovland, Tennessee Williams shaped the clay of his experiences not into a literal representation but into an uncanny sculpture, one that bore within it a truth half recognized, half intuited, and entirely ineffable. *Suddenly Last Summer* belonged to her no more than *The Rose Tattoo* belonged to Frank, even though, without them, neither of these plays would exist.

"You're not Catherine Holly," Tenn said to her now as, one by one, more patrons of the Waldorf restaurant turned to glance surreptitiously in their direction. "Your mother is not Violet Venable. None of us is, or ever was, Sebastian Venable. *Suddenly Last Summer* was not *for* you, Anja, or even about you. That play was the detritus of my psychotherapy, the slime that leaked from my head when they shrunk it. It was my way of making sense of my time in Barcelona, not Portofino. It was a war cry against the butchers who called themselves doctors and cut out my sister Rose's brain." He looked away. "It also happens to be the last best thing I wrote."

"I tried to exorcise that day from my dreams," said Anja. "I had almost forgotten it even happened."

"Maybe it didn't," Tenn said. "Who but us is left to say for sure?"

"It would come into my mind like a story I overheard, like a scene I had read in a cheap paperback. Not something that could have possibly happened to me, to my mother, to *us*. Then I look up at a movie screen and that horror flies back at me, the boys with their spears and those bells, the pile of bodies stabbing and biting! And your name blazed across it in triumph!"

"I'd hoped you'd never see that film," said Tenn, tenderly. "That *abortion* of a film. But, Anja, I wanted you at the play. I took great pride in it. *Suddenly Last Summer* was an exorcism of my own. I spent months in New York to get it staged perfectly. It was Frank who convinced me not to tell you in advance that it had some vague echoes of Portofino, Frank who asked me not to insist that you fly back for the premiere. He expected the play to close quickly and fade into obscurity, and who could blame him? A one-act freak show of cannibals and lobotomies and moral decay! He prayed for a flop, I'm sure of it, purely on your account. But then we got such excellent notices— from Brooks Atkinson no less; do you remember that one? 'A superb achievement. A genius of necromancy.' Those words meant the world to me—and by the time the film came around, faster than anyone thought possible, it was too late. We didn't see much of you in those years anyway, did we, when you were coming up so fast in the world? I seem to recall Frank writing you letters, attempting to reach you on the phone in various hotels, and getting no reply. Do you want me to describe the effect your vanishing act had on him?"

"I put his name on the list at every premiere. I used to watch the door, hoping he would step through it. But you kept him so busy. And Hovland—he demanded a great deal from me. When Frankie and I could finally find a time to speak, always late at night, always across oceans, I could hear the exhaustion in his voice. I begged him to come and live with me."

"Those are your excuses?"

"Frankie always had a plan, but it never came to pass," she said.

"I should have written you something then," said Tenn. "On the heels of that awful film, back when I still had the magic, back when the heart was still in fashion. Frankie urged me to, but—my last best thing . . ." He took a long, deep breath. "If you recall, we were with Miss Anja Blomgren at the first fork in her life. We were the ones who put you on this path you've been on. Isn't it almost romantic—in that sad way of romances—to be here together again, just the two of us? When maybe you can help me, the way Frank and I helped you?"

"You speak his name with such little effort," she said.

This took him aback, and for a few moments they sat in silence. It came as no surprise to Anja that Frank had tried to shield her from *Suddenly Last Summer*, or that Tenn did not think she needed shielding. Frank would always treat her like the damsel in distress no matter how much armor she displayed, whereas Tenn would credit her with more strength than she actually had. Perhaps these were the two types of men in the world: those who kept trying to save you, and those who would forever test you. It was still too soon to tell which type Pieter would turn out to be.

Finally, Tenn said: "I've been speaking of Frank Merlo—and writing about Frank Merlo—for a long while now. You would know this if you hadn't maintained such an untraversable distance."

"You left him in that cancer ward to rot," Anja said. Her hands began, again, to tremble. "When all he wanted was you. Just you. He wrote to me of your cruelty. Your absence. The other men you paraded around. It shocked me, how far you had fallen, the depths of your selfishness. I wanted to see you today so that I could judge you merely as weak rather than malicious, and so that I could forgive you, but it is too difficult when I hear you speak his name, and when I remember him as he was. Frank was a man of pure goodness, one of the very few I have known in this life. If you want to write a play with heart and muscle and poetry, write it about him. *For* him. Not for me."

"I've tried," said Tenn. "Each time, I've failed utterly."

"Try again."

He shook his head. "I can't get him right," Tenn said. "I thought I'd preserved him in amber as Mangiacavallo in *The Rose Tattoo*, but that was a Polaroid, now faded. How do I write about The Horse when, the last time I saw him, he was the skeleton of a sparrow? I wanted to do right by him in my memoirs. I wrote of our devotion to each other, of our final night together. It was my chance to tell the world of that goodness of his, of our long association, of his death that broke my life in two. But now here you are with your poison arrow, your accusations of mendacity. Of opportunism." He was slurring his words, growing more agitated by the minute. "What do you know of us, anyway?" he asked. "What, really, are you so certain of? I've written poems for Frank; shall I read you one? I gave Frank's ghost a voice and a name in *Something Cloudy, Something Clear*. Did you go to see the premiere of that play last July? No? You're in good company. No one else did, either."

Anja listened, regretting some, but not all, of what she had been wanting to say for twenty years. But she was thinking, suddenly, not of Frank—not of opening his letter in Madrid, not of calling the hospital in a panic and being told it was too late, not of vowing then and there never to speak to Tenn again—but of her mother. Anja had never gotten Bitte right, either; she weighed too much, she was impossible to account for, it was a burden even to make the attempt, and so she had given up trying. Tenn, apparently, had not. She watched him take off his glasses, wipe the lenses with his napkin, and put them back on. Without them, he looked a decade younger, even with the puffiness under his eyes and the deep lines that surrounded them. He began to eat ravenously the steak and potatoes that had long gone cold. It was then, maybe, watching him, her long-ago friend now a falling star, to whom she had finally said her piece, that she felt the crack in her anger. The first glimmer of sympathy, uncoupled from pity. Her hands went still.

The boy who had escorted him appeared in the window and gave Tenn a wave. He leaned on the side of a parked car and lit a cigarette. Anja was grateful for him. Tenn would need him, now, to navigate the streets.

"Write me something about Frank," she said. Their time was nearly up. "Something you haven't written before."

Tenn looked back and forth from Anja to the man in the window. "I had an encounter," he said. "This month in Key West. With Frankie. What I want to tell you is: The Horse was with me."

"Frank was there," Anja said, skeptically. "With you."

"Yes," said Tenn.

It was then that he began to cry, and she took his hands in hers for the second time that day, and the last time in this life. She looked over at the boy, ticked her head toward Tenn, but he just held his cigarette out as if to say, *When I'm done, lady.* He struck a model's pose, there on Park Avenue, in his cowboy boots and flared jeans and mane of bushy blond hair.

Tenn had slunk far down in his chair. "Is that your companion?" she asked him.

"That's Kurt, yes," he said. "He looks after me. Makes sure I get from place to place without a scene."

"That's good," she said.

"What did I say his name was?"

"Kurt."

"I think that was the *last* one," he said, and collapsed in laughter. "This one is Ted. Their names are never longer than one syllable."

Eventually, Ted came inside and stood discreetly near the entrance to the restaurant, his hands thrust in his pockets, a few feet from the maître d'. Tenn showed no signs of standing up. It was past three o'clock, and though Anja had nowhere she needed to get to, she was eager for escape. She planned to put on her sunglasses, call Pieter during his office hours, and spend the rest of the day in an air-conditioned museum.

"I will wait for you to send me something," she said to Tenn.

"Did I tell you what happened in Key West?"

"Next time," she said.

"You will hear from me," he said. "And then you'll visit me in Bangkok. I'll have Kurt find a grand hotel for you."

She asked him when he was leaving, though she sensed that this, like the reunion with Frank in Key West, was another of his fictions or fever dreams, that, though Tenn traveled often and widely, he had no credible plans to move himself, old and infirm, to the other side of the world.

"I'm leaving as soon as I possibly can."

She smiled at him. "Then I will come see you in Bangkok," she said.

Six months later, alone in his bedroom at the Hotel Elysée, four blocks from the Waldorf, he took one too many pinkies and died.

Anja heard the news on the radio in a taxi speeding up Sixth Avenue. She had chosen not to leave New York, having ultimately declined the lead role in Svoboda's play, which went instead to Jill Clayburgh. She chose *Sequence* instead, which meant she chose Hovland. He agreed to film just outside the city so she could be close to her astronomer.

A few months after Tenn's death, a large manila envelope arrived for Anja at Pieter's apartment building. Recognizing the Florida address, she opened it immediately in the lobby, the doorman watching her every move, as he always did, whenever the elusive Anja Bloom passed through. She pulled out a seventeen-page play entitled *Call It Joy*, dedicated to "A.B. and F.M." There was no letter or note attached.

Anja expected to see *Call It Joy* produced or published somewhere eventually, but the years went by and the biographies appeared, and the play was never mentioned. There was no record of the title in his archives or in his letters. She came to believe that she was in possession of the single surviving copy. She showed it only to Pieter, this gift that Tenn had given her and Frank alone. She kept it in its original envelope, postmarked April 11, 1983, at the back of the file cabinet in the apartment with all of her old marked-up scripts. And then, like so many things of great significance, it was forgotten.

"Until you, Sandrino," she says.

7.

MEN OF FEELING

No one wanted to call on a Portofino doctor, who weren't known for their discretion, so Sandro patched them up in private. He took care of himself first, and then, one at a time, he tended to the rest of them, sprawled on the floor of the women's muggy apartment off Via del Fondaco. With one hand, he held an ice pack on the side of Jack's head; with the other he unwrapped rolls of gauze, a safety pin between his lips. He poured iodine on their cuts and covered them in nylon bandages. He worked quietly, with calm and efficient determination. When he finished with Frank, he rubbed him above the ear with his knuckle the way he might do for a puppy.

They'd brought the Swedes back to their rented flat thinking it was the closest approximation of a home they had in the world, but, as the night went on, after they bathed and changed into clean clothes and took turns clutching Maja to their chests, they said they couldn't breathe between those walls. They couldn't bear to be left alone; they saw the boys' faces when they closed their eyes; their chants echoed in their heads; and so Frank offered to put them up at the Splendido for as long as they needed. Though Tenn was ready to be done with them—they were marked in some way, he declared to Frank; he called them *ill starred*—he reluctantly agreed.

They checked in the Swedes long after midnight to a room at the other end of their floor, sedated them with a couple of pinkies from Tenn's stash, and tucked them into twin beds separated by a nightstand. Bitte immediately threw off her covers and, eyes half closed, stumbled over to Anja's bed and curled up next to her, chin to shoulder, like a child frightened by a storm.

Frank kept them company from the armchair in the corner, his head in his hands, watching the Seconal work its magic on their breathing. First Anja's slowed, then Bitte's, to the same rhythm. It comforted him, their rising and falling chests, the animal sensuality of their snorts and drool and sudden jolts. Surely, he and Tenn painted a similar picture each night. The heat they generated was an unspoken code, a signal. What was the signal if not, *We belong here*. What was the code if not, *I'll protect you.* If only Frank could watch him and Tenn as he watched the women now, their bodies in their purest state, suppressing the rowdy forces of mind and memory. It was a love play in itself.

He dozed in and out, his dreams uneasy, haunted. At first light, he switched off the lamp and gently closed the door. His footsteps were loud in the wide hallway lit by flickering sconces. He thought, what happened at Testa del Lupo just hours before will not change me. He had already been hardened by life. In a jungle in the Solomon Islands, he'd knelt beside Thomas Brunner of Abilene, Texas, a boy his age, a fellow jarhead, cut down by enemy fire, blood spurting from his jugular. The bullet had missed Frank by less than a foot. In that foot was both a reprieve and a commandment: use well this gift of a future. Jack's demons were more obvious, black crows perched on his shoulders, pecking at his eyeballs. Life had already hardened all of them, and maybe that was what drew them to each other, how they could recognize each other at Truman's party. If it wasn't true for Anja two nights ago, it was true today. Testa del Lupo would change her—she had changed before Frank's eyes—the only question was how.

It took a few more hours of fitful sleep for Frank's hands to stop shaking. It took Tenn a go at the typewriter. They fetched coffees from the Splendido bar and carried the porcelain cups to a bench at the far end of the private garden, hidden from the other guests by a canopy of bougainvillea. Someone designed this garden for tranquility and protection: the bushes of soothing lavender and rosemary, the peekaboo views of the quiet sea far down the slope, the locked wooden gate two men tall. How many other lovers had stolen an hour to sit on this same block of carved stone, to throw one leg over the other's and huddle close, to idle in the silence of a long association whose terms were clear enough, only to disturb the peace with dreaded talk of what came next?

"I want a part in *Senso*," Frank said. He'd heard these words in his head so often, that they sounded disembodied spoken aloud.

"What kind of part?"

"Any part."

Tenn thought a moment. In this scene, a moment was too long.

"You surprise me," Tenn said. "Should I be surprised?"

When Frank didn't respond, Tenn kissed him, softly, on his left temple and pulled him tighter. "What about Anja?"

"Both of us, if you can," said Frank. "But, Tenn? Me first."

"Visconti's gone full opera again," he said. "From what I can gather. The set's in chaos."

"And here's not?"

Tenn mimed the crumpling of Visconti's letter and the tossing of it into the flowerbeds. "Chaos tends to find me," he said. "A hazard I should have warned you about before you hitched yourself to me. Too late now, I'm afraid. Listen. I'm thinking already. What would you say if I made you a soldier in the Risorgimento? There can never be too many soldiers in a war movie. I've only been conscripted to write the love scenes, but Bowles has a hand in the war scenes. He won't mind squeezing in another line or two. One look at you in uniform and he'll write you a ten-minute soliloquy."

"That sounds good."

"From what I've seen of the script so far, the soldiers do a lot of shouting and a lot of marching and a lot of drinking. I recall that in one scene they're standing around in their private quarters scrubbing their laundry—shirtless, no doubt, if I know Visconti—when Alida Valli barges in looking for her lover. You'll fit right in. How did I not think of this before? You forgive me?" He patted Frank's bare thigh.

"And Anja?"

"That's a tougher sell. She'll never pass for an Italian, not even a Venetian, not without shoe polish. Then again, Visconti wanted Brando to play Mahler—that's the *Austrian* officer, the *lead*, for Christ's sake—so he may not stand on ceremony with our apprentice."

"She'd make a fine Austrian," Frank said.

"She'd make a fine assassin."

Frank and Tenn agreed on one undeniable fact: Anja had an icy exterior—*an arresting chill*, Tenn called it—and it was too soon to tell how that translated to the screen. It was on the depth and density of the ice that Frank and Tenn disagreed. Frank believed the ice was thin, that all it would take to crack it, to melt it, and thereby free Anja from her mother's clutches, was love. Romantic love had the most potential, of course, but the love of a trusted friend—him, for example—love given or love received, might also do the trick. Tenn, on the other hand, believed that young Anja Blomgren was already frozen to the core, that some twisted thing had happened to her in Sweden, and that the damage was irreversible. This upset Frank, at which point Tenn said, "Oh, baby, don't you see? They're the lucky ones."

We are men of feeling, Tenn said to him, warm to the touch, live wires, and we would always be so. "Such is our lot in life. It's a curse, this state of being, but our particular sexual proclivity neither caused nor cured it, nor was it its symptom. Whether we fuck men or women does not factor." (Indeed, Tenn said, he counted some of the most fiercely heterosexual men he knew among the most deeply and painfully afflicted with the curse of feeling.) One of its few benedictions was that, in some—"think Brando," he said, "think Kazan, think Anna, think Tennessee Williams, think Frank Merlo"—it gave rise to the making of art, and this making, if not the art itself, provided temporary relief from the heat, the illusion of control over passion, a taste of power.

"You say, 'think Frank Merlo,'" said Frank, "but Frank Merlo hasn't done shit when it comes to art."

"Not yet, maybe," said Tenn, "which is why you've asked me what you've asked me."

"Five years too late, maybe."

"Or at just the right time."

Frank had paid close attention to Tenn's words. "*Temporary* relief," he'd said. "*Illusion* of control. *Taste* of power." Still, he'd take those terms any day of the week. They were a heck of a lot better than what he was doing now, which was treading water. Being taken by the shoulders and pointed in a direction—toward Rome, a Risorgimento uniform, a line or two, a chance—gave him air. It wounded his pride to ask Tenn for anything, but it was just this once, he'd never do it again, not unless it was absolutely necessary. He'd have done it a long time ago if he hadn't been caught up in the thrall and in the day-to-day tasks and plans and chores of Tenn's world: train tickets, hotel reservations, repairs on the Duncan Street house, stains on their white dinner jackets, a cold compress for Mother Edwina's feverish forehead, a last-minute sightseeing tour for Rose. He'd lost himself in their nightly entertainments and ministrations, the keeping happy of the other wives and the flirting with distinguished gentlemen, the after-hours fetching of pills from doctors easily bribed, the soothing of nerves, the demands for sex and the cruel refusals, all in support of the playwright and the theater and his and Tenn's common cause. Willingly, happily, Frank had played this part, and now the time had come—with Tenn's blessing, and with the promise of Anja's company—to take on a bigger role.

"I just hope Anja's going to be OK," Frank said. "In the head, I mean."

"She made it this far with that mother, she'll be just fine. Once something freezes, it can't get more frozen, it can only go the other direction. Who better than The Horse to melt her? I can hear it now: Drip drip drip. What a guide you'll be through the Land of Feeling! But I still maintain she's better off the way she is."

Frank thought a moment. "You're saying an iceberg in Antarctica is as cold as the ice cubes in a cocktail?"

"If you're going to be an artist, Frankie—even just an actor—your first lesson is not to be so literal."

The plan for Anja, which they concocted on that stone bench and had yet to run by her, had a number of steps. The first was to find a distraction for Bitte here in Portofino. Could they salvage her engagement to Signor Ricciardi? If not, did Truman know another rich eligible bachelor, preferably one with a black cat and a heart condition? If that was a no, they'd do a thorough sweep of the yachts. However they distracted Bitte, Tenn said, they had to do it fast, to "get the drawbridge down." Only then could they throw Anja over their shoulders, sneak her out of the castle under cover of night, and not stop running until they reached Verona.

In Verona, the three of them would join Paul and Ahmed as scheduled. Paul and Tenn needed to hole up to finish the *Senso* script before
Visconti's deadline at the end of the month. In the meantime, Frank
and Anja could explore the town, eat too much fried squid, pretend
they were Romeo and Juliet, steal away to Venice for a few days if they
could swing it, and run their *Senso* lines once Tenn and Paul had written them. If Frank visited a museum or library to educate himself on
the Risorgimento, all the better. By the first of September, all five
of them would drive to Rome in their matching Jaguar convertibles,
Tenn and Frank and Anja leading the way, Paul and Ahmed behind
them, the wind in their hair, their futures bright as the sunflowers on
the Tuscan hills.

Like most things, Anja's full liberation would eventually come down
to money. How much did she have and, more important, how much could
she access? Surely Frank and Tenn could convince her to accompany
them from Verona to Rome, but could she support herself after they left
Italy in the fall? It was that step of the plan that might prove the most
complicated. Tenn saw actress—or, at the very least, model—potential in
Anja, and he wanted her around long enough to solve the mystery at her
center, but he had not fallen for her decisively or romantically enough to
provide for her the way he had provided for so many others, Frank in-
cluded. It was possible Tenn would fall for her over time, given how necessary a person could come to seem simply by sticking around.

Tenn was generous with his money. He was also easily flattered.
More often than not, the two went hand in hand, and Frank had to
be there to protect him from the influence of an obvious bootlicker.
If Anja, who was incapable of flattery, even in the interest of self-
preservation, found herself in need, Frank would be forced to appeal
on her behalf to Tenn's other weakness: the damsel in distress. As
usual, Frank was getting ahead of himself. They had not yet arrived at
that step. First, they had to get the drawbridge down.

He went to Anja that very afternoon. She and Bitte had made no effort to check out of the Splendido, which meant one more night on Tenn's dime. Jack and Sandro and their memories of Testa del Lupo were, by then, more than halfway to their bungalow in Livorno. With them gone, Frank saw no reason to ever mention the horrible events again. If the Merlos of Peterstown, New Jersey, had taught him anything, it was to keep ugliness out—with happy talk, with food, with music and out-loud dreaming—until it forced its way in. Now was the time for looking forward into the thawing warmth of possibility. And so, in the hallway outside Anja's room, her mother safely behind the closed door, he handed her the ticket to the rest of her life.

Which she refused.

She was not yet ready, she said, for her life to begin. She needed more time.

"You're joking," Frank said.

She crossed her arms in defiance that could have been unease. Her elbows were still stained from the iodine Sandro had painted onto the cuts. Time, she explained, would help her determine whether her own vision for her life was the one she really wanted after all. She was referring to the portrait she'd painted for him in the water at Paraggi, the one of the gluttonous Madison Avenue secretary who gorged on ideas on her lunch break. She wondered if her imagination might come up with something better than this vision. She was still a girl, she said, and Frank should remember that a girl was always in a state of becoming. As she became, she had no intention of taking even the smallest step toward her mother's vision for her, the one in which she slaved for the camera and the audience and for the men behind them. She had been a slave long enough, she said, with a tick of her head toward the room where Bitte was supposedly sleeping, and it was the overly dramatic raising of her voice that convinced Frank, more than the bruises on her arm or her sunburnt skin, that this country had already made its mark on her.

"To be honest with you," she went on, "I do not consider acting much of an art to begin with. There is something of the childish about it, no? A game we play when we are small to entertain ourselves and our parents until we grow up and do something serious." She put her hand on his shoulder in a way he found almost maternal in its condescension. "Besides, I am acting right now. Are you not acting, as well? Do we not play our parts every minute of every day, even when we are alone? The myths we tell ourselves, the myths we allow our mothers and lovers to believe? It seems to take more patience than skill."

"You've never seen Vivien Leigh onstage," Frank said. "Or Maureen Stapleton. Tallulah Bankhead."

"And if I had?"

"You'd be transformed."

For a girl so smart, Anja was badly in need of an education, to see up close the art of the actress. She needed to witness the transformation, the *possession*. Frank had seen it many times, from just a few feet away in the wings. If you looked hard enough, you could see the demon in the act of possession, how it descended upon the woman, moved inside her, stretched the lines on her face, twisted her voice. You couldn't see that and call it a child's game. You couldn't see that and not call it art. All of this he said to Anja in the hallway of the Splendido, and the more his passion could not convince her, the more resentful of her he became.

"I guess I expected more gratitude," Frank said, finally. "Tenn and I don't have to do this for you, you know. Any of this." He opened his arms to indicate the hotel, but what he really meant, of course, was the privilege of her freedom, her education. Who was she to turn it down?

"I do not remember asking you to educate me," said Anja, her face an unscalable glacier. She went on, matter-of-factly, her arms still crossed, to recite a litany of other reasons for shoving Frank and Tenn's gift back into their arms without a hint of appreciation. Chief among them was that Testa del Lupo had shaken her and Bitte more deeply than she could describe. To Frank and Tenn it was a brawl, but to the two women it was a violation. How could he not see that? Bitte hadn't spoken a coherent sentence since the night of the attack. Anja could not leave her mother in such a state. "She's not a strong woman," she said. "She is my obligation. To dismiss that obligation, to dismiss everything that happened, is your arrogance. Your luxury. The way you fly about like bees, you and Tenn and men like you, we have seen it over and over, how you land on one pretty flower to suck all the nectar from it, and then move on to the next. I asked you this once already, and you did not answer. Let me ask it another way: do you ever think what becomes of the flower once you've sucked it dry?"

"I'm not the type to move on," said Frank.

"Neither am I," she said.

That evening, when the hotel manager called to relay Anja and Bitte's request to stay another night—not "one more night" but "another night"—Frank instructed him to stop charging Mr. Williams's account if the women did not check out the next day. They avoided each other for the rest of their time in Portofino, which was not an easy thing to do when Frank was kicking her and her mother out of their hotel, and when there was more to say, and when, either because of or despite her accusations—he still wasn't quite sure—he missed her.

THOUGH FRANK RARELY SAW the pages themselves, he knew Tenn worked on multiple projects at once, projects that changed shape from play to story to poem and back again. His current pages were charging him up, but whether they were *Battle* or *Orpheus* or something else he'd actually abandon, Frank was still not yet sure, though in time it would become obvious. As Tenn drafted these projects, he wrote letters charting their progress to Audrey Wood and Kazan and Bowles and to whatever producer or director or actress or reviewer he had business with at the time, or with whom he wished to have business in the future. There was constant chatter, and so much of it! So much arguing back and forth with black stains on white pages! Just the thought of all those voices, real and imaginary, barking at him from New York or Los Angeles or pulled from the darkest and deepest caves of the mind, begging for attention, never at rest, gave Frank a headache. Because Tenn sensed this, or because he needed his own refuge from the chatter, he kept Frank apart from it, in his own quiet and well-appointed mansion behind an unlocked door, where Frank was happy to explore its many rooms and entertain their guests and fix the leaky faucets and—if he felt like it, as he often did—dance on the beds. Tenn could visit him at any and all hours, but he could never live there; it was too quiet.

For Frank to ask for a part in *Senso* was to risk leaving the peaceful mansion for Tenn's noisy crowd. The moment he did it, he wished for the moment back. And then the moment he wished for it back, he hated himself for the wish.

It was almost luck, then, that Tenn didn't mention *Senso* again.

Without Anja's cooperation with the drawbridge plan, they had no reason to stay in Portofino. Verona was calling, *Senso* was calling, not to mention Mr. Moon and Anna and their apartment in Rome with the view of the Opera and the prehistoric plumbing. Now that Tenn was charged up with his new manuscript, he could write anywhere he could drag his typewriter. He could write up a tree in a jungle under artillery fire, Frank used to say, as long as he had a branch to set his Olivetti on, and if the tree was where the best words came, or where the words came best, it was up to Frank to send the telegram with

Mr. Williams's sincere regrets and to make Mr. Williams's increasingly preposterous excuses at the event he'd attend in his place and to find other ways to occupy himself until Mr. Williams climbed down from the tree and asked what day it was and how soon they could get the hell out of there.

The soonest, said Frank, was tomorrow.

"And what's today?"

"Tuesday."

"Then we leave Wednesday."

Frank made the arrangements for the ferry to Rapallo, where they'd pick up the Jag from the garage. He was grateful for the task. So far, he had spent his Tuesday walking over the hills to and from Paraggi to swim, both to kill the hours and because it was best not to be seen in Luca's truck.

They ordered room service and then stopped into the Delfino for an after-dinner drink and to bid farewell to Truman. If anyone knew the latest gossip about the man found at Testa del Lupo, it would be Miss Capote, and they were eager to find out just what stories, if any, still swirled around the little *paese*.

They found Truman alone at the bar, his legs dangling a foot above the floor, finishing off a screwdriver. Open in front of him was a book he wasn't reading. They took the empty seats on both sides of him. He looked sourly at Frank as Tenn said "my kind of library" and ordered three Campari and sodas.

The Delfino was busy for a Tuesday, though, in a resort town in the summer, every night was Saturday night, and everyone appeared to be engulfed in full-throated laughter or shouting at each other, all while eating and drinking with abandon, as if it would stay a Saturday in summer forever. It occurred to Frank that his life was not much different from this endless Saturday, that the Monday his father and brother spent every weekend dreading would never come for him as long as he stayed with Tenn.

"Our friend dropped this by," said Truman, and held up the book, a hardcover of *The Gallery* by John Horne Burns. "I tripped on it walking out of my apartment and nearly tumbled down the stairs. It was wrapped in brown paper, like a cut of raw meat or something indecent. I'm happy to say it's more of the latter than the former."

"It's that good?" Tenn asked.

"He considers himself a genius," said Frank.

"He's got a rare talent. Unfortunately, it's for making a story of degenerate soldiers, queer bars, and syphilis dull as the Pledge of Allegiance. No wonder Mailer praised it to the skies."

"You'd heard of it before now?"

"Believe it or not, Tenn, they still print the book pages even when you're not in them. Of course I've heard of it. It was all the rage the year after *Other Voices*. The Very Important War Novel Everyone Must Read and all that. The Dark Underbelly of Naples. The Tale Untold Until Now. The Voice of a Generation, they called him. If that sounds familiar, it's because it's the same moniker they'd given me not ten months before. It appears critics measure time by the fruit fly. If I had a competitive bone in my body, I'd have been seething." They all laughed. "Gore talked up the book all over town. It was his calling card. Then, when it started getting better notices than *The City and the Pillar*, he was suddenly struck dumb on the subject."

"Hysterical muteness," said Tenn.

"We both read *The City and the Pillar* the week it came out," said Frank. "It made me blush. I don't know how Gore got away with writing something like that."

"He didn't," Truman said. "Show me a *Times* review of a book by Gore Vidal since then. He's shunned until further notice. A Broadway musical with a blank marquee. If he wants to publish a word these days, he's forced to use an alias. He could take a lesson from Jack Burns. If you want to write a novel about queens in love and lust, just make it such a bore that no one notices, and they'll call it a Literary Masterpiece. They were this close to giving *The Gallery* a Pulitzer."

"That was five years ago," Tenn said. "Now he's just a washed-up drunk."

"My sources tell me he and *Il Dottore* have skipped town," said Truman. "I assume *Il Dottore* was the one who left the book as a parting gift. I'd have preferred a local amaro, or a treat for Bunky after the trauma those Swedes inflicted on him, but at least he put forth an effort."

"The effort would never have occurred to Jack," Frank said, wondering if Truman had even seen the bouquet of white roses he'd brought to his party.

"No, the Jack Burns passed out in my armchair didn't strike me as the paragon of manners," Truman said. "The grump doesn't know how good he has it, flitting around Liguria with *Il Dottore Bello* at his side. Driving, no doubt. One part bodyguard, one part big brother, one part Emily Post. You and I know how good we have it, though, don't we, Tenn? We could knock some sense into him."

"Add guardian angel to the list," said Tenn. "Then add a dozen more heroic qualities, and you have my Frankie."

Truman and Jack Dunphy had belonged to each other for as long as Tenn and Frank. The four of them had traveled all over Italy together, once, disastrously, to the island of Ischia, where they'd had a terrible row over something Frank could no longer remember. Jack Dunphy kept to himself mostly, the shy type, rarely glimpsed in public, ten years Truman's senior but going on thirty, as much the life of the party as a potted plant. "The old lady," as Tenn called him, was as withdrawn and serious as Truman was clubby and vicious. More often than not, Frank ended up stuck next to Jack Dunphy in the backseats of convertibles, where Jack would fade into the leather or wilt in the sun under his wide-brimmed hat, leaving Frank to watch the landscape pass blurrily by. Being compared with Jack, and even with Sandro, made Frank uneasy, not because he didn't like the guys—they were decent enough, as best he could tell—but because what he had with Tenn had come to seem bigger and fuller than either Sandro's anxious chaperoning or the domestic arrangement Truman was describing.

"My Jack's upstairs this very minute broiling me a hamburger," Truman said. "It's the meal I most miss when I'm here. A hamburger with a side of potato salad. The Italians are in a constant battle with mayonnaise. Mostly it horrifies them. We bring over our own jars, especially if we'll be in Sicily, where they don't even stock it. Give me a hamburger and potato salad with extra mayo and a post office with regular hours and I'm ready to defect. You don't know how many times I've walked to the piazza for stamps during business hours just to see the CHIUSO sign in the window and the clerk at his station shrugging as if there was a pit of crocodiles between him and the door."

"Those crocodiles may be invisible to us," said Tenn, "but for him they are very real. This is a country beyond convention, governed by mood, by fancy. By vanity. The only way to thrive in it is to govern yourself the same way. No wonder it so thoroughly and wantonly seduces the English and the Americans, the men in particular. Italy is everything the Anglo man is taught not to be: undisciplined, permissive. *Pretty.*"

"Pretty?" said Truman.

"I've seen this clerk and hundreds, maybe thousands, like him," said Tenn. "I can tell you he spent more than a few minutes in his bathroom mirror this morning to admire himself after putting on his postal uniform. He combed his hair and set it with spray. He stood proudly in that stiff dove-gray shirt, in that smart little cap. He rubbed his chin and turned his face from side to side, his own deep brown eyes enchanting him. The average Italian postal clerk is more conscious of beauty than the professional American landscape painter."

Frank listened with annoyance, not because Tenn noticed the clerk, of course—Frank had noticed him, too, how could he not, yesterday morning when he'd sent the telegram to Anna to check on Mr. Moon—but because they had something more important to discuss than the curious nature of the Italian male species, a topic he and Tenn had long exhausted. He decided to interrupt them, something he rarely did, otherwise they could go on all night.

"Sandro—*Il Dottore*—wants you to help Jack," he said to Truman. "You and Tenn both. He needs you. In all the . . . commotion the past few days I forgot that Sandro came to me. He thought I'd understand. I don't know what he needs you for exactly, but it's for something only another writer can do. Jack has a new book—"

"*The Strange Guy*," said Tenn.

"Something like that," Frank said.

"An autobiography?"

"Sandro is very worried," Frank went on. "Jack's other books flopped, and the publishers don't want this new one at all. But Jack won't let it go. He thinks it's more of a masterpiece than the first one. Sandro says he's going to keep drinking until the publisher agrees with him, and if he keeps drinking, it's going to kill him."

"Those novels didn't flop," Truman said. "They were drawn and quartered. The Voice of a Generation Gone Flat. Amidst my glee, I remember I almost felt sorry for him. Vanquishing a rival is, from time to time, bittersweet."

Thumbing through *The Gallery*, Tenn said, "I thought I'd at least *heard* of every fairy writer of some repute."

"You've been too busy with your starlets," said Truman. "Take my copy if you want. It's not even signed."

Tenn set the book back down on the bar. "Someone we know must have slept with him," he said indifferently. "Or is he a prude on top of everything? I can assure you I've never met a more joyless person." He picked up the book again. "On second thought," he said, handing it to Frank over Truman's head, "keep this for me, Frankie. A souvenir. We'll never see the man again. And no doubt we've seen the last of Sandro."

"You can't think of anything at all you're willing to do for him?" Frank asked. "I agree he's a nasty sort, don't get me wrong, I don't like him much, but if he's really so bad off, shouldn't we try to help? He's a fellow soldier. And he is—well, he's one of our kind, whether we want him to be or not."

Tenn looked at Truman. Truman looked at Tenn. "My Little Horse," Tenn said. "Sometimes I forget you're not a writer. Then you say something like this, and I'm reminded."

"What's that supposed to mean?"

"I think what your clod of a jockey here means is that *Il Dottore* is overreacting," said Truman.

"Precisely," said Tenn. "When you think of how Jack is now, think of me after *Summer and Smoke*." He walked over to Frank, put his arm around his shoulders, and turned to Truman. "We were in Fez," he began. "I was in a pit of depression so deep not even the African sun could find me. In the middle of the night I forced Frankie to pack up our things and drive us to Casablanca. But the pit was there, too, just as deep, filled with quicksand. I convinced myself that if I didn't get off the continent, it would swallow me up. I wasn't on the *verge* of a breakdown; I was broken and down and out. I was nearly catatonic,

babbling like an infant." He turned to Frank. "Did you call the au-
thorities, baby? Of course you didn't. He called the agency and booked
us on the next ship to Marseilles. He carried my bags onboard for me,
two on each arm, as if I were a cripple. The trip was a horror. It took
three days. I couldn't touch the food. I told the other passengers I was
dying of cholera. Frank held my sweaty hand under the table. In Marseilles, we switched boats for Rome. It wasn't until we breathed the air
off the Italian coast that I could start climbing my way out of the pit,
and there was Frankie at the top with his arm out, pulling me up onto
solid ground. If Sandro wants to save Jack, that's what he'll have to do:
acquaint himself with the mud. Roll around in it for a while. Build up
the muscles in his arms. Not pass his millstone off to people he hasn't
known for longer than a weekend, not to mention fellow writers with
dubious hopes for Jack's success. If we try to intervene, Frankie, what
you don't realize is that Jack will resent us for treating him like a charity case. He'll be humiliated. And in the end, when it all goes wrong,
he'll blame us."

"She has a point," said Truman.

Frank had not known Tenn to be unkind, but he did know him to
perform unkindness for his fellow writers. All the writers Frank knew
did it, as much for sport as to make themselves appear more confident
and self-assured than they really were. The unkindness armored them.
The only trouble was that, for Tenn at least, the armor fell away the
moment he was alone, leaving him with the fear of retribution and the
guilt of having mortally wounded someone who hadn't deserved it,
which was when he'd turn to Frank for reassurance that, no, he wasn't
a monster, that, yes, he'd singlehandedly made the careers of many, and
that, in the malice and enmity department, Truman was far worse.
Truman was as much Tenn's rival as he was Jack's, after all; for that
matter, so was Paul Bowles and Gore Vidal and Don Windham and

even Bill Inge. These rivals also happened to be his best friends, and the only ones, Tenn claimed, who understood him fully.

Frank longed so much for that full understanding of Tenn that, last summer, he'd spent a few hours a day in the air-conditioned public library in New Orleans attempting to write a play of his own. *Jersey Song*, he'd titled it, in double-thick all-capital letters, underlined, at the top of the page. He didn't have much school, but he read like a fiend—everything from Salvador Dalí's memoir to Joseph Campbell's *Hero with a Thousand Faces*—and people told him he composed the most entertaining letters. He was as much at home in a box seat at the symphony and the opera as he was doing the Lindy hop at the back of a Chelsea dance hall. For *Jersey Song*, he had in mind a traditional three-act structure, a leading lady inspired by his Aunt Marie (who'd be played by Anna Magnani, of course), and a rough outline for the set design, sketched in pencil on the back of the script. But *Jersey Song* never got sung. As a playwright, Frank chased words the way a dog chased birds. When he could finally come up with a line, he'd immediately cross it out. A letter he could toss off in his own voice no sweat, but when it came to putting a voice in someone else's mouth, he froze. His characters sounded like cheap knockoffs of Serafina Delle Rose and Stanley Kowalski. He left the library each afternoon with ink-stained fingers and forearms he'd scrub in the bathroom sink before Tenn could ask any questions.

The failed experiment with *Jersey Song* gave Frank greater respect for Tenn than he already had, but it also caused an earthquake in their otherwise happy French Quarter apartment. The earthquake was Frank's realization that not only was he not and never would be a writer, and not only was he not and never would be much of an actor or dancer, but, as none of those things, he had no natural place in Tenn's world.

Tenn had slept through that earthquake, but, the next morning, Frank noticed, the crack in the ground between them, the one only Frank could see, had grown into a crevasse. It was still possible to leap over, but the leap was more dangerous than it had been the night before; there was a great chance he'd fall into the crevasse and get himself stuck there. Tenn may have sensed this distance, but he had no idea Frank had tried and failed to write a play, let alone that its failure had led Frank to doubt their compatibility and to go so far as to question whether he had a place at all in Tenn's world. For Frank, though, the expansion was the omen he'd always feared would come. He stared down at the crevasse's jagged edges, the threatening darkness between them, with both fear and relief that the day had finally arrived. Every couple, he suspected, was separated by at least a crack; there was no such thing as solid ground or a perfect union, not in a war or a country and not among lovers; the trick, though, was not to acknowledge it. Once you did, once it jolted you awake, as it had for Frank, you became fixated on its progress, and the very act of tracking that progress ensured its inevitability.

It was also very possible that he was wrong about all of this, that the earthquake, and the crack, and the crevasse, and the leap over the edges, and the dog chasing after birds, weren't the right metaphors at all. Maybe it was Frank's inability to describe it accurately—the poverty of his language compared to the riches of Tenn's—that doomed him. If he was unable to describe a thing, if he couldn't settle on its metaphor, how could anyone else, including the man he loved, understand him? And what if the thing he was trying to describe, the thing he was so desperate to define so that he could hold it and protect it, was the very life he was leading with that man he loved? What then? They couldn't call the thing marriage, and, even if they could, Frank didn't want the word. At best, it was a mistranslation. At worst, it smelled of garages and empty milk bottles and the floor mats in his father's Chevy.

Marriage belonged to his cousins and to Luca and Teresa and to Ike and Mamie Eisenhower; it was not the proper word for what he had with Tenn, and it never would be. Neither was friendship; neither was love affair. Someday, someone would come up with the proper word. In the meantime, the only hope for a man of few words was in comparison, in the pointing out of two other men and saying, *That is us, too; they are the metaphor I was looking for.* Frank had yet to meet those men. They weren't Truman and Jack Dunphy; he'd seen enough of them in the past couple years to know that much. He still held out a hope, however vague, that they might be Sandro and Jack Burns.

"If Sandro can't handle him," Truman was saying, "some other sycophant will come along. I wouldn't be surprised if he had one waiting in the wings. As I'm sure you know all too well, Frankie, the only way to soothe a writer's ego is to stroke it. You can't train it to lower its expectations or to settle for less. Jack Burns didn't come to Italy to study at the University of Humility. He came here because his family and friends at home saw his guts splashed all over the newspapers, and he couldn't bear to face them. He wanted to live among a naïve people who'd treat him like the demigod he imagined himself to be, who'd be enthralled by the faint whiff of an American reputation. I don't blame him, really. I, too, have always depended on the kindness of strangers."

Frank shook his head.

"I wrote that as a punch line, you know," said Tenn, pleased, clearly, by Truman's invocation of Blanche DuBois. "But the audience never laughs. They identify too much with the character, with the tragic element. Every time I see them clutch their pearls and hear those sympathetic 'aww's from the seats, I consider the scene—the entire production!—a failure. They should be howling!"

"If it's any consolation," said Truman, "I agree with you that the scene is a failure."

Frank had never found the humor Tenn found in Blanche, and he certainly didn't find it in Jack. "It doesn't feel right to be laughing at him," he said. "He's in pain."

"You can only save one writer at a time," Tenn said, his hand on Frank's shoulder. "The weight of two of us would sink the lifeboat."

In the Marines, Frank had learned a different approach to rescue. Every man was his brother. To sit idly by while his brother was drowning was an act of treason. It didn't matter if your brother was a loudmouth or a screw-off or a mean son of a bitch, you still had to drag his sorry excuse for a body onto the boat before he went under. Instead of making this argument, which Frank knew he couldn't win, and which would only lead to Tenn and Truman mooning over him as a romantic soldier, he steered the conversation, as delicately as possible, toward what had happened at Testa del Lupo. It was clear, though, that Truman knew nothing more than they did about those events or had no intention of telling them if he did.

Meanwhile, the yachts pulled into the harbor and disgorged their hungry passengers onto dry land and then through the doors of the Delfino, which burst open every few minutes with another group in sundresses and straw hats. Everyone knew Truman. Not only was he patient with each of the women and men who came up to greet him, but he seemed to welcome their advances and to grow taller and more animated the longer they engaged him. In this way, Truman was more like Frank than Tenn, whose nerves often got the best of him in crowds, who shrank under the weight of too much attention at premieres and receptions. The whiskey and the pills helped up to a point, but only when Frank could calibrate and regulate them for Tenn; left to his own devices, Tenn drank too much of the whiskey and, to counteract the effects, popped too many of the pills, and by the end of the night he'd lose himself completely.

Truman was sorry they were leaving Portofino, he told them, after Jack Dunphy appeared briefly and admonishingly on the stairs. It was time for him to go up and claim his hamburger. Lady Dunphy did not feel up to guests tonight, Truman said, otherwise he'd invite them up for an espresso and to watch Truman digest his reheated sandwich. Truman promised to make it up to Frank and Tenn with an invitation to visit them again in Taormina, possibly in the fall, on their way to Morocco? If not, then in the late spring of '54, after the rainy season? Truman and Dunphy had already lived for three years in Sicily, in a vertiginous villa called Fontana Vecchia that had once belonged to D. H. Lawrence, where the rent was cheaper and the men darker and more accommodating than in the north. They were excellent hosts, Truman reminded them, and it was quieter in Taormina, more discreet.

If it were Frank's place to do so, he'd have put forth the idea that came to him as Truman went on and on pining for Sicily, which was that, since he and Dunphy had such spacious accommodations and such an appetite for guests, and since Frank and Tenn had already spent happy hours there a few summers back, they should invite Sandro and Jack to stay with them, or invite Jack alone. What better place, with the ghost of D. H. Lawrence looking on in benediction, to give their countryman a change of scene, a place to lick his wounds and dry out. But Frank was learning, ever so slowly, that other men's hearts, even Tenn's, weren't as big and simple and practical as his; if they were, they'd be drafting a telegram to be sent to the bungalow in Marina di Cecina. Frank wasn't always able to say out loud what was in his heart, but he was usually damn good at acting on his loving intentions. It frustrated him that he hadn't had much luck in Portofino so far—first with Anja, now with Jack—and so maybe it was a good thing that he and Tenn were moving on.

They said their goodbyes to Truman, who disappeared up the stairs of the Delfino, and walked tipsily through the piazza toward the Splendido. Neither wanted to hail a car. They were enjoying the chance to replace the horror of Testa del Lupo with the cool breeze from the harbor and the lights the booze made blurry and the man playing mandolin in the doorway of a shuttered *pasticceria*. Frank carried Truman's copy of *The Gallery*. When they came upon Anja and Bitte's apartment off Via del Fondaco, they were surprised to see one of the windows lit by a lamp and a shadow moving across it, since the women still had one final free night at the hotel. They stood a moment, watching the silhouette bend and straighten, bend and straighten, as if doing calisthenics. They did not ring the bell. Strange how much could pass between people in just a few days. Frank hoped he'd see Anja again, but, once they separated here, he'd have no way to find her. Her life had no clear direction. It would be up to her to seek him out and, finally, to express her gratitude for all that he and Tenn had tried to do for her.

The farther they got from the piazza, the darker and emptier the streets, the more at ease Frank felt walking with his arm around Tenn's waist. Never mind that Italian men sat in each other's laps and slobbered all over each other as a matter of custom; in the affection between queers, no matter how muted, there was an instantly recognizable difference. Frank shook his flashlight at the oncoming pedestrians, dazzling their eyes, both to identify them and to give him and Tenn a moment to unlink their arms and then wave a friendly, but not too friendly, *buona serata*. The drinks had not completely dulled their nerves. At every turn, they half expected to come upon the band of savage boys, or the *carabinieri* who'd decided to ask the Americans a few questions after all about the body found at Testa del Lupo. Frank quickened his pace.

Midway up the hill, Tenn took the flashlight and turned into a dark, narrow alley. "A shortcut," he said. The walls of the alley were covered in vegetation, a form of flowering ivy or kudzu that grew wildly all over town. It gave off a sharp, tangy scent—something like honeysuckle but much less sweet—that filled the air like smoke.

"Whatever this is would go great with gin," said Tenn, plucking off a flower.

The shortcut led, eventually, to a church and, behind it, a cemetery. Behind the cemetery, a cliff. "Oh well," said Tenn, with a grin in his voice. "Not such a great shortcut after all." They made their way slowly and clumsily down an uneven stone path toward the tallest structure in the distance, the mausoleum.

At the Splendido they had as comfortable a bed as money could buy in one of the grandest hotels of the world, but it was onto the muddy grass in front of the wall of skeletons that they fell, kissing madly, and where Frank, emboldened by the darkness and the wall that blocked the moon, pulled his pants down to his ankles. He switched off the flashlight. "Promise me," he said, his palms pressed to the firm ground, laughing, "after this: no more graveyards."

The only sounds were the Ligurian Sea bashing the rocks below and Tenn's sweet words in Frank's ear as he arranged himself behind him, just the right words, always at the tip of his tongue in these circumstances, to convince Frank of the joy his body brought him by the simple fact of its Frankness. His was not just any body; it was the body into which Frank Merlo had been miraculously born. It was the one and only Frank Merlo body that existed and would ever exist and could never be copied, and it pleased him so very much, its shameless revelation of itself again and again and again. Tenn had been looking for Frank's body all his life, he said, from the moment he'd first been pulled, as if by a wild undertow, to the body of another man (he could hardly recall who he was), and now that this body was entirely in his grasp, his arms locked so tightly around his chest that it squeezed his ribs and lungs and heart, he would never let it go.

THEY WOKE THE NEXT MORNING at the Splendido to a desperate telegram from Paul Bowles. He was having trouble with his part of the *Senso* script, and with Ahmed, and with his liver. DOWN TO

112 LBS, the telegram shouted. He begged Tenn to skip Verona altogether and drive back to him in Rome instead, right away, or else, implied the block letters, he would die of anxiety, frustration, malnourishment, heatstroke, and neglect. Ahmed was not chaperone material, not with so much kif around and street whores in cheap supply.

Writers in danger everywhere.

The new plan—the replacement for the drawbridge plan, which Frank and Tenn concocted on the spot—was for Paul and Ahmed to remain in Rome until Tenn and Frank rejoined them later that day. They'd taken an apartment on the same floor of 11 Via Firenze, just down the hall from the one he and Tenn shared with Mr. Moon. Tenn would work on his *Senso* love scenes on one of their two sunny fourth-floor terraces, Paul would complete his revisions on the terrace a few feet away, never out of Tenn's supervisory sight, and by the end of the week they'd both deliver their scripts by hand to Visconti, who was shooting on location nearby in Trastevere.

Whether or not those scripts would include dialogue from a horse-like soldier of the Risorgimento was never discussed. Frank was too ashamed to ask, to reopen the hands he'd put before Tenn in supplication in the hotel garden; it was also possible that Frank was afraid that his answer would be yes, and he'd have no choice but to put on the soldier's uniform and speak his lines. What if the costume didn't fit? What if he lost his voice? What if he wasn't any good?

He'd had a night to sleep on Anja's charges against him, and a sunrise swim to focus his mind. He resolved to clear his good name with her before they left Portofino. On the way to the harbor with Tenn and their luggage, he asked the driver to drop him off at her apartment on Via del Fondaco. After getting no response from buzzing her door, he left word for Anja with the landlady. When or whether Anja would receive that word, he didn't know.

It unsettled Frank to be out of favor with anyone for long, especially a woman. He wasn't accustomed to the guilt that bubbled up from it. The storms he'd had with his father and his brothers and cousins over the years, and with Tenn, earlier this summer especially, storms that shook the windows and kept him up at night and even drew blood, always passed quickly. But women, he knew, carried their storms with them.

The dark rages of women, in the face of which Frank was rarely brave, transformed him back into the little boy he'd been trying hard to grow out of, thumb in his mouth, crouched under the dining room table watching his mother's and aunt's skirts pass back and forth. Sometimes he didn't come home right away after hearing his mother call him from the front door; sometimes he corrected his father's English; for this, his mother would give him a hard smack on the *culetto* and a stream of curses; but then, moments later, she'd pull him to her breast, rest her head on top of his, and sob. The sobbing would go on for a few minutes until, as if remembering what he'd done wrong, she'd push him off her in a fury, only to find him later in the night and suffocate him again with a faceful of kisses. Frank never knew which mother he'd wake up to.

He'd spent entire summer afternoons studying her from under the table, listening in on her conversations with his sisters and Mrs. Covelli from next door, watching her in the rare moments she thought she was alone, when she'd sit in his father's recliner to smoke and sing and crack her knuckles, something he'd never seen a woman do before or since. What he came to learn about his mother was that she broke every pattern. There were times she kindly kept his dinner warm for whenever he showed up after her call, or when she laughed along with him, lustily, scornfully, at his father's butchered English. There was no way to predict or track her storms. The only thing about her that never changed was that she forgot nothing and forgave no one.

At the harbor, Tenn walked in wide circles around their stack of suitcases, checking his watch. The boat to Rapallo was late. He shielded his eyes from the afternoon sun, trying to spot the charter Frank had arranged. "You took your time," he said, when Frank showed up with a gelato he'd stopped for on the way down the hill. "You're sure this friend of Luca's will come through? It's quarter-past!"

"If you don't trust me to get us from one place to the next," Frank said, "you can look for a new travel agent."

"Don't be sour," Tenn said. "Not when we're about to spend hours together in tight conveyances."

By way of apology, Frank offered him a lick.

The mounting anxiety Frank felt had another cause: he was in no hurry to return to Rome. He was eager to see Mr. Moon, of course, and Anna, too, but otherwise, he was going back to a city and a summer plagued with storms. In the months before they escaped to Portofino, the same old argument had come between him and Tenn.

His name, this time, was Alvaro.

Frank had met Alvaro last summer, the summer of '52, and then the heat and the long solitary afternoons of the summer of '53 drove Frank straight back to him. He'd been tired of skulking around the apartment in hopes Tenn might finish his work early, of the weeks and weeks without so much as a love-smack on the ass from the man who shared his bed. He dreaded the drowsy siesta hours in the *centro storico* with its sad pulled-down grates and shiftless, starving cats. The sound of radios muffled behind shutters was enough to get him sobbing.

Alvaro had nothing to his name but hours in the day, and, like most Italians, his greatest talent was passing the time. Frank knew he could always find him in the Piazza dei Monti, and that Alvaro was always happy to be found, sitting on the top step of the fountain with his hands behind his back and his chest puffed out, ready for whatever came along. Alvaro demanded nothing from Frank but orders: drive me to Trastevere on your motorbike (*hop on, Signor Merlo!*), fetch me a cup of water (*here it is, Signor Merlo, nice and cold*), put your mouth here (*at your pleasure, Signor Merlo*). Alvaro had little patience for indecision, for hesitation, for sadness of any sort. A few hours of ordering this agreeable young man around, directing his various forms of attention for hours at a time, stanched Frank's restlessness. Every few days or so—it was wrong to be greedy, but oh how hungry Frank was for Alvaro every day that sultry June and July—he walked the few blocks to the Monti, locked eyes with him, ticked his head in the direction of the bar at the corner of the Piazza and Via dei Serpenti, and watched him bid a hasty goodbye to his friends for an afternoon and evening of *Il Duce*, Signor Merlo.

Frank returned from these episodes satisfied, temporarily well braced for the empty days ahead in the apartment, and grateful rather than desperate for whatever crumbs Tenn let fall from his plate. When Tenn seemed open to the telling, Frank recounted again for him, as he'd done after his first meeting with Alvaro the year before, all the particulars of the boy's puppy-like obedience and excitability, the dirt under his nails, his soft hairy belly. Tenn liked most to hear the ways in which Alvaro resembled Frank, and so these were the details Frank emphasized. When Tenn did not seem open to the telling, or Frank sensed he was spoiling for a fight, or that, in that moment, he was craving tenderness over titillation, he'd improvise a story about Alvaro spurning him or not showing up at all. To account for the missing hours, he'd describe a sightseeing trip that never happened or a nap on the beach he never took. Whether Tenn believed him or not didn't matter; they'd embrace and make love or head to Tre Scalini for a bite or the cinema for a late movie.

Most often that summer, though, Frank returned to the apartment to find Tenn in their bed with some skinny and bruised piece of trade he'd plucked from Via Nazionale out of loneliness and revenge. Then the storm would come. Tenn called Alvaro a filthy hustler, "the lowest scrap of trash on the heap," to which Frank pointed to the terrified trick at that very moment ransacking the sheets in search of his underwear. "Does this one even speak English?" Frank shouted. "Did you even ask his name?"

Tenn: Giovanni!

Frank: They're all Giovannis!

Tenn: Same as your Alvaro!

Frank: His family comes from the village of Sant'Angelo! Fifty miles from mine! He likes strawberry gelato! His mother is blind in one eye!

Tenn (*throwing up his hands*): The gallantry! The propriety! Such fine young gentlemen they are, too noble for the likes of me!

Frank: Every day I come for you first thing—you, Tenn! Not him! I come on my tiptoes so I don't disturb you, hoping, telling myself, maybe it's one of his good days. And what do I find? Tenn's in bad shape again. Drunk or sad or both. Every day since we got here. Needs something he can't tell me, I just know I don't have it, he doesn't even want it from me. So yes, I go find Alvaro. Isn't that what we've always done? And don't I make sure you're OK before I leave? Don't I kiss you on my way out the door?

Tenn: Just before you slam it shut!

Frank: Just after I check your pill bottles!

Tenn: Well, I'm tired of being treated like a stupid, unsatisfactory whore by the Bubu de Montparnasse!

Books thrown across the room. A table overturned. The neighbor banging her broom handle on the wall. A shattered vase. Silence so thick it choked the throat. The click of the bedroom doors, shut but not locked, in case forgiveness came early. Angry, fitful sleep. Dreams rueful and tender. Curtain. No applause.

In the morning, they basked in forgiveness. When done right, forgiveness costs a fortune. When it came to forgiveness, he and Tenn spent flamboyantly after every argument. To Frank's mind, their forgiveness for each other was a stockpile of gold coins in trunks in an endless vault. They'd spent nearly all of it those first two months of summer in Rome, before Portofino, and still it replenished itself, earning interest with every peaceful day that followed. With every declaration of forgiveness came a promise to behave more kindly, to give more thought to the feelings of the other, to remember they were lucky to be immune from the troublesome things that beleaguered most men—money, children, women—but not from jealousy. Didn't they used to know that? When did they forget?

It was in these moments, in the glow of a forgiveness morning, with the sopranos at the Opera below the apartment serenading them with their practice arias, their voices floating up to them like wishes, that Frank came closest to declaring his love for Tenn. The most he could offer, though, in the light of all that had been said, was forgiveness. It lasted a few hours, a day at most, and then the drama went up again: same lines, same props, same thunderous climax. The run lasted weeks, Alvaro growing more tan, more fond, Frank greedier, wilder, itchier, Tenn less open to the telling.

One morning in early July, Tenn told Frank, "I've booked a trip to Barcelona."

"By yourself?"

"Incredible as it seems to you, I am quite capable of applying for my own passage."

"You're going alone, I mean."

"Meglio solo che mal accompagnato" was his response, and with that he was gone.

It was not better for Frank to be alone, he found, those three long weeks Tenn spent in Spain. With Alvaro all to himself, he was at first ravenous with him, but then quickly Frank grew distracted and, finally, cruel. A going-nowhere boy, Frank called him. A waste of his time and money. Alvaro raised his arm to hit him. He spit at Frank's feet instead. His eyes were not angry, but afraid. Despondent. Betrayed. "Coward!" Frank shouted back, as Alvaro took off down the dark narrow street. Frank had demanded to be taken there and for Alvaro to kneel before him out in the open, but even this scene made him tired. He could only play the dictator for so long. It was not in his nature.

With all the time in the world, the entire apartment his playground, Frank did little but sleep and read novels and scribble the occasional postcard. He typed half a letter to a talent agent back in New York, then tore it up. There was no agent, no one in show business in the States, who wouldn't somehow, eventually, sniff out his affiliation with Tenn, and Frank was still young enough to think that a self-made man was the only kind worth being. Could it be that hard to make one's self out of one's self? Generations of American men, weaker than he, with less charm and drive, had done it, why not him? In the meantime, he stood at the open window and sang along with the sopranos. *Carmen*. This, too, got the neighbor's broom.

If Frank couldn't be trampled, if he couldn't make himself into something quite yet, he at least wanted to be useful to Tenn, as he'd always promised to be. So he arranged for Paul and Ahmed to meet Tenn in Barcelona, and then for the three of them to travel to Rome, and while all that was happening it was he who talked to the landlord about airing out the apartment at the end of the hallway for Paul and Ahmed to rent. It was Frank who plumped the pillows in their rooms and swept the terrace where Paul would work on the *Senso* script. When Tenn finally returned from Spain, that last week of July, he carried two armfuls of forgiveness, and what a lovely mess it was, the rose petals and the gold coins falling from him as he crossed the threshold, Paul and Ahmed behind him in the doorway like bridesmaids.

Tenn came back light from Barcelona. He'd left the blue devils behind, he said, and when he was free of them there was always the chance, however remote, that they'd never find their way back to him. Before Tenn, Frank had never heard of the blue devils. He'd had the *blues*, of course, which hung around for a while like rain clouds, but the sun always burned them off quick and he'd turn back to his old gay self. Tenn's blue devils were like wildcats, he said, who lived under his skin. And when you have wildcats living under your skin, they can wake at any moment, day or night, and make you shake and shudder and cry out and weep. The pills put them to sleep but never for long. They clawed and howled again without warning. Frank was one of the few who could tell when they'd awoken. He'd catch a glimpse of Tenn at a party, laughing or clinking his glass, carefree to the room of naked eyes, but there were the little paws scratching at his face, there was the anguished mewing. Frank would cross the room to stand beside him, put his arm around his waist. It helped, Tenn had told him, to have a Horse to hold him up under that ungainly weight.

In those three weeks in Barcelona, away from Frank, Tenn had added some pages to *Battle of Angels*. He'd watched a bullfight. He'd swum and eaten paella and spoken French. Franz Neuner, "the sexual impresario of Barcelona," according to Bowles, had procured some entertainment for him. Through it all, Tenn said, he'd been lonelier without his Frankie than he'd been with him, the kind of loneliness achievable and recognizable only by a separation. *Mal accompagnato*, it turned out, might not have been so bad. "What a sorry companion I make for anyone young and alive," Tenn had scrawled to Frank on a postcard. When it arrived, the day after his return, Frank took a match to it. He had no use for the words of the blue devils.

On the drive up to Portofino, Frank's head nuzzled in his lap, Tenn told him stories and they laughed for the first time in months. (He'd left the bullfight midway through, he admitted, because he was deeply offended by the spectacle. "It wasn't the cruelty to the bulls that was so hard to swallow"—he began to laugh then, and the ease of it, its anticipatory delight, its catlessness, got Frank laughing too—"It was the roly-poly matadors! You don't sit out in the heat, choking on the stench of bull blood, to look at pudgy figures bending and twisting.") All the way through Tuscany and into Liguria, Frank slept off and on, waking always to his voice. This was how it had been for years. This is how it could keep being.

And now they were going back to Rome. The boat to Rapallo was late, but here it came, rounding the harbor and headed toward them, a glorified canoe helmed by a skeletal shirtless man well into his seventies.

"This old hat rack is Luca's cousin?" Tenn asked.

"He might have said uncle."

"Or *nonno*."

The old man waved them over to the launch. "You can fit all this?" Frank said to him, gesturing at their stacks of luggage.

"No problem!" he said brightly, smiling with his clapped hands and his missing front teeth. He proceeded to open various secret compartments in the hull, tuck the bags in at expert angles, and somehow the little boat swallowed every one of them with room to spare. *"Allora!"* he said, when he slammed the doors shut.

They set off, Frank and Tenn behind the old man on an uncushioned wood plank, as transfixed by the deep knots of muscle in his back, muscles neither of them would ever develop sitting at a desk or even dancing with a professional troupe, as they were by the shoulders of Portofino itself, those twin mountains on both sides of the harbor trying as best they could to hide the orange and gold town from the curious world. It was just as they were turning away from the town toward the open water that Frank spotted Anja rushing out of the Delfino.

"Stop!" Frank said to the old man. *"Fermo!"*

"Che succede?"

"Just stop right here for one minute. Don't move. *Non si muova.*"

She wasn't watching where she was going. She looked back and forth from the piazza to the water, scanning the boats and the faces of the tourists waiting for them along the embankment, her hand on top of her head to keep her hat from flying off. She collided with a little boy and didn't stop to see if he was OK. In her other hand, she carried a small white suitcase.

"At long last," said Tenn. "The string of pearls is broken."

"She's coming with us," Frank said.

"WHAT DID YOU do for a living?" the new nurse asked Frank. That was how they spoke of his life now, all of the nurses, in the past tense. He didn't correct this one. She was moving him to a private room, making conversation so he wouldn't ask why.

"I slept with Tennessee Williams," he said.

That old joke.

"How nice," she said. She had her hand on his lower back, lifting him onto his feet. She'd brought a wheelchair just in case. "What do you say, want to do this the easy way?"

Her nametag said Fay Newton. She had a wide face and close-set eyes like an owl. "I can walk, Fig," he said. It made him smile, an owl called Fig Newton. Maybe it was the gas.

He walked around the ward to wish the other guys good luck. There were ten of them now. It was the middle of the day and most were asleep. He sat on the edge of their beds to catch his breath between goodbyes. Frank was the only one with lung cancer. The rest of them had it in the liver or the brain. As bad off as he was, plenty worse had come through.

"You gettin' sprung?" asked Blind Sid. Every guy had a sick name. They gave them out to pass the time.

"That's what they tell me," said Frank. Blind Sid could use a little hope.

"Good for you," he said. "I don't want to see you back in here."

"You won't see me no ways," Frank said, in his best James Cagney.

Blind Sid had been a carpenter for a living. Legs, the guy across from him, had been a postman. Pinky and Grumpy and Giggles had had office jobs. Robin Hood had sold real estate. Pluto had taught science at a high school in Teaneck. Muscles Marinara had managed a pizza shop. There was one colored guy they called Jazz. Cueball had painted houses. The Horse—he'd been an assistant. (Sometimes he said "secretary.") A long time ago, he'd driven a truck and danced and fought in the Marines and had walk-ons in some B movies. No, nothing they would have seen.

"Mr. Merlo," said Nurse Fig, from the doorway. "I've got to get you upstairs."

He patted sleeping Giggles on the chest. When he stood, the head rush got him a little dizzy. He steadied himself so the nurse wouldn't see. But the walk back across the ward did him in. "Just this once," he said, falling into the chair. "For you."

"You'll sleep better in your own room," she said in the elevator.

"I did fine down here."

"It's not a place you want to be forever," she said.

"So that's where you're taking me?" he asked. "A place I'll want to be forever?"

They went up. She parked him in front of a closed door, walked around the chair to open it, then pushed him into a small windowless white room. It contained a single bed, an armchair, an oxygen tank, and a low table piled high with cords and blinking machines. They'd already brought his flowers and cards and books up and arranged them on the nightstand like a still life.

"Not everybody has this luxury," Fig said. She pulled him up alongside the bed and hit the brake. "Someone's looking out for you."

"Who's footing the bill?"

"That's not for me to know," she said.

For the past few months, the thick of summer, Frank had been going back and forth from Tenn's apartment on Sixty-fifth Street to the cobalt unit at Memorial. They'd hand him a long white gown to put on and then he'd lie on his back on the long table like the Bride of Frankenstein, his arms at his sides, his head immobilized in a steel chamber. Four pins, thick as bolts, pressed against his jaw and temples to keep him still while the doctor positioned a giant metal eye at an angle just over his heart. "Ready?" he'd say, just as the eye shot two hundred beams of gamma radiation into his lungs at the precise locations of the tumors. Sometimes the visit lasted just a few minutes, sometimes more than an hour. When it was over, the nurse unbolted him from the chamber and sent him down to the ward to rest with the guys. He got there on his own two feet, never once accepting the wheelchair. If he had enough strength, he was free to leave the very same day, take a taxi back to Sixty-fifth Street, or sit on a bench in the park. If he was too weak, he'd stay the night in the ward, head home in the morning in time to catch Tenn at the typewriter, and then he'd sleep some more.

They told him the treatments could go on for months, for years. "All we can do is see where it hits you next," said the doctor, and once they did see where it hit him next, they'd hit it right back. The more Frank learned about the treatment, the simpler it became. The blurs would keep appearing on the X-rays of his lungs and his liver and his brain, but the eye would never run out of gamma rays to point at them. It was a race, and Frank had always been good at races. The quickest to the pin. A sprinter. A fighter.

He hated the sight of the black burns on his chest, his tender shriveled nipples, the ugly rashes, his skin flaky and dry and sore. Catching his own face in the mirror, the sunken cheeks, the bulging eyes, frightened him. But it was the fatigue he hated most of all. He longed to swim, to dance, to fuck. When he woke each day in Tenn's apartment, he vowed to do one of the three. But it was always already the early afternoon, and it took all his strength just to get from the bedroom to the living room sofa. He spent his days watching soap operas, Gigi on the cushion beside him licking his fingertips, Mr. Moon having died in April of '54, eight months after being disinvited to Truman's party. Tenn was always out somewhere. Friends called with nothing to say, brought him food he couldn't eat, stories he couldn't quite keep up with, as evening came on and he drifted in and out of consciousness. Still, this was a rhythm, a routine that could go on and on (months, years) and he didn't care what Al and Dan and Connie and the priest said, it was bad luck to write a will in this sorry state. Writing a will was the same as admitting the race was run. He'd do it eventually, he promised them, but only once Indian Summer came around.

Blind Sid was the one who'd told him about Indian Summer. Sid had been in and out of Memorial for ten years—"nine years longer than you," he reminded Frank, "so buckle up"—and he'd seen it all. Every guy who came through the ward, Sid said, had had a stretch of time—a few days, a week, a month, longer if he was lucky—when the cancer left his body, when his muscles suddenly kicked back in, when he could eat a bowl of spaghetti and meatballs without barfing it up, when his mouth filled with spit and his dick with blood. Sid was still waiting for his Indian Summer. He hoped that, when it came, his sight would come back with it. His daughter had grown into a young woman; he wanted to see her strawberry-blonde hair down to her shoulders. Like the weather, Sid said, you had no warning when Indian Summer would come on, but when it did, that was when you took care of your business, said your goodbyes, made your confessions, gave the wife one last good screw, because winter was about to flatten you and this time you weren't gettin' up.

All that was still to come, Frank had said to everyone who'd listen, though only Sid seemed to believe him. In the meantime, he'd settled into the rhythms of his shrunken world, the trips from Sixty-fifth Street ten blocks south to Memorial, from the cobalt unit to the ward, from the bedroom to the living room. He and Gigi kept to themselves while Tenn and Angel crossed in front of them, checking their watches, making their plans. Then, last week, without a goodbye, Angel flew off to Key West, and it was just Frank and Tenn alone together in the apartment. This, too, the strange and familiar rhythm of sharing a home with Tenn, Frank had settled into.

With Angel gone, Frank had hoped Tenn might sleep beside him on the queen-size bed. He longed for the fat and skin and sweat of another body cradling his, rocking him to sleep. No, it was not just any body he longed for; he longed for Tenn's body, Tenn's fat and Tenn's skin and Tenn's sweat, the soft brush of Tenn's mustache on the back of his neck. Tenn's was the body he came home to, the only one that could protect him.

"After you've swallowed all those pinkies," Frank had said, "my coughing won't wake you. You'll get through the night just fine if you just give it a try." He didn't want to beg, but it sounded a lot like begging. "Pretend it's 1953 and this is just a summer cold. Pretend you don't hate me."

"I could never hate you, Frankie," he said. He picked up the electric fan and his favorite pillow and headed for the living room sofa. "But you'll be more comfortable with that nice big bed all to yourself."

When Tenn shut the door to the bedroom, Frank crawled to the end of the bed, reached his arm out, and bolted himself in behind it.

Every night since, whether or not Tenn had come home from wherever he roamed in Manhattan, Frank turned that lock. Let him change his mind, he thought. Let him find his mercy—his compassion, his heart—but don't let him find the bedroom door open when he finally comes to comfort him. Let him not find Frank splayed before him on the bed like a whore. Let him wonder why the door had been locked at all. Let him bang his fists on it in fear that he couldn't get to Frank in time to save him. Let Frank hear his anguished pleas.

A week ago, in the morning, was the last time Frank had seen him. Tenn came into the bedroom while Frank was dressing. The car was downstairs for his nine o'clock appointment at Memorial.

"Let me help you," Tenn said.

"I can put on my own shirt," said Frank.

"As you like."

Frank was wearing only his fluffy white robe. The lifting of his shirt from the hanger knocked the wind out of him. The heat was already heavy on the windows, the fans whirring. He waited for Tenn to leave the room so he could remove the robe, but Tenn just stood there in the doorway, leaning his shoulder on the frame, staring. He stared at Frank the way you stare at a mouse you don't have the heart to sic the cat on. Their eyes met. And then, because Frank was already late, and because Tenn should see—for once, up close—the entirety of his ninety-eight pounds racked and gasping for air, the wreck of burnt bones the Little Horse had become, he let the robe drop to the floor.

"Jesus, Frankie," Tenn said. He fell to his knees.

He left town that day, or so Frank was told. *Milk Train* was opening in Virginia. Tenn would have gone anywhere, though, made any excuse, just to escape that apartment, to put distance between himself and the whining skeleton Frank had become. Frank knew him like a book.

He knew he paid for this private room on this quiet floor, for the oxygen tank, for the blinking machines and the better meals and the extra devotion of Nurse Fig, for the Bride of Frankenstein gown and the incinerating eye. He knew this was the most Tenn would do, here at the end of their long association. He had no more illusions. The only thing he didn't know was how soon Indian Summer would come, and if Tenn would come back in time for one last day in the sun.

8.

THE SURVIVAL HYPOTHESIS

The city, hateful as it is, has burst into bloom. In the park below Anja's apartment window, the tulips stand in proud formation. A row of purple, a row of pink, a row of yellow, the lawn at their feet a bright pool of green. A spiked iron fence protects the park. Twice a week, a team of men in orange shirts comes to caretake. They jump from their pickup truck, unlock the arched gate, fan out over the grass and mulch to spear the invading trash, skim and dredge the fountain, wipe the bird droppings from the statues, sweep the cobblestone pathways, and then they lock the gate behind them, throw the bag of trash into a pickup truck, and speed off.

If Anja is sitting at her window when the wind is high and blowing east, the spray from the fountain cools her face and neck and her bare arms. She closes her eyes, thinks of somewhere else. Every night at ten o'clock—she is often at the window at that time, just before she falls asleep—the jets and the fountain lights switch off with a sudden splash, plunging the entire square into darkness. Then, at ten thirty, even in heavy rain, the sprinklers pop on. She once thought it wasteful, all this attention to a park the Association opens to the public only six times a year. Now she wishes that the caretakers were the only ones permitted access, and that they worked on the weekends, too, when the scraps of paper pile up, attach themselves to the railings, and float in the water like unread messages. In two weeks, at the annual Memorial Day strings concert, the children will come trampling in for the start of the season, spilling their ice cream cones, scarring the grass, beheading the tulips with their sugary breaths.

Lately, Anja has taken to sleeping on the cushioned bench beneath her open window. The master bedroom has always been too stuffy, cooked by one too many radiators, their valves rusted shut. She endured the stuffiness for Pieter, who could never get warm enough. Their bed is perfect in its current state, adorned with the Amish quilt handmade for her as his gift for her seventieth birthday, the two king-size pillows plumped and unwrinkled, the top sheet folded in a straight line over the lip of the coverlet. That is how she left it, at least, many weeks ago. Sometimes she forgets about the room, tucked away in the back corner of the bloated apartment, far from the noise and color of the square. Anja can sleep anywhere. She has lost so much height that the length of her body, head to toe, is exactly equal to the length of the little bench.

The problem is that their heavy old wooden file cabinets remain in the distant bedroom, relics from the days Pieter lived alone in this apartment as a young professor, when he rented out the second bedroom to graduate students. His papers are gone, of course, but somewhere mixed up with her scripts and contracts and head shots and fan mail lies *Call It Joy*, which Sandrino and Trevor, mostly Trevor, insist is a treasure—a "guaranteed classic," Trevor calls it—despite her insistence to the contrary.

Oh, my dear boys, she thinks. Don't you know? A late work, completed in haste, out of desperation to prove yourself and reclaim your genius and spark a rebirth and win back the critics who abandoned you, while death looked over your shoulder, that is not a treasure. That is something you pray your friends will destroy.

They don't know, they don't believe her, so they press her. They resist her unromantic notions, as well they should. They question her objectivity, her perspective. In the weeks since the fruit fly lecture, these first warm Mondays of spring, they come to her in the city to make their case. Perhaps they think that the closer they get to the apartment that holds Tenn's manuscript, the more likely she will be to lead them up the hill and let them read it.

By they, she means Trevor. She always means Trevor. Each Monday evening, as she approaches the wine bar at the bottom of the hill, she can't help it, she hopes—just once is all she asks—that she will find Sandrino alone, without the chattering boy, waiting for her. She is always disappointed. For one thing, Sandrino is in love with Trevor. He reaches for his hand under the table; he never interrupts him; he gazes at him like a child at the magician who pulls the quarter from his ear. For another, they are both incapable of arriving on time.

Though the film series is over, they have kept up their Monday evening tradition. The maître d' puts a RESERVED sign on the one low table in the corner of the bar. The other patrons are perilously perched around them on high wobbly stools, hunched over their fifteen-dollar glasses of cabernet. The boys sit beside each other across from Anja on the banquette, their backs to the street, one of those cheerless battery-operated candles fake-flickering between them. What she would give for a real flame, for smoke, for dripping wax to dip her fingertips in, for a hand reaching for hers under the table. What she would give to hop onto one of those high barstools with no fear of it tipping over.

In as few words as possible, Anja has answered all of their television questions she once rebuffed. This, too, is on account of Trevor, who slips them between talk of aesthetics and art and weather, as if to trick her into confession. When she indulges him, what great pleasure it gives her to see the pleasure his pleasure gives Sandrino. She indulges Trevor not to unburden herself, but to see Sandrino's eyes go wide with the pride of having procured this living legend, this friend of his father's, for his zealous boyfriend.

Maybe, then, it is not Sandrino's indulgence, but her own. Are they comparable pleasures, being procured for and being procured? Whatever the case, these Monday evenings, the only break in her project of laziness, reacquaint Anja to the power she once had and mostly gave up, that of holding an audience in the thrall of her whims.

When every response is true, what leads her to say yes instead of no to the questions, to favor this reason over that reason as an explanation for her career decisions, to choose him rather than him or him or him when she is asked, so casually, what she misses? She misses them all. Her life without them is unbearable. Television questions force them into taxonomies, pressing her to admit he belongs in one period of time and he in another, when the truth is they were all one man smashed into pieces and scattered across her life. Each one contained the others. When Pieter cut his finger, Hovland's blood stained the knife. When Frank pulled her close behind him as they walked out of the surf at Paraggi, the body shielding her from the men's stares was the body of her father.

Q: "Don't you miss working?"

A: No.

Q: "How do you just let it all go?"

A: Pride.

Q: "You must be happier now than you were then?"

A: Yes.

Q: "Tell me *something* about it you miss."
A: Him.

Q: "Don't you miss working?"
A: Yes.
Q: "How do you just let it all go?"
A: Fear.
Q: "You must be happier now than you were then?"
A: No.
Q: "Tell me *something* about it you miss."
A: Him.

Q: "Don't you miss working?"
A: You make the mistake—everyone does—of concluding that the project of laziness on which I have recently embarked is not a form of work, to assume that if I am not acting I must be in a state of rot. I admit that I am no good at laziness. I have been an American too long, suspicious of indolence and directionless dreaming. That is why I will soon leave the country, as you know. That is why this city hates me—not for my fadedness, but for my wasted potential. Before I leave, though, I have a great deal of unlearning to do. To be successfully lazy you must be satisfied with what you already know and what you will never know. I am training myself to sit at my window in the company of the tulips, one more flower in the row, in full acceptance of my relative beauty and uselessness. My finishedness. It is excruciating. I cannot stop myself from considering my so-called contributions to the art; from assessing my capacity to reemerge; and, in my weakest moments, from looking back with syrupy fondness on my accolades and reviews and fans. It would be a triumph, I think, to achieve accep-

tance, to empty myself of myself without the convenience of death. I wonder if anyone has ever done it. I want to be the first.

Q: "How do you just let it all go?"

A: You buy two $2,500 tickets and fly to Los Angeles for a charity production of *Love Letters* starring a seventy-five-year-old Elizabeth Taylor. She has not done a play in twenty-three years, but this one is for AIDS, so she has made an exception. They wheel her onto the stage in a frock the color of cantaloupe and a gray chinchilla coat. The other ticket is for Scott, your new manager, whose lover died at forty from the disease and who bursts into tears when he sees Dame Liz in the flesh. Her earrings are so big and gold and heavy they make her head droop. Her back is shot, Scott says; she's held together with pins and plates; she's in terrible pain; she's hopped up on Vicodin. You jump to your feet to applaud her along with Scott and the tuxes and sequined gowns around you. Liz is so decrepit, you wonder if she can speak at all. You keep applauding because you do not want to find out whether or not she can go through with the performance, you hope they call the whole thing off, it has gone far enough, it is cruel to exploit her, a million dollars for AIDS victims or not. The first half is tortuous. Liz is out of tune. She delivers her lines with a cloying screech. You prefer to keep your eyes on James Earl Jones sitting beside her in his dark suit, impassive as a judge, indulging her out of respect. Then, midway through, something changes. Liz recalibrates, settles into the character of Melissa, who is growing old before your eyes. *I'm fat, I'm ugly, my hair is horrible!* she says, with a poignancy that is somehow both subtle and overwhelming. *They've put me on all sorts of new drugs, and half the time I don't make sense at all.* It could have become parody, but it does not. Liz rises above Melissa by inhabiting her without irony or self-awareness. At the curtain, she does what you are now certain she has planned to do all along: she rises triumphantly from her metal chair, as if cured by art, and takes a bow. So much for the pins and plates. So much for your misguided pity. She is radiant. Her neck is long, her earrings light as tin. She will save the world. Her talent is far beyond yours. Your own talent may be significant; you have even been compared to her; but you know your place. You will not let yourself be wheeled onto a stage unless you are certain you can stand up and dance across it.

Q: "You must be happier now than you were then?"

A: I do not want to insult you by keeping up the fiction that only the young believe happiness can be measured, let alone compared. Besides, what you really want to know is whether I would trade one time of my life for another, which of course I would. At this moment, I would trade my twenties for my childhood, my teenage years for any decade, my sixties for my forties. (Ask me in the next moment, and my answer will likely be different.) Today and tomorrow, though, my time in this moment, even in this body, I would not trade for anything. I suspect you boys feel the same. Pieter, Hovland, Frank, my father—I would not go back to any of them if it meant giving up the gamble of these last days or months or years of life. It would be an insult to think that because I am old and afraid of falling, and because I was once a star and a great beauty and a rover who scaled the Barabar caves, and because the only glitter left in my life is buried deep in the fibers of the carpet, and because you hear me say I am working hard to teach myself to become a tulip, that I have no faith in the brightness of my future.

Q: "Tell me *something* about it you miss."

A: You think I deserve a love story. This is the best I can do.

He came for someone else, but I was the one he chose. They are different things: being loved and being chosen. Being chosen is the more powerful drug. It enslaves you. And what you miss when it ends is not the man who did the choosing, but that rush of having been seen by him, and then plucked from the weeds, and then gathered up and hoarded and, yes, owned by him. These desires are out of fashion, but

that does not make them any less true. I am sorry to speak in generali-
ties. I am not trying to be elliptical. I am trying to tell you, in case you
do not already know, that you will be loved by many men but chosen by
only a few, and that knowing the difference will save you from making
a fool of yourself. Pieter loved me. Frank loved me. My father loved me.
You love me a little, in your own way. You should see yourselves, hanging on my words. Your wine is going warm. You see me not as I am, but
through a prism of projections. It pleases me to be loved; it makes me
what you call "happy" to act the part of the loved one for you, which is
what I did for them—Pieter and Frank and Tenn and my father, even
Sandro and Jack—for all those years. Hovland, though, was the only
one who saw me clearly, the only one who saw clear through me, which
is why he chose me, and also why he could not love me. I never acted for
Hovland. Not once. Not even the night we met, when he came looking
for someone else. I did not have to, once he chose me. What you see of
me on screen is what I see when I look at myself in the mirror; all Hovland did was turn his camera into a mirror.

"You don't miss seeing yourself, then?" Trevor asks her, interrupting. "I'd miss that for sure. I know Fabio here would." They both
laugh.

"*Me?* This guy can't walk by a mirror without making love to it,"
Sandrino says.

"And this guy's bathroom looks like a Sephora exploded," says
Trevor. "I didn't know a person could need more than one type of
blow dryer."

Sandrino makes a show of grabbing a fistful of his abundant hair,
pulling it above his head, and then letting it fall back into place exactly
as it was. "This does not happen by accident," he says.

The boys keep her later and later with their back-and-forth. Or she
keeps them. It is hard to say. Each week, as the bar thins out, and she
finally convinces them that she absolutely must go, playing the part of

the old lady (I need my sleep!), they walk her home, one on each side of her, to make sure the city causes her no harm. Their first Mondays in the wine bar, she was back long before the fountain shut off. She had plenty of time to sit in the fading light waiting for that up-sweeping westerly breeze, the tickle of spray on her skin a half-tender, half-vulgar violation. Now it is long past dark by the time they reach the top of her hill, and the fountain is still, and the sprinklers are churning away at their low work, and televisions have turned most of the windows in the square blue. She stands on the little stone path outside her door between the two tall boys, tired of talking and of refusing, again and again, their (Trevor's) requests to see the manuscript she should have destroyed years ago.

"You want to get rid of it?" asks Sandrino.

"Yes," she says.

"You don't want anyone but yourself to possess a copy of it?"

"Correct."

"But to just throw it in the fire, that would be—"

"Sacrilege," says Trevor. "Blasphemy. A *crime*."

"*Stai calma*," says Sandrino, patting him on the back.

"A mercy," says Anja.

"OK," says Sandrino. "We must show you respect. It is your wish. Your property."

"Thank you," she says.

"But I'm sure you agree we must also show respect to Tennessee Williams. Unless I am mistaken, he did not give you permission to destroy his work. What do you say we call him and ask him, in a way that is proper? Give him a chance to say goodbye?"

"This is your fancy talking again," says Anja.

Sandrino usually drinks one or two glasses of wine, but tonight, by her count, he refilled his glass four times. He has been more nervous lately, less forthcoming, less joyful, which Anja has attributed to his plans to spend the month of August in Italy. Does he fear losing Trevor to a summer fling? Does someone wait for him in Livorno, other than the ghosts of his father and mother? Will he miss her? She stops her own thoughts. *Television questions!* She is spending too much time in the company of these young romantic men. She should know better, how easily a mind and heart can be corrupted.

"What are you smiling at?" Trevor asks her.

"What I propose is a séance," Sandrino is saying. "Not now, not tonight. We need to plan to do it the correct way. Next Monday, instead of the wine bar."

"It's his idea," says Trevor.

"I did it before," says Sandrino. "Back home, with my *fidanzata.* I helped her believe."

"He never misses an opportunity to mention his ex-girlfriends," Trevor says. "Was this the one with the big feet or the one with all the birds?"

Sandrino ignores him, for once, mesmerized by his own diversion. "Here is how it is accomplished: we light many candles. We put a photograph of Tennessee Williams into a gold frame. We hold hands around a circle, with *Call It Joy* in the middle. We sprinkle flower petals on top maybe, but those are just for show. We have already something that he touched: the pages. Are they typed or did he write them with a pen? By pen is better. And, of course, we have you there, his friend from when he was living. He will want to talk to you again, yes? You made your peace with him the last time you saw him, in New York?"

"I suppose I did," says Anja.

"Good. We will ask him for his permission to read the manuscript. This will make you more calm, Anja. Less feelings of guilt. And when he gives it to us—how could he say no to us? We are his type, you said! Young and handsome! Ha ha!—we read the pages out loud together, each taking a part, with him there with us in the room, like a director. It will be beautiful."

"This is the best idea ever," Trevor says.

They both go quiet awaiting Anja's reaction. Purposefully, she drags out the suspense by looking over at the heavy-set man walking his miniature dog around the perimeter of the park. The man has stopped to monitor the suspicious scene of two tall men having cornered that old lady who never speaks to anyone. Didn't she used to have a natty old man with her to complete the pair? What became of him? The heavy-set man lives directly across the square from her. It is not a place where neighbors seek each other out as friends; it is a place where they make sure they know every owner's face but rarely acknowledge each other beyond a prim "good morning," where they engage each other only when there is a disturbance to the natural order: a concert in the park, a lost cat, a late-night invasion of tall interlopers on the stoop. Anja nods and smiles at the man, an all-clear.

"We burn the pages after we read them?" she asks Sandrino.

"Yes," he says. "That way, we receive them, but we do not preserve them."

"Unless you change your mind, of course, and you *want* to keep them," Trevor offers.

"Must they be special candles or will any cylindrical wax product suffice?" asks Anja, with mock seriousness. "I have some old birthday candles in a drawer. Shall I wear a veil?"

Sandrino narrows his eyes. "Are you making me a joke?" He is standing in her shadow, but she can still see the hurt on his face.

"Oh Sandrino," she says, "you really believe all this?" She touches his elbow. "Because it sounds to me like a stunt the two of you have cooked up."

"I'm not so talented an actor," Sandrino says. He ticks his head at his friend. "Him yes, but not me. Besides, I would not 'cook up' a stunt against you. I would not do anything to go against you."

"Then tell me," she says, her hand squeezing his arm. "Before I fall asleep here standing up. I would like to understand why my friend the neuroscientist believes there is a path from the material world to the spirit world." She will enjoy the music of his explanation. She wants back the boyish fervor that, just moments ago, returned the color and joy to his face. She wants him to be sweet on her again.

"I grew up believing," Sandrino says. "From the time I was a very young child. My *nonna* was always seeing people who were not there. To her, it was no fuss. They gave a kind of—fullness—to her life. For her, I pretended I saw them, too, because in her little room at the top of the stairs I felt—maybe it is your word—*chosen* by her, but if that is not what you mean by that word, then *blessed* is what I felt. Strong, at least, more strong than my sister or anybody else in the house, because I was her favorite. I hoped that one day I could stop pretending. I kept looking and listening for the people in the empty hallways. And then finally, I was ten years old, and in her bedroom I heard a voice that was not hers, except I was looking straight at her face. 'Is that your sister?' I asked; somehow I recognized her, even though she died before I was born; and she said yes, that is your Zia Carmela, and my *nonna* went back to her sewing like it happened to us every day. I was so happy! That one voice, a real voice, was all I needed to be convinced. It didn't make me afraid. No, I became less afraid of everything. Not so lonely anymore. More patient. More grown-up. And so, when the time came, that is why I picked neuroscience to study, to see if it could convince me why I should not believe anymore. Could the university scientists tell me my *nonna* and I were wrong? That we did not hear Zia Carmela say, clear as you are hearing me now, *E ora, dimmi tutto*? And so far, nothing I read in my courses tells me it is impossible that some fragment of our consciousness cannot continue after our flesh and bones rot away. And if the fragment can continue, there is no reason we cannot see it, hear it, feel it, or somehow communicate with it. The survival hypothesis, it is called. To me it is more than hypothesis. It is what I believe."

Later, on this cool May night, now Tuesday morning, Anja lies on the bench beside her window unable to sleep. She is in no way surprised that Sandrino and his poor demented *nonna* insisted on believing that some part of their dead floated among them, that they were desperately fighting their way back to them through the loud material muck. It also does not surprise her that he had not mentioned his belief in the survival hypothesis until now, that it took the guzzling of nearly an entire bottle of Sancerre for him to summon the courage to admit something so fantastic to a friend seemingly devoid of sentiment. Artist or not, Anja is still the partner of one of the more prominent quantum astronomers. Was.

She remembers the parties in Rome, Lugano, and San Remo, how they kept going and going, how they carried her from glittering room to glittering room beyond the hours she wanted to stay, how the Italians could never let you go, the words "good night" a lament, an apology, an admission of defeat. *Buona notte, buona notte*, she would mutter, her head bowed in shame, pushing her way through the door. No wonder Sandrino believes we do not end, that the party will always go on.

She calls him at his apartment the next day. He is surprised, and happy, to hear from her. She never calls him unless her annoyance at his lateness has turned to concern. She hears Trevor's voice in the background. She tells Sandrino that she has given his idea more thought and that, grudgingly, she will go along with it. "Monday is a holiday, though," she reminds him. "Memorial Day. There will be children and violins in the square. It will be loud."

"Memorial Day!" he says, delighted by the fittingness of the word.

He seeks Trevor's advice about the noise. A little violin music will fit the mood nicely, they decide together, but the children will not. "By dark they will be gone, no?" he asks. "For the séance it must be dark dark dark. No light at all except the light we bring. Even better if we start at the hour of midnight."

"Sandrino—"

"I'm sorry, you're right. Not midnight. I act silly. We will come at eight o'clock—we will not be late, I promise—and by the time we arrange all the pieces, the children will be gone to bed. Thank you for opening your house to us. We will bring wine and some food. Your only part to play is to unlock the door and produce for us the pages."

"I want to be clear," Anja says. "I am not a believer. I think of this night as my gift to you. To *you*, Sandrino, for your friendship, which has brought some joy to this year, to this city. I hope you will not ask more from me than that."

"That is funny," he says. She hears him close a door. She can no longer hear Trevor's voice. "In my mind, this is my gift to *you*. I tell myself, Anja will thank me when it's over. Finally, I will teach my friend something she does not already know! In the meantime, though, I want to make sure I explain one thing: we will not be looking back. We will be looking *through*."

"Cue the violins," she almost says, then stops herself. She has hurt his feelings once already. Instead she says, unconvincingly, maternally, though it is not her intention, "All right."

NINE MONTHS AGO, when Anja emptied the filing cabinets of Pieter's papers, she redistributed her own into multiple drawers. Her short-lived attempt at organization was a way of what her manager, Scott, called "taking stock," but the choices involved in the act of grouping and categorizing her documents—by film? by kind? by date?—overwhelmed her, and so the papers have remained in the half-coordinated state in which she left them.

Still, it does not take her long to find the yellow envelope inscribed in Tenn's looping hand, his Key West address in the upper left corner, the address of Pieter's New York apartment scribbled across the middle vivid as a photograph. In those letters and numbers are the lime-green window paint of their first shared home, the burnt smell of the neighbor's Turkish coffee, the gluey backs of the crumbling shower tiles. The pages of *Call It Joy* are curled at the edges. She resists the impulse to read the play again from start to finish. It is enough to see the words *Gisele, Frankie, bungalow, jukebox, Bangkok.* She slips the pages back in the envelope, carries it gingerly out of the bedroom, closes the door softly behind her as if someone were asleep on the bed, and sets it in the empty spot on the bookshelf that once held the novels of John Horne Burns.

The days pass slowly. She continues to fail miserably at her project of laziness, abandoning her post at the window for hours at a time to search websites for properties in places she has never lived: Malta, Sydney, Ljubljana. The listings are vague and overpromising, the sites cluttered with outdated statistics and dim photographs. She tries to limit her inquiries to more temperate zones, which are better for her skin and her frangible bones, and yet she feels continually pulled north. She cheats on Malta with Edinburgh, Sydney with Sendai, Ljubljana with Vancouver. They are all cities without associations or connections, without the lure of romance or memory. Glossy brochures arrive in the mail; agents leave breathy telephone messages entreating her to "come in." She enters her original name—Anja Blomgren—on the online forms, and when the mail and the messages come for that girl, it feels something like Sandrino's spirits pushing through.

On Monday, a large truck arrives and two men drop off stacks of white tables and folding chairs. A few minutes later, more cars

and vans line up behind it, and from them emerge women carrying sheet cakes from local bakeries, teenagers lugging large plastic
jugs of lemonade and water and coffee urns, and the musicians with
their instruments in leather cases. The tulips look on nervously
at the once-perfect grass already trampled, bracing themselves for
the onslaught. The newspaper called for rain, but so far Anja and
the flowers and the grass are out of luck: the weather is warm and
fine.

One by one, the front doors of the brownstones open and men appear with light sweaters tied around their necks, their wives ahead of
them pushing strollers over the cobblestones. As the sun sets, the
boxes of delivered pizza are opened, the lemon squares and cake slices
are devoured, and the coffee is poured into cheap Styrofoam cups that
will plague the park for the rest of the summer. The music plays on.
With each torch lit against the darkness, Anja's dread gathers force.
At precisely eight o'clock, her door buzzes.

Though it is only the second time Sandrino has been inside Anja's
apartment, he walks Trevor through it as if he has come triumphantly
home. He speaks with territorial pride of the fireplaces, the pocket
doors, the wainscoting, the intricate moldings along the arches, the
gold and marble inlays. "It just goes and goes," he says, taking Trevor's
hand and pulling him down the center hallway. Anja orients them to
Pieter's original four rooms and explains that, as the apartments around
them became available over the years, they bought them up and tore
down as many walls as they could to give the place an openness. She
insists she was not imperious or greedy. The more room she had in this
city, she says, the less likely she was to flee.

Sandrino cares less about the history of the apartment than about
finding the room best suited to his purposes. Eventually, he chooses
the parlor off the middle bedroom for its circular shape and wet bar
and tall windows, and because, with those windows open, the music

coming from outside is distinct but not intrusive. He sets the tote bags on the parlor floor.

"I made Trevor in charge of the food and drink," he whispers sheepishly, as he takes out three bottles of cheap red wine, from which he quickly scratches off the price tags, two containers of spreadable cheese in large white tubs, a box of plain water crackers, and a bag of pizza-flavored chips labeled FAMILY-SIZE in bright orange letters. He arranges these items on the bar and leads a series of toasts: to Anja, to his *nonna*, to Tennessee.

The wine is flat and sugary, the cheese unspeakable, but they help to blunt Anja's dread. She is hosting a children's party. She is indulging her boys in a harmless game. While she and Trevor look on, Sandrino clears a space on the floor in the middle of the room, unfolds a small rectangular Oriental rug with silk tassels at the short ends, and places one tall glass candle in each corner. The candles are imprinted with the faces of saints. When he requests pillows, Anja finally understands that he means for the three of them to sit on the floor. She refuses. Her legs. So they drag in a small card table from the guest room, and he places the rug and the candles on top of it.

He seats Anja at the head of the card table in the darkened room, with himself and Trevor across from each other in the middle. At his instruction, she places the envelope containing *Call It Joy* in the center between the lighted candles. Then Trevor takes a thin lumpy cigarette from his pocket and holds it up for them to admire. "Our medium has arrived," he says.

Sandrino turns to Anja. "This is OK?"

"You didn't ask her ahead of time?" says Trevor. He closes his fist over the joint.

"I'm sorry," says Sandrino. "So much on my mind!"

"Let me see it," Anja says. Maybe some magic will happen here after all.

The first time she smoked, she was with Frank and Tenn, the five of them lying around—on pillows! Oh, her young back!—in Rome, Ahmed passing her the kif as Frank looked on protectively. Since then, she had more than a few with Hovland to relax her into various roles. Once with Peter Fonda at a bar in Gramercy. Once with the doorman in Pieter's building. It was always men who introduced it into the proceedings, men who carried it with them or knew how to get it. Though she has smoked cigarettes with women in washrooms and film trailers and backstage dressing rooms all her life, never once has a woman pulled a marijuana cigarette from her purse and offered to share it with her. It would seem too tribal, Anja thinks; she herself would find it arrogant and, yes, a little queer.

She brings the joint to her nose, hoping for the sweet hay smell of kif, which permeated the apartment at Via Firenze for all her days there, but this offering of Trevor's is dry and flavorless. "We do this now?" she says, holding it above the candle flame. Sandrino cautiously nods. She fills her lungs with the sharp smoke, holds it in for a moment, closes her eyes, and then lets it out so gently that her breath barely disturbs the air.

"Holy shit," says Trevor. "She's a pro."

"No," she says, handing the joint back to him. "But I did learn to be elegant about it."

After they each partake twice, Sandrino places his right hand in her left and directs her to take Trevor's. They reach awkwardly across the table to complete the circle, keeping the envelope inside it and the candles at their elbows. Outside, the violins play a cheerful vivacious melody, a rite of spring. It is appropriate, says Sandrino, for this act of communion, this celebration, this happy reunion of old friends.

They stay quiet and still for a while, listening to the music and the stray voices from the square. When Sandrino begins to speak, repeating some sort of Italian chant Anja cannot translate, he squeezes her hand as if they are on a plane taking off. She has forgotten how the hands of young men are both strong and soft, their strength a promise for the future, their softness an echo of the past, so that they carry both with them until the softness is no longer necessary. Even Trevor's hands grip hers forcefully as Sandrino continues to chant. He says Tenn's name. He says her own. He introduces himself and Trevor to the empty room.

The walls sway with shadows. The candles have flavored the air cinnamon. Sandrino asks her to say something to Tenn that only he would understand. Something happy. It will reassure him that she is who he says she is, that the three of them can be trusted, that they have sought him out in friendship, with respect, with esteem.

She shakes her head.

"Please," he says. "It can be something small. Search your mind."

She goes back to Via Firenze. Frank is monitoring the effect that her first taste of kif is having on her. *I've never seen you laugh until now,* he tells her. *Really laugh. You were so serious before. You belong here in Rome with us.*

"The pale roses," she says to Sandrino now. "The pale roses at Gandolfo."

"Good," he says. "Say it one more time." As she does, he takes their hands, lays them on the envelope, and closes his eyes.

Anja does the same. It feels good to include Frank, to hear his voice. An extravagance. All of this is an extravagance.

"Now think of the last words Tennessee Williams spoke to you," Sandrino says. "Say them in your head."

I'm leaving as soon as I possibly can.

"Good," Sandrino repeats. "You're doing good." He pats her hand.

In the next city, she will miss Sandrino. Does he know she has stayed here this long because of him? When he gets back from Italy, it will be September, and she will be gone.

"Now we wait," he says.

"For what?" says Trevor.

"A disturbance."

Outside, they are replaying Beethoven's spring sonata, the piece that began the evening. It sounds mournful without a piano. How still the room is now, bracing for the disturbance. But when the disturbance does not come and does not come and does not come, and the music ends, and Sandrino shifts in his chair and he clears his throat and he repeats his chant, and Trevor sighs, and their sweaty hands slide off each other, Anja—she cannot help herself—starts to laugh. She bites her lip and shuts her eyes more tightly to stop the tears. Trevor starts laughing, too, and then, much to her relief, so does Sandrino.

Anja opens her eyes. There is Frank, standing in the window, his back to her, as if checking for rain. He says nothing, or he has nothing to say. It is not like him to be silent, to visit her and not offer the gift of his face, his voice. It is not like him to be angry with her, but she senses his anger in the room. She does not tell Sandrino what she is seeing, though she knows it will give him pleasure. She moves her lips silently. I am sorry we troubled you, she tells Frank. I am sorry I did not come when you needed me. I was afraid, she says. Tenn and I were more alike than you knew.

She blinks, and he is gone. How much of him will survive?

Sandrino lowers his head. He tried his best, he says, with a shrug. Some people don't want to be disturbed. And even if they do, he reasons, to reach them takes more than one attempt, especially if they are long dead. The fragment diffuses. Or it didn't survive at all. "Just because a man is famous," he says, "a big force in the world, in history, doesn't mean his chance to survive is better. A nothing person on the outside, I think, has the same chance as Tennessee Williams or a king . . ." He looks up at Anja. "Or you."

"That is logical," says Anja.

"Is it?" He laughs again.

"Yes."

"You think I am *pazzo*."

"Of course not."

"I actually do," Trevor says. Again they all laugh.

"I agree with Sandrino," Anja says. "The actual force of a person's consciousness is unknown and cannot be measured. It would not surprise me if it were much stronger or much weaker than the person imagined—the 'nothing person' or the 'something person.' And that if it were strong enough it could, as you say, *push through*."

"*Grazie*," he says.

"It makes me think of stars," Anja says. "When I was a girl, I was taught that most of the ones we see in the sky are long dead, that their light is just now reaching us, that when we gaze up at night we are looking into the past. It used to scare me, this notion of the sky as a vast, endless tomb. All that death flying back at us. But then Pieter taught me that it is not quite true. Only a small number of the thousands of stars we can see with our naked eyes have died. The dead light, though, is indistinguishable from the light of a living star. They burn side by side. You cannot tell the difference between them."

Anja has no respect for the act of looking back. It is a mark of weakness, of self-indulgence. The word "memorial" is cursed to her. When she seeks comfort or companionship from the dead, she thinks not of the men themselves, the four men who formed the constellation of her life, but of the stars. This was much too romantic an idea to admit to Pieter. It is possibly too romantic even for Sandrino. She can hardly admit it to herself. But she reasons, still, even now, that if she can watch the stars, it is not too much of a leap to imagine that she herself is being watched, and that whoever is doing the watching can see that she is, at every moment of her life, surrounded. They can see that her rooms are never empty.

"Maybe let's quit with all the stoner talk and get to the play?" Trevor says. "That's what we're all really here for, right?"

"Anja?"

She takes the envelope from Trevor's hands. She is delaying. Frank is gone again. All of them are gone. "To do this properly," she says, "we are going to need better wine."

9.

AN EDUCATION

For all their plan-making and manipulations in Portofino, Frank and Tenn did not discuss with much seriousness how long Anja would stay with them in Rome, or what their obligation was to her beyond a few introductions. She'd simply handed her little white suitcase to Luca's ancient cousin, sat beside him on the boat to Rapallo, taken the backseat in the Jag, and then the spare room in the apartment on Via Firenze. All the while, she maintained a silence that was both anxious and resolute, speaking only to ask how much farther it would be, and how soon she could meet their friends. She was evasive on the subject of her mother. All she said, after Tenn pressed her, was that Bitte had established a rapprochement with Signor Ricciardi, who'd locked her away in her old room above the kitchen, and that she likely wasn't even aware that Anja had left Portofino. Frank found her story more than a little implausible. Anja was more likely to drug her mother's chamomile tea and run as quickly as she could down Via del Fondaco than Bitte was to let her out of her sight. They'd learn the truth sooner or later.

When they introduced Anja to Paul and Ahmed as "the runaway," she didn't quibble with the description. They smoked some kif in their living room, sprawled out on pillows, and she fell instantly asleep. Frank carried her up the stairs and, for the second time in their short association, tucked her into a bed they'd provided for her. He unpacked her suitcase, as much to snoop as to help her feel at home. She'd brought cotton dresses in faded flowered prints, none of them white; some silver jewelry; an English Baedeker guide to Rome and Central Italy published in the thirties, heavily annotated in a faded language he assumed was Swedish; a small zippered bag of cosmetics and tonics; undergarments, stockings, and two pairs of shoes; and her passport. In the passport photo, her hair was boyishly short, her expression haunted and hard, her lips a thin line with a distant smile behind it. Her place of birth was listed as Malmö, her date of birth as June 2, 1936. Frank did the calculations twice, both times in disbelief: two months ago, she had turned seventeen.

His experience with women had led him to assume that most were a few years older than their stated age; still, the fact that Anja was five years younger, and little more than a child, filled him with fear. Suddenly, the fisherman was in the room beside him, and the boys from Testa del Lupo; suddenly Anja was walking out of the water at Paraggi in her transparent suit. Watching her sleep, a rush of tenderness, an urge to protect her, dissolved his fear, and the men vanished. And it occurred to him then, as he quickly and quietly reassembled her suitcase so as not to let on what he knew, that maybe Tenn wasn't so certain that Anja would make a great actress after all. Maybe he was so accommodating of her, so willing to give her a role in the little drama of their lives, because she gave Frank something to do. With Anja for a project, he'd spend less time, or no time at all, with Alvaro.

The next morning, they took her shopping on Via Condotti. The clothes she'd brought from Portofino were not flattering enough to meet Luchino Visconti later that afternoon and Anna Magnani as soon as possible afterward. In fact, Anja seemed to have packed her frumpiest frocks, as if she expected to audition for the role of milk-maid or housekeeper. Frank found her a sleeveless sundress with black and white polka dots splashed with pink roses, which the saleswoman at Gandolfo claimed was inspired by a painting by Renoir. The dress made Anja look slightly older, in her early twenties at least, especially with her hair pulled back, as the saleswoman suggested. Frank had yet to tell Tenn about the passport, and he wasn't sure he ever would. Keeping secrets from him gave Frank a charge.

Anja didn't hesitate to allow Tenn to pay for her dresses. She never promised, *One day I'll pay you back for your many kindnesses.* She took everything they offered her—the bed in their apartment, the morning coffee and *cornetti* Frank had brought back from the bakery down the block, Ahmed's rapidly dwindling kif—with the uncomplicated joy of feeling as though she deserved them. For this, Frank envied her. He kept a running tally in his mind of every penny Tenn had spent on him, every Key West utility bill paid out of the account he rarely checked, all the shirts and ties and cuff links purchased for parties on three continents. He accepted these only because he had the sincere intention to earn back the thousands of dollars they cost.

For her visit to the *Senso* set, which, on this day, was the blocked-off Vicolo del Cedro in Trastevere, Anja wore a simple butter-yellow shift dress. The three of them watched from the sidewalk, afraid to disturb the great Visconti, even though he was expecting them and had agreed, eagerly, to give Anja the once-over. Visconti had no part for her in this already bloated production, he said over the phone, not even a small one, he was up to his neck in Austrians as it was, but there was always the next film, whatever it might be, or the film after that. Alida Valli was proving satisfactory as Livia, but Ingrid Bergman had been his first choice, and Alida Valli was no Ingrid Bergman. Though

born a *baronessa*, Valli had a bohemian beauty ill suited to the lavish-
ness and decadence—"the wantonness!"—that Visconti wanted for
Senso, and that he could have gotten out of Bergman if she'd given him
a chance. Tenn had held the phone up so Frank could hear the man
rant. "It is easier to find love than it is to find a muse!" Visconti had
shouted, and then he shouted at someone else in the room, forgot his
conversation with Tenn altogether, and the line went dead.

Visconti sat in a folding chair in the middle of the alley, barking
directions at Valli and a pack of no-name actors in uniform. Valli's
character, Countess Livia Serpieri, had betrayed her Austrian lover,
Lieutenant Franz Mahler, which caused his death by firing squad, and
now she was roaming the streets of Verona undone by remorse and
grief. The Italian soldiers were on hand to harass and molest her, thus
adding a deserved degradation to her shocking downfall.

It was a fairly simple depiction of dissolution on an ancient cobblestone street, but nothing was simple with Visconti. Couldn't Alida
stagger a bit more wildly? "Livia Serpieri is not human anymore!"
Visconti called to her in his furious Italian. "She has turned animal!
She is a heart torn out by her own hands, flopping like a fish on the
ground!" And so Valli, in her heavy black coat and tangled veil, staggered and fell and got back onto her feet and then staggered and fell
again, dragging herself over the rough stones. Her lips trembled as if
she were freezing, but her face was glistening with sweat from the
humid August afternoon. An old woman ran out with a can of hair
spray and a handful of cotton pads to blot her cheeks and forehead and
touch up the men as well. Visconti walked out to adjust the soldiers'
shirts and hats before turning himself to Valli's hair, which he pulled
apart and mussed until it achieved the wreckage he was after. He held
her by the shoulders and whispered something in her ear. Then he sat
back down, folded one of his long legs over the other, put on his
glasses, and paged through a paperback as he waited for the actors to

return to their marks and the horses to cooperate with the soldiers in their carriage. By the time they were all in place and the scene was ready to reshoot, the light was wrong. It was just past the siesta hour, and the shadows were changing by the second.

It soon became obvious that, second choice or satisfactory, bohemian or *baronessa*, Alida Valli had Anja Blomgren in her thrall. Watching Anja closely, Frank saw that she followed every flicker of anguish on Valli's face, the angle of every calculated stagger, each twist of her torso as she writhed in the arms of the brutish soldiers. "She is marvelous," said Anja, wide-eyed, and her lips stayed half parted, words failing her in all three languages she knew. For the first time, Frank saw Anja for what she really was under all her hard and practiced defenses: a teenage girl, a child blushing at the discovery of a pure new pleasure. In this light, she was at her most beautiful, like a novice sanctified by her calling.

"Valli does have a fugitive energy," Tenn said. "Though I must agree she's no Bergman."

"The next Bergman might be you," said Frank to Anja.

"Not Garbo?" asked Tenn.

"What she is doing, it is—" Once again Anja's lips refused to close, but this time she couldn't find the word.

"Marvelous?"

"Marvelous!"

Tenn laughed. "We talked quite a bit in Portofino about your education," Tenn said. "Are you prepared for the hard work it takes to be someone else for a living?"

"Go easy on her," said Frank. "It's the first day of school."

Anja paid no attention to their chatter. She bit her fingernails and leaned in as far as she could to see Valli and Visconti through the harsh shadows between the film lights. The sun was fading fast. Valli shook her head when the men closed in around her. Then she fell to the ground again in a catlike crawl. She thrashed and beat her stomach with her fists and craned her neck to the sky, exposing her naked throat as if begging for one of them to cut it. A soldier grabbed her by the hair, she let out a guttural scream, and Anja jumped.

Visconti clapped his hands together once in triumph. Finis! The crowd of onlookers clapped as well, and they thought, for a moment, that the filming was over, until Visconti said no. Valli had done her part—*"Brava!"* he called out to her, and blew her a kiss—but the soldiers had not. He needed more menace from their faces.

The director sat back in his chair, but it was too dark for his paperback. He crossed both his arms and his legs. When he noticed Tenn, he gestured with his chin for the trio to approach.

"You are the protégée?" he said to Anja, standing, smiling handsomely, when she was introduced. He was a tall man, broad and imposing in the shoulders, with a strong jaw and slicked-back hair. Born a count, he was wealthier than any of them could hope to be, with all the time in the world to conform his films precisely to his vision.

"I am nothing yet," said Anja. Her eyes were still not on the director, but on his leading lady, quickly rebuttoning the coat she'd pulled apart just moments before. "And I could never be *that.*"

"That is my creation," Visconti said proudly. "Just wait until *Italia* sees how I've debauched their innocent sweetheart. The whole country will hate this film." He turned to Tenn. "They will love the *words*, of course. And the colors! Did I tell you what I was doing with the colors? It is the first—"

"How many movies has she played in?" Anja interrupted. "I want to see all of them."

Confused, Visconti looked at her and shrugged. "Thirty-six or so," he said. "After *Senso*, she might say no more often." As he said this, he put his hand on Anja's right cheek and looked more closely at her. He turned her head to one side and then to the other, to catch the light.

She barely registered his touch, though his large hand covered most of her right side from chin to eye to ear. She stood on her tiptoes, trying to see above his shoulder to where Valli was patting one of the horses. Visconti then took a step back to assess her from head to toe against the backdrop of the busy street. His face was agitated.

"This is her first time in the presence of a real actress at work," said Frank, by way of explanation.

"I saw actresses onstage in Sweden," she corrected him. "They bored me."

"Bored by Strindberg?" asked Visconti, incredulous. "You are even younger than you look."

"I don't know if it was Strindberg," said Anja. "We have other plays in our theaters besides *Miss Julie*. And I never said I was not young."

"Can we all at least agree that *The Dance of Death* is one of the three great modern dramas?" said Tenn, quickly, but the damage was done.

"She is hollow," Visconti said to Frank, later, when Frank pulled him aside. Anja and Tenn were barely out of earshot. "I don't have the time or the inclination to 'fill her up.' I don't even believe such a thing can be done. In the very special actresses, you see the fullness right away, no matter how young they come to you. I have seen it in girls in pigtails! The fullness overflows from them!" He lifted up his hands and shook his head. "Take Valli. She is not one of the greats, but the fullness is there. Anna Magnani. Rita Hayworth. These women, the too-much-ness of them, it electrifies me. I'm sorry, I do not see too much in your little Swede."

"You know this after one minute of conversation?" Frank asked. "What about a screen test?"

"*Boh*," he said, that infuriating Italian expression that meant, "How could *I* possibly know?" Invariably, it was uttered by a person—Frank's father, Alvaro, the teller at the Amexco office—whose very job it was to know.

"Ask Tenn about the women they've cast in his plays, he'll tell you: sometimes at first they seem like the wrong type, but then they learn his lines, they *swallow* them, and his words turn them into something else, something bigger than they were before. More full, maybe, as you call it."

"This has not been my experience," Visconti said. "Some actors, put them in any light, they don't glow." He was already distracted. There was a man on a bicycle doing circles in the middle of the set, disturbing the horses and scattering the crew. "*Vai via!*" he shouted at the man, shaking his fists. "The village idiot," he murmured to Frank. On the way back to his chair, he called over to Tenn: "Soon I will see pages from my American script, yes?"

"I'm making magic for you, *maestro!*" said Tenn.

If they were indeed to lead Anja's education, Frank and Tenn needed to start with the basics, including how to flatter a great director. You listened to him go on about his colors. You didn't throw all your attention on the leading lady you knew he considered second-rate. You did praise him for getting so much blood out of that particular stone, and then you showed a barely restrained pity for the stone herself. You hoped aloud that the stone worked again, maybe in a smaller picture better suited to her range. You looked the director in the eye, and then when he gazed upon you to accept the compliment and the pity, you shied away. You didn't mean to speak so boldly.

Tenn bid Visconti a quick farewell before he could ask any more questions about the stalled script. Then they crossed through the middle of his set so that Anja could finally take Alida Valli's hands in hers and tell her of her marvelous work while gazing with adoration into her royal gypsy eyes.

"He did not impress me," Anja said, as they walked off. It was the dinner hour, and they were winding their way through the narrow, jagged streets of Trastevere. "You really want this bully to film your words, Tennessee?"

"Bullishness is not the worst quality in an artist," said Tenn. "Its opposite is."

She thought for a moment. "Is that one of my lessons, too?" she asked. "Along with how to flirt and make the big man feel like the king?" Her tone was playful, but Frank caught the chill.

"Is it possible you are not inclined—romantically, that is—toward men?" Tenn asked. "You don't have to be shy about it. It's very much in fashion."

She laughed. "Because I find the leading lady transcendent and her director imperious to the point of nausea?"

"Yes. Because—I'm sorry to say it—she is a Garbo knockoff and he is famously, undeniably magnetic. So, it occurred to me just now that you may have Sapphic inclinations and, if so, they're distorting your perceptions, which are otherwise sharper than those of any twenty-two-year-old I've ever met."

"We should start telling people she's twenty-five," Frank thought aloud.

"This could work to your advantage, you know," Tenn went on. "As we speak, a grand tradition is forming: Marlene Dietrich, Tallulah Bankhead and, well, who am I to know or care which women are doing what to each other and why they'd want to do it in the first place?"

Anja, who rarely responded to a question right after you asked it, pondered this one longer than usual. "My inclinations are my own," she said finally, which meant everything and nothing and put an end to that line of questioning. Besides, after standing around for hours waiting for the nod from Visconti, they were all too hungry and over-heated and desperate for a drink to think straight about anything.

They were unfamiliar with the maze of Trastevere's streets, which were mostly deserted for the holiday month. They were darker than

anywhere else in Rome but for the bursts of light they'd come upon at
the turn of a corner, where they'd find a tiny restaurant packed to the
rafters. They stood at the front window of one of these places, one of
the few open this time of year, somewhere on the Via dei Genovesi,
and gazed lustily at the fat working-class men stuffing glistening
forkfuls of carbonara between their greasy lips and chasing it with
sweet wine.

"It's enough to make you fall in love with life again," said Frank,
dreamily.

"I didn't know you'd fallen out," said Tenn.

"To be old and round like those men, it's beautiful, don't you
think?"

Tenn and Anja looked at each other and laughed. "We better get
some food in him."

To be a romantic was to be seduced as easily by a beautiful boy as by
a room full of jowly stonemasons passing around jugs of cheap chianti.

Frank sweet-talked the maître d' into a table, and by the time the
first course of prosciutto and melon was set before them beside their
very own jug of wine wrapped in straw, he'd turned the entire episode
with Visconti into a short lesson for himself. He should trust Tenn's
instincts, as well as his own, over those of an agitated director and a
starstruck girl. Visconti had simply had a bad day; Anja was a naïf. He
made a toast to "the education of Anja Blomgren," and to "the success
of *Senso* and *Battle of Angels*" and to—it was then that he struggled;
he couldn't come up with a wish for himself, not one that he could
voice—"to Truman Capote for bringing us all together."

"And to the Little Horse," Tenn said. He leaned across the table
and kissed him, full on the mouth, and the coarse men behind them
guffawed as if it was a bit of drunken buffoonery. "May he grow old
and fat . . . but not yet!"

"To the Little Horse!" said Anja.

It wasn't until the wine kicked in with its heady fuzz that the weight of Frank's unsayable wish settled on him. He listened to Anja talk, on and on, ignoring her plate of fried artichokes, reminiscing, rapturously, about the power of Valli's overwrought performance, and wondered, again, if Tenn had given another moment's thought to his request in the garden of the Splendido. Frank was the nagging type, but he had too much pride to nag Tenn about *Senso*. He made his desire known, and now it was up to Tenn to fulfill it.

"Just a few days ago, you said acting was childish," Frank said. "Do you remember? Our conversation in Portofino?"

"Yes, I did," Anja said. "Am I not a child?"

"So you now believe it's worthy of you? That you're well suited to it?"

"Oh, how should I know?" she said. "I will outgrow it, that much is certain. By tomorrow, probably. In the meantime, I am willing to give it a try. I like what she did, all that rolling around on the street like a madwoman. It is very Italian. I suppose I am Italian in my aspirations, if not my inclinations."

THE NEXT MORNING, Frank called Anna. "Here is the program," he'd said. "It's time for you to meet our runaway." He didn't let on what had happened with Visconti the day before, as he didn't want to prejudice her first encounter with Anja. He suggested they meet for pizza at a place near Piazza Navona, just the four of them, at eight o'clock.

"Here is a better idea," Anna said. There was a filmmaker she'd been avoiding, someone trying to seduce her to star in his next project. He was a young Dane, reportedly handsome, with lofty ambitions but only a single film credit to his name. Had Frank heard of *Mirror*? No, he hadn't. No one had, and yet *Mirror* had earned heaps of praise from the French, which was Anna's main reason for putting him off. "He sounds to me like a better fit for your little Garbo," she said. "Unless I fall for him myself. Oh, Frankie *bello*, what do you say we all have dinner *insieme*, and we make it a little contest?"

"Anja can't compete with you," Frank said. "She's never acted a day in her life!"

"*Meglio così*," said Anna. "I prefer games I'm guaranteed to win."

"We were hoping you might help her, if you could, not intimidate her."

"They are the same," she said.

"Her mother does think she needs to be toughened up," Frank said. "But in my opinion, she's too tough as it is."

"*Basta!*" said Anna. "Enough of the trailer. I want to see the movie for myself. I will tell this Martin Hovland to meet us at the Osteria al Fontanone at nine thirty. Excellent fish. The owner is an old lover, Don Umberto. He is in Ostia, worth the drive. There is a bus but don't take it, it never comes. Hovland will pay the bill. In my experience, the *auteurs* who cry poor are always the ones with money. *Ciao ciao bello Frankuccio*. With me, you always do better than a pizza shop in Piazza Navona. Come at eight thirty, do you hear? We need time together before the Dane ruins the night. *Bah!*"

For two women whose names were off by only a consonant, Anna and Anja were more different than Jersey and Jupiter. It was something to walk with them around the courtyard garden of the Fontanone restaurant—Anna with her polio limp and full-bosomed laugh and those permanent smears, dark as bruises, under her eyes; impish Anja in her demure dress of pale roses, her face stretched tight from the pins pulling back her hair—an ox and a plover struggling for a common tongue. A native Italian, Anna could speak pidgin English but was uncomfortable doing so; Anja, a native Swede, spoke a botched Italian and an overly formal and heavily accented English she learned from a posh British tutor. They kept turning to Frank for help. He knew Italian and English well enough to translate, but he was keeping his distance so that the two women could forge a friendship separate from the ones they had with him and Tenn.

It wasn't working.

"Is that a riddle?" Anna asked Anja, who either pretended not to understand the question or was taking her typical eternity to answer it. Anna looked up at the sky in exasperation. To Frank, she said in Italian, "I asked her a simple question, 'Where did you grow up?' and she told me: a volcano. What does that mean? Is she playing a trick?"

"She might have said 'Malmö'?"

"No, not Malmö. My ears work fine. A *volcano*."

"It was a metaphor," said Anja to Frank, when Anna stepped away to link arms with Tenn. "I am sorry, I am not making a good impression on your friend. When I get nervous, I try too hard to be clever. She is very large to talk to. When she was describing one of her films to me—I think it was a film she was talking about, it might have been a story from her childhood?—I was remembering that when I was a young girl, my father gave me a book about volcanoes, a very scientific book with a section of history about Pompeii and Krakatoa. I used to pretend that there was a big volcano buried beneath our town, and that its mouth was directly beneath our house, and that I could control when it would blow up and melt everyone but me and him. It was more of a hope than a fantasy. When my mother or one of my teachers made me angry—usually my mother—I would stand very still and close my eyes and concentrate to try to make it explode. This made them crazy, me so calm with a little smile on my face. I was imagining a big bang was about to come and then they would all fly up into the sky. It was this I was trying to tell Anna to explain what it was like at home for me, but when I get nervous the right words do not come, and she is not a patient person."

"You don't seem nervous in the least," said Frank.

"I'm never nervous with you. With the rest, I am acting." She said this with that same little smile he recognized from the passport. It now had a faint sadness to it. "You're not acting, too?"

"No," said Frank. "I'm happy. This is a beautiful restaurant. My friends are with me. We have a project. Why not be happy?"

He and Tenn were putting too much pressure on her, Frank thought, for no good reason other than their impatience and his own unrelenting, unquenchable boredom. Was he so desperate for a purpose in life that he'd turned himself into Pygmalion, concocted an improbable future for this girl, and then set her on a path that divorced her from her own mother? What did he know, really, of Anja's true talents and desires, or of Bitte's character, other than what Anja herself, a child of seventeen, had constructed for him?

That was what he'd gone to her apartment to tell her the morning of their last day in Portofino: that her cynicism, the longer she nurtured it, would only keep her lonely and self-satisfied and small. He'd wanted to hold himself up to her as an example of a life free of the rot of cynicism, to remind her that despite knowing the horrors of war, the shame of sexual difference, the disappointment of failure of all stripes, he still trusted everyone who came along, he still gave over his heart, body and mind to them freely. This may have kept him scattered, or bored, or exposed, but it did not make him bitter. He'd gone to her apartment on the Via del Fondaco to make sure Anja knew he was happy, and that happiness was what he wanted for her, too.

Anna's ex-lover, Don Umberto, appeared and explained that they had two options for dinner seating at the Fontanone: a long table in the garden, where it was warmer but more fragrant and panoramic, or a round table on the first floor of the sixteenth-century villa, where it was cooler but a bit loud.

"We want both," Anna told him. "We will have *antipasti* in the garden—the good stuff, not the cubes of mortadella you chopped up last week—near the fountain where it is cool. Then we will be five people for dinner at nine thirty inside at the back table in the corner, under the round window. I explained this to you yesterday."

"*Certo*, Signora," said Umberto. "I wanted to be absolutely sure." The tips of his dark curls were matted with sweat at his temples. He put his hand on the small of Anna's back. "Now let me take you to meet the fish."

Umberto led them from the courtyard through an archway overflowing with red hibiscus. The garden was a maze of narrow stone paths thick with ferns and cattails and a rainbow of gaudy flowers imported from Africa and the Middle East. Thick slabs of cactus jutted up from beds of small white pebbles, blossoming amid the threats of thorns. Vines hung down from the trees, jungle-like, forming a kind of curtain they had to pull apart to reach the clearing in the center where, between two stout palm trees, stood a raised trough of shaved ice on which dozens of whole fish lay arranged in orderly rows. As they circled the trough, Umberto introduced each fish tenderly, as if they were members of his family. "Here is my beautiful *sugarello*, you can catch him only in summer; and here is the elegant *branzino*, he likes lemon and a little fresh rosemary . . ."

By the time they made it all the way around, Frank had grown hungry for each of them. How do you choose, when each has a delicious story and the same set of plaintive, uncomplaining eyes? Finally, to the single turbot, set apart from the others by his circular shape and tan coloring, fat and flat and grumpy, fond of orange and mint, he said, "You, right there, *rombo chiodato*, you're my guy," and Umberto scooped him up and whisked him off to the kitchen. It was not unlike walking through the Villa Borghese, the *ragazzi* on display on the low stone walls swinging their legs, waiting to be consumed.

The waiters arrived with trays of spritzes and the good *antipasti*: fried zucchini flowers stuffed with anchovies and ricotta, exotic varieties of mushrooms braised in white wine, calf's liver and caviar on little toasts. Frank wore a linen suit with a striped bow tie, Tenn an open-collared shirt with a jacket and a silk handkerchief Frank had monogrammed at a shop in the Monti. The garden was filling up with other patrons—not eating quite as well, not as smartly dressed—and, as always, Frank was conscious of their curious, admiring stares, the whispers of delight when they identified Anna or Tenn. Frank might as well enjoy the pleasures of proximity, he thought: the warm flush on his face as the stranger at the next table searched his eyes and cheekbones for recognition, the chance she'd mistake him for someone famous and get a thrill. If Frank could not be the fountain, he could at least feel the spray.

Martin Hovland arrived in short pants and a wrinkled shirt with rolled-up sleeves. He had not dressed to impress Anna Magnani or anyone else at the Fontanone, which of course caused the gawking patrons to turn their curiosity and envy squarely on him, the pale doughy-faced man who strode over to that glamorous quartet and helped himself to their company.

Hovland wasn't familiar with this restaurant, he explained, by way of apology for his dress, and he'd expected only to have the pleasure of a glass of wine with Signora Magnani before she flew off to her next engagement. He hadn't expected a dinner party, or the presence of the great Tennessee Williams. Frank liked him immediately, as much for the surprise of his boyish bubbliness as his cherubic features and endearing stutter. He'd expected Hovland to be like Anja: stern and severe and suspicious, but instead he was charmingly deferential, even to Frank, in whom he took what appeared to be a sincere interest. Was he "in the business" as well? Were his family farmers in Sicily, and what did they think of the agrarian reforms proposed by the

Italian government? Did he find it sad, as Hovland did, that the medium of film, unlike drama, could not accommodate improvisation or reimagination, that it was always the same film over and over and would never be anything but? His *Mirror* was not a "work" of art, Hovland said; it had stopped "working" the day it was finished; it was now a corpse.

"The work is the effect it has on the audience," Frank offered.

"Yes, fine," said Hovland. "That is what I'm supposed to feel as compensation. As consolation. But I'm not a generous man. I don't care what the audience feels or doesn't feel. If their hearts break or if they're left cold, what difference does it make to me? I care only how my ideas are translated onto celluloid. I care how they come together, my words and my cameras and my directions to the actors."

"And if nobody watches your film of ideas?" said Anna, barging into their conversation.

"That would be a happy dream," said Hovland, matching her Italian. "Releasing the film into the wild, signing the contract with the producer and the theaters, submitting myself to interviews by newspapers and critics and scholars, all of that is a necessary evil so that someone will pay me the money for the next one." He shook his head. "Mark my words: one day, if I have enough in the bank, I will make films for myself only."

"Will you be starring in them, too?" Tenn joked. "No actor I've ever met would want that job, no matter how much you pay him."

"Yes, please!" said Anna, also laughing. "Take all my work and put it in the closet!"

Hovland laughed, too. He spoke in that same ebullient tone, without any of Visconti's rage and pique, as if they were discussing the weather or recipes for cake. "If your work is not your reward," he said, "your film on a million screens will not satisfy you. It might as well be in that closet, playing on a loop for your dresses and shoes."

By then it was close to ten, they'd had more spritzes, and Don Umberto had led them inside the villa to the round table by the back window, where Anna directed the proceedings. She put Anja and Frank on either side of Hovland, Tenn directly across, and herself next to Tenn, as far as possible from the Dane, on whom she'd immediately given up. When it came to the matchmaking of actors and directors, it seemed, instinct was paramount.

Though Frank had explained to Hovland that Anja was at the beginning of her education as an actress, and that she had grown up less than fifty miles from Copenhagen in Malmö, and that she had orphaned herself for a career in film or theater, Hovland was so consumed by Anna and the men that he paid Anja only passing attention. Anja, too, was distracted. As Hovland talked—across the table to Anna, loudly, about the richness of the meals in France, where he was forced to spend far too much time in hotels—Anja's eyes darted back and forth from the kitchen, though she noticeably did not turn her head in that direction.

"What is it?" Frank mouthed.

The color had drained from her face. "Nothing," she said. She covered her shoulders with her shawl, though it was warmer in the villa, and gave Hovland, who still wasn't addressing her, a thin, anxious smile.

Frank leaned back to look toward the doorway to the kitchen. Two dark-skinned boys, Southern Italians or Africans, bone thin in their stained white T-shirts and work pants, leaned listlessly against the wall. One carried a broom; the other had a rag draped over his shoulder. After Umberto barked something at them and walked off, the taller one put the broom between his legs and pumped it in his direction. He then absently swept the ceramic tiles while the other ran the rag over the windowpanes in the French doors that separated the kitchen area from the back room. The whole time, they kept craning their necks to watch Anja, their attention solely on her. She adjusted her shawl, brought a glass of wine to her lips, and when she looked away they stuck out their tongues, doglike, panting, at her. It was irrational to think that these were two of the same tribe from Testa del Lupo, hundreds of miles off, but as Frank studied them, and Anja watched him study them, that is who the boys became, for Frank and for Anja, their gaping mouths crowded with white teeth sharp as spears, their birdlike bodies smeared not with fish guts but with mud and sweat and spit.

"It's all right," Frank whispered to Anja. His impulse was to reach across and reassure her, but he was trying not to make a scene. "Ignore them. You're safe here."

Instead she slid closer to Hovland, away from the direction of the kitchen. Hovland was now shouting over the din to Anna that he'd never film in Copenhagen or Brussels again, that his heart was set on Rome. The part he was writing for his next film required an Italian actress without inhibitions, someone who wasn't afraid to be loud, to play the wolf.

"Ah, another wolf," said Anna. "An original concept."

"They can't harm you," Frank said again to Anja, under his breath.

"I'm not scared," she told him. She had her arms folded petulantly across her chest.

"You know it's not them, don't you? It can't possibly be them."

"What are you two gossiping about?" Hovland asked, interrupting his own conversation with Anna. "Is our young lady sweet on someone?" He looked over at the boys. The sweeper winked, and then they giggled and he pushed the window washer through the heavy wooden door into the garden. Hovland put his hand on Anja's shoulder. "You're too sophisticated for the kitchen help."

"They're children!" she said.

"You can't be much older," said Hovland.

"I am twenty-two," she said, straightening in her chair.

Hovland squinted at her, then thought a moment. "Smart girl," he said, and took a drink. "Your secret is safe with me."

"I don't understand," she said to him.

"Those boys were staring, that's all," Frank said. "You can't blame them."

"They must have recognized Anna," said Tenn.

"No," Anja said, sharply. "It was *me* who recognized *them*."

"*Che cosa ha detto?*" asked Anna.

"You know those boys?" Hovland asked.

"Yes," said Anja. "They came here to devour me." The color returned to her face. "I've seen them before. All my life I've seen them." She pulled the shawl tighter, lowering her head.

"What is she talking about?" Hovland asked.

"Should I tell them about it, Frank?" Anja asked.

"No, I don't think so."

"It's not a pretty story," Tenn said.

"We don't need more pretty stories," Hovland said.

"It's a *hideous* story," Anja said. She was shivering now, or at least pretending to. The line between her reality and her act was never clear. It never would be. "No one will believe it, but it is all real. It is the world in which I live."

"*E dai!*" said Anna, throwing down her napkin on her plate of half-eaten pasta. "Out with it already! Before the fish comes."

The boys had been following her from the moment her mother, Maja, brought her to Turkey on holiday, Anja explained. They ran alongside the car that brought them to the hotel. They stood in the doorways with fans and candies. They lurked behind the pine trees at Patara beach, spying on them as they lay innocently on the sand. Briefly—Anja could admit this now—she and her mother enjoyed the boys' attention. They never expected that the boys would follow them

on their hike to the ruins, that they would gather in such large numbers, that there could be so many of those vampires, ten at first, their
faces ever-changing, and then more and more appearing, like ravenous
birds swooping down from their nests in the pines. Her mother should
not have allowed them to stay so late in the day; they should not have
fallen in love with the light on the ancient columns, the sound of the
sea waves crashing far off but clear as if they were at their feet; they
should have noticed they were the only ones left, that the shadows had
overtaken the field. They sucked her blood, Anja exclaimed, through
terrified tears, and here she paused to linger on Hovland's startled face.
Then, keeping her head still as a statue, she locked eyes with each of
them around the table, as if daring them to disbelieve her.

If it were not for the group of Americans who had come upon
them—navy men on a weekend furlough, they learned later, at the
filthy little hospital in Kaş, but to Anja and her mother they were angels sent by God Himself—Anja would still be there, she said, lying
facedown in the dirt, chunks of her flesh bitten off, left for dead,
wailing.

"And Maja? Your dear mother?" asked Frank. "What became
of her?"

"She is as good as dead," said Anja, matter-of-factly. "Confined to
an asylum outside Zurich."

"Extraordinary," said Hovland.

"Yes and no," said Anja. Her tears had dried, and with her composure came a kind of defiance. Even Anna, who didn't catch all the
words or their meaning, who watched grudgingly, envy and admiration warring within her, could see the effect Anja's delivery was having on the men, and on Hovland in particular. The fish they'd chosen
with such care sat on their plates untouched. "As I said, this is my
every day. Until it was no longer a metaphor, I did not realize how I
lived as a girl, how all girls live, surrounded by boys so hungry they

would eat you alive at their first chance. So I am grateful now to be a woman—are you not grateful, too, Anna?—to be older, to be moving toward invisibility."

"You are far from invisible," Hovland said.

"Oh," said Anja, blushing, as girlish in that moment as Frank had ever seen her. With expert precision, she lifted the delicate translucent spine from the center of her *branzino* and placed it on the side of her plate. "I have to wait a few years, then."

It turned out she didn't need their education at all.

Much later, it was Tenn who called it "the night Anja bloomed," and that is how they came to refer to it: she gave her first performance onstage at the table under the round window at the Osteria al Fontanone. She'd acted out her own version of the story of the horror at Testa del Lupo as if she'd memorized it in lines of poetry she'd written herself, from the crumbling statues strangled by weeds to the purple darkness falling fast over the cliff to the boys' sharp hot teeth tearing into her thigh. Was it a surprise that she'd cast herself as the damsel in distress, the strong American navy men as heroes, and her mother as the dog?

It was Hovland, completely under her spell, who drove her back to Via Firenze at the end of the night, in his rented Peugeot, which he'd driven all the way from Paris just for the chance to have a glass of wine with Anna Magnani. Anna herself stayed on at the Fontanone with Don Umberto. "I don't remember what broke us apart," she'd said, with a shrug, when they kissed her goodbye in the garden. "Maybe tonight it comes back to me."

Two years later, Anna played the lead in *The Rose Tattoo*—her first Hollywood film, direction by Daniel Mann, script by Tennessee Williams and Hal Kanter—and won an Oscar. The same year, Martin Hovland wrote and directed *Mercy*, which marked the debut of Anja Bloom in a supporting role. They'd been living together in seclusion outside Palermo, in the mountain village of Erice, site of the ancient Temple of Venus, where much of *Mercy* was filmed. *Mercy* flopped even with the French. It took a little while before Hovland could find funding for his next film, *Angle*, but when he did, he cast Anja as the star.

That night at the Fontanone, in the backseat of Hovland's Peugeot, and then later in the apartment, with Anja asleep in the next room and Paul and Ahmed passed out down the hall, one big happy family, Tenn was as tender as he'd ever been with Frank. It felt like the summer of 1949 again, their love new, the war finally fading into memory, Rome the holy city they pillaged together for the first time. Maybe the guilt of ignoring Frank's request for a part in *Senso* had caught up with Tenn now that Anja seemed, as suddenly as she had come, to be on her way. Maybe discussing the film of *The Rose Tattoo* with Anna brought Tenn back to the love he'd poured out for Frank in the character of Alvaro Mangiacavallo.

Tenn called it the song of the nightingales, what two men did with each other. When it was good, as it was that night, as it so often had been, he'd say, with boyish affection and gratitude, "the nightingales sang sweetly." Tenn was the undisputed master of words, but when the nightingales were singing, Frank was his equal. As long as Frank had his body, in all of its Frankness, he could tell Tenn exactly what he felt for him. He did not have Tenn's or Anja's fluency with words, with poetry, with the imagination. He had great fluency only in the language of the body. How cruel it was for it to fail so young.

WHEN IT STARTED, more than five years ago now, around the summer of '56, the time of *Sweet Bird of Youth*, he hid the failure from Tenn: the specks of blood in his cough, his weak limbs, the knives stabbing his lungs with every breath. At a workshop of *Sweet Bird* in

Miami, Frank felt dizzy, went to the men's room, and blacked out; when he returned to the studio, Tenn was furious with him for skipping out on the run-through. Dr. Jacobson had recently stuffed Tenn's palms with new prescriptions that gave him crazier thoughts than usual. The new pills convinced him that Frank was on the verge of leaving him; they fueled his paranoia that Frank had another man on the side, possibly one of his rivals in the theater, and that he'd fallen in with a dangerous lot. "You're a dope fiend!" Tenn snarled at Frank when he'd come home from one of the restless late-night walks he needed for air. None of Tenn's fears were rooted in reality. By that time, Frank was too tired to want anything from another man but a gentle embrace, something Tenn, alternately rageful and raving, looped on Dr. Feelgood's cocktail of barbiturates and speed, grew increasingly unwilling to give him.

They lived mostly apart after that dreadful summer of '56, stuck in the States, far from Italy, Frank in the Duncan Street house in Key West, Tenn in New York in the apartment on Sixty-fifth Street. In the days leading up to one of Tenn's return visits to Florida, Frank would try to sleep as much as he could to build up his strength. He blamed a nagging ulcer, a summer flu, for his pale skin and hunched-over posture. He blamed his thinness on the horse-grade antibiotics the doctor in town was treating him with, the all-liquid diet recommended by some boys at the club. He avoided eating in Tenn's presence, fearing the nausea that came on in waves after every meal. He wore dark billowy shirts to cover his atrophying arms and oversize linen pants to conceal the matchsticks he had for legs. When the nightingales sang, which they did hardly at all before they ceased completely, Frank made sure it was on nights Tenn had been drinking long and hard, so that the next morning he wouldn't remember how it had felt to push up against a rack of sick bones. If Tenn had only known the pain his weight caused Frank, how he had to fight for breath through all Tenn's pushing and twisting, he'd have never let the birds sing at all.

Frank's brief disappearances in those years, his resistance to sex when Tenn was sober, his constant fatigue and lightheadedness and flimsy excuses for his weight loss, his insistence on staying in Key West when Tenn traveled, only made Tenn's suspicions of drugs and love affairs grow stronger. In revenge for Frank's perceived betrayal, Tenn would leave the Duncan Street house unannounced and return in the middle of the night with a new boy, wake Frank up just to flaunt the boy in front of him, and then he'd fuck him in the next room with the doors and windows open so Frank could learn his lesson from their loud yowls and grunts.

It soon became necessary for Frank to live in a different house altogether.

He bought a bungalow on Bakers Lane, a ten-minute drive from Duncan Street. Between their two houses were ten long blocks and a public cemetery and fourteen years of codes and storms and ships and tunnels and nightingales. Frank dreaded every trip over this terrain, any return to the house they'd shared for a decade, which was the place he first met Freddy Nicklaus, the blond poet Tenn called Angel, the man who'd taken his place.

By the end of the 1950s, Frank Merlo no longer recognized his life. Most nights, he stayed home with a book and a pack of smokes and left the front door open in case friends dropped by. His TV, a gift from Tenn, he kept on with the sound all the way down. Gigi was his primary company. He wrote Anja letters filled with happy lies, and she replied with postcards from cities he'd never heard of. When she passed through Miami, early in '61, he declined her invitation to meet him at her hotel, afraid she would see in his body what he and Tenn could not. On his good nights, he chose a nightclub from the many booming options on Duval Street and drove himself to it. He still had a way with a spin and a twist and a shake. He still could manage a Lindy hop or two. He staggered home just as dawn was breaking, hope in his legs.

This went on for as long as it could. You can hide a thing from the world and from yourself—a pretty story or a hideous one, a fact, a crime, desire—but eventually you're sitting on the deck at the Magnolia Café with your friend Dan and these guys Mark and Brian who know Dan from somewhere and a bunch of other locals whose names you can't remember, and you're taking small bites of soft bread that you wash down with your second margarita of the afternoon and you're trying to show Dan with your two hands the size of the lizard you scooted out of your living room the night before but instead you start to choke and he asks if you're all right and you turn away and puke up so much blood it drips through the deck slats and pools on the white sand below. Then Dan takes you to the hospital and waits with you in the airless room and squeezes your hand when the old man points to the white bursts on the X-ray and scolds you for *waiting so long*, until you're *this far gone*, but you can't take your eyes off the bursts, which you couldn't possibly have seen before and yet they look familiar, as if from a dream; they don't shock you; you've always known those ghostly figures were there, crowding your heart.

The doctors promised Frank that a quick but serious operation would snuff out all the bursts once and for all. Once that happened, he could get back up to a solid weight. Six months tops, it would take. He was young enough, barely forty, the surgeon reassured him; he had plenty of time to recover; think of it as a "wake-up call." So Frank vowed to quit smoking. Live clean. Swim twice a day. And then, once this regimen made him the Horse again, once he was steady on his feet, he vowed his own revenge on Tenn for having treated him so barbarously these past few years when death had come knocking. The operation at Memorial Hospital would set this plan in motion. He booked himself on a late-night flight to New York City.

When Tenn heard about the scene at the café and the dire diagnosis and the flight that followed—not from Frank, but from Dan and Marion Vaccaro and God knows how many queens who'd rung him up to register their sorrow and confusion—he rushed to Frank's side in Manhattan, as if determined to foil his plan of revenge. It was Tenn's face Frank saw first when he woke from his surgery the next day. Every night during visiting hours, there was Tenn in the chair beside him, scribbling in his notebook, writing postcards he'd bought from the gift shop, gossiping, reminiscing, as if Memorial were another of their hotels and this one more of their adventures, just like old times.

It enraged Frank, Tenn's sudden transformation into Florence Nightingale, his gymnastic avoidance of Angel's name in his presence, his eleventh-hour ministry of remorse. Their friends came by with flowers and pinched faces and hugged Tenn as if he'd been the doting nurse from the start, as if he hadn't willfully blinded himself to Frank's wasting away before him, begging him to notice. "Get out of my room," he said to Tenn, in the days after that first operation. "Leave me alone once and for all. Go be with your Angel."

"Listen to yourself, Frankie," Tenn said. His weight on the bed was an insult, every tender word a finger jammed in his eye. "I'll come every day you're here."

"I say *I don't need you!*" Frank shouted the next day and the day after that, each time Tenn came through the door. His voice had gone both thin and hoarse from the tubes. He thrashed around feebly in his bed.

The operation was a success, said the surgeon. The bursts were gone. He had performed a kind of miracle. Frank had a life to lead once more. Tenn went back to his poet, and Frank flew home to Bakers Lane alone.

He got stronger. He made plans to visit Anja in Copenhagen or Marrakech or wherever she was. Then, from there, he'd light out for a new city on his own. Or he'd move straight to Rome, grow fat in Trastevere, reunite with Alvaro and spend his days lazing around the Piazza degli Zingari. Tenn agreed to keep him on salary in perpetuity, and of course he still had his 10 percent of *The Rose Tattoo* and *Cat* and *Camino Real*, which would keep growing. The money wouldn't hold forever, but it gave Frank all the more reason to take action. It was the beginning of the 1960s, and he had a chance for a new life.

A year had gone by since then. No Morocco, no Rome, no Anja, no more meat on his bones. The only time he'd left Key West since that first operation was to come back here to the cobalt unit at Memorial, where the surgeon told him—and this time he wasn't lying—he'd stay until the end.

10.

DIRECTION

| n Anja's front living room, on the night of Memorial Day, the single
copy of *Call It Joy* lies before them on the coffee table between the
family-size bag of those magnificent orange chips and two bottles of
Margaux. They sit alongside each other on the sofa, Anja between the
two boys. It is decided, after some debate, that Trevor will take Tenn's
lines, Sandrino will play Frank and the Young Patron, and Anja will
read the part of Gisele Larson, along with the author's note and the
stage directions.

First Draft for Anja Bloom
New York, November 1982

CALL IT JOY

(A Play in Two Parts)
By
Tennessee Williams
for F.M. and A.B.

CHARACTERS

TENNESSEE WILLIAMS, a playwright
GISELE LARSON, his lifelong friend,
proprietress of Gisele's Bar, Key West
YOUNG MALE BAR PATRON/MARK
FRANK MERLO/ANGELO

The set is divided into two rooms of equal size with
no partition, so that players may cross seamlessly from
one to the other. Stage right the darkened bedroom of a
modest Key West bungalow: an unmade queen-size bed with
white sheets and a lone rumpled pillow; a nightstand
strewn with books and pill bottles; a rocking chair; a
Japanese lantern with glass pendants; and a tall dresser
with most of its drawers half open, clothes spilling out
haphazardly. Stage left a comparatively spare, dimly lit
barroom with a working jukebox under a beefcake poster,
an empty dance floor, a wall clock that keeps real time
set to nine p.m., and saloon-style doors that swing into
the wings. On the bedroom side, a washroom door beside
the bed provides a parallel exit stage right. The wooden
bar, long enough for six stools, stands quarter-turned
to the audience at the same angle as the bed. A large
rectangular area rug—of any style but Oriental—spans the
middle of the proscenium, functioning as both decoration
and two-way portal.

This arrangement leaves an intentionally conspicuous
negative space upstage center, where the plain white wall
of the bedroom meets the dark-paneled wall of the bar. At
this intersection grows, fantastically, a large rose bush
in full flower. The roses must be red. While silk roses
are more practical, ideally the scent of live roses will
permeate the theater.

Audiences should consider this production, in
particular the character of Tennessee Williams,
as a corrective to the author's cowardice in hiding
behind August, the playwright and lead in last year's
Something Cloudy, Something Clear. This play must also be
considered an act of penance. Here, Frank Merlo is not a
brief and expedient memory wheeled cruelly onto the stage
in the violent throes of death, only to be dispensed back
into the darkness. In the eyes of Tennessee and Gisele,

Frank is as vital and horselike as the man who inspired
the creation of Alvaro Mangiacavallo in *The Rose Tattoo*.
Though some dialogue, names, genders, and setting details
have been changed, every word in these pages is true.

SCENE ONE

(With the rise of the curtain, offstage low male chatter,
as if from a crowded barroom. TENNESSEE, early seventies
but seeming older, haggard, gray-bearded, husky if not
stout, sits at the bar drinking a whiskey rocks. GISELE
is wiping down the bar. She has a mane of spectacular
blonde or white hair and wears a shiny blouse of silver
lamé or glittering sequins over designer blue jeans.
Though she appears a "tough customer," an understated
elegance belies the grubbiness of her establishment.

Throughout their conversation, Gisele waits on
customers invisible to the audience, nodding at them,
miming the taking of their money and the pouring of their
drinks, winking and smiling at them as she listens and
responds to Tennessee.)

TENNESSEE
This one didn't even bother with the
cover of night. Skipped out in the middle
of the afternoon, in plain sight. Took
my heart medications and the good liquor
and all the cash I didn't have the sense
to lock up.

GISELE
Jim, you said his name was?

TENN
Julian. "Call me Julie." Brains of a
starfish, but he came cheap. And like
most things that come cheap, he cost me
a fortune. Worst of all, he was a bore
in the sack.

GISELE
You won't miss him, then. Don't worry,
another will come along. They always do.

TENN

I sure will miss him when my heart conks
out! You think these town doctors care
I've got nothing for my blood pressure,
nothing for sleep, nothing to wake up?
Like a first-class criminal they treat
me. You should have seen me, half-loony,
all alone in my house, nobody looking
after me, my fingers shaking over the
keys. Julie used to rub my shoulders
while I worked, I'll miss that, and he
was a half-decent cook when he made the
effort. I kept hearing the front door
open, kept seeing his pinched little
face in the window, come back with a
gang of thugs for the rest of my worldly
possessions. How do I know what's a
hallucination and what's not? I need my
pills. I can't even drive in that state
of mind. So I walked down here looking
for you, but you were nowhere to be
found.

GISELE

They didn't tell you I was visiting my
brother?

TENN

Rafe told me. I sent you both a postcard.

GISELE

We didn't get it.

TENN

Maybe I didn't mail it. But I wrote it.
San Francisco, California 94114. When's
our Teddy coming back to us?

GISELE

He needs to get his strength up and put
on some weight. The doctors won't release
him until they can figure out the cause.

                TENN

More doctors! You notice they don't cure
people anymore? Their skills are in
placation. Appeasement. I've been sick
every day of my life and no doctor's
ever done a thing for me but get me
high. You should bring him home. So what
if he's skinny? Is that why you invited
me here?

                GISELE

I wanted to check on you. I haven't
seen you in a while. Rafe told me about
Julie. Said you were all torn up, worse
than he's seen you. Said the demons came
back again. He wanted me to give you
these.

(She pulls out a baggie of pills from her pocket)

He said these should tide you over.

                TENN

O, bless that beautiful man!

(He fumbles with the baggie, his hands trembling, and
chases two of the pills with the whiskey)

He'll be in for the late crowd?

                GISELE

As always. But listen, Tenn—will you
stay with me until then? Keep me
company? Can you do that? Your voice
is a comfort to me.

                TENN

Of course.

                GISELE

Seeing Teddy that way, it got me
remembering our good times here. The

three of us and Frankie. Those days
aren't coming back, Tenn. The nights I
don't see you, when you're away, I feel
like the only woman left alive. The
boys who come in all look alike: same
mustache, same white low-cut shirts with
their chest hair puffing out. They get
younger and younger and their pants
tighter and tighter.

(laughs)

I can't tell them apart.

(A disco song begins to play. She gestures toward the
jukebox.)

Take those two. Regulars. One of them's a
dark beer, the other's a scotch neat. Don't
ask me which is which. Either my eyesight's
slipping or they're identical twins.

TENN
Perhaps they've got the same daddy.

GISELE
(laughs)

We'll see by the end of the night.

TENN
(a beat. He stirs his drink with his fingers)

What do they say Teddy's got, the gay
cancer?

GISELE
They don't know for sure. Or they won't
say. Or he won't tell me the truth. But
it looks—(she interrupts herself). We
hope it's spared him. He might tell you.
Will you write him again?

                              TENN
          I will write him a long letter. Better
          yet, I will put said long letter into the
          mail. I will pay young Teddy's passage
          home and find him the best care
          available.

                             GISELE
          That's not necessary.

                              TENN
          This place can't provide you with much.

                             GISELE
          I'm getting by. Thank the Goddess for
          thirsty homosexuals.

(She refills his drink)

          These are on the house.

                              TENN
(He raises his glass to toast her)

          Who needs the Goddess when I have Her
          archangel!

(He stands, leans over the bar and kisses her on the
lips. Rather than sit back down, he remains standing,
swaying to the disco beat.)

                             GISELE
          Speed kicking in already?

                              TENN
(He addresses the following monologue to Gisele, even
after she leaves the room through the saloon-style doors
and returns, half listening to his drunken speed-fueled
rambling, which she does throughout. Every so often, she
refreshes his drink or nods at him.
     In the meantime, the YOUNG PATRON enters and exits the
bar through the same door, visiting the jukebox, dancing,

conversing with Gisele in mime. Each time he comes in, he
carries a drink in a different glass. He fits Gisele's
exact description of mustache, open-collared white shirt,
skintight pants. He doesn't glance at Tenn until he
becomes MARK later in the scene. It is essential that the
same actor plays each version of this man.)

> Key West is the only place that's been a
> home to me. The only place that provides
> me with the peace and quiet I need. With
> the right help, I can work and swim and
> sleep with no disturbance. I can't bear
> the winter or the holidays anywhere but
> on this queer little island. Did I tell
> you I'll be moving to Bangkok next
> month? You think that sounds strange,
> but let me tell you: they revere men of
> letters in the East, men who are taught
> in American universities. If I die out
> there, I want my ashes flown back and
> scattered in the Gulf of Mexico, as close
> as possible to where Hart Crane threw
> himself into the sea.
>   I called every boy I knew down here
> when Julie cleaned me out. I begged them
> to help me. I came to this very barstool
> seeking your counsel. I knew you were
> gone. I was hoping you'd come back early,
> hoping you'd bring Teddy, hoping for some
> good news. Rafe must have told you I got
> to crying. I'm not ashamed of it. I've
> never been ashamed to show emotion. Mark
> was here—you know Mark, the blond who
> sings torch songs at the Orchard—

(Gisele nods)

> I caught his big blue eyes drowning in
> pity for me. So I went to him

(He gets up out of his chair and walks toward the YOUNG
PATRON, who is standing by the jukebox)

and I took the umbrella out of his
daiquiri and I tucked it behind his ear.
"You feel sorry for me, do you?" I asked
him. He had *fear* in his eyes.

                    YOUNG PATRON/MARK
(fearfully)

    Of course not, Mister Williams.

                    TENN
    Then he saw I was teasing him and he
    took my hand and kissed it.

                    YOUNG PATRON/MARK
(kisses his hand)

                    TENN
(to Mark)

    All you boys suck up to me. I can
    make you a star with the snap of my
    fingers. Would you like to be a star,
    baby?

                    YOUNG PATRON/MARK
    I sure would.

                    TENN
    Then sing something special for me
    later.

                    YOUNG PATRON/MARK
    Anything for you, Mister Williams.

                    TENN
(to Gisele)

    He's a slut, of course, but very sweet
    about it. At the end of the night, he

did as I asked, he serenaded me right
here. We were the last ones in the bar—

                YOUNG PATRON/MARK
(sings the entirety of Irving Berlin's "What'll I Do,"
with backing)

                     TENN
(emotional, claps for him as he slowly exits)

     Mark was kind enough to drive me home

                  YOUNG PATRON
(walks back in carrying a different drink, so as to
indicate that he is no longer Mark)

                     TENN
     and the next night he was gone, too, off
     to sing his torch songs at some no-name
     piano bar on Islamorada. He wrote down
     the name of the place and the directions
     for me before he walked out.

(to the Young Patron)

     Don't you know I can get you gigs in New
     Orleans or New York?

(the Young Patron shakes his head, exits)

                    GISELE
     You're too good to these boys, Tenn. They
     take advantage.

                     TENN
(not quite listening to her)

     The critics say my plays are melancholy.
     They say I keep covering the same
     territory. But I tell you, I've never

written a play as melancholy as this
one you've got a front row seat for, this
melodrama of the old man in the disco bar.
There is no territory so bleak as this.

(stands)

You think I put on this suit and
chapeau, covered myself from head to
toe, to appear distinguished? It's to
hide the burst capillaries, the liver
spots, the knots of blue-black veins on
my legs. Look at my hands—they're as
gnarled as mangrove roots. Do you have
gloves I can borrow? A ski mask? No, it's
essential they know my identity. That
they recognize my face, my trademark
honey-soaked drawl.

(laughs bitterly)

If I'm too good to these boys, Gisele,
it's not for their sake. It's not
charity. Their touch, brief and phony as
it is, is the only thing capable of
expelling the demons. Such relief, for
just a moment, it's as sweet as love.
That's who comes into this bar night after
night—boys eager to play the role of
exorcist. The kinder ones wait until the
sex is through to take my money.

GISELE
Rafe said he couldn't get you to stop
talking this way. He tried, though,
didn't he? You were telling him stories
about Frank.

TENN
I unloaded that on him, too, did I? I
don't remember. Oh, the blue devils have
really come home to roost. I can't shake

them alone. It's Frankie I go back to,
more and more. The same goddamned
territory. If I could find my way out of
it, don't you think I would? Wouldn't
anybody?

                    FRANK
(enters, stands at the jukebox, not far from the
Young Patron, beside the rose bush. He wears tight
blue jeans and a white T-shirt, his hair slicked back
fifties-style. He keeps his head down, but looks up
from time to time, knowingly, at Tenn, who has yet to
notice him)

                    TENN
        I do recall Rafe saying he had
        something to lift my spirits. How kind
        he was to come through. How kind you
        both are. I wish I deserved such
        kindness.

(notices Frank, stares at him for a long moment,
transfixed)

        Who is that man?

                    GISELE
(after a quick glimpse)

        Hmm, that's one I haven't seen before.

                    TENN

        You don't see what I see?

                    GISELE

        What do you see?

                    TENN

        He's the spitting image!

                         GISELE
         Spitting image of who, Tenn?

                          TENN
         Of Frankie!

                         GISELE
         (looks more closely at him)

                  Well, now that you say it.

                          FRANK
         (holds Tenn's gaze, runs his fingers through his hair,
         smiles coyly, flirtatiously, seductively)

                          TENN
         (takes a step toward the man, trancelike, looks him up
         and down, still transfixed)

                         GISELE
                  You all right, Tenn? Let me get you some
                  water. Better yet, let me find somebody
                  to drive you home. I won't hold you
                  hostage any longer. I'm feeling a little
                  better. Teddy wouldn't want me moping
                  over him.

         (exits)

                          FRANK
         (walks toward Tenn, hands in his pockets, stands before
         him at arm's length)

                  Hello, Tenn.

                          TENN
         (looks behind and around him, guiltily)

                  Frankie?

         (tenderly, in amazement)

What are you doing here?

                    FRANK
I wanted to see you again. I've missed
you.

                    TENN
(holds the man's shoulders, as much to keep himself
standing as to touch him to make sure he's not a
hallucination. He rubs his arms, squeezes his muscles.
He lays his palms, priestlike, on his cheeks)

    But how can it be?

                    FRANK
I've been here all night, waiting, hoping
you'd recognize me. I didn't know if you
would, it's been so many years. You've
been doing a lot of talking over there,
Tenn. A lot of feeling sorry for
yourself.

                    TENN
I don't understand.

(rubs his eyes)

    What was in those pills? Where's Rafe?

                    FRANK
I look pretty good, don't you think?

(turns around, shows off his body)

                    TENN
You look—you're all better.

                    FRANK
(winks)

    Strong as a horse.

                              TENN
(Impulsively, emotionally, Tenn embraces him. Tenn holds
him tightly, both of them swaying. He kisses the top of
his head and down to his ears and lips. The two men
fall passionately against the jukebox. Gisele enters,
sees them, shakes her head bemusedly, goes about
her work.)

                              FRANK
          Can you please take me home now? To our
          old place? I've missed it oh so much.

                              TENN
          I'll take you anywhere you want, Frankie.

                              FRANK
          Then take me home.

(Frank grabs him by the front of his belt and pulls him,
still kissing passionately, into the bedroom. As they
cross into it stage right, the lights come on, including
the bedside lamp. Tenn throws off his suit jacket, and
they fall upon the bed. Frank lies back on it, his
T-shirt riding up to reveal taut muscular abdominals.
Meanwhile, and throughout the rest of Scene One, Gisele
continues her work at the bar, the YOUNG PATRON walks in
and out with different drinks, conversing with her in
mime, playing the jukebox, etc.)

                              TENN
          You stayed young.

                              FRANK
          Because I never left you. I was with you
          every day. You just couldn't see me until
          now.

(He kicks off his shoes and slowly undoes the button of
his jeans)

                              TENN
          Sit up, Frankie. I want to see your face.

                              FRANK
But my face is not my best feature.

(laughs, turns over on his stomach, and, in the style of a
striptease, starts to pull his jeans down over his buttocks
with his thumbs. Tenn stops him before any skin is exposed.
Playfully he turns him back over, and they lie beside each
other, Tenn propping his head up with his elbow)

                              TENN
        Come on, Frankie. Talk to me.

                              FRANK
        I'd rather hear you talk.

                              TENN
        But I've been talking too much, you said.

                              FRANK
(bites the nail on his right thumb, flicks it onto the floor)

        What's the use of talking, anyway? I
        don't have too long. I wish I did. I wish
        I could stay with you forever.

                              TENN
(looking down the length of Frank's body. He traces a
scar that runs from his hip across his abdomen)

        When did they open you up?

                              FRANK
(a pause)

        You don't remember?

                              TENN
(covers the scar with his palm)

        I wasn't there when you needed me. I
        didn't trust you. I treated you like a
        whore and a thief. But I've been punished

for it, Frankie, punished with a lifetime
of suffering, with one flop of a play
after another. Without you I've been
wandering, cursed as a—

                    FRANK
Don't say that, Tenn.

                    TENN
Do you forgive me?

                    FRANK
(without hesitation)

    Of course I forgive you.

(He takes Tenn's hand, tenderly, and squeezes it)

                    TENN
The Rose Tattoo was the only goddamn
thing I wrote that had anything to say
about love.

                    FRANK
(laughs)

    Now you're really talking crazy.

                    TENN
(beseechingly)

    Did you hate me, Frankie? By the end? I
    don't blame you if you did.

                    FRANK
I never hated you.

                    TENN
How can I believe you?

                    FRANK
Believe me. It's all right. It's in the
past.

(He pulls his T-shirt over his head and switches off the
lamp. The room and the bar are now equally dim.)

> See? The past. You don't have to worry
> about it anymore.

> TENN
> How long do you have?

> FRANK
> Until morning. A few more hours. Enough
> time for all of it.

(He unbuttons Tenn's shirt but leaves it on him)

> TENN
> You can't even look at me. I'm so old and
> ugly now.

> FRANK
(runs his hand up and down Tenn's bare chest)

> You're as handsome as the day we met.

(He leans in to kiss him on the lips)

> The best day of my life, you know. Do
> you remember what I was wearing?

> TENN
> Will you say you love me?

> FRANK
(without hesitation)

> I love you. I bet you don't even
> remember where I first saw you.

> TENN
> Will you say, "I love you, Tenn"?

> FRANK
(laughs)

Is there someone else here you think I'm
talking to?

                    TENN
Just say it, please, Frankie. Just like
that.

                    FRANK
(takes Tenn's face in his hands)

I love you, Tenn.

(releases him, tenderly)

That better?

(The curtain begins to lower. Gisele stops wiping down
the bar so that she can watch and listen.)

                    TENN
Just keep saying it. Will you do that for
me? Keep saying those words, like you
just did? I won't ask any more favors.
You've done so much already.

                    GISELE
(flicks a light switch behind the bar. BLACKOUT)

                  SCENE TWO
(The next day. The bar clock is set to two p.m. Light
fills the entire stage. The curtain opens on Gisele
sitting behind the bar, her hair pulled up and secured
with pins, wearing a more modest blouse. She drinks a cup
of coffee and turns the pages of a newspaper unfolded on
the bar while the Young Patron mops the floor. Tenn is
alone in bed, asleep, in a white undershirt. A sheet
covers his torso. The offstage sound of a flushed toilet
and running water wakes him. He sits up on his palms and
looks around, bewildered. The door beside the bed opens
and Frank enters, his hair tousled and no longer slick,
wearing only a pair of boxer shorts, clearly in a hurry.

In his left ear is a tiny diamond stud he was not wearing
in Scene One.)

                         FRANK
(smiling down at Tenn as he crosses the room)

         You're awake.

                         TENN
(regards him quizzically)

                         FRANK
(Scanning the room, he finds his jeans thrown across the
rocker, and pulls them up over his boxers. He picks up
his shirt from the floor and puts that on as well.)

         Shoes!

(He puts his hands on his hips, somewhat mincingly)

         If I were my new leather sandals, where
         would I be hiding?

(He squats down and locates them under the bed. He sits
beside Tenn to put them on. He pats Tenn's leg kindly but
patronizingly.)

         I'm all set to go. But I can be back in
         a few days if you want.

                         TENN
         Who the fuck are you?

                         FRANK
         You don't remember? I'm Frankie!

                         TENN
         Get that thing out of your ear.

                         FRANK
         Oh shit.

(He removes it)

>Sorry, man. Frank would've never worn an
>earring, would he? Too butch for that. I
>hear no one could tell he was a fairy—
>not to mention a butch bottom!

                    TENN
(leaps up and grabs him by the throat. Tries to push
him against the wall, but the young man is too solid.
He elbows Tenn in the stomach to stop him from choking
him. Tenn gasps, falls back on the bed, breathing
heavily)

                    FRANK
>Relax, man! What's your jazz?

(He steps back, holding his arms out defensively)

                    TENN
>Get the FUCK out of my house! Don't call
>yourself Frankie.

                    FRANK
>But I am! I was! Don't tell me you didn't
>feel it. I know you did. You gotta admit
>it. Even I felt it.

(laughs)

>Some kind of magic, wouldn't you say?

(Tenn regards him with stunned horror. Frank gathers his
breath and speaks more gently, puts his arms down.)

>I swear, man, I didn't mean any harm by
>it. I give you my word. And listen, I
>gotta drive to my sister's in Lauderdale.
>I can come back next week if you want. I
>don't mind the drive. We can do this all
>over again. No earring, I promise. I'll
>butch it up again for you.

                    TENN
        What do you want from me? Money?

                    FRANK
        No, sir! No need for it.

                    TENN
        I don't understand. Are you on dope?
        Where are my pills?

                    FRANK
        I don't take pills. Clean living

                    TENN
        What kind of monster are you? I'm an old
        man. I'm sick. You could have killed me.
        Why did you do this?

(sorrowfully, a wail)

        Why didn't you just kill me?

                    FRANK
(He stares down at him for a long moment, conveying a
pity not unlike compassion. His hands again on his hips,
he shakes his head.)

        Tennessee Williams!

(He jogs across the stage, into the bar and through the
saloon doors)

                    TENN
(clambering to his feet and standing at the edge of the
bedroom, calling out again)

        Why did you do this to me? Tell me!

                    FRANK
(from offstage)

        Ask Gisele!

(At the sound of her name, Gisele lifts her head for a moment before going back to her reading. Tenn—confused, agitated—hastily puts on his clothes from the night before, which are in a pile on the floor beside the bed. He grabs the pill bottles on the nightstand, opens them and shakes them. They are all empty. He throws them to the floor. He fishes out Rafe's pills from his pants pocket and swallows them dry before hurrying into the bar. When he sees Gisele at the bar, he stops.)

                    GISELE
(mischievously)

      You got my present.

                    TENN
      A hustler? That's what you call a
      present?

                    GISELE
      He's not a hustler. He's a friend of
      Rafe's from Miami. His name is Angelo.
      He came in a few weeks ago for the first
      time. You were in New York, I think, or
      maybe Chicago. I've been keeping a close
      eye on you, Tenn. Since Frank, and since
      Teddy moved away, I've been trying to get
      to you. To reach you. But I don't have
      those powers anymore. When I saw this
      man, Angelo, I did a double take. I
      thought, oh, there's the Horse, he's here
      to dance. Simple as that, like it was
      1955. I couldn't take my eyes off the
      man. Put him in Frank's clothes, I
      thought, slick back his hair, he's his
      exact copy. I showed him and Rafe photos
      of him. I have so many photos of the
      four of us—what will I do with them? I
      talked to the kid all night. He's a
      dancer who wants to act, just like Frank
      was. He got that dreamy look about the
      movies the way Frank used to. He has

that same sweetness, that *intuition*. He's
nothing like Frank when he talks, but
when he's just standing there? He took my
breath away.

TENN

So you thought it would be a good idea
to whore him out to me?

GISELE

I wanted to give you some joy. Did it
work?

TENN

(looks over, dreamily, at the bed)

It did. And it did not. I knew and I did
not. But even when I knew, it didn't
matter. I was in Frankie's arms again.

(a beat)

Can you call that joy?

GISELE

Yes, I think you can. A writer can live
on illusions. They can be enough. I might
be a writer, too.

TENN

He told me he loved me. He said it, plain
as day. Like it came easy. "I love you,
Tenn." That's when I knew for sure it
wasn't Frank. There's your illusion: the
words, not the body.

GISELE

I don't understand.

TENN

You don't understand because you are not
aware that Frankie Merlo never once in

our fifteen years together said those
words to me. He wasn't hoarding them. He
wasn't being miserly. He could have said
the words anytime he wanted. "I love
you, Tenn." How easy it would have been!
His heart was plenty big enough for love.
He told everyone he loved them, everyone
but me. Because he was incapable of
lying. Frank was many things, but a liar
wasn't one of them.

                    GISELE
You've believed that all this time?
That Frank didn't love you? You still
believe it?

                    TENN
(dreamily, distractedly)

You may have helped me after all, Gisele.
You've given me the idea for a play more
melancholy than that one about the old man
in the bar. This one stars that same man.
He even looks a bit like me. He once was a
big name in certain circles. What nobody
knows is that he's lived all his years
without once having been loved by another
human being. Not his mother, certainly not
his father, not a single one of his lovers.
They all used him in one way or another.
Do you think I'll get back to Broadway
with this one? What shall I call it?

                    GISELE
Frank must have told you a thousand
times. You just couldn't hear him.

                    TENN
Women have slit their wrists for love
of you. You have Rafe. You have your
brother. How much longer, do you think,

          will Teddy last? What are you doing here
          with me, with these queens, when you
          should be with him? I've never had
          anyone. Only illusions. You've kindly
          reminded me of that.

(walks toward the door)

          I'll find Teddy the best doctor in the
          country. He'll be well taken care of.
          Treated like a prince. Then I'm going to
          Bangkok, and I promise you this, I'm
          never coming back.

                    CURTAIN

"Wow," SAYS TREVOR, after he delivers the play's final line. He sits back against the sofa, still holding the page in his hand. "It's even worse than you said."

A throbbing at Anja's temples has replaced the pot's gentle woolliness. At the end of Scene One, she excused herself to drink a large glass of water and swallow three aspirin and check her face in the bathroom mirror. She applied some light makeup, a bit of tightening cream under her eyes, and pinned up her hair in case she grew queasier than she already was. When she returned, she found the boys kissing passionately at the end of the sofa, Sandrino's hand on the back of Trevor's head smashing his face harder into his own. "Method acting?" she joked.

The mood is darker now, the square empty and quiet except for the hiss of the fountain.

"I kept waiting to feel something," Trevor says. "For the first few pages, I almost did, but then, as it went on and on, I just wanted the guy to shut up and die already. The whole thing was so self-indulgent."

He looks to Anja for approval, but all she is willing to give him at this moment is a blank stare.

"He writes on the front page, 'first draft,'" says Sandrino. "He would have made it better."

"Think about somebody seeing this play in fifty years," Trevor continues. "By then, no one will know the name Tennessee Williams. For a work of literature to be great, it has to be timeless. You don't need a history lesson to understand Blanche DuBois or Maggie the Cat. They just *are*. Everything you need to know about them's in the script." He folds his arms petulantly, his face miserable, as if personally aggrieved.

"Why did you expect any different," says Anja, "when I told you I had read it?"

He looks at her sheepishly. "I thought you were hiding something—"

"—Even though I told him you would not do that," Sandrino cuts in.

"I might do that," Anja says. "But not in this case."

"All right," says Trevor, "so I had these fantasies that we'd put on this great never-before-seen play together."

Finally, thinks Anja, he admits what she has known all along.

"I don't mean I'd be in it or anything," he goes on, "but that me and Sandro, we'd drive you around places, be like your secretaries. And all these people would come to see it, and be crying at the end. And when you won a Tony for producing it or directing it or even starring in it or whatever, you'd thank us in your acceptance speech. I know it's stupid, but that's what I was expecting."

"That was very childish of you," Anja says.

"What can I say? I'm a child."

"I am curious," says Anja. "Why is it not enough for you that here on these pieces of paper, disintegrating before our eyes, are the words of a writer you claim to revere, words only you and three other people in the world have had the privilege to read? Words that could very well constitute the last play Tennessee Williams ever wrote? Why do you need more than that privilege? My curiosity is sincere."

"I don't know," he says. "I mean, of course it's a huge deal, and I'm super grateful for the privilege, I really am, but—"

"But it's more important to you that Anja Bloom says your name at the Tony Awards."

"No, that's not it. That's not totally fair." He goes back to his cheap wine, leaving her what's left of the second bottle of Margaux. "The point is: Is a play still a play if it's not performed? If only four people have read it, and three of them are sitting here in this apartment? Don't you think Tennessee Williams would want this play put on no matter what, even with its flaws? OK fine, maybe not put on but, at the very least, turned over to a biographer by now? The fact that you're hoarding it, that you want to *destroy* it seems—" He stops himself, shrugs, takes a sip of the wine. "Well, I'm just saying."

"Just saying what?" she presses him. "Tell me how it seems to you, my hoarding."

"Please don't," Sandrino says to Trevor. "We are the guests of my friend."

"No, Sandrino," says Anja. "I would like to know."

"It seems *self*ish," Trevor says. "Like, *really* selfish. Like, I mean, I one-hundred-percent agree that the play isn't great. You were totally right about that. And I'm disappointed, not only because it won't win any Tonys, but because, I don't know, I wanted to believe Tennessee Williams made this amazingly beautiful work of art right before he died, that he left the world this one last incredible gift, and that, because you knew him personally, and had this personal history with him, you were too blind to see its true value. And then here comes me and Sandro to open your eyes to it. OK, so that didn't happen. I'm getting over it as we speak. I'm mourning that little daydream here in real time." He smiles at her. "But I guess what I'm saying is, just because the play's kind of crappy is no reason to stuff it in a closet. It's definitely no reason to destroy it. You're always saying you like to argue, so tell me, how is that not selfish?"

Sandrino tries to answer for her, but she stops him.

"Because I wanted to protect him," Anja says.

"From what, embarrassment?"

She nods.

"He wrote some pretty bad plays in his time, especially in the seventies. This one's actually not *much* worse than the one-acts I saw in Provincetown last fall. Have you ever actually SEEN *Something Cloudy, Something Clear*? It's no day at the beach."

"I am not referring to Tenn," she says. "I am referring to Frank."

"I don't understand."

"Frank did love him, whether he said the words or not. I saw the two of them up close. I lived in their little apartment. I knew Frank's heart. No one should be led to believe otherwise. When I read this play the first time, I imagined what would happen if it was mounted. I did not want people to start digging into Frank's life, to write articles about him, to bother his family in their grief, to print his picture next to the bad reviews. He did not deserve that. He still does not deserve that. The less attention the world pays to Frank in that way, the better. Let him rest in peace."

"Well, it's way too late for that now," Trevor says, looking confused. "Have you ever Googled him? It's not like Frank Merlo's some big secret."

"I am aware of that," Anja says. Her head is pounding. "I've read the books."

"Then what about Frank were you trying to protect?"

With the sweep of her arm she scatters the cursed pages to the floor. "Goddammit!" she says. The suddenness of the act, the force of her anger, the word itself, takes her by surprise. "I wanted Tenn to get him *right*. To bring Frank back to life just as he was. It was his last chance! When I received the play in New York, twenty years after Frank died, I hoped to find in it the man I knew: his goodness, his love. It was like a child's love, suffocating, endless. Do you see that in these pages?"

"To me, at least, it looks like he tried?" offers Sandrino.

"No," Anja says. "He did not try. In here there is the double of Frank with his earring and his scar. There is the symbol of Frank with its aromatic roses. There is the memory of Frank, blurred by Tenn's guilt and Tenn's longing and Tenn's desire. Mostly guilt. Instead of the real Frank, there is instead—you are right, Trevor—the real Tennessee, an old man talking and talking about himself, begging us to feel sorry for him, making excuses. But we feel nothing. We just want him to—how did you put it?—shut up and die." She gathers the pages from the floor and stuffs them back in the envelope. "When I read this thirty years ago, it made me furious. Now I remember why."

"So what are you going to do with it?"

"What we discussed," she says. She goes to the kitchen and opens and closes drawers. "May I borrow your lighter?"

"It's cashed," Trevor says.

"What a pity." She turns to the oven and flicks on the burner. The flames shoot up with a pop and then settle. In the guest bathroom is a metal wastebasket.

"Can we just talk about this for five more minutes?" asks Trevor. "Will you at least let me try to convince you, now that I've read it, to contact his archives? You don't really have a reason not to, from what I've heard. I bet they won't even do anything with it. They'll barely know it's there."

"Then it will not matter if they never get it."

"But—" Sandrino says, waving his arms in that way Italians do to generate words. "But—it is a piece of history you kill. To erase it, *poof!*, like it never happened—do you feel you are . . . authorized . . . for that?"

"He's right," says Trevor. "Just because Tenn gave it to you doesn't mean it's yours."

"He did not just 'give it to me,'" she argues. "He made it *for* me. Did you not see my name at the top of the page? But even if he had not, you are both too sophisticated to think that art belongs to the artist. Or have I overestimated you?"

"I still think you have a responsibility," Trevor says.

"To whom?"

"To history!" Sandrino repeats. "To give history all the evidence. I think of this play like an experiment. It did not go right, but still it should be recorded. If the fruit flies—"

"I assure you," says Anja, interrupting. "There is no woman fitting Gisele's description in all of Key West. Her character is a version of me and—more than that—a vehicle for me. A small vehicle, as it turns out. At the time he wrote this, remember, I drew very big audiences. Tennessee was hoping I would fall in love with Gisele and that I would want to play her, and that people would flock to see me, and it would revive the corpse that was his career."

"Ah," says Trevor, smugly. "But the part was too small for you, so you stuck it in a drawer."

"Of course not!" Anja says. "I am not so vain. If it was a great part, I would have taken it, no matter how small it was."

She notices the self-satisfaction on Trevor's face, the doubt on Sandrino's. She considers, for a moment, as the burner crackles, the veracity of the statement she has just made. She wants to believe she is telling the truth, that her dismissal of the play back in 1983 was on account of Frank, and the merits of the script itself, and not her own ego. Was she so ambitious then? Is she still? The turquoise flames undulate like waves. They watch her, wondering what she will do. Is it possible that she, too, was hoping—then and now—to pull from the manuscript a work of great genius, her own shiny new vehicle? Has she been holding on to it for all these years, neglecting to hand it over to the archives or to some ardent and scrappy young Williams scholar, in hopes that one day she might turn it into her own triumph?

Who's she kidding, Sandrino tells her, she could draw a big crowd today if she wanted.

In fact, adds Trevor, she'd draw the biggest audience of her career, because nobody, especially Americans, can resist a comeback. She is not Elizabeth Taylor, Trevor goes on, as she shuts off the burner (she will give them five minutes); she is uniquely herself. There is no one else like her, and there is no one better to put Tenn's last words about Frank into perspective, to do right by her old friend.

What a story it would be, they say (this time it is both of them, their eyes wide and dreamy); the great Anja Bloom emerges from seclusion to produce and direct and star in the lost last play of Tennessee Williams. It gives you the chills to imagine, does it not? Yes, it does, they say. Yes, it's no *Streetcar.* Yes, Hovland is not here to direct it. Yes, it's got these warts. The warts are the story.

"I do not want to 'come back,' as you call it, in a story of warts," says Anja, the spell they are putting on her already breaking. "I do not want to come back at all. What I want—what I have been wanting for years—is to leave this place. It has no hold on me now."

"If that were really true," says Trevor, "you'd already be gone."

11.

ARRANGEMENTS

Jack Burns was the last person Frank expected to intrude on him in Rome. It was the morning after the Fontanone dinner, and they were all standing around the Via Firenze living room, Frank and Tenn and Anna and Anja and Paul and Ahmed, hands on their hips, deciding how to kill the day. Any other August, they'd have escaped by now to a *pensione* in Rimini, but, for the foreseeable future, the *Senso* script was holding Tenn and Paul hostage. Tomorrow, Anna was off to Sicily to visit her family for the Ferragosto holiday, and Anja had an appointment with Hovland—she would not call it a date, but who knew where it would lead?—to see St. Peter's for the first time. Today was the last time they would all be in town together.

Tenn insisted that he and Paul had not made enough progress on the script to justify an afternoon of faffing around Rome. Paul countered that not even ditchdiggers worked on Saturdays, and besides, was not the mind like a field, and like a field must not the mind go fallow for periods of time if we were to rely on its continued fertility?

Anna and Anja nodded loudly, their first moment of harmony since meeting the night before. Ahmed mentioned the benefits of stretching the mind with kif on its days off, so that when it snapped back it had a different shape, a little wider on one side and longer on the other. Laughing along, Tenn said that, by this point, Paul's mind was more than sufficiently stretched, and, as for his fertile field, Tenn was happy to let it go fallow, but first it had to produce an edible crop. What's more, Tenn went on—it was around then that the buzzer sounded with what would be Jack's telegram—he did not appreciate Paul's comparison of their heady hours to those of common laborers, or their poetic words to ditches.

"A proper lunch is reason enough to take a break," said Anna. "The artist and the ditchdigger, neither one can live without food, on that we can agree, no?"

"Followed by a nap, I assume," replied Tenn.

"*Certo*," said Anna. "Very reasonable. In this country, labor is for the morning and for the evening. Daytime is for food and for sleep, and the night is for love."

"*Brava*, Signora Magnani!" Paul said.

Frank read the telegram and handed it to Tenn.

```
SERIOUSLY ILL PROBABLY DONE FOR NEED YOU LV-2324
RIGHT AWAY = JACK B
```

"You make it sound so orderly," said Anja. "That's not how Rome feels on the streets."

"You have been on the streets?" Anna asked her. She took out a tube of lipstick and applied it as she spoke. "I did not say 'orderly.' I have no fetish for orderly. I said *reasonable*. We Italians are accused of excess, but the reality is that we are the only culture that has perfected the art of moderation."

"You'll find St. Peter's Cathedral a prime example of Italian moderation," said Tenn to Anja.

Frank stepped into the front hallway to place a call to Livorno. He expected Sandro to answer in a shaking, tearful panic, but instead, after the first ring, it was Jack himself.

"I already gave up on you," Jack whispered. A Burnsian hello if Frank ever heard one. "How soon can you get here?"

"Are you feeling better?" Frank asked. "You don't sound too terrible."

"The shivers have mostly stopped," he said, though Frank could hear them in his voice. "The double vision's gone. But something's still not right. It's not the DTs. It's not VD either; I've seen enough of both to know. And it's not just a fever. I'm not the paranoid type. Will you guys come? We have a guest room."

"What's Sandro saying?"

"That I should sleep and stay out of the sun and quit drinking. Same old saw. I was in bed all day yesterday and what good did it do. He doesn't know I wired you. He went for a swim and I snuck out. You have the address. He likes a surprise. He's fond of you, and Tenn he likes enough. Please say you'll come, Frank. Come today."

"Can you get Sandro on the phone?"

"He's out in the garden," Jack said. "He's pissed off at me. He's got me cooped up like a criminal. Hold on." There was a sound like a suitcase tumbling down stairs. "Look, I know I'm no peach. You think I'm an ass. I can't change that. But I'm telling you I need you to come here, that I'm in a bad way. Why don't you believe me?"

Jack's desperation fit the telegram but not the man they'd met a week ago in Portofino, the man with no vocabulary for need or self-reproach, whose face was always half turned away from you even when he looked you straight on.

"It's just that I'm sure you're not as bad off as you think," Frank said. "It's the fever talking. I had a fever so bad once I saw rabbits flying across the room. You should listen to *Il Dottore*. If he tells you to stay in bed and quit drinking, then maybe—"

"He's not a real doctor."

"And we are?" said Frank. "Listen: there must be a hospital nearby. Get a second opinion if it'll ease your mind."

"He called another doctor," Jack said. He lowered his voice again. "He was here yesterday, some quack from the navy base. Asked a bunch of dumb questions, blamed the heat, repeated verbatim every word Sandro said. They're in cahoots!"

The living room at Via Firenze erupted in laughter. Frank could hear the clinking of glasses and the rattle of the window blinds being pulled up. The hall doorway filled with the afternoon light.

"If you let me talk to Sandro, there's a good chance Tenn and I could make it over there soon," said Frank, growing impatient. "He won't be angry. I promise. You can't think straight right now, but he can."

"I'm not seeing flying bunnies," Jack said. "I'm telling you, it's not just a fever. They're plotting something!" The shiver in his voice was more pronounced. "Leave today, please. Not tomorrow. Come see for yourself. Sandro's very fond of you. Did I give you the address?"

"You did," said Frank.

"Our backyard is ten steps from the water," Jack said. "On a clear day, you can see Elba."

"Exile does look better from a distance," said Frank, hoping for a laugh.

"He's coming in," Jack said, and the line went dead.

Frank stood for a moment in the light, torn by his distaste for Jack and his natural instinct to speed to another man's—in this case, Sandro's—rescue. He owed the doctor more than he owed Jack, of course, for tending to them in Portofino. To Jack he owed nothing at all. Was he tricking him? Had Jack truly gone mad and done something to hurt Sandro, and was that why he couldn't put him on the phone? Marina di Cecina was a three-hour drive—four hours tops—on an August Saturday.

"We have a compromise," Tenn said, when Frank stepped back into the living room. "Anna's going to fix lunch for us while Paul and I make some headway on the script. You and Ahmed will smoke a little kif down the hall, and Anja will learn from Chef Magnani how to make an *amatriciana*. Everybody wins."

"Not such a good deal for Anna," said Frank. "You surprise me." He came up behind her and wrapped his arms around her chest. She lay her head back on his shoulder and kissed him many times on the cheek.

"This is not charity," Anna said. She extended her right arm as if casting a spell. "I am putting you all under my obligation. For the rest of today and tonight, after Tenn and Paul make their headway, we do what Anna says, we go where Anna goes, we sleep when Anna says we sleep. This will be the most expensive lunch of your lifetime." She broke free of Frank, grabbed Paul's hand, and pulled him and Tenn across the room into Tenn's study. "Now get to work!"

Frank followed them. He told Tenn of his conversation with Jack. "He's even more of a hysteric than we thought" was Tenn's response, with almost a grudging admiration. "Or he's just bored. You're not seriously considering driving all the way out there, are you? Indulging his neuroses?"

"A busman's holiday is still a holiday," Frank said, playfully.

"How can a man be so beautiful and so cruel?" Tenn said. He leaned over, kissed him, and looked him in the eyes. "Lucky for me, you don't mean a word of it."

"I don't," said Frank, as Tenn gathered his papers from his desk. "But it did get me thinking." He watched Tenn stick a pencil in his mouth and arrange himself at the desk behind the typewriter.

"Thinking about what, baby?"

"How bored I am here. In Rome. With nothing to do."

"I can't stop you from saving every writer in distress," Tenn said, "if it gives you a purpose in life." He said this absently as he loaded the typewriter with a clean sheet of paper. Behind them on the sofa, Paul scribbled in his notebook pretending not to listen.

Genuine cruelty between lovers was like this: accidental, off-hand, overheard. Frank's confession of boredom, Tenn's instinctual dismissal, both sharp less in their accuracy than in their casualness. Two men could get used to living with this sort of cruelty as long as there was enough tenderness to blunt it and the nightingales kept singing and they smashed enough vases. If Jack was telling the truth, Frank wouldn't mind playing nurse for him and Sandro for a little while.

In the kitchen, Anna was up on the step stool in her heels pulling down pots from the cupboards. "I can make my autograph in the dust!" she declared, and directed Anja to wash them. Frank closed the door on the unfolding scene.

"I'd have thought you'd want to stay here with us," Tenn said to Frank, "for the night at least, before we lose the girls. Anna will not be happy with you."

"It could be real," Frank said. "You didn't hear Jack on the phone. You wouldn't have recognized his voice. Sandro could be a monster for all we know. A week ago they were strangers. If something happened, I couldn't live with myself."

"Sounds like you've already made up your mind," Tenn said. He handed Paul the page he'd been typing and then sat back with his arms crossed in thought. "It's fine with me, Frankie. The mystery has sought you out, and now you must solve it. I won't need the car. Will you take Mr. Moon? Let him run on the beach?"

"I had the same idea," Frank said.

"Keep your bag packed," Paul interrupted. "Visconti waits for no man."

Frank's entire body flushed warm. He looked over at the back of Tenn's head. "What do I care about Visconti?"

"He didn't run it by you?" Paul asked.

"Run what by me?"

Tenn was still focused on the page he was typing. Without turning his head, he said, "It's up to the great director, not to me. He still has to approve." When he finally looked up at Frank, pencil dangling from his mouth, his hair a mess of curls from Anna's tousling, on his face was a mischievous joy. "I didn't want you to get your hopes up, baby," he said.

"So—you really wrote me in? An actual part? You found a way?" Frank asked. If he asked enough versions of the question, he might get the answer he wanted. He took a step toward Tenn, about to pounce, then steadied himself. "In all the commotion with Anja, I thought you forgot."

"It's not *Hamlet*," Paul said. "It's just a—"

"I don't want to know!" Frank interrupted, his hands in the air, trying and failing to tame the grin that had run wild all over his face. "Don't tell me *one single thing* about it until we hear from Visconti."

"He's not an easy man to please," said Paul. "Visconti, I mean."

"Listen to Paul," said Tenn.

"I'll leave the telegram in the hall," Frank said, half listening. "It has Jack's number on it. If Visconti wants me, you call me there, and I'll jump in the car and rush back, I don't care if Jack's gasping for his last breath, I'll come."

"Please, Frankie," said Tenn. "Try not to dwell on it. There's a reason I didn't tell you. Your heart—it breaks so easily."

"This heart?" He beat his chest like a gorilla. "This heart is stronger than you think!" He cranked open the window and belted out Puccini—"*Un bel dì, vedremo / levarsi un fil di fumo / sull'estremo confin del mare*—Take that, sopranos!"

"Lucky for you this part requires no singing," said Paul.

Frank reached over and goosed Paul so hard his notebook and pen went flying. Then he sat beside him on the sofa and watched them both at work—the back of Tenn's head bobbing as he pounded the keys, Paul's eyelids fluttering to stay awake. He allowed himself to imagine putting on the blue jacket of a Risorgimento soldier and clasping the wide gold belt across it. He stood tall beside his brothers-in-arms and summoned his pride for his country. Then he transformed into a hungry peasant, his undershirt torn at the seams, dirt smeared across his chest. Then he was a carriage driver, then an angry idiot on a bike for a moment of comic relief, then the brother of Alida Valli come back on a horse to save her.

Could he wait another second for Visconti's call?

Could he learn to ride a horse?

"In every other circumstance, your heavy breathing would excite me," said Tenn, swiveling around in his chair. He pushed his glasses onto the bridge of his nose. "But in this case, it's just distracting. Why don't you go find Ahmed before you go? You drive better a little high."

For the few days, at most, that Frank planned to stay in Livorno, he needed only his bathing suit, a couple linen shirts, a pair of pants for the evenings, and the loafers already on his feet. From the nightstand, he grabbed the book he'd been reading on the French Revolution and stuffed it into his valise along with his shaving bag, a half-empty bottle of Vitalis, and biscuits for Mr. Moon. On a whim, he slipped a deck of Italian playing cards into the front pocket.

"What is that nonsense?" said Anna, when she saw him carry the valise into the hallway. When he explained, she said, of course, if someone is sick you must go to him right away, *immediately*, just as soon as you have a lunch of pasta and day-old bread and a nap afterward so that you can stay awake for the drive, and also after the last night in Rome of your best friend Anna who loves you and needs you probably more than this Jack Burns she hears is not such a good guy anyway.

Of course he would not miss Anja's first *amatriciana*, he told her. But after that, while they took naps, he'd drive to Livorno, and with any luck he'd be back in the next day or two for the leftovers.

"Anna taught me her secret," said Anja. She looked as comfortable in her sauce-splattered apron as Frank would look in an evening gown. Her hair was pulled back the way it was the night he met her, though the heat and the steam and the sweat on her temples had made it unruly.

"Let me guess," said Frank. "Her secret is *love*. That's what every Italian lady says—my mother, my *zia*—when you ask her what makes her sauce so good, she says, 'it's the love.'"

The women looked at each other and laughed, allies at last.

"Not quite," Anna said. "We tell you love because we know it's what you want to hear."

"It's the *anger*," said Anja.

AFTER FUMBLING WITH THE MAP led to a few wrong turns, Frank eventually found the bungalow on Via Baldissera, a paved road that ended in the sand of the Ligurian Sea. If he drove any farther, he'd crash into a beached fishing boat and a scatter of families with small children watching the sunset from chairs and blankets.

He parked the Jaguar in the dirt on the side of a modest *villino* with a wraparound balcony and carried his bag and a bouquet of flowers to the front door. He knocked, got no answer, knocked louder. The door, unlocked, led directly to a sitting room that looked more abandoned than empty: a white leather sofa, ashtrays and magazines and books on a coffee table, a wet towel thrown over a wooden chair. He stepped in. The air was stale and close. Mr. Moon howled and pulled him back toward the street.

He followed a path of mismatched flagstones that ran the length of the far side of the house. When he reached the backyard, he found Jack in what appeared to be a ladies' wide-brimmed hat squatting among the flowers in the garden, pulling weeds, looking as healthy and pink and perturbed as they'd left him in Portofino. Off to the side under a pergola in a folding chair sat Sandro reading the *Corriere della Sera.*

The bouquet seemed silly in Frank's hand, not only because of the explosion of colorful flowers Jack was already tending to but because he was clearly too healthy to have earned them. The washed-up American author was dressed for a summer evening promenade: tan linen pants a few inches too short above the ankle, a blue button-down shirt with the sleeves rolled up, a checkered scarf tied around his neck, all of which failed to cover or hide the only visible evidence of illness, which was that his entire body had been burnt lobster red.

If I leave first thing in the morning, Frank thought, I can catch Anna before she leaves for Sicily.

"Is this what you call a deathbed?" Frank asked.

Sandro looked up, tossed the paper on the table and, arms out, rushed to him, his face a cartoon of joyful surprise. He'd also spent too much time in the sun, but it had only turned him a darker shade of brown. He hugged Frank tightly and then kissed him hard on the lips as he held his face in his hands. "You are bread falling from the sky," he said, "and we are starving!"

Jack stood, creakily, and steadied himself on the large palm tree that shaded them all. There was an empty tumbler on the ground behind the tree, half hidden by a leaf.

In a flurry, Sandro explained that Villino Brunella belonged to his family, who lived a few miles away. He and Jack chose this place over their own private *pensione* in Ischia to save money, which turned out to be a very good idea after the surprise expense of Portofino, and because they could stay as long as they wanted, and because Sandro had been raised not far from here and was familiar with the region. The help used to stay in Villino Brunella, but now *they* were the help, Sandro joked, *they* were the poor relations in need of shelter from the fierceness of the August sun. "Look at what it did to my Jack," he said. "This is why we hide back here under the trees and the grapes."

"You're not angry that Jack invited me?" Frank asked.

"What angry? Now we can celebrate that he is feeling better. We had a big little scare."

Jack walked slowly over to Frank, wiping his hand on his pants, and held it out for him to shake. It felt both clammy and hot at the same time. "Really great of you to come," he said.

"Doesn't he look good?" Sandro asked. He was on the ground now with Mr. Moon, rubbing him expertly under his neck, which sent the dog into an ecstatic stupor. "If you saw this man two nights ago you would scream the way I screamed, so loud it waked the neighbor. But every day he gets a little bit better, and this afternoon he is able to work on the weeds after a good long rest. The red skin burn is not so good but I tell him he glows like an Indian and I am the cowboy. And here you are, another cowboy for us to play western with. Will you have a drink? Do you want to watch the sunset? How long can you stay? Where is Tenn? The extra room is already made up for Marika but she stays at my mother's house with Lucky so Jack can sleep. No guests come except my mother. She sleeps on top of the covers but otherwise the bed has not been used."

"I'll take a drink," said Frank. "But I won't stay long. Just for dinner. You won't believe who's waiting for me back in Rome."

"I will make your drink and then you will tell me about your famous friends," Sandro said, dancing his way into the house, Mr. Moon at his heels. "Only one thing you say wrong: you are staying the night with us, no excuses. I don't care if it's Marlon Brando himself who waits for you."

"What's the big idea?" Frank asked Jack, with barely restrained agitation, when Sandro was out of earshot. "This isn't exactly the scene you described. You make me drive all the way here for a bad case of sunburn?"

"Ask him one fact he read in that newspaper," Jack said, defiantly. "I promise he can't tell you. He's been sitting there all day looking over the top of the page waiting for me to keel over. *Hoping* I'll keel over."

"He was reading when I walked in," said Frank, moving closer to him. "He didn't even notice me until I spoke." He pressed his left palm behind Jack's neck and his right against his forehead, the way his mother used to do. He felt an equal heat on both palms, but he couldn't tell if it came from the burn or a fever. He still had that bump on his right temple from Testa del Lupo.

"I'm burning alive, aren't I?" said Jack, his eyes wet and bloodshot. "He's putting something in my broth. It tastes like chalk. What he did before didn't take so now he's trying something else. Don't drink what he's bringing you, Frank. Spill it and I'll replace it myself."

"You'll forgive me if this all sounds crazy."

"Then watch, at least watch, how he keeps me in his sight at all times. I'm too weak to walk far. His cousin took the car. Drive me back to Rome with you tonight, after he goes to sleep. Take me to a real hospital. If I could find his pills I'd drug him myself. Do you have any of Tenn's on you?"

"Jack," said Frank. He narrowed his eyes.

"You don't believe me!"

"Is that your glass hiding over there behind the tree?"

"So what if it is? You want me to get the DTs on top of everything?"

Jack's raving had to have a rational explanation, and possibly it was that very bad sunburn did not mix well with whiskey.

"It's the only thing that calms me down," he said. He shambled over to the chair Sandro had been sitting in. "Watch how he watches me," he said again, breathing hard, as panicked as a man with a gun to his head, and then, as Sandro walked out with a tray of drinks, he rubbed his eyes of his tears and sat up straight.

"I brought something for each of us," Sandro said. "Campari and soda for Frankie, a Dubonnet for me, and some mineral water for the patient."

Frank reached for Jack's water glass. "You don't mind?" he asked Sandro. "I'm very parched from the drive."

Unbothered, Sandro said, "Of course!" He turned to Jack, and with a tender, "I will get you another, *amore*," he went back into the house.

"Not *every* drink is poisoned," said Jack, grouchily, when he saw Frank's face. "He won't try anything now that you're here. You're my shield."

"You'll keep getting stronger, then," said Frank. "And then you can drive off on your own."

"I'm not playing a game," Jack said.

After Sandro returned with Jack's water, which went untouched, the three of them sat at the table and bathed in the cooling mercy of the sunset. The light through the leaves mottled their faces; for a moment, Sandro would glow, only to be thrown the next moment into a sinister shadow that covered half of his face. The table was round and

made of wrought iron, painted white, with four wide armchairs of
gaudily elaborate design. The fourth chair sat off to the side, turned
toward the west, flecked with rust, and inconsolably empty of Tenn.
Frank had yet to develop an armor against the sudden ache for him
that overtook him at moments like this, when his absence felt less like
a habit than an affliction.

When Jack slumped, Sandro offered a pillow. When he rolled
down and buttoned his shirtsleeves, he offered a blanket. When he
didn't touch the cheese and salumi Sandro had brought out, he suggested a cup of broth. This struck Frank as the appropriate level of
concern, neither too little nor too much, and yet, each time, Jack
flared his eyes at him as if to say, "Now do you believe me?"

The story of Anja's escape from Portofino, and her impromptu audition with Martin Hovland, didn't surprise them in the least. From
the beginning, they said, they'd expected Anja to attach herself to
Tenn, and to use Frank to get closer to him.

"She's a parasite," said Jack. "A bounder. She'll devour the both of
you and then move on to the next man who can get her one step closer
to the Great White Way."

"She's just a kid," Frank said, defensively. "And I'm mad for her.
She's smarter than all of us put together."

"I adore her!" said Sandro.

"She has no interest in the theater," Frank went on. "It's film that
captivates her. Tenn can get her only so far in that department."

"Which is why she's already moved on to this director fellow," said
Jack. "That took her how long, two days? She's got you under her
spell, but, believe me, I met a hundred girls like her in the States, back
when I was a high-muck-a-muck. Rubbing their ginches up on my leg
as if that could swing me their way. If you ask me, all women are
bounders, when you really think about it. They have to be for their
own survival. Without a man, how far can they get?"

"Your life with Tennessee has much glamour," Sandro said. "Jack and me, we prefer the quiet of the country." He nuzzled Mr. Moon. "I learn that I make better talk with animals than with people."

"What'd you get rid of Lucky for, then?" Jack sniped.

"Lucky stays at my mother's with Marika," Sandro explained to Frank. "They keep her company better than us. Three times a day Marika comes here in the car, makes us a meal, and we—I—take Lucky for a walk on the beach. I want Lucky to stay all the time but he is not a quiet dog. All night he barks at the birds. We can't have that. Jack needs to rest. When he is done resting, I will bring Lucky back, and then together we will chase him on the sand."

"That makes sense to me," said Frank. "Doesn't that sound reasonable, Jack?"

Jack looked at his watch. "Marika's late."

"You're hungry?" Sandro said, hopefully.

"No."

"I gave her the night free," Sandro said. "I bought some fish to grill, and we have plenty of fruit and vegetables." To Frank he said, shaking his head, "For the patient, I'm sorry to say, this week it's broth and water only."

"No wonder I'm so weak!" said Jack. Suddenly he lunged forward, grabbed Frank's drink, and took a big swig before Sandro wrenched it away from him. "I can't take it anymore! I'm a prisoner! First he banishes the dog; now the cook!"

This time it was Sandro who made eyes with Frank, except his glowed with supplication. "You must tell him to listen to me," he said, clasping his hands together as if about to pray. "I am at the end of my rope. He is improved—since Thursday he is *very much* improved—but still I worry day and night."

"What happened Thursday?"

Jack sat back in his chair, licking the Campari that had splashed across his lips. Then his entire body erupted in a fit of shivers. "I'm fucking freezing," he said, and stood. "I'm going in." On the way, he snatched the tumbler from its hiding spot under the tree and threw it against the stone wall that separated Villino Brunella from its neighbor to the east.

"I'll go in, too," Frank said to Sandro.

"No," he said. "Please stay here. Enjoy the breeze. I will put him to bed." He assured Frank there was nothing more he could do tonight, that this was how it had been between them, more or less, not just since Thursday but since the letter about his book from the New York editor.

"Is he really going to be OK?"

"Yes," said Sandro, and then, instead of following Jack inside, he stayed with Frank in the garden. He looked, suddenly, very tired. "Yesterday I bring the navy doctor to confirm what I knew already. Heatstroke. Heatstroke is grave, but it is not impossible to cure if you do what you are supposed to do, if you let me give you an ice bath, if you drink the water I pour for you all day, if you sit still when I wave the fan on you. He does none of these things. He is out of the worst danger now, but he is too much a pighead to believe it. He keeps the stroke going just to spite me!"

"You're sure it's just heatstroke?" said Frank. "That bump on his head"—he tapped his right temple—"That has nothing to do with it? It hasn't gone down even a little bit since last week."

Sandro dismissed this. "I see many bumps like that. Some, they last a year. Sooner or later, they go down. No. The fault is my own. I wanted to go for a sail, to take Jack on my father's boat. To show off, maybe. To prove to him something—what, I don't know. To be romantic. I wanted so badly for him to have a little joy. Because of his book. Because he is a man in pain. This was Thursday. You remember how it was on Thursday? The sun here was terrible. Thirty-eight, thirty-nine degrees, no clouds, some wind, but then, all of a sudden there is no wind at all, and we are very far out. I should know better. I should not take the risk. I am used to the boat in the middle of the water, but he is not. The reflection makes like a torch on the skin. I got us back fast as I could, but it was not fast enough. For him, I am never fast enough at anything, you see. When we arrived at the dock, he collapsed and nearly fell back in the water headfirst. I was very afraid. He was confused, babbling like a crazy person. I stuck my fingers on his tongue to keep him from swallowing it. The tears fell from my face onto his. He was dehydrated. After I stabilized him with help from some people on the beach—it took hours, Frankie; I carried him to a café for the shade—I told him it was my tears and my hand in his mouth that saved him, and he said, 'Next time let me die.' To hear such a thing from the man you love! It is like a knife in the neck."

"Now he thinks you're trying to kill him," said Frank, matter-of-factly. "And I almost believed him!" Then, he couldn't help it, he laughed. The laugh echoed across the garden, through the windows of the house where Jack was banging around, over the cypress trees.

Sandro was not laughing. "I know," he said. "I heard his crazy talk when you called." He gave Frank a sheepish look. "I'm sorry."

"You mean you *both* set me up to come here?" Frank asked. "Why not just invite me? Why these tricks?" He stood. His keys were still in his pocket. "What kind of people are you?"

"I did not know about the telegram," said Sandro, his hands above him in surrender. "I promise you. I went to swim, and when I am swimming Jack sends it to you in secret. I admit, when I heard him on the telephone with you, I thought, he is smart to call Frank. Frank is the man to call when there is an emergency. I should have called you right back to tell you there was no emergency. But I did not. That is why I am sorry. I was at the end of my rope. And now that you are here, you can talk to him the way I asked you to do in Portofino. You can build him up, tell him how it is for Tennessee Williams when the editors don't accept his great plays, when there are more boos from the audience than clapping. This will inspire him. He will not feel so alone. He doesn't believe me when I try to comfort him. He calls me a simpleton. He says I don't know a book from a blueberry."

"He's cruel to you."

"He's a man in pain," Sandro said again. "In the head, in the body, all pain. He feels too much. He was not always this way. I wish to turn back the clock to take you to Firenze so you can meet him the night I met him. The weeks and months after. This is what I'm afraid of, Frankie: if you don't help him, I will lose that man forever."

"It sounds like he wants to be lost."

Sandro rubbed his face. "That is what I think, too," he said. He had not shaved that day, or maybe the day before, either; on his chin was a patch of gray stubble. Again he looked at Frank with those wide supplicating eyes. "But he should not get what he wants. Not if it brings harm to him. That is why we keep our friends and lovers, is it not? To protect us from ourselves?"

JACK SLEPT MOST OF the next day, Sunday, while Frank and Sandro took turns checking his breathing. Frank soon discovered that there was not much else to do in Marina di Cecina but doze and read and chase Mr. Moon and haggle for the best fish and walk back and forth to the ocean and watch your friend's chest rise and fall, the whole time waiting for the phone to ring and Visconti to change your life.

Jack took shallow breaths. He frequently jolted awake into a stupor. More than once, he called for his mother. Despite the heat, there was no sweat on his face or the sheets. They kept the blinds drawn to keep the awful light away. At Sandro's direction, Frank forced him to drink large glasses of water in small sips. He wouldn't drink anything Sandro put before him. In one of the glasses, Sandro had dissolved what he called a mild sedative, saying, "What he needs most of all is to sleep." Frank didn't question him.

Villino Brunella may have been the housekeepers' quarters, but it still came with a private beach. The rocky and gray-black sand was volcanic, according to Marika, the remains of the eruption of the Cala Rossa ten million years ago. Marika had come in the early afternoon, eyed Sandro warmly as she stocked the cabinets with groceries, rearranged the flowers Frank had brought with a few cut stems from the garden, and swept up the shards of glass from the patio. *"Dov'è Lucky?"* Frank asked her, from the doorway.

"I'll bring him tonight when Signor Burns is awake," she said, brightly, in Italian. "The little *mostro* cheers him up."

"He'll have a friend," Frank said, meaning Mr. Moon, who hadn't left Sandro's side since they'd arrived.

"He needs one of those," said Marika. "He is very lonely."

"The dog?"

She thought a moment. Her hands, bony beyond her age, gripped the top of the broom handle. "All of them," she said, and went back to sweeping.

When Frank checked on Jack later that afternoon, he was surprised to find him sitting at his desk. He was writing what appeared to be a letter but might have been a manuscript. "You're up!" Frank said, cheered by the familiar sight of a man at a desk hunched over his pages.

"So to speak," Jack said. He was writing with slow deliberation, crossing out words here and there, as Frank waited for him to come up for air. "Listen," he said, setting his pen down. He turned to face Frank, still keeping his head and shoulders bent forward like a gargoyle. "I sure am grateful to you for coming down here and looking after me. It's a damned decent gesture on your part. First-class."

"What can I say?" said Frank, inching closer for a peek at the pages, hoping, for all their sakes, that they were the first of a new manuscript. "I'm a sucker for a damsel in distress."

Jack laughed, a sound so rare that Frank couldn't be sure he wasn't just clearing his throat. "I got a little schizo there for a while. But my head's on straight again now." He pressed the base of his left palm under his chin and the base of his right against his temple, and pretended to screw his head back into place. Instead of reassuring Frank, this burst of playfulness gave him pause. "You'll stay another day, though, to get the all-clear?"

"I don't think I'm necessary," said Frank. The room was dark and humid and fusty. "You want some air? I'll keep the light at a minimum."

"I can handle it," Jack said, but when the breeze did rush in, cool and clean, with the fading sun, he shivered and reached for one of the many blankets on his bed. "Salty," he said, lapping up the air. Then he sank back into the chair, nearly missing the edge of it. "Christ, I'm so fucking thirsty."

There was a glass of cloudy water on his bedside table. All day Jack had slept without taking the pill Sandro had crushed into it. Frank nearly handed it to him anyway, and then said, "A fly got in here. Let me get you a fresh one."

"You might as well bring in the entire pitcher," said Jack, picking up the pen again. "And tell *him* to leave me be for a while, will you?"

Frank found Sandro on the beach dozing in a chair, shirtless, a pack of cigarettes and a magazine and Mr. Moon at his feet. The news of Jack's progress brought relief to his face. Since he'd already gotten plenty of sleep without it, Frank asked, should he still give him the drink with the sedative? Sandro thought a moment. In his opinion, he said, a man still woozy and shivering could use one more night, at least, but probably two, of deep restoration. By Wednesday, for sure, he insisted, he'll be good as new. Until then, to rush was not smart.

Frank returned to Jack's room to find him back in bed wrapped like a mummy in the blankets, fast asleep, breathing deeply. The pages and the pen were gone from the desk. He set the cloudy glass and a pitcher of fresh water on the nightstand, shut the window most of the way, and closed the door firmly behind him.

Sandro showed up soon after with Mr. Moon, and later the two of them ate a light dinner on the patio: more grilled fish, a plate of Marika's finger-rolled *busiate*, bread from the bakery at the end of the block. Their attention was fixed on the house, alert to any movement from Jack. The haze of clouds made for not so much a sunset but an intermittently perceptible dimming—no blaze of color in the dying of this particular day, no glory wrought from its inevitable crash. This was, for the vacationers in Marina di Cecina, for the man expecting good news from Rome that could have come at any moment but did not, a day hardly worth its price.

When it was finally dark, Frank and Sandro closed themselves in the kitchen, poured shots of anisette into their espressos, and turned the portable radio on low. At Frank's suggestion, they played *briscola* for money with the deck of Italian cards he'd brought from Rome. Tonight, Sandro had all the luck. He won the first round by twenty points and the next by eighteen. Frank pushed the stack of lire toward him in theatrical frustration.

Whether it was the cards or the anisette or Jack's improved condition Frank didn't know, but the heaviness had lifted from Sandro's shoulders. Maybe it hovered just above him, between the top of his head and the ceiling, ready to descend at any moment, but for now he sat up straight in his chair, and he tapped his feet to Nilla Pizzi who sang too slow for tapping, and he talked of the future as if it were bright. He was only thirty-one years old, he said. His father had lived to ninety-six, a miracle of health. Jack would be his lifelong friend. His children and grandchildren would read *The Gallery*—all of Jack's books, he corrected himself—in the original English. Every August, the two of them would travel to an exotic place as far as their money would take them, a place where they had no one to answer to: Lisbon, Cairo, Beirut. The rest of the year, he'd be happy enough with his animals, and Jack would have his typewriter.

When Frank asked whose children Sandro was referring to, he said, matter-of-factly, "Mine." He hoped at least one of his sons, if he was so lucky to have sons, would take over his veterinary practice, but, if not, they could do something else, anything else, that required an education. He wanted even his daughters to learn English, which was the key that would unlock the world for the next generation. He said all this as he racked up more points in *briscola*, collecting aces and threes hand over fist. When he noticed the bewilderment on Frank's face, he said, "There is always a woman in the picture, no?"

His woman lived not far from here, Sandro said, in San Vincenzo. She was a schoolteacher, the younger sister of his *compare* Nunzio, known to Sandro since he was in short pants. Her name was Floria. It was Floria who'd taught him the importance of English, she who gave him lessons in grammar when he visited. It was difficult to make time for her, but he managed. He never spoke of this woman in front of Jack, but he knew of her and that, sooner or later, perhaps once they married or the first child was born, she would require more of Sandro than she did now, more than she had over these last three years of the men's affiliation. Beyond that, Sandro said, he and Jack would have their Augusts, and maybe more. Because if he wanted to take these holiday trips with his friend, the famous American writer, who was she to complain?

Frank was no stranger to arrangements, but this one was not so simple to organize in his head. Why had Sandro not mentioned it until now? Why had Jack not mentioned it at all? How many lives could a person lead at one time, and how did you keep them from crashing into each other? Meanwhile, he lost track of the game. San-dro continued to amass his fortunes, chattering on amiably about a change of luck, a clear day tomorrow, another night of restful sleep to the sound of the waves. Frank's thoughts turned to Jane Bowles, wife of Paul, whose very existence he'd all but forgotten in the haze of kif and Ahmed and the parade of Ahmeds before him. At least Jane was off having love affairs with women; he doubted that the same was true of this Floria, that she had adventures far beyond conjugating verbs for children in some one-room schoolhouse in San Vincenzo.

"When will you see her again?" Frank asked.

"Floria?" He shrugged. "Next month sometime. After I drive Jack home to Firenze. She likes me to come on Sundays. I spend many hours on the train."

"All that back and forth would make me tired," said Frank.

"No, I don't think it would," Sandro said. "Not you. Not us. We are not the tired kind. The switching, the in-between, the this and the that, it gives us life. You can't tell me you don't know what I'm talking about."

"I'm not sure that I do."

Sandro leaned forward, clutching his cards to his chest. "The fact that some men choose to live in chains when they could be free."

Frank considered this. "You don't think that all you've done is add another chain?"

"You mean Jack?"

"I mean either one of them. You break free of one just to tie your-self to the other."

Frank had come close to this double knot with Alvaro. Just as Tenn expected Frank's time and attention, so Alvaro had come to expect them of Frank. Worse: Frank came to demand equally precious things of Alvaro—his immediate availability, his unfailing good humor, his complete submission—and when Alvaro could not or did not provide them, Frank felt forsaken. The contract too closely resembled the negotiations and obligations of love. It was better to enter into no more than one such contract, even an unspoken one. It was better to remember the boys for their elbows and scars, not their hearts.

He started to say this to Sandro, in so many words, but in the middle of it, they heard Jack knocking around in his room. He appeared in the kitchen doorway moments later barefoot, still mummified in the blanket, shielding his eyes from the lamplight. It was past ten o'clock. He had slept, off and on, for nearly twenty-four hours, with or without Sandro's pills. "I'm starving," he said.

"That's very good!" said Sandro. He stood and, giving Jack no chance to resist, grabbed his shoulders and kissed him on the lips.

Jack pushed him away, as if by instinct. "My sunburn!" he said, rubbing those assaulted shoulders. He sat down in Sandro's chair and poured a shot of anisette in his empty espresso cup.

"Take small sips," Sandro said. "Don't drink it all in one gulp."

"I will make you some pasta," Frank said. "I'm hungry again myself. It's the ocean air. You too, Sandro?"

"For pasta?" he said. "Always."

They had plenty of fresh tomatoes and vegetables, but Frank wanted to fix for Jack the dish his mother used to make when he was coming off a fever: long pasta with butter, olive oil, cheese and extra red pepper. The butter, otherwise unnecessary, was there to soothe the soul, the red pepper to kill the germs. As he boiled the water and grated the block of parmigiano and uncovered the strips of dried linguini that Marika had left them, Jack and Sandro fell into a wordless game of *scopa*. Whether or not Sandro intended it, Jack won most of the tricks. He smiled smugly when he swept up a four of clubs and a three of cups with his *settebello*. "I guess things are looking up for me," he said.

His forehead was cool to the touch. When he let the blanket fall, he didn't shiver. He devoured two bowls of the pasta (which turned out perfectly, with just enough bite, the sauce clinging to the noodles as they raised them to their lips, their lips glistening with butter), and he continued to win at *scopa* even after Frank joined in. He told an off-color joke about a Marine that got him laughing in that grunting way of his; he'd heard it from an officer in his company, a gentle giant of a guy named Abernathy, somebody he'd lost touch with and wished to see again.

If tonight were the first night Frank had met this Jack Burns, he'd scarcely have imagined him to be anything but an amiable fellow soldier who must have passed out on the beach. Jack even poured them each a shot and toasted his "two able nursemaids, who brought me back from the brink." He felt renewed, he said. "I have shed my chrysalis," he said, triumphantly, pointing to the blanket on the kitchen floor. And yet, when Frank turned to Sandro expecting to see relief, he saw that the heaviness had descended again.

FRANK WOKE THE NEXT DAY close to noon in the same clothes, with no memory of how or when he made it to bed. He made an espresso for himself, ate a *cornetto* left for him on the kitchen counter, and set out with his dog. On the beach, he immediately encountered Sandro and Jack, who had just returned to the umbrellas from a walk. The day was hazy and windless, the clouds again shielding them—or at least attempting to shield them—from the violent sun.

"You are looking very well," Frank said to Jack. He wore a wide-brimmed hat and, over his bathing trunks, a long-sleeved shirt printed with loud geometric shapes.

"I'm stealing your name," said Jack, puffing out his chest. "I am the Horse now."

"I keep telling him not to push," said Sandro, "but one thing does not change: he still ignores my advice."

"Tenn won't stand for you being the Horse," said Frank. "*I* won't stand for it. How about we call you"—he remembered the blanket—"the butterfly."

He made a sour face. "Am I so delicate?"

"Yes," said Sandro. "The name is perfect. Blond hair, blue eyes, white teeth, red skin. And that shirt! A color explosion!"

"You might as well just call me a fairy."

"Would it be the first time?" Frank teased, and, playfully, Jack kicked sand at his feet. Mr. Moon barked at him in rebuke.

"Call me what you want," said Jack. He tossed the hat to the ground and unbuttoned his shirt. "I'm going for a swim."

"Is that wise?"

"Certainly not," Jack said, but before they could stop him, he'd stripped off the shirt and sprinted for the water.

Sandro and Frank rushed toward him, but they couldn't catch him. They stood at the edge of the surf, lifeguarding, Mr. Moon beside them splashing maniacally. Jack ran in a few yards, where it was still shallow and translucent, then dove into a cresting wave. He appeared on the surface moments later, bobbing, to catch his breath. Then he backstroked north. Just as they lost sight of him, he turned around and headed back south. He made this loop a number of times, always just about to disappear, then reversing course. The water was frigid. The shock to the system was worth it, though, for the view Frank had seen yesterday: the tropical aquamarine of the wide shoal against the ancient black sand, the pastels of the sleepy town beyond.

Sandro kept shouting to Jack and waving him back to shore. When, finally, after twenty minutes, he headed in, Sandro rushed to the house, grabbed a large towel, and held the towel before him like a matador. Jack stepped into it, smiling broadly, shivering.

This shivering, the natural kind, stopped soon enough. They sat for hours under the umbrellas. The beach was close enough to the house that they could hear the phone if it rang. It did not ring. Frank took out his binoculars so Jack could point him in the direction of Elba.

Though little could be made of Elba but a blurry blotch of green, Frank still spent a while gazing at its peaks, imagining the terror of solitary confinement on an island, even a beautiful one in the middle of the Tyrrhenian, even one that, according to Jack, was almost a hundred miles wide. Though Frank vaguely recalled that Napoleon had armies of men with him, he pictured the great man wandering alone up and down the mountains in his muddy uniform, foraging for food like a Neanderthal, crying unabashedly, growing mad, his glory years slipping further and further into memory. In Frank's mind, Napoleon was still out there, trudging around in his black boots; if he kept his binoculars trained long enough on the island, he might just spot him emerging from a cave.

Frank wanted to talk more about Napoleon, but Jack kept bringing the conversation back to Shelley, the poet, who'd been shipwrecked on this same coast a few hundred miles north, between here and Portofino, a month before he turned thirty. Frank admitted he knew nothing of Shelley, that he had no appetite left for poetry after eating up novels and plays and history and opera, that even these he hadn't found a taste for until he'd come back from the war, a time when beauty was all he was after. "I guess I'm still in that time," he said.

"And why not," said Sandro.

Jack, who wasn't much for beauty, had loved every kind of book and every kind of writer for as long as he could remember, he said, as long as they were any good. He'd brushed up on Shelley in the days leading up to their trip here because, unlike Keats, the poet hadn't stuck with him, either. He still didn't love Shelley the way he loved Keats—"the way every fairy schoolboy loves Keats," he said—but he had come to appreciate him. In fact, the evening of the day he'd arrived at Villino Brunella, he'd recited one of Shelley's poems, "To Night," alone in the twilight of the empty beach in order to summon his ghost. He wanted something from Shelley's ghost, he said, but he wasn't sure what. His permission, maybe. His protection. His blessing, at least. Jack figured, we're two writers stranded here on the same shore, we might as well get to know each other.

"This I did not know," said Sandro.

"Do you have to know everything?" Jack said.

"You don't come across as the mystical type," said Frank.

"Because I'm not a sentimentalist," he said. "And yet you call me a butterfly." He smiled. "You want to know the most fun this butterfly had in Africa, during the war? It wasn't gazing at the orange sunsets over the fever trees. It was watching the guys who got diarrhea from being too lazy to scald their mess gear rush past my tent, tearing down their britches. To me, this was a perfect comedy."

"This is why you recovered!" Sandro said, with awe in his voice. "Because the dead poet, you prayed to him, like we pray to the saints for intercession."

"I choose to believe it was the whiskey and the Campari and the anisette that healed me," said Jack. "But just in case—" He stood and stepped out from under the shade of the umbrella. Their only company were the sullen teenagers and the families many yards away on the public beach. Jack turned northward, dug his feet into the sand, extended his arms, and recited:

Death will come when thou art dead,
Soon, too soon—

Sleep will come when thou art fled;
Of neither would I ask the boon
I ask of thee, belovèd Night—
Swift be thine approaching flight,
Come soon, soon!

"Bravo!" said Sandro, as Jack took a bow. "What is the meaning?"

"Don't ask me," said Frank.

Jack looked down at them, shaking his head. "It's the last stanza of the poem. He's describing the refuge of darkness, of sleep specifically, a refuge that the day, that light, can never give you. The poem's about wanting it always to be night, because only at night can you be completely hidden. And how death is the ultimate night, but you don't want that quite yet. You want a close approximation that's not so permanent."

"It sounds like Shelley had some secrets," said Frank.

"So I was right," said Sandro. "It was fate for you to read this poem before you needed sleep. The saints could not have done better."

Later, after lunch and just before they all took refuge in sleep, when Sandro was out in the garden, Frank followed Jack into his bedroom. "When I walked in on you yesterday," he asked him, "what were you writing? You can tell me it's none of my business."

"It's none of your business," he said, his good humor suddenly gone, as quickly as it had come on. He removed his shirt—there were blisters on his shoulders Frank hadn't noticed earlier—and climbed into bed. "I told Marika to make us steaks tonight. I'm sick of all this fish. Could you get the shades?"

"I'm going back to Rome in the morning," Frank said, making the decision as he spoke the words. A wave of relief washed over him. "I hope I've been of some help."

"Not the way he wants you to be," Jack said, his face turned away, half buried in the pillow. With that grim snigger, he said, "He thinks a pep talk can raise the dead. I tell you, I hate the sight of him. The *idea* of him." He pulled the blanket tighter. "Listen, I meant what I said before. It was big of you to come. Brotherly. I won't forget it."

Frank called Tenn to let him know he was coming back, but there was no answer. He napped, played with the dogs on the beach before the dinner of roasted beef and zucchini blossoms and fresh green beans in tomato sauce. The three of them made a brief *passagiata* up and down the Viale della Vittoria, nodding at the men walking toward them. Afterward, their hands sticky with gelato, they played more *scopa*, more *briscola*, at the kitchen table. Sandro begged Frank to stay one more night, the heaviness so thick on him now it hunched him over. He said there was music in the piazza on Tuesdays; the younger men would come out for it; Mr. Moon and Lucky were just getting to know each other. Frank declined. He thought to himself: I am going to Rome to be a soldier, to gussy myself up like Napoleon, to swim against sleep, to try a new thing. He avoided being alone with Sandro. He had more than done his part for him. For both of them. By eleven thirty, all three lay in their separate beds.

FRANK WOKE IN THE MIDDLE of the night to the howling of the dogs. He heard a door slam and someone shouting in the next room, which was Jack's room. Moments later his own door burst open. Sandro.

They rushed to Jack, disoriented by the dogs jumping in the doorway and at the foot of his bed. He tried to speak but all that came out was wheezing. He couldn't get enough air to form a word. There was panic in his eyes. The lid of his right eye had gone slack. His sheets were drenched in sweat.

"What's happening?" Frank asked.

"I don't know!" said Sandro. "I came in to check on him. I find him like this. Worse than the first night. He doesn't respond."

"We have to get him to a hospital."

"I called Dr. Vassallo," said Sandro.

"Jack said he's a quack."

"He is not a quack!"

Jack closed his eyes. When they touched his arm to rouse him, it was stiff as a block of wood.

"I'm taking him to the hospital," said Frank.

They wrapped him in a dry sheet and a blanket. His legs were as wooden as his arms. They lifted him off the bed and slung him over Sandro's shoulder. He carried him out the front door and across the street to Frank's car. They laid him in the backseat. The dogs chased them when they sped down Via Baldissera. Jack's legs shook violently and kicked the back of Frank's seat. Sandro didn't know the way to the hospital. They had to stop and ask an old man on Viale Galliano. He pointed them in the opposite direction. "You grew up in this fucking place," said Frank, swerving the car around. "You don't know fuck-all about anything!"

"I'm sorry, I'm sorry," Sandro said. He got on his knees and turned in his seat to face backward. He watched Jack as Frank drove, one hand on the headrest, the other gripping Jack's wrist. "His *impulso* is very high," he said.

Eventually, Frank spotted the cross on the roof of the little hospital. He pulled up to the front, parked between two ambulances, and two nuns appeared. They helped get Jack inside. His arms and legs were useless. His body, red and blistered and stinking with sweat, had grown very heavy.

A nurse wheeled Jack on a stretcher down a long hall. Someone used the word *coma*. It was the same word in Italian as in English. They were asked a lot of questions as they waited for a doctor to emerge from the hall. Sandro claimed to be Jack's physician, a good friend of his family. Who Frank was didn't matter; he stood off to the side, listening. There was no one else in the waiting room. The nurses seemed happy to have Frank to talk to.

The doctor came out and declared Jack dehydrated but, otherwise, in no immediate danger. The sun had poisoned him, he said, but it would not kill him. They were filling him with fluids. They had a way to ease his breathing. They'd keep an eye on him and monitor his blood pressure and his oxygen and they had no doubt he'd wake up any minute. Jack was an American citizen, Sandro told him, an important one. The doctor replied that everyone who came into the hospital was important, no matter what country they came from. Still, they put a call through to the American consulate in Florence to inform them of the situation.

"Should I see if there's something Tenn can do?" Frank asked.

"Like what?"

Frank couldn't think of anything.

Sandro repeated the doctor's words, "He will wake up any minute," and so they waited. One hour, then two at the foot of Jack's bed brought no change. The day wore on. Nurses came in and out, throwing around the word *coma* as casually as his name.

Frank drove back to the house to get Jack some clean clothes and to find Mr. Moon. Marika was in the kitchen chopping onions. When he told her, in his best Italian, what had happened, she shrieked, steadied herself with the help of the counter, and then went back to the onions. "He is not a healthy man," she said. "He should go back to America and leave poor Signor Nencini alone." She turned to face Frank, holding up the knife. "You know, it's because of him that Signor is that way—" She shook her head. "Before he showed up—"

"Where are the dogs?"

She hadn't seen them. When she arrived, she said, she found the front door wide open letting in the flies.

Frank went to Jack's closet, took out a pair of pants, a long-sleeved shirt, and a clean pair of briefs, folded them neatly, and set them on the desk to take with him. The room smelled rancid. He opened the windows and stripped the sheets from the bed. "Wash these," he said to Marika, gruffly, and tossed the sheets on the kitchen floor on his way into the garden.

"Did anyone call?" he asked, from the doorway.

Marika said that no one ever calls.

It was then he saw the blood on the flagstones. "What happened here?" he called back to her.

She came out, wiping her hands on her apron. "This is from Signor Burns?" she asked.

"No," said Frank. "He wasn't bleeding. We didn't even come out this way."

They followed the trail of blood to the side of the house, where it stopped among the weeds. They retraced it back into the house through the kitchen. There were small smears in the corner beyond the table that Marika somehow hadn't noticed. There were little spots in the hall and on the rug at the foot of Jack's bed. When you're look-ing for blood, you see it everywhere. They followed it out the front door and looked up and down the block. In the throng of the bicycles and scooters and mothers carrying picnic baskets, it was Marika who saw, farther down the street away from the beach, the two animal shapes—one black, one brown—moving in circles under a palm tree. Frank ran toward them.

Lucky was fighting Mr. Moon for the small white bird in his mouth. It was from his right hind paw, which he kept raised as he limped and lunged at Mr. Moon, that the blood had dripped. Frank and Marika looked on impotently as he whimpered and growled and butted Mr. Moon's head with his. Finally, he managed to tear half of the dried-out bird from Mr. Moon's teeth, and the two retired to their separate sides of the tree, a carpet of white feathers and bird guts between them.

"*Che schifo,*" said Marika, wrinkling her nose.

Frank pointed to Lucky's paw. "Jack's whiskey glass," he said. "You didn't get all the pieces."

"*O Dio!*" she said. "Even the dog he makes suffer!"

She carried Lucky back to the house as Mr. Moon trotted beside Frank, tail wagging in triumph. The glass was still wedged deep in Lucky's paw. He wouldn't let Marika or Frank touch it without whelping and kicking. They needed Sandro.

It was after two when Frank arrived back at the hospital with Jack's clothes; a pair of his shoes and ankle socks; Percy Bysshe Shelley's *Poems and Lyrics,* which he'd spotted on his nightstand; and four *panini* wrapped in wax paper. Marika had insisted on making the sandwiches of prosciutto and cheese with extra tomatoes and pepper, the way Sandro liked them. She would not leave the house, she'd said, until they returned; she'd clean up all the blood and air out the rooms and sit with Lucky until he calmed down. She was more worried about the dog than she was about Signor Burns because, according to her, "*L'erba cattiva non muore mai.*"

Her words gave Frank a kind of comfort. *Bad grass never dies.* She was right that it kept growing back, thicker and tougher than before. This is what he was thinking, with vague hope, as he again watched Jack's shallow breaths. The past few hours had not changed his condition. The doctor no longer spoke with the same confidence. Multiple times he used the words *colpo apoplettico,* which Frank needed Sandro to translate.

"Stroke," he said. He paced up and down the narrow space between Jack's bed and the windowless wall, his hands on his head. While

Frank was gone, he'd called a brain specialist in Volterra, a family friend, an expert in the field. Volterra was only one hour's drive. He should have called him three days ago, he said, instead of that quack Vassallo.

"You told me Vassallo wasn't a quack," said Frank.

"He's not!" His face went red. Then he began to cry. "I did everything wrong."

Frank tried to convince him he'd done the best he could, but, as he searched for words of reassurance, he wasn't sure how true they were. He thought of the cloudy water in the glass, the sailing trip Sandro insisted on despite the conditions, the wrong turn on the way to the hospital. Floria. The bump on the right temple. If Tenn were in Jack's condition, Frank would have caught up to him before he jumped into the ocean yesterday. He would have dived in after him. He would have never lost sight of him. He remembered the fear in Jack's voice when he'd called him in Rome three days ago, and the hatred he expressed so matter-of-factly for the man now standing over his bed. What was Sandro really doing in his room in the middle of the night? Was anyone ever who he said he was?

"Should I write to the mother?" Sandro asked. "She is the only one who matters to him."

They decided that they should wait for the specialist to offer his assessment first, that by the time the cable reached Mrs. Burns in Andover, Jack would be much improved and she would have worried for nothing. It would be up to Jack to write to her, as he did regularly, and describe, in his own words, his harrowing days and nights, his miraculous recovery.

Who knows, Frank told Sandro, this episode might work its way into Jack's next book. To pass the time, he told him of Baron de Charlus's pale yellow suit in *Camino Real*, which Frank had spotted on an old dandy mincing down Hudson Street, then pointed out to Tenn.

The body of Alvaro Mangiacavallo in *The Rose Tattoo*? That was Frank's horse body, muscle for muscle, down to the giant head and broad shoulders. That first name itself, Alvaro? He was Frank's lover of many summers, yes, Sandro knew that already, but he was also Tenn's gesture of permission, of understanding, of forgiveness.

To all of this Sandro responded, with quiet defeat, that he had yet to see a single trace of himself in the words Jack had published.

They ate their *panini* in distracted silence, the juice from the tomatoes dripping onto their laps, each tick of the wall clock on the half hour like the breaking of bad news. Then, just after five, Jack stirred. His first movement since they'd brought him in. They stood and shouted for the doctor, for the nurse, for anyone. Sandro took Jack's hand and squeezed it as they waited, saying his name over and over, calling him back to him. Jack did not respond. His face was pale, all his Indian color suddenly gone. His legs jerked forward. He threw his head back against the pillow. His eyes popped open, as if from a terrible dream, but he didn't seem to see Sandro and Frank, though they were inches from his face, assuring him he was going to be just fine. This all happened in the same terrible moment. He threw his head back again and, when he did, a yellow-gray foam, thick as snot, oozed from between his lips. Frank gasped. Sandro stuffed his hand in Jack's mouth to hold his tongue down. The doctor rushed in and pushed them both out of his way.

Would it have made a difference if the brain specialist from Volterra had arrived before the seizures? No one could say. What if Jack hadn't gone swimming the day before, or drunk so much liquor the past few years, or spent that extra hour in the sun? No one could say. If that nameless boy at Testa del Lupo hadn't bashed the side of his head with a rock, what then? What if Jack never stepped foot in Africa, or abandoned his home country, or chose to flood his brain with words as a way to make a living? No one could say, though Sandro kept asking. He asked the doctor, and the specialist who finally turned up, and Frank, as if the answers could change the outcome, which was that the man he loved, John Horne Burns, was dead at thirty-six. Which was that Sandro had failed to keep him alive.

Frank believed in destiny, that every moment of a life was a piece of a jigsaw puzzle, and that death was the final piece of the puzzle snapped into place. You could move all the little pieces around, try to fit them one way or another, but sooner or later, depending on your luck, they fit together in the exact way they were meant to from the moment you dumped the pieces on the table, whether or not you liked the picture they ultimately formed. Maybe this was why Frank floated from the Marines to the stage to the film set, from women to men, from man to man, from driving a truck in Jersey to ironing shirts for the greatest playwright of the twentieth century. And maybe this was why, now, he had no tears for Jack Burns. The puzzle of him had been solved—he was dead at thirty-six, a washed-up drunk—and in that solution was a kind of relief.

Once the hospital informed the American consulate, and they cabled a message to Jack's parents, and arrangements were made for Jack's body to be evaluated in Livorno and then, with due process, shipped home to Massachusetts, Sandro had no other part to play. On Jack he had no official claim. His name would never appear beside Jack's anywhere but private letters and the backs of photographs. The family, and the state, took over. Sandro stopped asking questions of the doctors, of Frank. His footsteps echoed down the halls of the hospital. He sat silently beside Frank on the fifteen-minute drive back to the bungalow. By then it was night. The piazza was loud with horns and cymbals and the jerky syncopations of jazz.

In the corner of the kitchen, on the hard ceramic floor, Marika held Lucky down as Sandro pried the glass from his paw. He poured an antiseptic into the wound and bandaged it, and then Lucky trotted away into the other room to find Mr. Moon, still holding up his hind leg but otherwise good as new. They were leaving Marina di Cecina in the morning, Sandro said. He ordered Marika to clean out the kitchen and to take the leftover food to his mother's house as soon as his cousin returned the car. In the meantime, every floor in the house was to be mopped, every wall and surface scrubbed, every sheet and towel and window washed. He didn't care if it took her all night. They would leave this place as if they'd never set foot here, and he would never return. Marika set about these tasks without complaint.

Frank couldn't bear to spend another night in that cursed house. His bag was already packed from the night before. He dragged Mr. Moon out to the front seat of the car and locked him in. He left Jack's clothes and shoes and his book of poems on his nightstand.

He found Sandro sitting at the table at the back of the garden, staring at the water. There was barely enough moon to light Frank's way to him across the uneven stones. He told the man he was damned sorry. He'd gotten a bad break. Standing over him, his hand on his shoulder, he had the simultaneous urge to embrace him and to knock him senseless. Before either urge won out, he promised to write him with their forwarding address once he and Tenn left the country.

Sandro nodded.

Frank needed one more thing to say, some way to cut through the darkness. He decided on, "Jack was a great writer," choosing, deliberately, that word—great—that had come so easily to Sandro in Portofino when describing him the night they met. "He'll live forever in his books." To Frank's mind, this put a harmless, charitable end to their brief association.

"He was a big child," Sandro replied. He shrugged off Frank's hand. "You know what he called it, that thing between his legs he never let me touch? His *pickle*. Like a little boy. It was a joke to him: us. For a man, he was all brains and no body. To take care of the dog was more easy." He stood. "What I have been thinking, sitting here alone, waiting to see how fast you would leave me, listening to the music that will go on and on, is that right now Jack is where he wants to be. And he is happy in that place to blame me for everything bad that came to him."

He did not wait for Frank to drive off. By the time Frank turned the car around, he was gone.

THE ROADS OUT OF LIVORNO were empty. Mr. Moon, curled in a ball on the seat beside Frank, began to snore. The dark mountains were lit by hotels with poolside terraces. Frank flew around the sharp curves and switchbacks, cursing the obstructed miles that stood like a punishment between him and Tenn. Until he described the gruesome scene to him—their new friend, five years younger than Tenn, just six years older than Frank, convulsing on a squeaky metal cot, blood vessels bursting in his brain, while Frank looked dumbly on—the fact of it would not touch him.

On the outskirts of Rome, he felt a custodial affection for the prostitutes who waited in the roadside parking lots in front of the dance halls and gas stations. Their shamelessness, their open transactions, were a welcome change from the hushed subterfuges of the bungalow in Marina di Cecina. If Frank pulled over and paid one of the softer girls for her valuable time—as he'd done twice last summer, when the urge, or was it the boredom, came over him—she would gladly oblige, and then, an hour or so later, they'd both be on their way, their debt to each other tidily satisfied. No Sunday trip to her schoolhouse. No promise of August in Egypt. His mood suddenly lightened. It was the honesty of Rome, of cities in general, that drew Frank to them. The beach, the country, the mountains, the saltbox suburbs of Jersey, these were fertile ground for secrets and mysteries, for gossip and petty betrayals. The city's ground was too rocky for all that. You got away with everything. Besides, you had opera tickets that night. Movie lines to go over. Some of the guys in the bar knew you by a different name.

The apartment was empty. Lamps were left on, Anja's bed was made, but Tenn's (theirs) was not. Frank pressed his ear to Paul and Ahmed's door at the end of the hall and heard silence. He walked down to Tre Scalini, and the wavy-haired bartender, Sergio, said he hadn't seen Tenn all weekend. He went from bar to bar in the Monti and then the secret bars in the narrow alleys over by the Colosseum, the ones with the dimly lit back rooms and the false doors to basement stairways, all of them shuttered or shuttering.

Tenn was nowhere and everywhere. On the walk back to Via Firenze, the men who approached Frank each took on Tenn's proportions and features: his upside-down V mustache a little bushier than Frank liked it, his rounded cheeks, the slight lean on his left hip, the swing of his right arm as he pulled a handkerchief from his blazer pocket. Frank hurried toward him. But then, as he got closer, the man transformed into someone who bore no resemblance at all to Tenn, the man Frank knew best in the world, whose face he longed to see, whose arms he longed to hold him, with growing desperation. No mustache on this guy on Via Serpenti. Sunken eyes, crooked nose. All he could offer Frank was a halfhearted leer and a last-ditch look back over his shoulder when he crossed at the next block.

Before climbing into their empty bed, Frank made it up carefully, tucking in the corners of the sheets and pulling down the quilted coverlet he wouldn't need on this humid night. He left the lamp on in the sitting room and taped a note to the wall so as not to startle Tenn if he got home before morning. He lay awake for a long time, fighting sleep because—he could admit this now—he was afraid. The fear was an unfamiliar one, without direction or shape. It gathered in his chest and hardened in his throat, like he'd swallowed a small animal and it had worked its way back up through his windpipe and got stuck there, cutting off his air. He felt he understood, for the first time in all their years together, the terror of death that Tenn claimed to feel every day, the irrational certainty that it was coming straight for him at high speed.

He sat up against the headboard, sweating through his T-shirt, stinking from the beach and the hospital and the drive and the swampy Roman streets. The muscle and bone drained from his legs, leaving them hollow and tingling. He considered driving back to the edge of the city to stay in a hotel with one of the girls. He considered waking Paul and Ahmed, but his pride didn't allow him to seek their help, and besides, what would he tell them? The blue devils have finally come for me? A man I hardly knew died before my eyes, and now I can't sleep? That was the entire story, and yet it was not the half of it. If only that shadow in the open doorway was Tenn crossing the room to throw his body on top of his in protection. If only that distant click was his key in the lock. Only then would Frank be safe.

He opened the top drawer of Tenn's dresser and thumbed through his pill bottles until he found the pinkies. If the pinkies could chase Tenn's blue devils away, they might do the same for his. He gulped one down and then, when it had no immediate effect, swallowed another. He stood there a moment, regarding himself in the mirror, waiting. The wildcat did not budge from his throat. He couldn't brave returning to the bed, where the terror had first seized him. Then suddenly the floor buckled and sloped toward the window. He slid toward it. Gripping the frame for balance, he scanned the deserted streets below, the swaying rooftop gardens, the silent dome of the Opera. Two cats ran from one end of Via Firenze to the other. Another cat shot out from an alley and overtook them with a piercing yowl. The last thing Frank remembered from that night was thinking, *At this hour, Rome is a cat's playground.*

The next morning, when Tenn found him sprawled there on the hard stone tiles, he fell to his knees, gathered him up in his arms, and kissed him into consciousness. He stuffed an upper in his mouth to pull him out of the pinkies' fog. How happy he was to see Frank, he said, how awful it must have been to watch the poor bastard die. Everything would be better, he said, now that they were reunited. The nightingales sang sweetly that morning, as if to banish death itself, because, no matter what his state, no matter how violent the storms had been, the return of the Little Horse always brought Tenn joy. Every man had one superb talent, one unique purpose. Frank's was to bring joy. Why else had he kept staring at chairs in Marina di Cecina, wishing for Tenn to appear in them, if not so he could offer him joy?

And yet Frank believed now, after almost a decade turning it over in his head, that this morning in Rome was the first hour of their long and fateful end. The sight of Frank passed out on the tiles after having "ransacked" his drawer of pills—it gave Tenn the germ of an answer, however wrongheaded and paranoid, for why, in the months and years that immediately followed, Frank grew moody and cold and started drinking and smoking more than he had ever done, for why he stayed in Key West, for why he seemed thinner, quieter, adrift. It gave Tenn all the reason he needed to watch Frank more closely, to study his moods, and because Tenn saw himself in these moods, he recoiled from them. Tenn was always looking for trouble, whether in his own body—his digestion, his heart, his white blood cell count—or in the ways the people around him, his friends and family and lovers, treated each other, how they loved with anger and fought with tenderness and conned their souls into submission. Something was always wrong. Something was always about to go wrong. Something that seemed right couldn't possibly be *all* right. The tunnel in which Tenn lived was cluttered with calamities and ailments and heartbreaks strung to-gether with the colored lights of poetry. For light and comedy and music, for the fleeting uncomplicated joys of desire and laughter, he had always turned to Frank. And when Frank could no longer offer these, he pushed him away.

The night Jack Burns died gave Frank an answer, too, the one he'd long been after, the one all his hours of introspection had been de-signed for. It had come just before he'd left Villino Brunella, when he stood beside Sandro in the garden, his hand lying on his shoulder in a feeble attempt at comfort, just before the man bitterly shrugged it off. Like most long-sought answers, this one was the most obvious. The answer followed him over the narrow mountain roads out of Livorno, past the gaping mouths of the *puttane*, into the apartment he'd burst through in hopes of surprising Tenn. It followed him from there to Bakers Lane and to the cancer ward at Memorial. Frank had been wrong about joy. As purposes went, joy was, at best, incomplete. Frank Merlo was not here on earth just to bring joy to the great Tennessee Williams.

He was here to keep him alive.

12.

HIM

The Fredrik A. Blomgren Theater opened in Malmö fifteen years ago today, the eighteenth of December, the anniversary of his death. Though Anja is not in the habit of tracking such milestones, she cannot ignore the date on her plane ticket to Provincetown. She must have noticed when her travel agent arranged the trip that it fell on this day—in fact, that is likely why she agreed to it—but the significance of the date does not register until the woman at the security checkpoint hands the ticket back to her.

She passes the flight rebuking the familiarity of the view from her tiny window. She has never seen the coastline of Sweden from the air, but surely it must be identical to these snow-tipped houses and icy harbors ringed with trawlers. If Anja were the sentimental type, she would search the frozen towns for the illuminated glass atrium of the Blomgren Theater, which today, at this very moment, four thousand miles to the north and east, hosts its annual birthday celebration. Instead she pulls down the shade. She takes out the paperback of *Something Cloudy, Something Clear*, which, though slim, she has struggled to read a second time. The bookmark is a slip of paper with the name, address and phone number of a different theater, of sorts, one much more intimate than her father's, where she will be taken upon her arrival in Provincetown.

Anja wrote the large checks that funded the construction of the FAB—as the Blomgren Theater has become known—the hiring of its staff, and its first five deliberately eclectic seasons of opera, Scandinavian folk music, satirical comedies, French farces, and children's educational programming. Only performances that her father loved or would have loved. No Strindberg, Shakespeare, ballet, or solo piano recitals, none of which, to Anja's recollection, meant much to him. The director dutifully mails Anja biannual reports that include audited budgets, glossy photos from recent shows, patron testimonials, handwritten letters from local government officials, and proposals for future productions. Anja participates remotely in administrative meetings once conducted by phone, now on Skype, so that the director can walk her virtually up and down the aisles, showing off the additions and renovations, the bright faces of the little girls and boys learning to sing.

Anja's cheery reaction to the children is for the director's benefit. At the sight of the teenagers in the studio classrooms, though, Anja must avert her eyes. No, she says politely, she would not like to speak to Lina—*a prodigy if we ever saw one! She reminds everyone of you!*—to accept her gratitude. She would prefer to proceed with the business at hand. With the help of the city and other private donors, the FAB has reached a point of healthy financial sustainability, and, when Anja dies, its endowment will skyrocket. Lina will have a home on its grand stage for as long as she pleases.

"It's an honor," says Keith, when he greets Anja at the terminal. He holds a bouquet of pink winter tulips. "May I give you a hug?" he asks, his sizable arms already around her, the flowers crushed between

them, his abrasive shaved head grazing her temple. "We're ten minutes max by car. Or did you want to stop at your hotel first?"

"I'm not staying the night."

"Oh right, I'm sorry. You're not on vacation!"

Her small satchel contains only the two plays, a notebook, a half-
drunk bottle of lemon water, and the red hat and gloves she bought at
the end of the previous winter. She puts them on as she steps outside
and Keith leads her to his car.

"I can't believe you've never been to P-town!" he's saying. "It's a
place of pure magic, especially in the winter. Totally quiet. No tourists. The real people stay on year-round: the artists, the poets, the
Portuguese fishermen. It's the only true community I've ever known."
He points through the windshield at the tall tower that dominates the
landscape. "You see the monument? That stack of bricks has guided
misfits here for a hundred years. And the light! If we have time, I'll
drive you to Herring Cove for the sunset. You can't leave here without
seeing the light."

The road is bumpy and empty and surrounded by windswept dunes
and wild brush glittering with ice. Snow narrows it on both sides.
They are halfway to their destination before they pass another car,
and when they do, the old man behind the wheel waves at Keith and
gives Anja a curious stare. "Don't worry," he says. "Nobody knows
you're here. It's *killing* me, believe me, not to tell, but if I fu—if I mess
this up, I'll never forgive myself."

"You can say fuck," she says. "I am not a nun."

"Of course not," he says. "I'm sorry. Fuck, I fucked up already."

She laughs.

"All day I kept telling myself, 'be professional, Keith, just *be professional*.' But this whole thing is so intense. Not just the play, but you
directing it, and at the A-House of all random places. You're not just
teasing us, are you? You think it's really going to happen?"

"Against my better judgment," she says.

The place is not at all random, she explains. Tennessee Williams and Frank Merlo saw each other for the first time on the porch sometime in the late forties. A one-night stand that lasted fifteen years—or sixteen, or fourteen, depending on who told the story. Depending on how you defined "lasted."

Keith claims to know this bit of history, both from *Memoirs*, which he "swallowed whole" the year it came out, and from his new friends Sandro and Trevor. After numerous phone calls and emails, they showed up at his doorstep three months ago, the day after Anja received the permission to produce *Call It Joy* from the University of the South.

They turn onto what Keith calls the main drag, which consists of one souvenir shop and bar and theater and restaurant smashed up against another. Though most of the businesses are closed for the off-season, wreaths and white lights and red bows decorate the doors and windows. A display of giant gift-wrapped presents in rainbow colors occupies the main square.

"Frank liked it here," Anja says. "What he didn't like, I remember, was that there was no opera. He wanted to come back one day, but he never made it. As far as I know."

"I can ask around," says Keith. "The old queens in this town know all the gossip. They're basically living history."

"Like me," Anja says.

"No, I didn't mean that!" he says. "I'm sorry!" He parks the car on the edge of a snowbank and turns to her. "Really, you don't even look that old, especially up close. Oh my gosh, that came out wrong, too. I'm usually better at this."

"Please try to relax," she says. "You are making me nervous, and I am not a nervous person."

"I'm so sorry," he says again.

He guides her on foot around the corner, down a narrow street, and there, to her left, is the porch with the white posts, no more than fifty feet wide, next to the sign for the Atlantic House Bar. She gazes at it a moment before taking the two wide steps up onto it, gripping the post for balance. Without this little porch, Anja Blomgren would exist, but Anja Bloom would not. If Tennessee and Frank had never seen each other across these planks of wobbly wood—was it here? was it over there?—they would not have traveled through Italy together, and they would not have taken her to Testa del Lupo, and she would not have run away with them, seeking their protection, and if none of those things had happened, who would she be?

"One thing I've always wondered," says Keith, thumbing through his ring of keys for the one to the locked front door. "If you don't mind me asking—"

"Why did I stop making films?"

"No," he says, with a smile. "Well, *yes*, but I feel like everyone knows that. If by some miracle I got to be somebody's muse, especially a great director like Martin Hovland, I'd never act for anybody else, either. Luckily I just do costumes now." He pushes the door open and switches on the lights, revealing a cramped windowless barroom with low ceilings and wood-slatted walls adorned with nets and buoys and ship wheels and other nautical flourishes. She walks through it, testing the sight lines. "It's freezing in here, I know," says Keith. "We're only open on weekends this time of year. And pay no attention to the stale beer smell; it goes away once the cleaners come."

Though the space is larger than its exterior suggests, she doubts the assurance of the new owner, Sally, that it can "easily" accommodate an audience of two hundred. "That would need to serve as one half of the stage," she says, pointing to the large bar and row of stools that take up the left side of the main room. "The other half would go beside it. No other configuration is possible."

"I'm sure that'll work," says Keith. "Sally told me, 'Give Anja Bloom whatever she wants. Tell her we'll knock down walls if that's what it takes. Just make it happen.' If her sister didn't up and die this week, she'd be here instead of me. And I'm telling you, she considered skipping the funeral."

After years of wrangling, Sally has recently purchased the Atlantic House and vows to return it to its former glory, the days when it hosted the likes of Ella Fitzgerald and Billie Holiday, back when it appealed to patrons other than shirtless men and bachelorette parties. What better way to usher in the new era, wrote Sally in her letter, than with this astonishingly original and groundbreaking buried treasure of a play from the greatest American playwright of the twentieth century, starring and directed by one of its finest actresses?

"The space is far from ideal," Anja says. She notes the tacky stained-glass window in the far corner. She reaches up to run her hand along a large wooden oar hanging inexplicably from the ceiling. "But it does have meaning."

"Oh, we've got meaning up the wazoo," Keith says, and leads her through another door to show her the framed photo of a young Tennessee striding naked across the beach. "We didn't just hang that because you were checking the place out. It's been in that spot as long as I've been coming. It's like he's been here the whole time waiting for you. Anybody can put on a play in an actual theater. This place takes *imagination*."

The FAB seats two hundred and ninety-nine guests, Anja tells him, in eighteen rows of plush fixed seats. Its cedar proscenium stage spans forty by thirty-six feet across, complete with a classic red velvet curtain and state-of-the-art soundboard and his-and-hers dressing rooms. The entire Atlantic House bar could fit in its wings alone.

"Oh," he says, deflated. "Are you trying to decide between your own theater and here? Because that's like apples and oranges."

"No," she says. Then, "I don't think so." Then, definitively, "No. But it is on my mind. The FAB has meaning, too. Of a different sort. I built it, but—this will sound strange—I have never seen it in person." She walks over to the bar. "Do these work? I am craving a beer."

"You fit right in," says Keith. He gets behind the bar and pulls the darkest draft they have, one for her and then one for himself.

"You were going to ask me something," she says.

The beer is pleasantly warm, fortifying. The foam tickles her lips. When she turns to scan the room from what would be Tenn's spot at Gisele's Bar, the stool squeaks. She sees the audience elbow to elbow in folding chairs, their faces eager and trustful. The air is rich with roses. Has she grown sentimental? This is no place to mount the forgotten final play of Tennessee Williams, even with its warts. This is no place for the return of Anja Bloom. Worst of all, it is no place to bring Frank back to, Frank who loved the finer things, Frank of the grand dreams. The idea is too romantic, the corruptive influence of Sandrino, of Trevor. She must fight it. She must come to her senses. She will. It is not too late.

"Oh," says Keith. "Never mind my question. It's probably not appropriate."

"You want to know if I'm happy," she offers.

"Aha!" he says, playfully. "Wrong again. Who believes in happiness after forty? No. I may be a star-fucker, but the life choices of celebrities don't actually interest me. The thing is, and this is truly embarrassing, I'm a closet filmmaker. I even have a degree from Chapman, not that it's done me any good. All my stuff is terrible. Anyway, Hovland—he was a genius, no question—but what I'm wondering is, didn't you ever want someone different? Just once? His work was so antirealist, so cut off from history, almost *hostile* to it, like god forbid it had a cultural correlation, god forbid you had dialogue that wasn't allegorical. But what was the allegory?"

She sits up straighter on the stool.

He puts his hands up, as if in surrender, for emphasis. "I'm saying this as a huge Hovland fan. Really! I own the entire Criterion Collection. I've seen you die a horrible death in every single movie. This professor at Chapman—I hope you don't mind me saying this—she called them *snuff films*. She said Hovland was either a horrible misogynist or you had a death wish, or both."

"If that's how you were taught," Anja says, "I am not surprised your films are terrible."

"Ouch," he says. "Fuck, I deserve that." He pours himself another beer. "Please, don't tell Sally I badgered you. Pretend you weren't annoyed."

"You are not badgering me," she says.

"Then, hey, between you and me and the horseshoes: did you or did you not want to cheat on Martin Hovland with another director?"

"I was loyal to him."

"But . . . ?"

She thinks a moment. "I decided at a young age on loyalty above all. Above taste, above preference, above politics. Loyalty above what every manager said was best for my career or my 'image,' neither of which ever meant a fig to me."

"Loyalty above art?"

"If it came to that, yes. But it did not."

"All that loyalty, just because Hovland discovered you?"

She looks at him. *The life choices of celebrities don't actually interest me*, he had said. He meant gossip. Freudian speculations. Taxonomies. She takes him at his word. So she says, "Yes."

"No" is equally true.

So is this, which will forever remain unspoken:

He came to her in the mornings, when her mother was asleep. Bitte was an insomniac, a word Anja did not learn until later, at her aunt's apartment in Vienna, where she was forced to share a bed with her. For the first years of her life, his was the face Anja woke to, placid and kind and delightfully creased. When he smiled, she liked to trace with her fingers the lines that radiated, leaflike, from the corners of his eyes. Some curved down into his thick red beard, others up to merge with the lines in his forehead, still others ran back behind his ear-lobes. Her father. Fredrik. Pappa. Together they passed their brief hour in the mornings, sitting drowsily across from each other at the kitchen table inventing stories about the creatures that hid in the woods behind their house and the potions and spells and tricks Anja could use to defeat them on her way to school. Mornings when school was out, or he held her back to keep him company, they retreated to the farthest corner of the house, where he taught her songs on his guitar, and put on his records of German and Italian operas, and jumped on the furniture acting the part of the Skalunda Giant or the menacing Varulv or the cross-eyed troll in their made-up plays. The loud creak of Bitte's footsteps on the stairs was their signal to stop. He rushed to greet her, and then to fix her breakfast of coffee and toast with melted butter and blackberry jam, and then to disappear again to give her peace. He worked nights making deliveries. Later, he took a second job in a warehouse. There was never enough money. If he slept, he did it in the afternoons, when Anja was at school, or, he told her, across the front seat of his little truck, the heat on, between stops. Meanwhile, Bitte took trains to Stockholm and to Copenhagen to apprentice with photographers and painters and sculptors. She was in search of her medium. The search required time and space. She rented a studio above a furniture store in the city, where she kept her expensive supplies and half-finished pieces, and where, on occasion, she brought Anja to model for her practice drawings. Once, an older man painted Anja's portrait while her mother stood crouched behind him, her hand on his thigh for balance, to watch his strokes up close. The portrait took weeks. The boredom was agony. Anja grew accustomed to scrutiny. She grew into a statue. More men came to paint and dress and sculpt her. They arranged her in Greek positions. Bitte's hand moved up their legs. Over time, the creases in her father's skin deepened, his beard lost its softness and color, his eyes their serenity. *It has become necessary to leave him behind*, Bitte told her. He was useless to them. That they loved him—which they did— did not factor. She had married him out of love, and that love had not diminished; it had merely proven wildly insufficient. *My parents were right*, Bitte said. She was rescuing Anja from a meager man. So, mother and daughter began to make their secret preparations, and all the while Pappa drove his little truck and packed and unpacked boxes in the warehouse unknowing, and all the while he melted the butter for her toast and slathered it with the blackberry jam—like a housemaid, Bitte said—and all the while he came to Anja in the mornings with his crinkling leaf face, and they listened to comedy shows on the radio. And then one night, while he was out making his deliveries, she and her mother took a taxi to the ship. They would return to visit him, Bitte promised her, but not for many years. During that time, it was important not to write him any letters. To do so would open his wounds over and over, said Bitte, and to open his wounds would be cruel. The one long letter Bitte wrote in explanation, and which Anja signed with her own hand, would be enough. Her words would not come as a surprise. He was nothing special as a man, Bitte reminded Anja, but he was not stupid and he was not blind. From the beginning of their marriage, he was aware that he could not keep her—them— forever. That is why he had transformed himself into the maid, the clown, the bumbling troll. To provide a service. To make himself necessary. To borrow time. Bitte was grateful to him, she said; she had been as loyal as could be expected; but gratitude and loyalty were reasons less sufficient than love to keep yourself planted in rocky soil.

Remember that. They would return to him someday, Bitte promised Anja again, wiping her face of tears, when they left Malmö for Paris, and once more when they left Paris for Vienna, but by the time they left Vienna for Portofino, he had driven his truck to the beach at Ribersborg and frozen to death inside it.

"And after he died?" Keith presses. "Even then, you didn't give yourself permission to play?"

"I had all the permission I needed to do anything I wanted," Anja says. "I was in no mood to play. I was grieving. I am still grieving for him."

KEITH PUSHES OPEN ANOTHER DOOR to show her, just for fun, the expansive back porch, which is covered in nearly a foot of untouched snow. Abandoned tiki torches and striped umbrellas poke up through the drifts. Sally calls him on his cellphone to check on the progress of the site visit. They will charge a fortune for the tickets, she tells them on speaker, and all the money will go into the coffers of the annual Tennessee Williams Theater Festival. Whatever build-out or restorations are required for the Atlantic House will be complete in time for the Festival next September. She has not rescued this historic shithole as a retirement plan, says Sally. She is in the business of creative placemaking. Together with the Festival, and the Fine Arts Work Center, and the Norman Mailer House, all within spitting distance, she will put the literary arts at the forefront of Provincetown's identity once again, and she is thrilled to have the legendary Anja Bloom as a partner and a thought leader and a coinvestor in this artistic renaissance.

Keith holds the barking phone face-up on his palm like a tray of cookies. Anja looks helplessly between it and him.

"You're a force, hon!" he shouts at his palm.

Already the play has gone from dim prospect to foregone conclusion, from Anja's indulgence of Sandrino (not Trevor) to the cultural reawakening of a town whose face she has yet to see up close. Anja has rarely decided quickly on matters of art. She used to keep Hovland waiting months for her responses to his scripts and treatments, needing the time to immerse herself in the world he had designed, both to interrogate it and to submit to it, so that she could come back to him fluent in its language and color, armed to refine its rhythms and contours. The only occasion on which she acted on instinct over a long process of immersion and negotiation was the construction of the FAB. The idea came to her in a dream, and by the time she woke from it, she had built Pappa a theater.

"That's spelled H-U-N, by the way," Keith says, when he hangs up on Sally. "Seriously, though, that woman is on a mission. You couldn't have appeared at a better moment in time."

"What is 'creative placemaking'?"

"Nonprofit speak. Sally's just come from running a big museum in Chicago. I'm her Gal on the Ground here. My job is to nod and fetch and make sure she doesn't step in dog shit. The new money in town treats her like a carpetbagger, but the truth is that her family's lived here for decades. Thank god she's a certified dyke, and Portuguese on top of that, and not greedy, otherwise she'd be dead in the water for staying away most of her life. Provincetown may be spitting up glitter and GHB, but the place has a soul, and so does she." He lowers his voice to a whisper. "What I can't wait for, though, are the looks on the guys' faces when they show up this summer and find out the biggest club in Gayville is now the town cultural center."

Anja needs an hour to herself, she tells him. Walking down the main street, hooded into facelessness, she peers into the houses and shops and empty restaurants. She expects dusty dioramas, sets abandoned mid-scene, but everywhere she looks there are signs of life. She is

admiring a large oil painting in the window of a darkened gallery—
three shirtless boys, heads bowed, backs taut, pulling their fishing nets
to shore, the moon the color of lemon—when a man suddenly crosses
the room behind it putting on a sweater. At the bend of a narrow side
street she looks down into a basement café filled with construction
workers hunched over their wax-paper lunches. One of the men senses
her gaze, looks up, and toasts her with his half-eaten sandwich. As she
walks past a darkened store selling homemade jewelry, up come the
blinds and on come the lights and a young woman with braided hair
flips the sign to OPEN.

Anja steps into the store for warmth and pretends to consider a
necklace of hammered pewter coins as a Christmas gift for a niece she
does not have. The two of you are close in age, she tells the young
woman behind the counter; she has been living with her for many
months, but now she is finally going back to school. New York City.
Anja wishes to give her niece an amulet, of sorts, some token to protect her from the creatures that hide in the alleyways. The young
woman laughs. She suggests pepper spray instead. She is not a city
girl, she tells Anja; she was born on the Cape and still hasn't found a
good reason to leave it. Her braids are as tight as the rope the boys in
the painting are pulling, will keep pulling forever, the nets overflowing with fish, the boys never coming to rest under the lemon moon.
She holds the necklace against her chest so that Anja can picture her
niece in it. The style is not to her own taste, Anja says, but her niece
is the whimsical type, and coins are said to bring good fortune, so yes,
she will take it.

The town cannot see Anja's face, but she can see hers. It is the face
of the girl who resembles the niece Anja will never have. Her cheeks
are round and burnt, her forehead a high wall battered by waves. Her
eyes are downcast not from shame but self-protection; look at them
straight on, and you will dive into them without permission. The girl

behind the counter wraps the tacky necklace in soft tissue paper scented with lavender. She hands Anja a flyer for a political action group she runs on Tuesday evenings above the shop. She watches Anja from the window as she descends the three slick steps. No one would believe Anja if she told them this town had a girl's face. Look how hard it is working, she thinks, to convince itself of its maleness: its shores a fist swollen at the knuckles, its tall bald monument, this street she's walking on a long throat choking as it bellows.

She meets Keith back at the Atlantic House at the appointed time. He drives her to Herring Cove to watch the sunset before her evening flight. They sit beside each other in his front seat facing the beach. She senses other cars pull up next to them in the parking lot, the drone of their engines, arms finding their way around shoulders, breath fogging the windows, but she cannot take her eyes from the burning sky, the flat slate sea. She has seen the likes of it before; she has never seen anything like it.

These days, there is nothing more simple than flying through clouds, over deep oceans, across great distances. The world is a small pond, the continents lily pads, women like her splashing from one to the other jolly as frogs. It is not as it used to be, back when there was no money and Anja was forced to rely on the largesse of obscure aunts and vague strangers, back when her obligation was to someone who was not herself. How heavy Anja was in those years after she left Malmö, dragged from station to station, shined up between arrivals and departures like silver from a velvet case. When her aunt in Vienna told her what her mother had kept hidden—that her father had died for love of them, a vagrant's death, completely unaware of Anja's miserable regret—she began to understand the power of rootlessness. No place had a claim on her. She released her remaining obligation, left her sleeping in their shared bed in the apartment in Portofino. She carried a suitcase down to the dock, stared out at the harbor much as she is staring now. Her fear of flight had turned to lust. And that is when, predictably, her men began to appear, those smashed pieces of Pappa, each offering her his version of home, until, one by one, they left her, just as she had left him.

Was it necessary for her men to ask her, as each of them did, why she never went back to Malmö? Was her resolve never to return, which hardened over the years, not a signal in itself to refrain from asking? Strange how her men were the most susceptible to the television questions. You don't want to see your theater in person? That moving memorial? That enormous stage? That moonlit atrium? The singing children? The orchestra pit? The wings? The sopranos? The elaborate sets? That heavy curtain? Those studios? Those box seats? Those handsome ushers? The catwalks? The lobby? That marquee? Your father's name—FREDRIK ALMAR BLOMGREN—in lights? How can you say you don't deserve it? How can you be serious when you say you are unfit—you, of all people, the great Anja Bloom!—to walk through the door?

13.

GABRIELE ROSSINI

When the call from Visconti did not come after many weeks—by then it was early September—Frank concocted another visit to the *Senso* set, which had moved north to Vicenza. In the meantime, Visconti had rejected all of Paul's scenes and put Tenn in charge of the revisions. *Senso* was based on the novella by Camillo Boito, but fidelity to the original was not the task for which the director needed Tennessee Williams. He needed Tenn to swell the hearts of the viewers, to infuse the dialogue with the passion of the film's soaring score, and to make the romantic drama at its core as powerful as the war in the backdrop. Frank was too superstitious to ask Tenn what exactly his part might now become with this promising development.

They'd gotten another letter from Truman, who'd just arrived in Venice on Arturo Lopez's yacht, which made the timing of a trip to nearby Vicenza not only right, but fated. No one was in a rush to see Truman, but the gossip he carried with him from Portofino was too tantalizing to resist. Frank argued that Tenn could work on the revi-

sions in the hotel, while Anja gazed upon Alida Valli and Frank hung
around the set trying to catch Visconti's eye.

Tenn agreed to this plan immediately. He'd been looking for another escape from Rome anyway, now that Anna was in Sicily and
Paul and Ahmed had moved on. He'd just sent all three acts of *Orpheus
Descending* to the typist, and was spending much of his days skulking
around the apartment consumed with shame and regret. He spoke of
the *Orpheus* draft as if it were his own shit smeared across paper, shit
that could never be spun into gold, shit that would sink his career,
which, he insisted, had died with *Streetcar* with no hope of resuscita-
tion. He was suffering from physical fits of suffocation—"air hunger,"
he called them—and Frank could do nothing to feed him or calm
him. The ends of seasons always brought on the blue devils. He
stuffed rags into the cracks of the windowpanes to keep out the sound
of the opera rehearsals; *il teatro* had switched to rehearsing the flutes,
and the bouncy notes had taken up permanent lodging in Tenn's head.
So he was happy for Frank to make some calls to Vicenza to find a
decent hotel, and then, while he was at it—why not?—to book the
Excelsior in Venice for the weekend after.

When they arrived at the ancient Vicenza hotel, Tenn had a message waiting. He looked at Frank, folded the slip of paper in half, and
stuck it in the pocket of his blazer. "Truman," he said, rolling his eyes.
"He wants to meet for dinner, but tonight I want us to dine *à deux*."

In their room on the top floor, after he set up his typewriter and
Anja was safely installed at the other end of the hall, he led Frank by
the hand out to the balcony. The room overlooked a small patio enclosed by tall cypress trees and, in the middle distance, a sky-blue
clock face on a tall brick campanile.

"What is it?" Frank asked.

Tenn pulled the slip of paper from his pocket and read it aloud.
The message was not from Truman; it was from Visconti. He wanted

Frank on the set first thing in the morning, prepared for his scene on the footpath with Alida and the washerwomen. With some last-minute revision from Tenn, the complication now fit nicely into the plot and pacing of *Senso*.

He held the letter against his chest as Frank leaned in to kiss him. "I'm so relieved," Tenn confessed. "It could have gone either way." Visconti had another actor up for the part, he explained, someone with a few credits, but Frank had the *sprezzatura* he was after. "He remembered your magnetism, your fire, from the set in Trastevere. He needs Alida to feel the temptation and the danger."

Frank drank in the words. Magnetism. Fire. *Sprezzatura*. Temptation. Danger. He fell against Tenn on the railing of the balcony, the sun setting over the tower, the gawkers on the patio hissing up at them with their beaten eyes. When Anja knocked on their door soon after, they went quiet and still on the creaky bed until her footsteps trailed off down the hall.

Hours later, Frank went in search of her. He and Tenn had run the lines—sixteen between them—again and again, but he wanted the rehearsal to go on, with Anja as his sparring partner. She didn't answer her door. The innkeeper hadn't seen her go out. Up and down the Contrà Cavour, Frank peered into the shops and bars, the clock tower everywhere he turned like a guide, a promise, an admonishment. The streets were glazed and shiny. Had it rained? He found Anja sitting alone in the window of an empty trattoria. For a moment he stood beside a streetlamp. She tore a chunk of bread into pieces she didn't eat. She sat tall against the chair, staring straight ahead at the blankness of the opposite wall. If Frank didn't know her, he'd take her for a bored child waiting on her father to pay their bill, sneaking sips of wine from the glass left behind on the table.

Frank needed the distraction of her. Her reassurance. Here he was on the last night of his life as he knew it, and she alone understood how it felt to have the future open up before you in the exact way you both orchestrated and feared. What if Visconti laughed at him? What if he discovered in him a great talent? What if film after film pulled him apart from Tenn? How could Frank watch over him if he was off on his own?

Anja turned to him. She must have sensed his gaze of questions. When she recognized him, standing in the spotlight with his hands deep in his pockets, a girlish smile broke out across her face, and she beckoned him in.

Frank hadn't eaten since they'd left Rome. The trattoria was about to close, but they fixed him a plate of pasta and brought him a carafe of dark red wine. As he ate and drank, and the wine and Anja's company worked their soothing effects, she read over the scene Tenn had just hastily rewritten for him and Alida Valli.

"It's not much," he said, embarrassed, suddenly, by the flimsiness of the lines, the two onionskin pages so precious and fine they could float out the window on a breath of air. And yet these scant few lines contained more words than Frank Merlo had ever spoken on film.

Anja set the pages aside. Then her face went dark, fretful, as if she'd just been told very bad news. She folded her hands on the table.

"Anja?"

She looked up. *"What is it?"* she said, sharply. She stood, knocking over the chair, and pointed toward the back of the restaurant at the waiter, who was wiping down tables. *"Can't you see there's a fire?"*

"Oh God," Frank said. "We're doing this now." He wiped his mouth. "Give me a second." He tossed the napkin on the floor and got to his feet. Addressing Countess Livia Serpieri he said, *"Your friend, in the granary, he's not safe."* He said the line as menacingly as he could muster, as Tenn had instructed him, with the faintest of undercurrents of tenderness in the word "friend."

A flash of panic flew across Anja's—Livia's—face. Then, her fear masked by defiant confusion, she said, *"I don't know who you could be referring to, Signor. I have no friends here. Only servants."*

"I thought you might want to know where the little mouse ran off to," said Frank, with mock nonchalance. Tenn had given his character a name: Gabriele Rossini. It was Gabriele Rossini he was trying to become.

"What do you want from me?" Livia asked, through clenched teeth, whispering so that the washerwomen couldn't hear.

The waiter had stopped his cleaning to behold this strange interaction. He stood with his hand on his hip and his eyes fixed on their little performance. Frank could see him out of the corner of his eye, and even this audience of one, the young man's head cocked in bemusement, thrilled him. Distracted him. What would it be like tomorrow, when Visconti switched on the camera? What if it rained? What if the light was wrong?

"You already memorized this?" Frank asked. "It took you two minutes?"

"Memorized what?" said Anja, refusing to break character. "Are you mad, young man?" She clenched her teeth again. "You talked of a mouse in the granary, and I asked you, Signor, *what do you want from me?*"

Then Frank couldn't help it—those flared nostrils of hers, her awkward improvisation, the waiter calling the cook out from the kitchen to watch them—he started to laugh. Livia narrowed her eyes at him, wrathfully. She pushed the table aside. Now was not the time for horsing around. She needed him to be serious.

Frank covered his face with his hands for composure. When he

removed them, he made his best effort to regard Livia Serpieri with
the lasciviousness the moment required. It was time for Gabriele Rossini to exploit the Countess's wantonness, to put her in her rightful
place. But again, his body convulsed in laughter, and this time Anja's
did, too.

"Frank!" she whined, throwing up her hands, rather like an Italian, like Alida Valli would have done if this were the set and not
the window of an empty trattoria on a rainy night in Vicenza. Anja
couldn't stop smiling. She couldn't resist him, she said. That look on
his face, like a boy who'd eaten too much chocolate. It was too funny
for her to imagine Frank as anyone but Frank. "It is not your fault,"
she said. "Still—are we here to practice or are we here to joke
around?"

"I want to practice," he said.

"Good boy," she said.

Earlier, with Tenn, Frank had gone stiff and anxious and breath-
less. He kept forgetting the lines. He'd needed the pages in front of
him as they maneuvered around the twin beds in their hotel room.
The words knocked around in his head in a jumble; they couldn't
make their way to his body. The words came easier with Anja, but no
matter how many times they acted out the scene, he couldn't keep
from laughing, even after the waiter lost interest and went back to his
cleaning.

"Could this mean I'm ready?" Frank asked, hopefully.

"No," said Anja. He'd still not convinced her he was Gabriele. He
shouldn't need a costume.

"The costume will help, though, right?"

"Maybe," she said.

The waiter started going from table to table, blowing out the
candles. Frank and Anja stepped out onto Cavour. She took his arm as

they walked back. In front of the hotel, in the middle of the empty street, she stopped and turned to him. *"What is it?"* she began again.

This time, he was ready for her.

At the end, she said, "Bravo!" and clapped, which sent off a scatter of pigeons.

He bowed.

"Try this trick," Anja said. "When you say those lines to Alida tomorrow—today—pretend you are speaking to me. Pretend you are in this street, with no one around but me and the birds."

"Grazie, maestra," he said, and bowed again.

In the hallway, at the door of his room, he kissed her good night on both cheeks and turned away, but for a moment she lingered, and he thought she might start up the lines again, one last time, but instead she stood there with her head bowed and her hands clasped behind her back, not moving and not speaking, like a girl he'd taken to a movie and walked gallantly to her parents' front porch, and who was now expecting more.

"Is something wrong?" he asked.

"Of course not," she said, the brief spell breaking. "To leave your company, it is just—always difficult." And she walked away.

At four a.m., Tenn came out to the balcony, where Frank lay awake in his chair. "Oh, Frankie," he said, his arms folded, shivering. "You didn't sleep at all?"

Tenn sat beside him in his bathrobe, his hand on Frank's naked thigh, as the sky lightened. It was chilly, but he'd been too lazy and agitated to search the room for a blanket. Now he crawled onto Tenn's lap and curled in on himself and he let Tenn cover him with his soft robe. The chair squeaked and strained under their weight.

"We're getting too old and fat for this kind of thing," Tenn said, holding him more tightly as the sky turned flamingo pink.

After a while, he led Frank by the hand to his bed. He wanted to get some work done. Frank lay under the covers watching him at his desk, and only then, to the soothing familiarity of his tapping fingers, could he finally catch a few hours of sleep.

THE DAY WAS BRIGHT AND WARM. They drove the twenty miles north to Villa Godi, the sprawling Palladian palazzo where Visconti had assembled his crew. He offered a halfhearted wave as Frank, Tenn, and Anja crossed the great lawn. They waited in one of the courtyards, drinking coffee from small metal thermoses. Frank stood at the table of pastries, nervously gorging himself, one eye on the movements of the cameramen, the other on his shaking right leg. Where was Alida? Would Farley be here, too? His lips were oily from the buttery *cornetti*. There were no napkins. He wiped his mouth on his sleeve. He went over the lines again in his head. Visconti shouted something at a cameraman. In place of lights, they'd arranged large metallic shades on movable posts. Soldiers milled around in their uniforms, scratching their balls and attaching and reattaching the chinstraps of their helmets. Tenn lit a cigarette. Frank smoked three. When would he be fitted into his costume? Anja pinched his side, and he jumped.

Truman arrived in a baggy white sweater that swallowed his tiny frame and a polka-dot scarf tied around his neck in a flouncy knot. What a queen, Frank thought. He stood taller and squared his shoulders. Today he was the bold brutish seducer of a countess. He gave Truman swift awkward kisses on both cheeks, nearly knocking off his thick glasses. The four of them sat together on wicker chairs at the base of a stone column, waiting to be told something.

"The ennui of the movie set," Truman said, rolling up his sleeves to his wrists. He sipped on iced water from a long straw, both hands wrapped around the glass. Though she sat to his immediate right, he had yet to acknowledge Anja. "Hours of standing around for five minutes of action."

"Like cruising the Villa Borghese," said Tenn.

Truman's hair was lighter than it had been just a month ago in Portofino, which he blamed on the long sun-splashed August days on the decks of Lopez's yacht. He seemed incapable of speaking of much else but his trip around the Italian peninsula on *La Gaviota*, which employed a crew of twenty-six, "eight more than Visconti's got with him today." He turned to Anja. "It's a pity your mother's back with Signor Ricciardi. A billionaire homosexual can never have too many beards."

"How does she find herself?" asked Anja, feigning dispassion.

"Well fed," said Truman. He puffed out his cheeks. "Italian men prefer their wives fat and their mistresses fatter."

"Which is she?"

"She wanted to invite you to the ceremony," Truman said. "But you left no forwarding address." He waved at Alida Valli, who had just appeared on one of the terraces, but Anja didn't seem to notice her.

"It was a small affair," Truman went on, "hastily thrown together, though it's safe to say not for an improper reason." He laughed. "Ricciardi's a widower, as you must remember from the months and months you lived under his expansive roof. His first wife was a *baronessa* from the north. Lombardia, I believe. They say your mother resembles the *baronessa* in the face, if not in the fortune. It's almost noble, in a way, how he evened things out by marrying down."

"And to be so forgiving of Bitte after the sea-wolf incident," said Tenn. "This widower's heart is either very strong or very weak."

"In both cases, my mother wins," Anja said.

Truman raised his now-empty glass to her. "From where I sit, you both emerged victorious. Tenn tells me you've taken up with a dashing Danish auteur. He must be the real McCoy, or else I'd surely have heard of him. But don't worry—obscurity is a disease soon cured by mediocrity. Is there wine?"

"It's ten o'clock," said Frank, to Truman's blank stare. He added, quickly, "It's martini hour, of course!" which got the much-needed laugh.

Frank had learned early on how to keep up with the back-and-forth among Tenn's set—it was never too early to drink, it was never too late for another—but today his heart and mind and eyes were elsewhere. He watched Visconti pull a chair onto the grass under the shade of a tree and sit with the script in his lap. He watched him scribble onto the pages and shake his head and screw up his face and cross out what appeared to be entire lines with his pen. He watched Truman get up and walk over toward him, pick up a chair of his own along the way, and plant it beside him. He watched Visconti light up at the sight of the little man, then double over in laughter, then, after a few minutes, shoo him away, as if to say, enough games, I have work to do.

All that watching and waiting Frank did, from the day Paul told him he'd been written into the film to now, and yet, when his moment finally came, it caught him by surprise. It was early afternoon by then, and they'd already walked twice through the courtyard to look at the statues and fountains and the terraced gardens. They were bored and hungry, and Frank was smoking another cigarette and telling Truman what had ultimately become of Jack Burns and *Il Dottore*. Truman had read about it in the papers, of course—the death of the American author John Horne Burns was, briefly, the talk of *La Gaviota* as it rounded the coast of Sicily, he said—but he had no idea that Frank had been anywhere close to Marina di Cecina, let alone at Jack's bedside as he thrashed and frothed. "I told everyone on the yacht that he was murdered," Truman said. "And no one who'd met him registered the slightest surprise."

"Sandro didn't murder him," Frank said. "But he did kill him."

"There's a difference?" said Visconti's voice.

He greeted each of them warmly, and he even held Anja's hands in his for a moment longer to say how glad he was to see her in Vicenza. It was time for Frank to get into makeup, he said, but before that it was time for them to join him for lunch. He'd used the morning to shoot some establishing shots of the view from the steps of the palazzo, but now that Farley had shown up, and the horses had calmed down, he was ready for the new scene Tennessee had added.

The courtyard was suddenly filled with dozens of crew and actors in and out of uniform dining together at the tables. The pastries had been replaced with large bowls of pasta and fried fish and olives and cheese, vases of wildflowers expertly arranged, and bottles of water and wine. Visconti's table, the only one covered with a linen cloth, was set up in the shade beside his piles of books and papers. "You were talking of murder and killing," he said to Frank. "Not what I expected from such a sweet-faced young man."

"Frankie's inborn gallantry uniquely qualifies him to detect subterfuge in others, even at its most subtle," said Tenn. "He's convinced John Horne Burns died not from some poisonous potion the doctor mixed into his whiskey, but from—what was your diagnosis, Frankie?— *malignant neglect.*"

"In Portofino, Sandro was the picture of patience and benevolence," said Truman. "I suppose that should have made any of us suspicious."

"I witnessed it all firsthand in Livorno," Frank said, pouring himself a glass of wine.

"Tell it," Anja said to him, sensing, moments before Frank himself had, the attention the director was paying him. He'd motioned for Frank to sit beside him, after all. His chair was turned slightly toward his shaking right leg. Anja had had her moment at the Fontanone to impress her director with a story; this was his. His story did not require vampires for embellishment or misdirection; he could tell it just as it happened. But without her there to prompt him, he might have missed his chance.

Frank spoke of the garden and the trail of dog blood and of Shelley, but mostly he spoke of Sandro's incompetence: the quack from the naval base he called too soon and the specialist from Volterra he called too late and the cloudy glass on the nightstand and the forced dinners of broth and water. He spoke of Floria. Sandro was not evil, Frank said, opening his hands as if in supplication, as if he, on Sandro's behalf, were pleading for mercy. He did not even consider Sandro cruel. He was incapable of striking a blow to the head of his lover, but he could lose sight of him when he swam out to sea. He could pretend that the swelling on his lover's temple might last another day or might last the year, all the while expecting to see him again next August in Cairo and the August after that in Beirut and for many Augusts more. This was what Frank meant by killing that was not murder, by the deliberate blinding of the eye, by malignant neglect. Sandro was arrogant, he said to them. Had they ever met a doctor who wasn't? He'd convinced himself that Jack was courting death, and then ignored all evidence to the contrary so that his wish might be fulfilled.

"I found Jack at his desk writing the day he died," Frank said.

"A suicide note?" asked Anja.

"I don't think so," said Frank. "He was feeling better. Coming *back* to life. At the time, I thought, you don't write a letter to someone unless you plan to be around for the response. Now—" At this, Frank stood, the better to make his point, to hold the crowd, to show off his chest in his tight shirt to Visconti—"sitting here at a table of true artists, I'm thinking, isn't everything you write—your plays, your stories, your scripts"—he looked at each of the men in turn—"a way of reaching into the future? Of claiming it for yourself? You imagine having tomorrow to finish it. You imagine an audience reading it and watching it."

"Frankie's right," said Tenn, admiring him. "They say artists crave immortality. I say we don't give a fuck about the next life. It's this one we want more of."

"More and more!" said Truman.

"The doctor—I understand he was of a lower class than the American," said Visconti.

"Yes," Frank said. "Even to call Sandro a doctor is an exaggeration. He's more of a country catchall."

"Well, that explains everything," Visconti said, without elaborating, uninterested in talk of immortality. He stood and squeezed Frank's shoulders. "You see *quella bionda là*," he said, pointing to the young woman carrying a stepstool. "She will get you into your makeup and costume. I will collect the stars. We shoot in one hour."

THE BLONDE PUT HIM in a baggy three-piece suit: brown wool pants, maroon vest, and a long matching corduroy jacket buttoned in just one place, at the top, below a black necktie undone at the throat. A different woman handed him a tan fedora not to wear, but to carry, so that he could hold it against his heart, as if pained, as he threatened the Countess. They—these women of Visconti's crew—ministered to Frank as attentively as they had to Valli and the soldiers back in Trastevere, fussing with his collar and dabbing his cheeks with powder and even lacing his black boots. They took a step back, regarded him, took another step back, and then they came close again to adjust his cuffs and apply a gluelike substance to his brows. In the shade of the tent, Frank—Gabriele Rossini, the village merchant in his best suit—stood with his arms outstretched as the women circled him, wanting all this to go on, though he was sweating, as much from nerves as from the weight of the heavy fabric.

Soon, though, he was pushed from the shelter of the tent onto the path beside the low wall where the washerwomen stood ready to hang their laundry. There, in the sun, Alida Valli waited for him in her blue and white petticoat, carrying a parasol, a black shawl draped over her shoulders.

"*Piacere*," said Alida, absently, at Visconti's introduction. That they'd already met, and briefly exchanged pleasantries, in Trastevere, didn't matter; for stars to remember you, you had to have been of some use to them. Alida's eyes were fixed not on her costar, but on the horizon, where clouds of black smoke had begun to appear above the garden wall

Visconti and one of his assistant directors, Franco Zeffirelli, took their places behind the camera, which was set up on the grass beside the path. First Visconti peered through the lens, then he gave Zeffirelli a look, and then Zeffirelli nodded and Visconti took his place. The camera, perched on a tripod, was tall and wide as a gorilla, Visconti with his arms around its waist and his head on its shoulder as if to comfort it. He directed Tenn and Anja and Truman to sit on the far stone wall beside him with the rest of the crew, outside the range of his camera, where they watched Frank pace in anticipation of his cue to action.

Should Frank look at Tenn, crossing his legs and trying not to lock eyes with him? Should he try to catch Anja's eye, which followed Alida's every graceful glide, every girlish twirl of her parasol? Should he banter with Alida herself, or was her avoidance of him part of a code he didn't understand, a way of coming to the scene pure of association? Only Truman had the courage to meet Frank's eyes, and wave his little paw, and call out something Frank couldn't hear, just as Visconti barked his orders, and the ladies came rushing to him to dab his and Alida's sweaty faces, and the camera began to roll.

After all Frank's fussing, all his hours of practice and sleeplessness, how easy it was for him, that day on the gravel path of the Villa Godi, to disappear into the body of Gabriele Rossini. It came as naturally as if he'd never read Tenn's typed words on the onionskin pages, as if, for his entire life, the man called Gabriele Rossini had been dressed in the costume of a working-class wop from Jersey named Frank Merlo. The lines came to Frank with the same ease as they did when he asked a young woman to dance. He didn't need Anja's trick. He gazed at the frantic, beseeching face of Alida Valli and held the Countess there, on the ropes, for a delicious moment. And then he let his gaze travel, slowly, hungrily, down the length of her heaving, corseted body as he said, *"He can't stay here forever, Signora."*

"Swine!" said Livia. *"Tell me what you've done with him!"*

Gabriele folded his arms. The fire raged in the distance, behind her, as she tried to pull away. The wind was blowing the fire toward the villa. The sheets drying on the line snapped in the breeze. In moments, Livia believed, the men would discover her lover, Franz Mahler, in the granary. Gabriele could save her from ruin, but it would cost her. He was telling her how. He was a poor man of evil design, she a noblewoman who'd already debased herself. Each of them had met their match.

"When grain catches fire . . ." said Gabriele, and paused—

Already he was approaching his final line. So far, he and Alida had accomplished their scene in one take. Along the way, he'd lost awareness of who watched him, if the cameras were even still rolling, if Visconti had fallen asleep, if Tenn and Anja and Truman had jumped off the ledge. None of that would matter. This was how extinguishment felt. Maybe this was how it was for Tenn to burrow his way through the tunnel. Whatever this sensation was, this delicious rush, Frank wanted more and more and more of it. Gabriele Rossini would soon die in that fire, never to be heard from again, and Livia Serpieri, lucky, for once, and for the last time in *Senso*, would be spared. But, at this moment, neither of them knew their fate.

"It explodes."

14.

SUDDEN MOVEMENT

The house sits atop a high green ridge—the broker does not call it a cliff, though it is most certainly a cliff—and faces west over the sea. From the edge of the ridge to the private beach is a journey that requires fifty-seven stairs. When the weather allows, Anja takes the stairs slowly, gripping the reinforced handrail. She is in no hurry. The descent is a greater challenge than the climb. With each steep step she feels the deep downward pull, strong as the tide. If she does not stop herself at the landings, she will tumble all the way to the rocks, lie splintered and bleeding on the sand, and that is not how all this will end. At the bottom, she removes her shoes and all of her clothes and swims. Over the nine months she has lived here, the water temperature has yet to rise above frigid. She craves the shiver that shoots through her as she dives into the waves. One day it will be the shiver that stops her heart, and then she will simply float until the sharks devour her. That will be better.

The house occupies four thousand square feet of the ten wooded acres now deeded to her. It swallows all of the apartment furniture and leaves many empty corners and closets to spare. The broker emphasized the house's durability, openness, and innovation: the box shapes connected by glass breezeways, concrete floors and walls, exposed beams, floor-to-ceiling windows overlooking the water, the flat roof engineered to withstand more than six feet of snow. It is the roof's flatness that had given Anja pause, but then the broker explained the science behind how it could bear all that weight, and how pitched roofs were lazy and all too common in these parts and made for sloped ceilings on which she would constantly be hitting her head. Anja signed the papers on that first visit, and she moved in by the end of the month. Her one disappointment in the house is that it faces west instead of east, but there are no houses on the peninsula's eastern shore. The land there is protected. If she wants to see the sun rise over the opposite horizon, she needs to drive. On the weekends, there is a bus.

There is a little town she rarely goes into, though it pleases her to know it is there. Besides, everything can be delivered nowadays: groceries, books, films, clothes, the Arab man who untangles the knots in her back and legs and cracks her bones. When going into town is required, Ray, a hired man, takes her in his noiseless hybrid car. Ray waits in the lot outside the office of her new doctor, her new dentist, her new post office, her new colorist, whose name also happens to be Ray. It is the doctor who prescribed the Arab man, the doctor who promised the massage and chiropractic treatments would help her walk with less pain. So far, she feels no difference. He warns her about all those dangerous stairs. She should never have told him about them. She is tempting fate, says the doctor. The weather here changes in an instant.

"Do you have someone looking out for you?" he asks.

"No."

He writes down the name and number of a private nurse. "You don't want the state involved," he says. "You have no family at all?"

"No."

"No friends nearby?"

"No."

"Surely—" He stops himself.

"Surely what?"

"No . . . devoted fans?"

This she ignores.

He gives her the name of an alarm service. All it requires, he says brightly, is the wearing of a discreet necklace she can tuck into her blouse. No one will see it. The necklace detects sudden movement and impact. Once alerted, the paramedics arrive within minutes, even all the way out there. "You should consider it."

She does not consider it.

She sits on the patio watching the team of men mow the lawn and prune the trees. She pays them a sizable monthly fee to maintain the grounds. They look out for her. So do the Rays. So does the postman. So does her manager and her line producer and Sandrino, all of whom call her on Skype regularly, if at odd hours. They crane their necks to peer over her shoulder as she talks, trying to catch her in the act of something, looking for clues. They know where she lives but not how to find her.

She wants tulips in all of those beds, she says to one of the gardeners. What is spring without tulips? But the time to plant them is long past, he tells her. Summer is around the corner. They will plant the bulbs in the fall, he says, rows and rows of them, in alternating colors, just as she described.

And roses, she says.

Of course, he says; fall is also the time for roses. He asks—people are always asking—what else she wants.

15.

HIGH WATER

From Vicenza, they drove as far San Giuliano, parked the Jag in a garage, and hired a private *vaporetto* to take them directly to the Excelsior. Frank and Tenn had stayed in this same grand hotel two years ago, in the midst of one of their summer storms. Now, under clear skies, under the rainbow of Tenn's gift of *Senso*, it looked even grander. Out of superstition, Frank arranged for a suite in the southern wing, which had a view of the city, because last time they'd had a beach view in the northern wing. The nightingales had been quiet then. This year, if Frank had his way, they'd sing through the night and into the morning, and so he slipped the man at the front desk one hundred thousand lire in exchange for the invented crisis that forced Signora Blomgren to move from her original suite next door to the other side of the building.

It was a Saturday in September, and the beach was crowded. The three of them lay beside each other on orange chairs and took turns swimming and fetching *granitas* from the bar. Frank didn't remember having ever slept as soundly as he did in that chair, the sun gently painting his skin with its fine golden brushes. His arms sliced through the water with great force, his lungs filling and refilling with nourishing air. He could swim clear across the Adriatic, strap a Slav on his back, carry him back to the shores of the Lido, and still have breath to spare. As far as the eye could see (his eyes could see all the way to Russia, to California), gorgeous brown limbs surrounded him. "*Bravo, ragazzo,*" Visconti had said, only yesterday, and clapped him on the back. Frank could still feel the force of his hand on his shoulder blades. When you lived your life in triumph, it possessed your body as entirely and unshakably as guilt or shame or fear. This was better.

Anja's trip to Vicenza had not been as successful as Frank's. The evening of the *Senso* shoot, she'd declined Truman's offer to drive her to Portofino, stay with him above the Delfino for the rest of September, and make peace with her mother. She'd failed again to catch the eye of Alida Valli, who retreated into the Castello immediately after her scene on the gravel path with Frank. What she wanted more than anything, she'd told Frank, was to stroll arm in arm with him and Tenn through the streets of Venice, and so, after dinner, they fulfilled her request. Frank and Tenn wore linen suits with bright ties, Frank in a dark jacket, Tenn in beige, Anja in her Renoir dress from Gandolfo. They'd all eaten too much and needed to move their legs. They walked lazily from the dock to Piazza San Marco, where they stopped for a while to smoke and consult the useless map in search of a route to the Palazzo Gritti, which, if Frank remembered correctly, had a pleasant veranda.

"This city weighed heavily on me two years ago," Tenn said, "but it has a delicacy to it now." He ran his hand along the smooth stone as they turned onto a street so narrow it barely fit them three across. "It's that quality I love most in people and in cities," he went on. "Delicacy. Lightness. I have found it so scarcely."

In his new body, soaked in triumph, Frank understood that Tenn was referring to Key West—their home—and to him, his home. Now was the time for Frank to say that he saw those same qualities in Tenn, and that they were among the many sources of his love. But then they turned another corner and came upon a pack of tourists drunkenly weaving, lost, loud, their voices echoing up to the swirling bats, and the moment, like so many before it, passed.

Anja's hand in Frank's was delicate, childlike. She allowed him to pull her along, to point out dresses and furs and jewelry in the storefront dioramas. She told him that, as soon as they returned to Rome, she was moving into Hovland's rooms by the Colosseum. From there, he would take her to Erice, where she would stay for as many months as they could stand each other. Beyond Sicily, she said, her life was a diary of blank pages. "But I am glad to leave you," she said. "It is not that I will not miss you, or that I am not grateful. I want Hovland to leave me, too. Eventually. I need to find out if I can survive alone, without my mother, without my aunt's money, without men." She preferred to learn this while she was still young, she said. She didn't want to be one of those women who went through life in constant fear that the ice beneath her feet might suddenly give way. "What a tragedy it would be never to take that plunge," she said, "to never know how long I would last in the frigid water."

They gave up on Palazzo Gritti. On their way to Harry's Bar, they came upon Piazza San Marco again, but this time it was flooded above their ankles. A sign of luck, Frank decided. The *acqua alta* had not spilled onto the Venetian streets two summers ago. The winds had stayed calm. Now the flags in the square flapped madly in the breeze of the *scirocco*, and they were sloshing their way barefoot through the warm overblown Adriatic, their shoes and socks in their hands, their pants rolled to just below the knee, the hem of Anja's dress skimming the surface of the water as she kept it from flying up.

"Stop laughing at us!" Frank, doubled-over in laughter, shouted at the pigeons.

"They don't understand English," Anja joked.

"*Vaffunculo, piccioni,*" Frank shouted again, shaking his fists at them. "We'll eat you for breakfast!"

At Harry's Bar, they dried their feet with towels and drank *amari* for warmth and to help with their digestion. When their stomachs settled, they ordered martinis. It grew very late very fast. They watched the Aga Khan stumble out alone onto the Calle Vallaresso. The bar was filled with young men in silk shirts and gold necklaces, their hair, like Frank's, slicked back and shining. They overheard the bartender tell a disappointed old woman, her neck and ears dripping with diamonds, that she'd just missed Truman Capote by a matter of days.

"This place is where the good and bad queens of the continent go to die," Tenn said.

"It's heaven," said Frank. The last time they were here, they'd argued in the toilets before they'd ordered their first drink. They'd spent the rest of the night on opposite sides of the room, glaring at each other, daring the other to be the first to make peace. This was better.

"I need to walk some more," said Anja.

So off they went again, taking the long way around the Piazza, away from the sea, though they needed the *vaporetto* to take them back to their hotel. They were too drunk to remember to look up at the street names or to read the map or to care that they'd gotten themselves immediately lost. At this hour, the side streets were mostly empty. Gone were the cries of children, the thrash of the motorized sweepers. Gone were the women and the girls. They passed packs of boys on scooters; gondoliers stowing their boats for the night; the lone young man leaning one shoulder against the grate of a storefront, his head bowed to hide his face from the light. This man's double appeared again on the next street, and then again on the next, unless they were going in circles, in which case there he was again, the same young handsome man with his shoulder on the grate of the *pasticceria*, lifting his head at the exact moment Frank lifted his.

"Do you know about our game?" Frank asked Anja.

"Frankie, no," Tenn said.

"Don't be such a prude," he said, playfully. "Come on, let's play. It's the perfect time of night."

"What game?" Anja asked.

"The game called cruising," said Frank. "The winner is whichever one of us picks up the best-looking boy."

"That's enough, Frankie," Tenn said.

"It's the art of queens," Frank went on. He couldn't get his words out without slurring, but he was too happy, too giddy, to apologize for anything, and they had only one more night in Venice. Besides, this was a celebration. He was going to be a star. *They* were going to be stars, Frank Merlo and Anja Blomgren. Him first, then her. They'd join Tenn in his constellation, and the three of them would light up the world.

"You speak our language, don't you?" Frank asked her.

"I don't know if I do," she said. "Maybe if you point me in the direction of the *vaporetto*, I will walk on ahead, and I will see you for breakfast in the morning."

"You think *I* know how to get to the *vaporetto*?" Frank said, laughing. It was all so terribly funny. "There must be a bar open somewhere."

"I have had too much already," Anja said. "Perhaps you have, too?"

"A bar to ask *the way to* the *vaporetto*," Frank said. What a beautiful word, he thought, *vaporetto*, like little vapor, like breath. A little breath would carry them across the lagoon to their grand bed in their grand hotel, where he and Tenn and some boy of astonishing beauty would make love to the crashing of the waves, the boy in his gold necklace, Tenn with his gasping hunger, Frank between their bucking bodies gleefully extinguished.

"We go straight, then right," said Tenn, holding the map. "Toward the campanile."

The game, the first time they had played it, had been Frank's idea. Nine times out of ten, he won by a mile. Alvaro. Mario. Pierre. Walid. Names offered and forgotten in the same moment. Frank was at his most alluring when he cruised the street or the beach or the piers, those stages for his wrestler's physique, his square jaw, his legs. Oh, how the boys praised his dark eyes, his sultry mouth! Tenn did not have the same allure. When they cruised together, the boys saw only Frank. That power enlarged him. But he felt no guilt. He knew how the power shifted once they got the boys back to the apartment the hotel the house, their disappointment upon seeing what Frank had between his legs, the happy surprise of what Tenn had between his. Once they removed their clothes, Frank was the first to switch off the lamp. Then the fumbling in the dark, the anonymous limbs, the scrambling for position, and, finally, that sweet extinguishment. The power between them evened out. This was better.

"There!" said Anja. The only one paying attention, she was the first to spot the turn to the Piazza San Marco.

Too tired to remove their shoes or to roll up their pants or to look for a way around the *acqua alta*, they let the water rush over them. On the other side of the square, they found a guy willing to ferry them to the Excelsior on a private boat. He gave them towels to dry their feet and a blanket for their legs. They sat on the leather banquette, Frank in the middle with his arms around Tenn and Anja, holding them close to keep warm. Tenn fell immediately asleep. Anja was shivering. The wind had undone her hair. It lashed Frank's face as they sped across the lagoon toward the breaking sun. How would they fill this day? And the next?

"The New York Ballet is performing at the Opera," Frank said. "What do you say I get us tickets when we're back in Rome?"

"I have never seen a ballet."

"Well, then it's time," Frank said. "I used to think the ballet was a bore. Then I educated myself. I couldn't afford the shows, so I'd sweet-talk my way into City Center to watch them rehearse. Once I saw up close what those guys could do, and found out I could move like that, too—without much effort either, if you want to know the truth—all I wanted was to keep doing it."

"Your next part will be in a musical," she said.

"Wouldn't that be a gas?"

"Can you sing?"

"You tell me," Frank said, and, in his best Maria Callas, belted out "Pace, Pace, Mio Dio" until he lost his breath, and they doubled over in giggles. The driver turned and glared.

Tenn let out a snort and nuzzled closer. "Frankie," he said. "You're scaring the fish."

"Perhaps the soprano is beyond your range," said Anja.

"I've heard that before," said Frank. "Just give me a few lessons, though. I pick things up easy. We'll take them together in New York. Unless you've got a natural voice, too, on top of everything?"

"Is that your way of tricking me into singing for you?"

"Yes?"

She ran her thumb and forefinger across her lips as if to zip them shut.

That they would never see each other in New York, that this was the end and not the beginning of their nights together, was inconceivable to Frank then. They slunk down on the banquette and whispered like lovers in the back row of a movie theater, Tenn's sleeping head now in Frank's lap. Frank stroked his curls. Anja tucked the end of the blanket under his head to make a pillow on Frank's knee. She wanted to see their house on Duncan Street, she said, and Frank said yes, of course, she was welcome to visit and stay with them anytime, to sit in the shade of the banana trees and the Australian pines, but once she came all the way to

Key West, shouldn't she continue on with them to all the other light and delicate places they frequented—to New Orleans, to Provincetown, to London—and wasn't it exciting to imagine what other cities they'd meet each other in, the three of them, over the long years of their lives?

When he told her that *Senso* would likely premiere at the Venice Film Festival next September, she promised to come back for it from wherever she was in the world. She could still be in Erice with Hovland, she said, or there might be no Hovland at all. Who knows? She might be living in Venice already, working at La Fenice as a cigarette girl. She'd take a train or a boat or a plane, she'd walk barefoot if she had to, whatever it took to be in the audience on the night Frank Merlo spoke his first words on screen.

When he explained that those words—*"Your friend, in the granary, he's not safe"*—would be dubbed into Italian for the Venice premiere, and that it would take a few months, at least, before the English version with Frank's actual voice would be released in the States, Anja pouted. "It is too long to wait," she said.

"My first fan," Frank said.

"Second," said Tenn.

"I should've known you were eavesdropping," Frank said.

"How else can I find out what's really going on," said Tenn, his eyes still closed. "A cigarette girl? Where'd you get that idea?"

"Anna told me that is how Lana Turner was discovered."

"You're already discovered!" said Frank.

Anja thought a moment, her eyes fixed on the sky, which was now a dark and fuzzy pink. The stars were dwindling by the second. "Anna told me, 'It takes more than one man to make your life.'"

When they arrived at the Excelsior, the other guests were coming down the stairs in their silk robes, looking for breakfast. Frank and Tenn slept into the early afternoon, and upon waking, the nightingales sang—for them and them alone—a brief and perfect song.

They drove back to Via Firenze the next day. Anja gathered her suitcase, her dresses, the vase of Murano glass she bought with her own money—everything she owned—and loaded them into Hovland's Peugeot for the two-kilometer trip to the Colosseum. As a parting gift, Frank handed her two tickets to the ballet for Friday, the eighteenth of September, less than two weeks away, the soonest they were available. She and Hovland were to come to the apartment at six p.m., smoke the last of the kif with them, and then the quartet would walk down Via Firenze to the Opera.

"My first ballet and my first double date," Anja said. She kissed him, and then Tenn, on both cheeks, before turning again to Frank. She held him by the shoulders, looking up at him clumsily, as if to steady herself. For a moment, one foot hanging off the edge of the curb, she laid her head on his chest. She then stepped into the car, and she and Hovland sped away.

When the evening of the eighteenth came, Frank and Tenn waited in their tuxes until seven. Frank paced the hallway, cursing Hovland's cheap apartment, which he'd never seen, for not having a dedicated phone. The only way to reach them was to drive over themselves, but there was no time, and besides, it was unseemly to chase down a person you'd given a gift to, as if to enforce it, as if she owed you something for a kindness she never asked for.

At seven thirty, they walked to the Opera alone. Throughout the performance, Frank trained his eye on the guys he recognized from City Center, conjuring Anja so that he could point out for her the force of their legs, the lightness of the girls they tossed and caught, the deceptive ease of all that twirling and leaping. But the seats beside him remained stubbornly, puzzlingly, empty. The next morning, he took a taxi to Hovland's address. The landlady informed him that Signor had been gone for almost two weeks, and that, no, he'd never had a woman living with him; if he had, she'd have known about it. The place was too small even for one, she said.

By the time Frank learned what had happened to Anja—that, the morning she moved out of Via Firenze, Hovland drove them straight to Civitavecchia, where they boarded a ferry to Palermo, and then hired a car to take them up the mountain to Erice—he'd already forgiven her. He blamed her age, her sex, the ice at her core. He was still high on his triumph, immune, however briefly, to petty grievances and disappointments, to the disappearing act the girl would come to perfect after years of practice. Once you've abandoned a mother, Frank reasoned, you can abandon anyone. He missed her, but they had the Venice premiere to look forward to—the year would pass in the blink of an eye—and, in the meantime, he had work to do.

Visconti sent Tenn letters and telegrams and called him at odd hours from Verona and Mantua. He even showed up once at Via Firenze, dragging along the beleaguered Suso, author of the Italian version of the *Senso* script, as if putting yet another writer in the room was going to help matters. He'd shot more scenes all over the country, but the film was not coming together. He'd gone so far over budget that further costs, further delays, became meaningless. Frank read his letters out loud to Tenn and listened in on their conversations, trying to devise a way for Gabriele Rossini to rescue the film and make himself a hero for Visconti, but Frank's ideas, according to Tenn, were either too expensive to pull off or too minor to make a difference.

Frank arranged for short trips to Naples and Positano, where Tenn could work with fewer distractions, and where Visconti couldn't so easily track him down. The days wore on. Tenn was growing tired of the story, he said to Frank, and of Visconti's perfectionism. He began to refer to *Senso* as the "wop *Gone with the Wind*." He wanted desperately to be free of it, to devote his full energy to the drafts of what would become *Cat on a Hot Tin Roof*, to *Battle of Angels*, to anything else. Even Italy he was weary of. This mess of a film could only be solved by a change of scene, Tenn said. So, in early October, they sailed together to Spain.

In Madrid, in Málaga, Tenn worked in the hotel at all hours and Frank went out dancing. He told the boys he met that he was an actor. The name of the film dropped from his lips like a jewel. "It's like an Italian *Gone with the Wind*," he said, proudly.

"What a great idea!" they said.

By winter, they were back in Key West. To the house on Duncan Street came a long letter from Visconti, posted from Ischia. Frank read it with Mr. Moon in his lap and Tenn standing behind him, his hand on his shoulder. To understand Livia Serpieri, Visconti explained, the audience did not need further evidence of her wantonness, more foreshadowing of her dissolution. The film was already too long. For these reasons, the decision to cut the Vicenza scene, and others Tenn had written, was an easy one. He assured Tenn that the rest of his beautiful dialogue—especially the scene between Livia and Franz and the prostitute in Verona—remained intact. Those scenes were among the finest in the film. He made no mention of Frank, or of Gabriele, by name. He had no regrets to send to him or to anyone. When Tenn left the room, Frank read the letter again, but he still couldn't find himself in it.

At the world premiere of *Senso* nearly a year later, September 2, 1954, Anja was in London with Hovland and Tenn was on his way to Taormina and Frank was sitting with strangers in the back row of the crowded hall in Venice. The swooning public filled every seat and the gentlemen stood in the aisles while Visconti paced up and down the gallery, shaking hands with Rock Hudson and Scott David and the reporters asking for his comments on *Senso* and *Rear Window* and the rebirth of Italian cinema and his chances of winning the Golden Lion.

Whether or not Visconti noticed Frank, he did not approach him. Frank sank lower in his chair, ignoring the strangers to his right and left, his dry throat, his pounding chest. Anja had urged him not to go at all. He belonged in Taormina with Tenn, she said; he belonged in England with her; he belonged in Rome with Anna; he belonged anywhere but in Venice.

Frank had promised her he would not show up at the Festival, that he'd swim and write and practice the monologue she mailed him from Ostrovsky's *Diary of a Scoundrel*. Instead he booked one night at the shabbiest hotel in Santa Croce and the late train there and the early train back, and now here he was in the hall as the lights came down and the music drowned his thoughts and the crowd erupted in applause. The screen lit up with the title of the film and the crowd applauded. The names Alida Valli and Farley Granger appeared and the crowd applauded. The name Tennessee Williams appeared and the crowd applauded and, for the first and only time, Frank did, too. Then the film began, and their hands went quiet.

When Countess Livia Serpieri began to make her way down the gravel path toward the fire, the crowd did not see a young country merchant in a three-piece suit call to her and pull her aside. They did not hear their exchange, or see her pull away from him and run off. Frank watched for the flicker in the film that marked the moment he was cut, the seam that proved he had once been a part of the story. But there was no seam. The sequence was smooth. Visconti was a perfectionist, after all. The Countess ran down the path unmolested, past the washerwomen, the sheets floating like ghosts, just as they had on that day in September. How could the people around him know that a man named Gabriele Rossini stood hiding behind that high stone wall, watching her every move, waiting for his moment to strike, if they couldn't see him? In that scene, now gone forever, he'd enthralled Livia. She'd spoken his name in fear, clutching her shawl. Frank wished he had someone he could tell.

16

CALL IT JOY

F our days before the dress rehearsal, Anja arrives at the hotel in Provincetown. Her manager has chosen a place close to the commotion of the Atlantic House but secluded and expensive enough to ensure her privacy. They put her in an octagonal room called the Moroccan Tower, which they have filled with pan-African rugs and statues and tapestries. For a moment, she pretends they have done this in homage to her deathbed scene in *Runaway*, but of course this room is available to anyone with the money to pay for it.

On the drive from the Moroccan Tower to the Atlantic House, she passes under banners splashed with photos of herself and Tenn from the sixties, their young faces smiling at each other across the traffic. The actors playing Tenn and Frank/Angelo and Young Patron/Mark did not qualify for the banners. They are locals—"no-names," Keith calls them—chosen so as not to distract from the true stars: Tennessee Williams as playwright and subject, Anja Bloom as Gisele Larson and Director.

Sally waits for her on the porch of the A-House. She has proven as formidable as Keith warned. She priced the tickets for the once-in-a-lifetime show at one thousand dollars each, with the proceeds split 50/50 between the Theater Festival and the forthcoming Atlantic House Cultural Center, due to break ground next spring. To make those proceeds "meaningfully transformative" for both nonprofits, Sally convinced Anja to fund all of the play's production costs, including the salaries of the actors, set designers, and line producer. She made the tickets available only by private invitation. After their payments were confirmed, Sally emailed the guest list to Anja annotated with biographical sketches and notes on their future donor potential. She refers to the play as a "seed event." The guests are supporters of various arts organizations and other liberal causes; the president of Pieter's university; and a few politicians, including two current and former Massachusetts state senators; they are developers and socialites and media and the Swedish-born actress Ann-Margret, whose fan mail Anja still occasionally receives.

With Sally and Keith and David, the Festival director, looking on from across the dance floor of the club, Anja leads her cast in the first official table read. The set is half constructed behind them: the bed, the jukebox, the extravagant rose bush. The actors have had weeks to memorize their lines, but this is the first time they have all met in person.

Anja closes her eyes and listens to their voices and intonations, scrawling notes blind onto a legal pad. She saves the faces and the bodies for later rehearsals. Just as Tenn begins his Bangkok soliloquy, she hears the creak of the door, and in walks Sandrino with Trevor, sheepishly, from the porch. The read was scheduled for ten o'clock, and it is now past eleven. Sandrino blows her a kiss. They take their seats beside the others. She closes her eyes again.

She has not seen Sandrino since the night of the séance. She left him and the city without notice. When he heard nothing from her for weeks, he came to her apartment and found it emptied out and sold. Eventually, she mailed him a handwritten letter. Now they keep in touch the newfangled way. It breaks his heart, he says, every time he thinks of the city without her in it.

By the time Sandrino returned from Italy in September, Trevor had taken up with a married advertising executive sixteen years his senior. Trevor is currently waiting around for the man to leave his wife, and then they, too, will make a fresh start somewhere else. Sandrino feels abandoned, he tells Anja on Skype. His face on the screen is dark and grainy; he needs more lamps. He loves no one in the city quite the way he loves her and Trevor, and he still has two more years left in his program. He clings to the hope that Trevor will come to his senses. In his mind, this week in romantic Provincetown, and the debut of the play the two of them helped usher into the world, is his last chance to relight the fire.

When Mark starts serenading Tenn with "What'll I Do?" Sandrino rests his head on Trevor's perfidious shoulder. Trevor shrugs him off, and, in that moment, Anja decides the song is all wrong and must be changed. "I find 'What'll I Do?' too expository and on-target for a man mourning his lost love, do you not agree?" she asks the cast, and of course, yes, absolutely, they do agree with her. She suggests "Danny Boy" instead, "one of Tenn's favorites," and again they nod vigorously. Mark calls it a "genius move," which it is not; at best, it is a mitigating move. The men in the cast are collegial and loose and flirty with each other, but with Anja they are tentative, timid, deferential. She was hoping at least one of them would fight her, that they would guard with some fierceness the words and intentions of Tennessee Williams, whom they claim to idolize. But, for now, they go along with every one of her admittedly capricious directorial adjustments.

Her task for the rest of the day is to work with the two other leads.

To her frustration, the best Tenn can offer her is a caricature of the drawling Southern drunkard. He has educated himself with tell-all memoirs and YouTube videos of Tennessee Williams at his most dissolute. He has made the common mistake of conflating him with the blinkered and babbling Truman Capote as interviewed on *The Stanley Siegel Show*; or maybe he is doing Blanche DuBois at her most hysterical. When he chooses to cling to this interpretation despite Anja's correctives, she reminds him, sensing the first hints of his resistance, that she is the only one in this room who knew the real Tennessee Williams. The man did not hate himself, she preaches to him; he enjoyed his life, his work, his men, his fame, his starlets, his travels, his triumph over his family, his body, his wit, his money.

"But, with respect," says the actor. "That guy you're describing is not the character in the play."

"Do not be fooled," she says. "The last thing the world needs is another cartoon of Tennessee Williams. The portrait he painted of the man at Gisele's Bar is cartoon enough. It is my job to find the shadows in it. It is your job to ensure the audience can see and feel those shadows."

With young Angelo, she takes a different approach. Though he has Frank's wrestler body, his dark eyes, and even his large teeth, his version of Frank is barely distinguishable from his version of Angelo, which is barely distinguishable from himself. When she asks him, with as much patience as she can muster, "Are you acting at all?" he bursts into tears.

At the time Anja let Sally make the casting decisions, she was trying to distance herself from the production. Her only stipulation was that Sally not hire Trevor, no matter how talented or well suited he might prove, to play Mark. Now, at Sally's prodding, and Sandrino's fanciful urging, Anja is again at the play's center, and she regrets not having at least chosen her own actors. Still, she works closely with her three men through dinner, late into the night, and all the next day. They confess they are intimidated by her and by this opportunity to make names for themselves. They are aware that not a single person in the audience has paid all that money to see them. After winning the part, Mark had nightmares about forgetting his lines; Tenn upped his appointments with his acting coach and his therapist; Angelo started smoking again. Once they admit these anxieties to her, they improve. Tenn's shadows appear in flashes. When he says, "Perhaps they've got the same daddy," with all of the real Tenn's merry wickedness, even Anja manages a laugh. When Frank tells Tenn, tenderly, "I never hated you," just before the lights come down on Scene One, she forgets, briefly, that none of this is real.

Because the nights are warm, and she cannot get enough of the sea air, and the drivers are Bulgarian teenagers who have never heard of her, she takes pedicabs back and forth from the hotel to the theater. The streets are crowded with men walking in packs, or hand in hand, some with children on their shoulders. They sit on each other's laps on the ledge outside the pizza shop and greet each other with kisses on the lips. A troupe of shirtless men in high-heeled boots rides by on bicycles, their matching white boas trailing behind them like wings. The men here are not all young; many of the faces are ravaged, gray-bearded. They are not all beautiful or fragile or ashamed or threatened, but the town folds itself in on each and every one of them nonetheless, as if to shield them.

A *Boston Globe* reporter comes to the set to ask her questions she has already answered in *The New Yorker* and *The New York Times* and *Variety*. Why did she hide the play for so long? How does it feel to be back onstage? Might this be another *Streetcar*? Instead she tells the reporter about the real Frank Merlo. The truck driver who loved Maria Callas. The fifteen years of tenderness and hostility and competition and adoration and suspicion he had with Tennessee Williams, the alchemy of which produced the playwright's greatest works: *Cat on a Hot Tin Roof* yes yes, but also *The Rose Tattoo* and *Night of the Iguana* and *Orpheus Descending* and *Camino Real* and *Sweet Bird of Youth* and *Suddenly Last Summer*. All of these plays came into being during the Frankie years; nothing of consequence came after Frankie was gone. She asks the reporter—a child playing dress-up with a press pass and a recording app on her phone—if she can name a single Williams play after 1963. She cannot. Frank's story has yet to be written, Anja tells her, to which the reporter replies, "Are there any plans to make *Call It Joy* into a movie?"

Anja sends her away. The first dress rehearsal is about to start, exactly twenty-four hours before the real thing. The room has filled with roses. Keith fits her into her Gisele costume of blue jeans and silver sequins. He tries three blonde wigs of varying lengths, then settles finally on Anja's natural hair, which he teases and sprays with a stiffener as she autographs a stack of programs for his friends shut out by the unaffordable tickets. The light and sound guys knock over the bedside lamp with their cables. At Anja's insistence, the only audience permitted at the dress rehearsal are Sally, Keith, Trevor, and Sandrino.

Anja wishes for a proper curtain—swags that hang from the ceiling, tiebacks with gold tassels, a pulley—but, as the play drags on, forced and stilted, it becomes clear that the hastily sewn fabric Keith pulls across the set is the least of its problems. Tenn backslides into his cartoon. Angelo goes stiff.

When the end comes, mercifully, even the sound guy averts his eyes from Anja. Sandrino and Trevor slip out without a goodbye. Sally suggests to the cast that they try another dress rehearsal first thing in the morning, before the cleaners and the caterers and the decorators arrive to transform the club.

"Call it a matinee," says Sally, with manufactured brightness. The actors groan.

Anja refuses to do the morning dress rehearsal. The only difference between tonight's rehearsal and tomorrow morning's, she tells Sally, will be the sunlight in the windows.

She pulls Anja aside. Under her breath, she asks, "What can we do?"

They need another week, another month, a new venue, a new cast. They need a new play. "Return their money," Anja says.

"No, seriously."

"I am quite serious," says Anja. "Give me a figure—whatever amount is not recoverable—and I will write you a check."

Sally considers this. She looks out at the rows of empty chairs. She takes a few moments to decide how to respond. Perhaps she is thinking of the reporters, the live bodies of the donors, the white tablecloths and canapés, Ann-Margret. "Sleep on it," Sally says. "Who knows—the sunlight of a P-town morning may make a difference after all."

"It is plausible that I will have had a bad fall overnight," says Anja. "I am an old woman, you know."

"Let's hope it doesn't come to that."

"My offer stands," she says.

The cast is milling about by the door. For men who smell defeat, they are strangely buoyant. Perhaps they are as relieved as Anja that the entire ordeal will soon be over. Perhaps they will jump for joy when Sally tells them of the play's cancellation due to Anja's tumble down the steps of the Moroccan Tower.

They have waited around to invite her out for a nightcap. "To mark the eve of the play's historic debut," says Tenn. It is a Friday night in Provincetown, the first of the autumn, the harvest moon. He knows a quiet bar nearby with an outdoor patio and fire pits and strong cocktails.

"It's called the Shipwreck," Mark says, laughing. "Sounds about right, don't you think?"

"Bite your tongue, Twinkie," Tenn says.

"I will meet you there," Anja says. She writes down the directions on the back of a program and tucks it into the front pocket of her jeans, which are far too tight. She cannot wait to get out of them. She cannot wait to go home.

Her dressing room is one of the A-House's restrooms into which Keith has crammed a cushioned club chair and an extra mirror beside the urinal. The walls are covered in old postcards and photos of men baring their chests, spreading their legs, presenting their hairless backsides. They watch her lasciviously as she removes her makeup and ties back her starchy hair. They invite her to best-body contests in the seventies and eighties with the promise of cash prizes. She senses their disapproval as she changes out of her shiny sequined top into a cardigan sweater and plain beige skirt and sturdy shoes. She wonders how many of the men in the photos survived those awful decades. When Sally returns this room, this place, to what she calls respectability, they will be lost again.

Anja walks onto the porch, and there is Sandrino alone in the dark, leaning, ghostlike, against the railing. He is waiting for her. Everyone else has gone ahead.

"Can I walk with you?" he asks.

"Of course," she says, taking his arm. "You may escort me to my chariot. These kids work extremely hard. I tip them extravagantly. Did I tell you I am learning Bulgarian? *Dobar večher, priyatno mi e.* Good evening, nice to meet you."

"You won't need a pedicab," he says. "The Shipwreck's around the block. Do your legs hurt you again?"

"I am not going to the bar," she says. "It is too painful to face them. The poor boys, they try their best, but they are making fools of themselves. And of me. And of Tennessee! If he could see it . . ."

"Is that what you think is happening?"

"You cannot possibly disagree," she says. "The play is a disaster. Every part of it."

"I don't disagree with that," he says. "Even me, a dumb scientist, can see it does not 'come off.'"

"Thank you," she says. "I am relieved to hear the words no one else has the courage to say to me."

The pull each other closer, as they walk down chilly Commercial, which tonight is busy with weekend tourists on their postdinner promenade. Their eyes are on Sandrino, surely thinking what a kind boy he is for taking his grandmother out on the town. Her head is wrapped in a flowered silk scarf tied under her chin. One of the banners flies above them.

They sit on a bench in front of the post office so that she can scan up and down the street for a Bulgarian. *Zdravei*, she thinks. *Svoboden li si?*

"Trevor and I were having a talk," Sandrino says. He tucks his hair behind his ear. "Not about us. '*Us*'—it is finished. He is in love like never before, he tells me, straight into my face, like I will be happy to hear this news. I tell him he watches too much of the *Mad Men*, and he gets angry, his executive boyfriend is more handsome and more deep than the man on the show, he says, but it's OK. We make up and fight, make up and fight a hundred times a day. You don't approve of Trevor, I know, you never did approve, so it won't hurt either one of you to tell you what he said tonight about the play, what we talked about after the rehearsal. What he said was that the problem is not the actors or the words of Tennessee Williams. The problem—it was Trevor who said it first—is you."

Anja laughs. The pettiness of fellow actors has never surprised or bothered or thwarted her. In fact, she has Hovland and Tenn and Anna—and yes, her mother—to thank for preparing her, and suiting her with armor, for such acts of war. "And what does Sandrino say on this subject?"

He turns to her. Most men his age would not look her in the eye, but that is what he does. "What I say is that the play needs something from you, but you do not give it."

"And I suppose you and Trevor have helpfully identified that 'something' for me as well?"

Before Sandrino can respond, she mounts her case against them. She defends her hours with the cast, the months of email exchanges with the line producer and the Festival director, the site visit, the reading and rereading of Tenn's impenetrable final one-act plays. She has given everything, she asserts, but, as she speaks the words, she recognizes them as untrue.

"My father had an expression," says Sandrino. "He used to tell me, 'If you are on the dance floor, you should be dancing.' I see you in your costume on the stage behind the bar, wiping it down with a rag, I hear Tenn call you 'Gisele,' I hear you speak back to him, but you are not Gisele, you are not even there. I wonder, sitting in the audience, where did Anja Bloom go? You give this play your time, but not your faith. Not your *respect*."

This is what Sandrino wants her to consider, Sandrino who speaks in Trevor's voice: that she has not given *Call It Joy* what she and Hovland gave each other in every film, not what Tenn tried for in his lines, which was the will to make it great. When it came to art, what mattered more, the ambition or the result of that ambition?

She did not have an answer.

"You and Trevor are not the only ones who think this?" she asks him.

Again, he does not look away.

"No one spoke up. None of the actors. Not Sally. Not Keith. Not one of them has any guts."

"You are who you are," Sandrino says, matter-of-factly. "You are the great Anja Bloom! You are the director!"

"That is naïve," she says, furious with him, with all of them, with herself. "No one said a word to me because my name is on the checks."

She thinks back to her most recent conversation with Sally after the dress rehearsal, memorable now for the woman's lack of reassurance, her absence of admiration for the stamp Anja had put on the play. For all the actors' fawning over her "genius" decisions, they did not once praise her performance. She blamed their shyness and immaturity, Tenn's self-indulgent script, the rushed rehearsals. Not once did she consider her own unworthiness. It embarrasses her now, her disregard for the character of Gisele Larson, for Tenn's conception of her, for her role in his life. Anja had dismissed Gisele as a mere functionary, the grout between the tiles. Was she more?

"Hovland had his expressions, too," she tells Sandrino. "When he sensed anything other than my full commitment to a scene, he stopped the cameras and waved his arms and turned his face into a big frown. 'What a sad day it is today,' he would say to everyone on the set, 'the day ambivalence murdered Anja Bloom.' His greatest insult was to call someone 'Hamlet.' He did not tolerate the slightest ambivalence from the characters he wrote or the actors who played them. His characters and his actors were famous for their force of will and commitment and singleness of purpose." She shakes her head. "To watch a Hovland film was to watch a runaway train."

"He was a good teacher," Sandrino says.

Anja can admit this now to herself, if not to Sandrino: in the years after Hovland died, she was too cowardly to perform without him. She was afraid to act alone. She cultivated this fear. It was an easy substitute for her grief over losing him. Pieter did not try to change her mind. When, finally, Pieter had her full attention, he wanted her to stand still, to choose him. Pieter wanted her mind all to himself, and for that he required her body. He wanted to come home each night and find her there, the newspapers and journals opened before her on the table. Her fear of performing without Hovland was a dog guarding the door, holding her in, shutting out everyone but Pieter. Then Pieter died, and fear proved an insufficient substitute for the new grief that overwhelmed her. She needed something stronger than fear. Pride. Arrogance.

"There is nothing we can do now," she says to Sandrino.

"We can go to the bar," he says. "You can buy the boys a cocktail. Or we can smoke a little, all of us—it can't hurt. To make the mood lighter. To laugh. We have not been laughing enough. And you can talk, the four of you together, about Gisele. Angelo is a very good actor, we think. *I* think. He is better than Tenn. Trevor is too jealous to admit it, but it is true. Every second of the play is torture to Trevor because he is not on the stage." Sandrino shrugs. "Maybe I will have a love affair with Angelo, for spite."

"Will everyone still be at the bar?"

"Yes."

"Trevor, too?"

"No," says Sandrino. "He went to sleep."

"Wake him up," she says.

It is eight o'clock in the morning on the day of the premiere of *Call It Joy*, and the second and final dress rehearsal, hastily arranged at the Shipwreck, has come to an end. Anja unlocks the front door of the A-House to let in the grumbling cleaners, who have been waiting on the porch for them to finish. Overnight, with the cooperation of Sandrino and Trevor and the rest of the cast, she has cooked up changes in the production, of which Sally knows nothing. She will see them soon enough.

Still half drunk, and more than a little high, Keith drives her back to her hotel on his way to his apartment. They both need rest before the five o'clock hair and makeup call. When she crosses the lobby in the clothes she left in the night before, her hair unpinned, the young man at the desk gives her a conspiratorial wink.

On her back on the pink bedspread, unable to sleep, she cannot stop scripting every possible worst-case scenario: flubbed lines, boos, yawns. She longs for the mercy of an electrical fire. To distract herself from these thoughts, here in the Moroccan Tower, she goes back to the set of *Runaway* in Marrakech in 1963. She conjures the heat, the crowds, that nasty spitting camel. She sees herself in the photo on the camel taken by Hovland, the one she sent with her letter to Frank in New York, the letter he returned to her with his plea scrawled across the back—*Come now please I need you.* His last words to her.

All throughout her days here, Frank has been coming to her. On the streets of Provincetown, in her dreams, in the opera music Keith plays in the club. She looks across the porch of the Atlantic House, and there he is leaning against the wooden post, waiting for Tenn to notice him.

And why should Frank not come to her? She has brought him into the light.

She must sleep. She has been awake for nearly twenty-four hours. The lines in her face are ghastly. She is not above vanity. She lies perfectly still, careful not to disturb the maid's sculptural arrangement of the pillows. She counts the wood slats in the cupola of the Tower, the threads of fringe hanging from the rim of the shade of the chandelier. Not since she was a girl, with her mother and father in the next room, has she had such trouble calming the beat of her heart. Her impression on the bedspread is itself an imposition. How heavy she feels now. It is suddenly very important that she keep the room pristine, that she leave no trace. At this hour tomorrow, she will be home.

It is the thought of her new home, the brightness of the morning sun in her wall of windows, the sea just fifty-seven steps down, that finally gives her the peace she needs to sleep. When she wakes, it is already time to head back into town.

Backstage, Tenn paces and puffs on an electronic cigarette. Angelo sits in the corner on the floor with his eyes closed and his legs crossed and his head bobbing. She leaves them be. She stands behind the curtain for a moment, her hand on the flimsy fabric, listening to the rumble of the crowd she has yet to glimpse. Keith reports that every seat is filled. People are standing three-deep against the back wall. One hundred and thirty thousand dollars and counting, says Sally, her seed money and more, and that is before the silent auction she engineered at the last minute. Every so often, Sally's forced laugh rises above the din. She is furious with Anja, but Anja will not budge from her decision. This is good practice for your future with artists, Anja told her. If you hire them for their will and ambition, do not be surprised when they exert them.

At the appointed time, ten minutes after eight, fashionably late, the overhead lights flash. The audience bursts into applause as they scramble to their seats. Then they go quiet. Reverential. The only sound is the squeaking of the chairs and the overhead fans. As Hovland used to do on the first day of filming, Anja goes to each of the actors, one by one, takes their hands in hers, and thanks them for their work.

In her blonde wig and glittering sequined top, altered and expertly stuffed by Keith, Trevor is unrecognizable as himself and unmistakable as Gisele Lemonade, the bartender and proprietress of Key West's legendary Club Gisele. His face is pale, even under the thick foundation, pink rouge, and blue eye shadow. He is still going over his lines. When he looks up at Anja, blinking, his lashes open and close like butterfly wings. With the help of the Shipwreck's cocktails and one small hit of Angelo's pot, they reinvented Gisele together. She went from the middle-aged woman of "understated elegance" to the brash drag queen who loves and misses her brother, who wants to give Tenn some joy, who makes her living from illusion. She went from Anja Bloom's comeback to the debut of Trevor Halley. It is better.

"If you forget something, just make it up," Anja whispers to him. *Her.* "No one will know the difference."

The houselights go down, and the spotlight comes on, ready for Anja to step into it.

"You're about to disappoint a lot of people," Trevor says.

When she pushes through the curtain and steps onto the stage, dressed not as the barmaid described in the program but in a simple pink silk dress, a necklace of pewter coins, her hair arranged in a loose chignon, carrying a cordless microphone, the audience leaps to their feet. They did not expect her to greet them.

She is there, she tries to say, to explain. "Thank you," she mouths, and waves, and takes a humble bow. She holds out her hands before her to quiet the crowd, to get them to sit and listen to her announcement, but they do not sit, they do not stop clapping. They hold their phones over their heads. She takes another bow, though she has yet to do a thing to deserve it. The lights are bright. Her eyes dazzle. She can see mostly darkness. Then the lights flash again, on and off this time, strobelike. The crowd claps louder, in sync, whistling and stomping their feet, until the lights stay on, and suddenly she can see all their faces. There is Scott, all the way from New York, standing on his tiptoes in the back row. There is a woman, house right, who might be Ann-Margret. There is the university president, whom she met briefly at Pieter's memorial. There, on the aisle of the third row, is Sandrino, dressed in a suit, blowing her kisses with both hands. The empty seat beside him belongs to her. She does not recognize the other faces. She has been away for so long. She has made the world a stranger. She scans each row, looking for someone, but there is no one to look for, not him, not any one of them.

She is at the start of the next thing. She tried laziness and failed. She was no good at being alone. Can she admit now, finally, how greedily she snatched up Sandrino the day he appeared, like some starving Baba Yaga? How she courted his affection and attention, and encouraged—no, luxuriated in—his television questions? How happy she was to dab at the brown salt his boots dripped onto her rug? He is the only one in this room she trusts with her address. Even Scott sends her mail from New York to a PO Box in the town.

What comes next after arrogance? What follows pride? She has bought a house on the edge of a cliff. Shrink-wrapped boxes of milk and fruit arrive each week on her doorstep. In the spring, there will be tulips and roses. The town is a twelve-minute drive through protective miles of dunes and woods, ten acres of which belong to her. For nearly a year she has been testing the town's embrace, and, so far, it still looks upon her as kindly, girlishly, as it did on her first visit. The locals and tourists who recognize her in the café across from the post office, and the jewelry store next to the hair salon, and on the steps in front of Ray's salon, leave her mostly alone. They regard her with the same bland curiosity they have for the men in boots and boas flying by on their bicycles. She is nothing special here. Just another misfit.

Tonight's debut of *Call It Joy* is the first theater performance Anja has attended in her new town. The testing of an embrace requires care, caution. She has yet to appear at a political action meeting, or one of the weekly summer parades and festivals, but the Rays keep her informed of the goings-on in case something appeals to her. There is still, to their knowledge, no opera. Once this night finally ends, she will propose to Sally that she bring in a company. A soprano, at least, to sing a few selections. Another "seed event," if that is how she prefers to view it. If Sally does not cooperate, Anja will find another theater. One with perfect sound. Or she will build the opera house herself, and it will be grand.

She is auditioning the next substitute for grief. Love did not prove sufficient. Neither did fame, or money, or fear. Neither did all of these at once. Eventually, something will stick. The right formula. And if it does not stick, if no such formula exists, then she will know with certainty what she has long suspected and ignored, which is that the auditions were the closest she would come. In the meantime, she has the rest of her life to contend with.

In the lexicon of stars, Anja Bloom is a has-been. These people now at her feet are gazing up at dead light. If they recognize it as such, they are kind enough not to let on. Most do not know the difference. They want to believe in Anja Bloom's greatness as much as Anja Bloom has wanted to believe in it. But it is possible her greatness ended with Hovland, that any talent she possessed as an actress was conditional, relational. Alchemical. It is possible she has been dead for some time.

These possibilities do not scare her or sadden her as much as she imagined they might. In fact, she feels that relief that comes when possibilities are taken away. Perhaps the crowd senses her relief. Her lightness. They let her go on standing before them on the stage, accomplishing only the taking of her bows, the mouthing of her thank-yous. They will not let her tell them she will not be performing tonight or any other night. She never was Elizabeth Taylor. They will not let her get to the speech she has been writing in her mind since 1982, her speech about Tennessee Williams and his fifteen years of alchemy, of greatness, with Frank Merlo.

The last time she saw Tenn, she will say to them, he was nearly the age she is now. He was as much of a has-been as she has become. Like her, he was living with the curse of having once been great, and the burden of the belief that greatness was still possible. They will not like hearing this. They will groan, for sure, thinking her haughty or falsely modest. But the difference between us, she will say, is that Tenn kept working. His light was dead, but every day he made the attempt to revive it. The stonemason, Frank used to call him. He showed up each morning, got down on his knees, and he *worked*. And after Frank, he wrote through twenty years of fear and grief and loneliness and failure. Plays and stories and scripts and poems. She has read them all. He was not a coward. He did not hide himself away like she did. *Call It Joy* is not his best play. It is not even a good play. She wanted it to be better. But Tenn wrote it for Frank, and for that reason alone, she believes it is worth putting into the world.

She hopes they enjoy it. She is grateful for their generous donations. They will make a difference to this town she has come to love. She apologizes if she disappointed them. She has already gone on too long. The lights will go down now, and she will take her seat beside her friend. She will see them again after the show. She is sure they will have questions.

17.

INDIAN SUMMER

When he came for him, his fear filled the room. Frank was on the bed gasping like a hooked fish. Something was wrong with his oxygen tank. Nurse Fig was supposed to fix it. Instead, in came Tenn. The sight of Frank flailing and wheezing stopped him dead. His shadow covered the walls and the floor from the doorway to the edge of the bed.

"Get the damned nurse," Frank said, each word cutting off his air. He knocked over the roses on the nightstand. He slipped on the spilled water trying to save the vase. Tenn's shadow disappeared. An orderly came to sweep up the glass.

Of this scene, Frank remembered only the shadow. How it stopped just short of him, then retreated. He was too doped-up on morphine to recall anything else. But he'd known the shadow was not death. It was too afraid, too dark. When death came, it would come as a brightness, a seduction. "Ecstasy," Father Kelly had promised him. "Look at the faces of the saints," he'd said, pulling a set of cards from his sleeve like a magician. "See how they welcome death like a lover. Do the saints look afraid to you?" He'd given Frank the cards to keep next to the flowers. Now they were soaked.

He woke to Tenn beside him in the chair, his fat soft fingers entwined with his. Holding his hand as he slept. He was telling Frank what happened when he'd walked into his hospital room like it was gossip from a night at the Monster.

"I ran into the hall screeching, 'He's in there gasping like a hooked fish!'" said Tenn. "That's what got them moving, baby. My tears and carrying-on. If you want a hospital to pay you any attention, you've got to play the hysteric. They ignore you otherwise. You have too much pride for that, but by God I will not have you die of pride."

Tenn thought he could just come back from—where'd he go again? Yes, Frank remembered: Abingdon, Virginia. *Milk Train*. Audrey. Clare Luce—and he'd just forgive him lickety-split for his vanishing act. And why should he not think that?

Frank breathed easier from the new tank. When he tried to sit up, though, all the strength left his arms. He fell back onto the bed. A bomb exploded in his lower back, shattering his bones. He cried out. Nurse Fig appeared with another injection. He made a fist when he saw the needle. His entire fist fit in Tenn's hand, clasped over it as he went under. Tenn continued to talk. "You've had a parade today, baby," he was saying. "All the people coming in and out of here. See all these chairs? You're the hottest ticket in town."

When Frank woke again, the room was filled with men. Al and Dan and his uncle and Father Kelly and Tenn. They'd even wheeled up Blind Sid from the ward. Frank knew every face. He'd been swimming. He heard their voices from the bottom of the ocean. He lifted his head above the surf to see who'd come around to see him. *Ciao ciao ragazzi, what's the program?* They were talking to each other across his bed. They seemed not to know he was lying there on top of it. Al's arms were folded across his muscled chest. Tenn leaned over and patted Sid on his shoulder. His uncle was reading the newspaper. Frank dove back in. The water was warm. Taormina. Wildwood in July. His mind got clear. When he came up again, Tenn was the only one left.

The swimming had done him good. He felt rested, stronger. He sat up in bed without any explosions. He was sweating for the first time in the week Tenn had been gone. He threw off the covers.

"Frankie!" Tenn said. The sudden movement startled him. He closed his book. *The Letters of Vincent Van Gogh*. "How are you feeling?"

Frank looked around. It wouldn't take much to set up a desk in here. Take out a few chairs, push the bed up against the wall. Plenty of space. "You must miss your typewriter," he said.

"Not in the least," said Tenn. He leaned forward. "The color's come back to your face."

"I need to walk," Frank said. He unhooked himself from the tank. His lungs filled with the hospital air, stale but sweet. His feet found the floor. Tenn helped him stand. "Take me outside," Frank said. His legs had enough in them to get him out of the room. He walked toward the chair by the door. He didn't need the wall to steady him.

"Careful, Frankie," said Tenn, following close behind, preparing to catch him, his breath on his neck, his hand on his hip bone. The bone jutted out like a shelf.

Slowly the room filled with water. He was nowhere near Taormina; he was in Memorial Hospital, and the water was rising, and now it was up to his elbows, and now it was up to his neck. Tenn called to him. He stretched out his arms and floated, listening to him repeat his name. He kicked and swam toward the door. Beyond the door was the beach. Somebody there had a cigarette. It felt good to kick and to stretch his arms. But it tired him out fast. He needed to rest. He tried sitting in the chair, but the water came up to his lips, and he jumped up again. He had to keep swimming or he'd drown. He swam from chair to chair. Then back to his bed. Then the chair again. Then the doorway. Each time he tested his ability to propel himself upward, he passed the test. He could make it all the way to the beach if he kicked faster, if he didn't tire himself out.

When Tenn wasn't looking, he dove through the door into the hallway. But he swam straight into Nurse Fig. She dragged him back inside. She pulled him toward the bed.

"No," he said, fighting her off. "I'll drown there."

"We won't let that happen," she said.

"I'm telling you, I have to keep moving," Frank said. His limbs buzzed. He was becoming a shark. "It's the summer. I want to be outside."

"It's September, sweetheart," she said. "We call that the fall. There's even a little chill in the air today."

"Frank is correct that it's not yet autumn, Miss Newton," said Tenn. "There are still three days left of summer, if I'm not mistaken."

To Frank, she said, "Your mother would never forgive us if we let you catch cold."

"Wouldn't you agree he's much improved from the morning?" Tenn asked her. "When you left him here alone for nearly an hour with a faulty oxygen tank? Look at those roses in his cheeks. I'd like to take him outside, if you don't mind. And even if you *do* mind, it's my understanding that this is a hospital and not a prison."

"Mr. Merlo is in our care and in the care of his family," Nurse Fig said firmly, gathering the bedcovers from the floor. "I can't authorize that."

"His family is not paying his bills," said Tenn.

"I'll get him some fresh sheets," she said. "If you'd like to speak to Doctor Fallon—"

"What I'd like is for you to bring us a wheelchair," said Tenn. "One of those electric ones, so he can drive. Driving calms him. It gives him happiness. Can we give him a little happiness?"

She ignored him.

"Do it, do it!" Tenn shouted, stamping his feet. He grabbed fistfuls of his hair with both hands and pulled at it as he snarled at her. "Immediately!" When she turned her back, he gave Frank a wink and snarled again. He stamped and roared: "Do you hear me, Miss Newton!?"

Frank laughed. "They should give you a Tony," he said, after she walked out.

Tenn tapped his shirt pocket, where he kept his cigarettes. "Put something on, baby," he said. "She was right about the chill."

IT WAS THE MIDDLE OF the afternoon, and Frank was riding circles around the sycamores in St. Catherine's Park. Tenn watched him from a bench, hunched over with his elbows on his knees and his face in his hands, the shiny sunlit windows of Memorial behind him. He called out for Frank to slow down, to look out for the dips in the asphalt and the broken bottles and that little girl on the trike. He didn't have to warn him. Frank saw every divot, every glint of glass, every pigtail, every falling leaf, every pigeon, every sad stare.

At least the women met his eyes before they glanced away. A flash of sympathy, of concern, of morbid curiosity. The men just checked their watches. What did Frank care? He lapped up every breath of the delicious air, rich with earth and trash and fumes and dog shit. So what if he got a little dizzy circling the trees? It was worth the nausea, the risk of fainting, to feel that chill on the tip of his nose, that tilt of the chair on the curve. If only this claptrap could move a little faster. If only he could push the wheels with his own strong arms out of the city, take one last trip south through Jersey, waving goodbye to the shore, and roll himself all the way to the Keys.

Instead, ten minutes steering the electric chair nearly crippled him. He parked beside Tenn to rest for a bit. Tenn helped him onto the bench. He slung his leg over Tenn's thigh and rested his head on his shoulder, and together they watched the men pass by, their favorite pastime, the choosing of the fish from the bed of ice, the catching the eye of the deer before it leapt into the woods. None of these men would touch them now, of course. They shunned the sickness they could sense from twenty feet off. An old man of fifty-two on the bench holding a skeleton on his lap, better not to look their way at all, better to pick up the pace. Frank nudged closer, covering his head with Tenn's scarf. The chill had seeped into him.

In the years they summered in Italy, they used to daydream about staying on after the season. They dreamed themselves onto a farm in Sicily, some tract of lush and fragrant land far from the constraints and temptations of a city. They'd hide their address from everyone but Anna. She could visit as long as she rode in on a donkey. (Oh, how they laughed when they pictured Anna in her black silk dress and high heels, slapping the donkey's cheeks to get him to hurry up!) On their little farm, Frank would learn the native arts of cheese and oil and bread, and Tenn would spend his long days in the tunnel. The nights and afternoons would belong to the nightingales.

Each summer they daydreamed of the farm, and each September, when the time came for Frank to book the tickets to the next place, the new city—Berlin, Amsterdam, Lisbon—they found it impossible to resist the lure of those unspoiled streets, those secret bars, those operas and beaches and parks and alleyways. The daydream was never enough. Frank longed for the next place as much—maybe more— than Tenn did. And then, once they grew tired of the next place, as they always did, they longed for Duncan Street, the closest place they'd had to a home.

"I think I would have been happy on the farm," Frank said.

"Which farm is that, Frankie?"

"The farm in Sicily."

Tenn thought a moment. "Oh yes—our little *paradiso* with the geese and the goats and the young gardener-chauffeur."

"And the lake nearby for swimming," Frank said. "It was a good plan."

"It was," said Tenn.

"I'd have gotten along good with the geese and the goats."

"Not to mention the young gardener-chauffeur," Tenn said, with a laugh. "There's his cousin Raffaelo right there!" He pointed, discreetly, to a teenage boy carrying a soccer ball. "What do you think of him?"

Frank said he did not want to think of Raffaelo.

"You get along with everyone," Tenn said. "Even that awful nurse."

"She's not so bad," said Frank. "She's just doing her job."

"See what I mean?"

"I think I was cut out for the domestic life," Frank said. "More than . . . We should have stayed in one place, maybe, for more than a few months."

"We had Duncan Street."

"For a while."

"I don't want to fight with you, Frankie."

He had no fight in him, either. He watched young Raffaelo try to bounce the soccer ball from knee to knee. The kid had no talent for it. The ball kept hitting him in the face or sailing into the grass. His feet weren't quick enough. He was leaning too far forward.

"I'll take my cigarette now," Frank said.

"Are you sure you can handle it?"

"No."

But he could. The smoke was so much sweeter than the air. His chest swelled with the pleasures of it, its invigorating rush, the tingle on his lips. Just this morning, he was alone on his hospital bed too tired to read the cards that came for him. He was fiddling with the tubes in his nose, trying to get more air that wasn't coming. Something was wrong. And then, or so Tenn told him, he was gasping like a hooked fish. Those words spoken in Tenn's voice, that image of how he'd found him when, finally, he'd shown up to pay his respects, stuck in Frank's mind. A hooked fish. He could taste the metal on his tongue, the blood from the gash in his lip. Now the smoke purified his mouth, his throat, his lungs, his heart. He took the smoke into him in precious sips. Any more and he'd choke.

They passed the cigarette back and forth. It was the closest they'd come in years to a kiss.

"I went cold on you," Frank said. "After *Senso*. I want you to know you didn't imagine it."

"It never once occurred to me that I imagined it," Tenn said.

"Was I so obvious?"

"After all this time, Frankie, you still don't know how transparent you are. It's one of your finest qualities, your absence of artifice. The sincerity of your rages and affections. It's what's always attracted me to men from the sunburnt countries." He laughed. "You boys think you're hiding something, but whatever it is you're attempting to conceal is as plain as your Roman nose."

"I'd have made a terrible actor, is what you're saying."

"Frankie, that's not—"

"I'm trying to say I'm sorry," he said.

He couldn't bear to hear what Tenn might be tempted to say next: that Frank would have made a fine leading man, that he'd needed just one more lucky break, that he should have stayed in closer touch with

Anja, that he'd have gladly intervened again if Frank had only swallowed his pride and asked. All of this had run through Frank's own mind over the years since Venice. "Visconti tossed me aside like I was a nothing," he said now. "Even having you as my—patron—wasn't enough to keep me in his film. That's what a nothing I was. But I didn't blame him. I didn't even blame myself. I blamed you."

"You talk of this blame as if it's news to me."

"Nothing is ever news to you. Maybe that's why I stopped talking."

"You gave up so easily, Frankie. After making such a fuss about *Senso*, you let it defeat you, like you didn't want it much anyway. Like acting was just another plan—like your play, and your dancing, like Anja—another dress shirt you were fitting yourself for. And now you tell me that wasn't the life you wanted after all, that you'd have been happier on a farm we invented after too much Margaux and kif. And I suppose you blame me for that, too. For the farm that never was."

"I did," said Frank. "But I don't anymore."

"Well, call that news, then."

"You don't understand," said Frank. "You've been gone—off in Virginia, on the town with Angel, wherever it is you go now—and I've been back there, back in that time. Because that's what the guys in the ward told me to do, to put myself in my body back when it was strongest. The most healthy. Happiest. Putting myself in my body was supposed to give me energy. It was supposed to give me my fight back. It worked for them, they said. For me, though, it made everything worse. The pain, the fatigue, the soreness in my bones. It made me miss you. It made me call out your name when I should have been cursing it. So I tried to take myself out of that body, but I couldn't; once I was back there, I couldn't let it go. I didn't want to let it go. Those months after Truman's party. Rome and Livorno and Vicenza and Venice. Waiting for Visconti to call. The three of us on the Lido. The *acqua alta*. I was at the beginning of something. I used to thank

Anja for putting me there. And Truman. Even Sandro and Jack. I used to thank Jack for dying in front of me. It woke me up."

"You thanked everyone but me."

"Isn't that how it goes?"

"Not always."

"Well—" Frank said.

If he were to script the moment to say the words—*I love you, Tenn*—finally, to his face, in a way that convinced him that he meant them, and always had, wouldn't it be now? Like the aria Maria Callas might sing at the end of the opera, just before she plunges the dagger in. Like Maggie the Cat in the upstairs room as the curtain slowly falls. But to say the words here, under the swaying sycamores, in the first hours of Indian Summer, after fifteen years of holding them back, was the same as giving up. He wasn't ready.

For months, Frank had been burning terror like fuel. Terror had given him the energy to go back and forth from Key West to New York, from the apartment to the hospital. Terror burned slower, colder, than fury had. He felt himself coming to the end of the terror, just as he'd once come to the end of the fury. What was next? What came after terror? Ecstasy? Not yet. Between now and the final brightness, he needed something else to live on. He chose the words, the ones he knew, as surely as his Roman nose, Tenn most wanted to hear, the ones he'd flown back from Virginia desperate for, the ones he'd written for his leading ladies but could never write for him.

"I'm thanking you now," Frank said. He meant it tenderly, but it didn't come off. Might as well have another storm, then, for old times' sake. So he said, "You showed up in time for that, at least."

HE DIDN'T REMEMBER how he made it back to his room. Did Nurse Fig come to claim him from the park? Did he zip down the hallways again, in and out of the elevator, slaloming the abandoned gurneys? For the third time that day, he woke to Tenn beside him in the chair, those chubby fingers clasped over his.

The shadow of fear covered every wall now. People came in and out, whispering. His mother smoothed his sweaty hair. He had crisp new sheets. The stack of machines blinked and sighed. The tank fed him the purest of air. But the shadow never moved.

Again the room began to fill with water. Again Frank stood, scared, surging with purpose, threw the covers off the bed, and swam toward the door. Again, the moment he sat in the chair to rest, the water choked his lungs, and he forced himself to jump up and swim back to the bed, and then back to the chair, and then to the bed again.

This went on and on. It was more difficult than it had been before to move his arms. His stride was slower. The wooden slats in the back of the chair dug into the knobs of his spine. The new sheets burned his skin. He lifted his arms and legs to cool them. His gown covered almost nothing. He felt ashamed, obscene.

"Frankie, try to lie still," said Tenn.

"I'm too restless," he said.

He had to swim again. But when he planted his palms on the mattress to lift himself, his wrists collapsed. Explosions everywhere. He fell back onto the bed. The end of Indian Summer already, so soon.

"Those visitors tired you out," Tenn said.

"I'm glad they're gone," said Frank, closing his eyes.

"And the park tired you out."

"Yes."

"And me."

"A little," he said. Teasing. Could Tenn see the smile on his face? The bombs kept going off, two and three at a time now, pulverizing his bones. He let go of Tenn's hand. He turned on his side away from him. When he woke next, he didn't want the shadow to be the first thing he saw, even if it was attached to Tenn.

"Frankie, do you want me to leave you now?" he asked.

He did not. He never had. Still, they'd left each other again and again. They rarely asked permission. They simply declared their leave-taking, and the next morning they woke in some other place. They kept their lives pleasantly separate, as they expected two men might need and want to do. It still had no name, the nature of their long association, their fifteen years—a lifetime!—of trips and plans and nightingales and cautious public affections. Maybe it never would. Maybe they invented it. Was Frank really cut out for the domestic life, or would he have always longed for the stars? How astonishing that he still didn't know, that he was as much a stranger to himself on this last day as he'd been that night on the porch of the Atlantic House.

"Frankie, do you want me to leave you now?" Tenn asked again.

"No," he said. He did not. He never had. Not in Rome, not on Duncan Street, not these last weeks in New York when he'd been back in his body, strong as a horse, and all the boys were looking their way.

"No," Frank said again. "I'm used to you."

A NOTE TO THE READER

I first met Frank Merlo in the pages of Dotson Rader's memoir, *Tennessee: Cry of the Heart*, which I picked up on a whim at a used bookstore in Wilmington, Delaware, in 1997. I remember standing in the aisle of the store reading about this working-class gay Italian guy from New Jersey who'd been the lover of Tennessee Williams, and who died at forty after days of waiting for one last visit from the great writer with whom he'd spent most of his adult life. There I was, a twenty-five-year-old working-class gay Italian guy from Delaware with dreams of being a writer myself, feeling an instant kinship—which eventually became an obsession—with both men: the neurotic and ambitious Tenn and the steadfast and searching Frank. I knew I wanted to write about these guys, but I didn't yet know how.

The book, later a film, that taught me I could write fiction about real people was Christopher Bram's *Gods and Monsters*, an interpretation of the last days of James Whale, director of *Frankenstein*. My first attempt at such "alternative history fiction," as it's come to be called, was the short story "The Last Days of Tennessee," which, despite multiple revisions, went nowhere, and caused me to abandon the notion of making Merlo and Williams into fictional characters. I kept in touch with them over the next twelve years, though: As I wrote novels about other people, I read and reread Williams's work and the numerous biographies and tell-alls about him and his time with Merlo, continually struck by the fact that it was during the "Frankie Years"—roughly 1947 to 1963—that Williams wrote all of his major plays after *Streetcar*. Once Frank was gone, Williams descended into what he called in his *Memoirs* "a seven-year depression," though, in truth, those bluest of devils stuck around until his death in 1983, and during those twenty years he never wrote another truly great play. I kept asking myself, what was the alchemy between these two very different men that produced such transcendent classics as *Cat on a Hot Tin Roof, Suddenly Last Summer, The Rose Tattoo, Camino Real*, and others? How must it have been for Frank to live in the shadow of that genre-defining artist, playing his supporting role, deferring his own dreams? I kept looking for a way to dramatize their long association in narrative, to write into the fictional spaces between what was "known" about them, not only to explore the particular dynamic between Frank Merlo and Tennessee Williams, but to discover something—I still wasn't sure what—about relationships in general.

Ultimately, it was a letter—more accurately, a series of letters—that provided the way in.

The first of these letters was from Williams to Elia Kazan, sent from Barcelona in July 1953:

> I had to leave Rome [for Spain] as Frank's behavior toward me
> became almost insufferable. He seemed to be playing Bubu
> de Montparnasse and to expect me to accept the role of one
> of Bubu's less satisfactory whores. . . . Then I had it out with

him, verbally, and flew to Barcelona the next day. . . . He is sunk into such a pit of habit and inertia and basic contempt for himself or his position in life which I think he, consciously or unconsciously, holds me responsible for and almost if not quite hates me for. That old cocksucker Wilde uttered a true thing when he said, Each man kills the thing he loves. The killing is not voluntary but we sure in hell do it. And burn for it. I have given up faith in happy solutions to problems between two people but I shall try to think of something just the same and to work it out if it can be this coming year. . . . And maybe it will all clear up again as it has before and we'll go right along as we have been going. So far I haven't thought of anything else.

Williams returned from this fateful trip to Barcelona in late July, but he makes no journal entries during the period in Rome between *"circa Tuesday 28 July or Wednesday, 29 July 1953"* and *"Friday, 7 August 1953"*; during that time, it is entirely conceivable that he and Merlo could have accepted the invitation from Truman Capote to visit him in Portofino. Williams references Capote's recent invitation in a letter to Maria Britneva, mostly to complain about Truman's explicit exclusion of their beloved dog, Mr. Moon.

These letters got Frank and Tenn to the party, but I didn't know who they'd meet there, or what that "missing" weekend, smack in the middle of a stormy summer, might reveal to me. I'd been a longtime fan of John Horne Burns's novel, *The Gallery*, and I knew that not only had he taken up with an Italian doctor named Sandro Nencini in Florence around that time, but that he died under mysterious circumstances ten days later. We know that Jack sent a letter to his mother dated 5 August 1953 from Marina di Cecina, but there is no evidence that he and Sandro did *not* take a turn northward up the Ligurian coast to Portofino during their documented road trip from Florence to Livorno in that same span of days—and so to Truman's party I sent them as well.

I thought four leading men might be enough for one book, but then I came upon the June 1953 letter from Truman Capote to David O. Selznick, an excerpt from which appears as an epigraph to the novel. Capote's throwaway scrap of gossip about the scandalous mother-daughter duo in Portofino that same summer stuck with me, but I wasn't sure what, if anything, to do with it until, quite by chance, I met a certain legendary actress at a dinner party. An impromptu conversation with this actress, who is also an accomplished director— one in which we discussed the particular loneliness of life in Boston, the art of fiction itself, and a memorable encounter she had with Tennessee Williams and his dog in a hotel lobby in Paris—inspired me to invent the characters of Anja and Bitte Blomgren. Ironically, it was only after the entirely fictional Anja entered the narrative that the plot began to take shape, and that I was able both to imagine more fully Frank's inner life and to venture an answer as to how "each man kills the thing he loves." As a character, Anja started out as a potential muse for Tenn, but the more I got to know her, the more I saw that she belonged to Frank. Somehow, by another strange alchemy, watching Anja struggle with fame in her final years taught me something about how Frank struggled in his short life with the anxieties of anonymity.

I have researched the lives and work of Tennessee Williams (1911–1983), Frank Merlo (1922–1963), Truman Capote (1924–1984), and John Horne Burns (1916–1953) in an attempt to deepen my understanding of them, but my goal for *Leading Men* was neither to reproduce what is "known" about them nor to put forth any divergent theories. I have made every effort to stay true to the locations and dates in which the real-life versions of these characters lived and traveled, taking no deliberate liberties for the sake of convenience or dramatic effect.

While some significant figures have been omitted—most notably Maria Britneva, who accompanied Williams and Merlo to Verona to work on the *Senso* script—to the best of my ability, I have not allowed anyone who couldn't possibly have been in a scene to make an appearance. According to Burns biographer David Margolick, Sandro Nencini died in 2005 in Italy, leaving behind at least one child. He, too, is my own interpretation and invention.

On the twenty-year journey from that used bookstore in Wilmington to the novel you now hold in your hands, I was guided by multiple signs and chance encounters (meeting Liv Ullmann being just one of them) that helped convince me I was on the right track. On a trip to Italy many years ago, my partner and I spent a happy weekend at the Hotel Opera in Rome; only later, upon reading the letters Williams sent in the summer of 1953, did the street address of that hotel stand out: 11 Via Firenze, the very same walls of Frank and Tenn's apartment. St. Stephen's Church in Boston, which I still pass every day on my walk to the grocery store, turned out to be the site of John Horne Burns's memorial service (which only four people attended). Most spookily: During my interview in Chicago with Tony Narducci, the man who calls himself "the last living lover of Tennessee Williams," a full decade after I'd written what became *Call It Joy*, he told me the story of meeting a drunk and despondent Williams at the Monster Discotheque in Key West in 1982, where the first words Williams spoke to him were that he was a dead ringer for a young Frank Merlo. It was Tony's resemblance to Frank that prompted Williams to invite Tony back to his house that night, and then the two men spent six more months together.

Though writers are grateful for such coincidences and magical thinking, they're not what give us permission to tell stories; nor are they what keep us returning again and again to the people we create on the page. We do it because we fall in love, as I did with Frank Merlo, a real person who lived and breathed and died too young, and as I did with Anja Bloom, our mutual imaginary friend who made sure I didn't forget him.

ACKNOWLEDGMENTS

I am deeply grateful to the John Simon Guggenheim Foundation, the MacDowell Colony, and the Massachusetts Cultural Council for their generous support of *Leading Men*.

To research the novel, I turned first to multiple works by Williams, in particular *Suddenly Last Summer, The Rose Tattoo, Orpheus Descending*, the script of *Senso, Memoirs, Collected Stories*, and the fascinating late plays collected in Volumes IV–VIII of *The Theater of Tennessee Williams*, published by New Directions.

I also happily devoured Williams's extensive and extraordinary *Notebooks*, gorgeously edited by Margaret Bradham Thornton, and published by Yale University Press; New Directions' *The Selected Letters of Tennessee Williams, Vol. II (1945–1957)*; and *Five O'Clock Angel: Letters of Tennessee Williams to Maria St. Just*. For a sense of Capote and Jack Dunphy, I turned to *Too Brief a Treat: The Letters of Truman Capote*, edited by Gerald Clarke, and Clarke's wonderful *Capote: A Biography*.

John Lahr's world-class 2014 biography, *Tennessee Williams: Mad Pilgrimage of the Flesh* also proved essential, as did James Grissom's *Follies of*

God: Tennessee Williams and the Women of the Fog, and our off-the-record conversation over drinks in Manhattan in 2015. Though its biographical period predates Williams's time with Frank, Lyle Leverich's classic *Tom: The Unknown Tennessee Williams* was also useful.

To explore the character and sensibility of John Horne "Jack" Burns, I (re)read his published novels—*The Gallery, Lucifer with a Book*, and *A Cry of Children*. I then visited Box 1238 of the Howard Gotlieb Archival Research Center at Boston University, which houses the manuscript of *The Stranger's Guise*, as well as Burns's letters and selected family photographs. In the meantime, David Margolick's excellent *Dreadful: The Short Life and Gay Times of John Horne Burns* (Other Press, 2013) appeared, and provided a rock-solid and insightful basis for understanding and appreciating this misunderstood and underappreciated writer. On a 2015 trip to Italy, I visited "Villino Brunella" and "La Bicocca," where I was given a memorable tour of Burns's apartment and neighborhood.

Though the vast majority of the dialogue in *Leading Men* is my own invention, some words and phrases have been transposed directly or paraphrased from the sources mentioned above. This includes the very last line of the novel—"I'm used to you."—which, as Williams recorded in *Memoirs*, Merlo is reported to have said to him on the last day of his life.

I am grateful to the following people who generously went out of their way to connect me to someone or something important in the lives of Merlo, Williams, and Burns:

David Kaplan, founder and director of the Provincetown Tennessee Williams Theater Festival, guided me with great wisdom not only toward the production of the entirely fictional *Call It Joy*, but toward a better understanding of Williams's work itself. Kaplan's *Tennessee Williams in Provincetown* deepened this understanding. He also led me to Thomas Keith's article "You Are Not the Playwright I Was Expecting" in the September 2011 issue of *American Theatre* magazine, which proved especially useful for appreciating the experimentations in Williams's "post-Frank" period.

Professor Alessandro Clericuzio, of the University of Perugia, author of *Tennessee Williams and Italy*, was my proxy at the Luchino Visconti archive in Rome, where we read Williams's typed and handwritten drafts of the *Senso* script.

Anthony Narducci sat with me for hours at a coffee shop in Chicago in January 2017, talking candidly about his time with Williams, specifically about how Williams came to terms with his relationship with Frank Merlo. Narducci's own gripping memoir, *In the Frightened Heart of Me: Tennessee Williams's Last Year*, provided great insight into the broken man Anja meets at the Waldorf in the summer of 1982.

The late Thomas D. Burns, Esq., Jack's younger brother, was gracious enough to host me for a long and candid interview some years ago at his law offices in Boston. Howard Medwed kindly made the introduction and set up the interview.

Extended and ongoing conversations with Christopher Bram, Maud Casey, Chip Cheek, Robert Cohen, Stacey D'Erasmo, Katherine Fausset, Antonia Fusco, Sonya Larson, Margot Livesey, Thomas Mallon, Stephen McCauley, Heidi Pitlor, Whitney Scharer, Sebastian Stuart, Michelle Toth, Barbara Shapiro, and Dawn Tripp gave me the permission, guidance, and direction(s) that ultimately proved necessary.

My friends, colleagues, and students at GrubStreet, Warren Wilson, and Bread Loaf—especially Debra Allbery, Lisa Borders, Eve Bridburg, Michael Collier, Jennifer Grotz, and Ellen Bryant Voigt—provided unending support, inspiration, and crucial feedback on early drafts.

For various kindnesses, indulgences, and talents—including gifts of time, space, translations, and additional research help—I thank Boris Deliradev, Christopher Dufault, Arthur Egeli, Brian Halley, Gary and Paul Hickox, Karl Krueger, Aaron Lecklider, Elizabeth Kostova, Matthew Limpede, Elinor Lipman, Mameve Medwed, Elisa Piccinelli, Rebecca Smith, Isabel Walsh, Dito van Reigersberg, Noah Whitford, and the friendly staff of Provincetown Public Library, The Chellidency NYC, and Caffè Loro.

Janet Silver and Paul Slovak not only brought *Leading Men* into the world—they made it immeasurably better with their wise and insightful feedback, their fierce advocacy, and their commitment. I am forever indebted to them and to everyone at Viking.

The love, faith, and unquestioning support of Michael Borum, my leading man of twenty-one years and counting, made this book possible.

A PENGUIN READERS GUIDE TO

LEADING MEN

Christopher Castellani

An Introduction to
Leading Men

Two lovers locking eyes across a room: this was theater, yes, but it was something else, too. Brightness, maybe.

In July of 1953, at a glittering party thrown by Truman Capote, the literary and film elites of the age gather in Portofino, Italy, for a night of drinking, gossip, and dancing. Truman himself lords over the revelry, while the American novelist John Horne Burns stumbles through the door on the arm of his Italian lover, Sandro, and Tennessee Williams parades around the man he calls Little Horse—his longtime partner Frank Merlo—a working-class, Italian American man from New Jersey.

There, in the fog of smoke and boozy conversation, Frank and Tenn have a lively exchange with Anja Blomgren, a young, enigmatic Swedish beauty and aspiring actress, and decide to take her under their wing. Their chance encounter and the events that transpire in the following week—shaped by personalities like Luchino Visconti, Anna Magnani, and Paul Bowles—will go on to alter the rest of each of their lives.

A decade later, a terminally ill Frank revisits the tempestuous events of that fateful summer from his deathbed in Manhattan and reflects on his fifteen-year romance with Tennessee, in which he transformed himself and sacrificed his own artistic ambitions to play the roles of lover, caretaker, and muse. Tennessee was on his most productive and successful run—the era of *Cat on a Hot Tin Roof, Night of the Iguana, Suddenly Last Summer*, among others—during their time together, and never penned another hit in the decades that followed. Losing an untimely battle with cancer, Frank waits anxiously for his former partner to visit him one final time.

In present-day America, Anja is settled into a quiet retirement after enjoying a long and successful film career as the leading lady for renowned Danish film director Martin Hovland. That is, until a young man connected to her time in Italy, Sandrino, lures her back into the spotlight after he discovers she possesses the only surviving copy of Tennessee's final play.

What keeps two people together and what breaks them apart? Can we save someone else if we can't save ourselves? What does it take to endure the pressure of expectations that accompanies a generation-defining talent? *Leading Men* seamlessly weaves fact and fiction to intimately resurrect Frank and Tenn's relationship and explore the tensions between public figures and their private lives. In a deeply affecting portrait of the burdens of fame and the complex negotiations of life in the shadows of greatness, Castellani creates an unforgettable leading lady in Anja Bloom and reveals the hidden machinery of one of the great literary love stories of the twentieth century.

Questions and Topics for Discussion

1. This novel is a fictionalized account based on the lives of real people, some of whom, like Tennessee Williams and Truman Capote, are very famous for their roles in elite literary circles. How did the author's characterizations of these people surprise you? Did they differ substantially from what you imagined?

2. What is your opinion of Frank and Tenn's relationship, and why do you think it endured for so long? What do they bring to, and take from, each other? Do you view them as codependent—and, if so, in an ultimately positive or negative way? Which of them do you believe needs the other more?

3. *Leading Men* examines the trappings and pitfalls of living in close proximity to celebrity, ambition, and excess, both for famous artists and those who inspire and support them. How did your understanding of this kind of relationship evolve over the course of the novel? How did this dynamic function in different partnerships (Anja and Martin, Frank and Tenn, Jack and Sandro)?

4. The title of the book is *Leading Men*, but much of the novel hinges on Anja, the enigmatic Swedish muse and actress. Did knowing Anja's story enhance your understanding of Frank, and vice versa? How do you think Anja's experiences with her own set of leading men—Martin; her husband, Pieter; Sandrino; her father—relate to the larger themes in the novel?

5. Castellani portrays several queer relationships in the novel, including those between Frank and Tennessee, Jack Burns and Sandro Nencini, Jack Dunphy and Truman Capote, and Sandrino and Trevor, each with its own set of norms. And there are more unconventional groupings—young Trevor and Sandrino with aging Anja; Frank and Tenn's surprising alliance with teenage Anja; and even the brief and notorious love triangle between Anja, her mother, and an Italian fisherman. What did you find compelling about these love stories? What differences, if any, did you notice between the relationships set in the mid-twentieth century, those that are more recent, and our current historical moment?

6. What did you make of *Call It Joy*, Tennessee's "lost" play? What did it reveal to you about the man who wrote it?